NO RETURN

Ava Bardoff—
she's the most beautiful woman on earth—
and the only one who
knows the mind-stunning secret of

THE STYX COMPLEX

"Warning: once picked up, it can't be put down."
—Barbara A. Bannon, *Publishers Weekly*

THE STYX COMPLEX

RUSSELL RHODES

BANTAM BOOKS · TORONTO · NEW YORK · LONDON

THE STYX COMPLEX

*A Bantam Book / published by arrangement with
Dodd, Mead & Company*

PRINTING HISTORY
Dodd, Mead edition published May 1977.
Bantam edition / April 1978

ISBN 0-553-11380-1

Published simultaneously in the United States and Canada

*Bantam Books are published by Bantam Books, Inc. Its trade-
mark, consisting of the words "Bantam Books" and the por-
trayal of a bantam, is registered in the United States Patent
Office and in other countries. Marca Registrada. Bantam
Books, Inc., 666 Fifth Avenue, New York, New York 10019.*

PRINTED IN THE UNITED STATES OF AMERICA

To Manolita

THE STYX COMPLEX

In late 1974 a bewildering series of deaths occurred among the diplomatic corps, security forces, and armed services of the major world powers and the oil-producing nations. Sovereigns, cabinet ministers, generals, and a great many others of high rank and station fell sudden prey to fatal cerebral hemorrhages. This strange phenomenon lasted approximately one year.

Lacking evidence to the contrary, it was postulated at the time that this rash of deaths was directly attributable to the strain under which these men and women worked during this most difficult and confused political and economic period.

Evidence that subsequently came to light may have contradicted this assumption, yet all efforts by the World Health Society to open an inquiry into this serious matter were repeatedly thwarted by executive order in those countries concerned.

Excerpt from a report to the Society, "Mental Health Under Tension," 27 October 1976, by Dr. Emlyn Blackwood, World Health Society, Geneva, Switzerland.

1

"Faster," he urged the uniformed chauffeur. "Can't this damn thing go any faster?"

The long, black limousine with the U.S. government seal emblazoned on its door swerved out of its lane, nearly forcing a horn-blaring tanker into the highway divider, and continued its erratic, high-speed weaving through traffic to plunge into the Midtown Tunnel toward Manhattan's East Side. Undersecretary George Martin leaned forward in the back seat. The perspiration beading his forehead could not be attributed to the modest temperature of the early evening in July nor to a malfunction of the official car's air-conditioning system. Wiping his face with a damp, mangled handkerchief, Martin looked at his watch for the hundredth time since leaving Kennedy International Airport.

"Come on, come on," Martin pushed. "Let's move it."

"I can move the car, sir, but not the traffic," his chauffeur replied patiently. "Shall I go directly to the Waldorf?"

"Of course not, you fool," he almost shrieked, "to the Bardoff Building." Martin rubbed a hand over his eyes and sank back against the cushioned upholstery of the Lincoln Continental. "Sorry, I didn't mean to bite your head off; it was the plane's fault, not yours. But I've got to get to Bardoff before seven."

"Then the Bardoff Building it is, Mr. Martin."

The dirt-streaked tiles of the tunnel walls flashed past as the undersecretary stared straight ahead in numb panic, gripping the handle of his attaché case with white knuckles.

The Bardoff Building rose fifty-three stories, a slender needle of blue glass and stainless steel on the northeast corner of Fifth Avenue and Sixty-second Street overlooking Central Park. It was the proudest gem in the glittering business empire worn like a tiara by Ava Bardoff, *Madame* Ava Bardoff, the genius and undisputed leader of the cosmetic and fashion world today. The House of Bardoff counted all of the great and most of the nearly great among its vast clientele. Tonight Madame was entertaining in the executive penthouse. The invitation lists to her receptions read like pages out of the *Social Register,* New York, Washington, *and* Boston. Few ever found themselves otherwise occupied or too busy to attend.

Ava Bardoff stood surrounded by disciples at the far end of the long living room under a large, full-length portrait of herself done over twenty years ago by Spain's most renowned surrealist artist. She appeared even younger today than when it had been painted. She looked a ravishing, exciting woman of perhaps thirty-five, although everyone there knew she must be at least in her fifties. It was her secret of apparent eternal youth that had brought the vain flocking to her doors and was the basis for the phenomenal worldwide growth of the House of Bardoff over the last twenty years.

Madame was of medium height and had a full, well-developed but controlled figure. Honey blonde hair fell softly around her face in a casual but carefully styled arrangement to accentuate her complexion, which had the smooth texture and youthful glow of a teen-ager's. The features of her face were elegant and strong, as was her approach to life. Despite the summer season, tonight she wore a slender black silk kaftan from her new collection, generously embroidered with tiny diamonds and garnets.

Flanking her on the right and left stood what could only be described as two beautiful young men, flawless in build and features. Madame Bardoff was never seen without dedicated and well-kept young men in close attendance, which gave rise to jealous rumors that her youthful appearance and vitality could be attributed directly to insatiable nymphomania. "Let the insignificant whisper," she had once said, laughing, in her deep, throaty voice while affectionately tracing the half-open lips of her young escort with the tip of a scarlet fingernail. "Ava Bardoff lives while others wither. Where Bardoff leads, they will follow."

And follow they did—the rich, the political, the social—all revolving about her this evening. A senior U.S. senator kissed her extended hand with humbled respect. A Wall Street financier whispered the recommendation of a soon-to-be-published report in her bejeweled ear while she nodded graciously to those less intimate who watched enviously from across the room. She took the arm of the Iranian ambassador, acknowledging the small, dark velvet ring case he presented her. Madame Ava Bardoff smiled generously, almost condescendingly, to the wealthy and political around her, knowing that youth and beauty were the supreme power, a power she held firmly in her own two hands.

Undersecretary George Martin burst from the elevator on the fifty-third floor at precisely 6:45. He was overtaken halfway down the long carpeted hall and restrained by a handsome and diplomatic receptionist. "I'm sorry Mr. Martin, but your name has not been included on Madame Bardoff's guest list tonight. If you'll wait here, I'll check with . . ."

Martin tried to push him aside. "I've got to see her now, right now, damn you."

Another equally attractive but more muscular receptionist hurried toward the two struggling men as Martin shook himself free and pushed through the doors into the crowded penthouse living room. The two receptionists stood helpless, not daring to cause a potentially embarrassing scene. They began moving inconspicuously around the perimeter of the room hoping to cut off Martin before he reached the admiring circle about Ava Bardoff.

She looked up in surprise as he broke through the ring. Her eyes darted briefly to the ashen faces of the receptionists behind him and dismissed them with an imperceptible order.

"Why Mr. Undersecretary, I had not expected to see you this evening. What a delightful surprise." Madame extended her hand, which he brought quickly to his lips. "Gentlemen, have you all met Undersecretary George Martin?" she asked, looking around her at the others.

"I must talk to you . . . now. Please, Ava," he said under his breath.

They stared at each other meaningfully for several seconds and then a look of compassion crossed her face. "Come," she said, excusing herself from her admirers. George Martin followed Ava Bardoff across the room to a wall of sliding glass doors leading onto the apparently empty penthouse terrace. One of the beautiful young men moved before her to open the door. Ava's nod indicated her desire for complete privacy; he slid the door shut behind them and stood watching from inside. The second young Adonis joined him.

Madame Bardoff and George Martin crossed to the railing and, while ostensibly looking over the panoramic view of Manhattan spread out below them, carried on an unheard, but not unseen, conversation. At times Martin gestured wildly and at others seemed almost to be pleading. Madame Bardoff, her back to the penthouse living room, listened calmly and occasionally shook her head sympathetically. Once or twice she reached out to console him.

"Ava Bardoff is one of the most understanding and discreet women I know," one guest told another as they watched the terrace. "No wonder she's become the crying towel for the entire diplomatic corps."

George Martin raised both hands as if to strike her but instead clutched at his head, reeled, and cried out. Madame Bardoff moved forward to help him, but too late. He staggered back away from her against the low terrace railing, slipped sideways, the agonizing scream shattering the July evening as he plunged fifty-three floors to the street below.

Three nights later, Sarah Dilworth walked down the long corridor to Gate 32A at Orly Airport in Paris, where the Air France plane from New York to Nice waited. The man directly behind looked appreciatively at her legs as the heels of her shoes clicked sharply over the marble floor and he smiled in anticipation of the company he would enjoy on the last part of his trip from New York. He caught up with her and touched her arm.

"Excuse me, but I noticed you on the flight coming over from the States. Have you been to Nice before?" he tried for openers.

Sarah was amused by this obvious pick-up attempt and looked him over out of the corner of her eye as she walked on. Actually, he's not bad, she thought, noting his strong cleft chin and the unkempt sandy hair that fell over his soft brown eyes. A bit rugged perhaps, but he looks nice enough . . . certainly good for a drink and a laugh.

"Yes, I have been to Nice before," she replied to his question, "but all the action is in Cannes and St. Tropez. That's where we usually stay."

"We?" he asked tentatively, anticipating a jealous husband or lover to complicate his plan.

"I'm sorry," she said in slight confusion, "I meant where *I* usually stay. I was thinking of my parents."

"Oh, well, in that case you must tell me all about Cannes and St. Tropez." Peter Kent took her arm confidently as they passed through the gate toward the waiting plane.

Through the glass wall of the airport corridor over Gate 32A another man watched Sarah and Peter walk to the plane. He was rugged-looking with a strong cleft chin; unkempt sandy hair fell over his brown eyes. He turned to his companion and smiled. "Right on schedule." The other laughed.

Air France Flight 404 knifed through the thin, star-filled night sky, racing toward its fashionable destination on the Mediterranean coast. It was approaching its objective almost as fast as Peter Kent was approaching his. He ordered a third double Scotch for Sarah.

"I think you're trying to get me drunk," Sarah laughed while gulping down the remains of number two. "I'll just bet you've got some pretty naughty thoughts whirling around in that brain of yours."

"You do me a grave injustice," he answered in mock outrage while trying to affect a shocked look. "I do not go about seducing strange young women."

"*Strange?*" she exclaimed in surprise. "You've been pumping me about my life for the last hour. Is there anything about me you *don't* know by now? One would think you were a master spy. By the way, you aren't a spy, are you?" she asked coyly.

Peter looked appreciatively at her while the stewardess fumbled awkwardly with their new drinks. Sarah was a plain, naturally attractive girl in her mid-twenties. She had a delicate face with sleepy green eyes and long, straight black hair that fell halfway to her waist, a slim waist around which both of Peter's strong hands would fit with little trouble. Her breasts were youthful and firm, and her slender hips ran smoothly to the long, graceful legs that had first attracted his attention. She could be a smash sensation, he thought, if she'd put a little effort into jazzing herself up. But Sarah was in conflict with life. She dressed almost as if she were still in finishing school, dressed just the way her father had last seen her. She wore not a trace of makeup, her sweater and skirt combination had passed from the fashion scene years ago, and as for jewelry, even to Peter her single strand of pearls seemed woefully inadequate. Sarah Dilworth was a lovely understatement.

"You're not answering me," she said, poking Peter in the ribs and rousing him from his thoughts. "So am I to assume you *are* a spy?"

"No," he laughed, "just a humble reporter."

"Oh," Sarah said flatly. He could see her disappointment and feel the wall of cool reserve suddenly erected between them.

"Just my luck," he said wistfully. "Spies are 'in' this season and nobody wants to know a reporter." They sat in silence for a minute or two. "Okay," Peter Kent said finally, "I admit I did recognize you at Orly; after all, the daughter of a late U.S. ambassador to the Court of St. James isn't very easy *not* to recognize . . . particularly when she's gone around the world for the last few years breaking up nightclubs, jumping into fountains, and smashing up cars. Can you believe I've always wanted to meet you, not as a news item, but as the kind of woman I could really swing with? It's as simple as that."

Sarah looked hard at him. She rather liked Peter Kent and was eager—perhaps overly eager—to accept his story at face value. She was tired of most of the international set in the south of France; Peter promised to be a happy change. Her defenses relaxed. Why not give him a chance? He was fun, genuinely seemed to like her, and had a warm, cosy feel about him.

"Would you like me to disappear?" he asked.

Sarah smiled. "No, I guess not. I'm just very sensitive about you so-called gentlemen of the press. I like to lead the life I lead, and lead it without editorial comment. Besides, if you leave, Mrs. Van Schuyler will just take your seat and I won't get anything more to drink." Sarah indicated an elegant, silver-haired matron in deep conversation with her seat companion several rows behind them. The conversation was a distinctly one-way affair. "She talked my ear off all the way from New York to Paris. If you need some gossip for your paper, plug her in; she's the world's greatest unpaid columnist. Maybe she can tell you why the first-class section of this plane is off limits; she was furious about not being able to sit up there. Would the mystery of Flight 404 fascinate your readers?"

"I'm afraid whatever readers I have are going to have to be satisfied with my coverage of the art auction in Cannes Thursday; that's why I'm here. How about you?"

"Personal curiosity or professional?" she asked.

"Strictly personal." He smiled, running his hand lightly over hers.

"I come to St. Tropez every year in August," she said. "I don't know why; I suppose it's just a habit . . . we always came here before."

"Stop me if you know something I don't," he said, "but isn't this July?"

"Of course it is, you fool." Sarah laughed. "I'm early this year because of my godmother." She sobered quickly and took a gulp of her drink. "I witnessed an accident several days ago that shook me up a lot. I'm okay now—who wouldn't be after all those needles and pills—but Ava insisted I get away from New York and come stay with her at her clinic for a rest. So, here I am," she smiled again, "spending August in July."

"Clinic? Ava? Not the famous Ava Bardoff?" Peter asked.

"There's only one. She's my godmother and some-times she's my boss. In other words, occasionally I do a little publicity for the House of Bardoff and in return I'm horribly spoiled."

Peter thought for a minute. "My God, that 'accident' you witnessed; it wasn't the suicide plunge Undersecre-tary Martin took, was it? You were there . . . on the terrace?"

"Please, let's not talk about it," Sarah begged, shak-ing her head. "I'm so confused I don't know what I did or didn't see anymore. Besides, I hate talking about death. Everyone dies sooner or later, so why make such a big thing out of it?" Her voice began to rise. "It's fate, isn't it—some people die and some are left behind?" Peter felt her hand tighten under his and drain of warmth; her words seemed more directed at proving a point to the world in general than to him. "Well, I'm not going to be left behind, not again. I can go anywhere, do anything I want, and I'm going to do it, do it without getting tied up with anyone; that's how you . . ." She paused in mid-sentence, and her voice dropped almost to a whisper. "I've got lots of friends; I won't be alone."

During this emotional outburst Peter remembered the black newspaper headlines four years ago shriek-ing to the world of the death of Sarah's parents, both buried under an avalanche of stone and snow while skiing. He remembered the pictures of the desolate girl standing in the small Alpine cemetery. Despite Peter's curiosity about Martin, investigating the death of his superior was not his mission, and he decided not to hurt his new friend further by pressing the matter. He lifted her hand to his lips.

"Okay," he said cheerfully, "let's talk about us. How about dinner tomorrow night? I'll pick you up. Where does Godmother Bardoff live?"

His flippant reference to the great Ava Bardoff amused Sarah and she began to relax. "The clinic's in the hills behind St. Tropez, but I don't think you'd better come out; from what she said, things are going to be very busy there for the next few weeks, and Ava's not at all keen about unexpected visitors dropping by. I'll call you tomorrow morning and we'll meet at a marvelous little out-of-the-way restaurant; no one I know will be there. Okay?"

"Ashamed of me?"

"Don't be silly; I wouldn't be suggesting my favorite place if I were. It's very intimate," she teased, pressing her leg against his. "I hope you're up to it."

Peter smiled at what he took to be an open invitation. He scribbled his number on a piece of paper. "Now who has the naughty mind?" he asked, handing it to her. "I'm ready for anything you can dream up, and more."

"Is that a challenge?" Sarah whispered in a low, husky voice and then laughed.

Before he could reply, another voice broke into their conversation. "Excuse me, I wonder if you'd be kind enough to help me with my father. I'm afraid he's had another of his attacks."

Peter and Sarah looked up at the worried face of the man standing in the aisle and then over to the old gentleman slumped forward in his seat quietly moaning. They had watched sympathetically as the young man helped his father board the plane at Paris; the two had taken the seats across from theirs on the plane.

"If you could just help me get him back to the toilet, I'd be most grateful."

"Is it serious?" Peter asked.

"Shouldn't you call the stewardess?" Sarah added. "There may be a doctor aboard who . . ."

"No," the stranger broke in gently, "I know what to do, he's had this trouble before. If you'd just . . ." He looked imploringly at Peter.

Peter Kent handed his glass to Sarah and folded the tray before him up into the seat ahead. "Okay," he said, "I'll be glad to help."

Together the two men eased the elderly, white-haired invalid out of his seat and stumbled awkwardly down the narrow aisle, half carrying him toward the tail of the plane. As Peter pulled open the toilet door with his free hand, his mind puzzled abstractly over the fact that such an old-looking man weighed so much and, from what he could feel, had such a muscled and firm body beneath his rumpled clothing. Peter's brain suddenly clicked and his highly trained instincts shouted a warning, but too late. He felt himself being shoved roughly forward. Peter rebounded like an un-coiling spring from the far wall, trying to turn with fists clenched in the confining space of the tiny chamber. Before he could face his assailant, a needle jabbed into the carotid artery of his neck.

The silent struggle took less than a few seconds; Peter Kent crumpled motionless onto the seat, staring up with glassy eyes. His assailant placed the hypodermic in the basin and then reached up behind his own head and slowly, carefully pealed off the thin plastic mask of the elderly invalid to reveal the face of Peter Kent beneath. He looked down at his double, his lips twisted in a sneering smile. The switch of clothing was done quickly and the mask of the old man skillfully pressed over the other's limp features. A new Peter Kent opened the door to the light knock of his accomplice and together they helped the sick old man back to his seat. Then he crossed the aisle to join Sarah.

"How is he?" she asked, looking up at the now familiar face with concern.

"Not too good, I'm afraid," the substitute Peter Kent replied. "Don't worry yourself; his son can handle things from now on. He's had the pilot call ahead for an ambulance."

"But he's unconscious," Sarah protested, leaning across Peter to get a better look at the unmoving figure slumped in the window seat across the aisle, his face turned partially to the wall. Her eyes strained to see the rise and fall of his chest, but since the reading lights of both father and son had been extinguished, she could detect nothing. "Why don't they see if there's a doctor on board who can . . ."

Peter took Sarah's shoulders and gently pushed her back into her seat. "Stop worrying; it's none of our business. The old man will be okay. His son gave him a shot of something to get him to sleep and an ambulance is waiting in Nice."

"But . . ." Sarah protested.

"But nothing," Peter cut in. "Everything's under control. All you'll do is upset everyone, so relax."

Sarah sat back, took a gulp of her drink, and stared at the half-empty glass she put back on the tray. "Well, I just hope I never have a son like that," she said in annoyance, picturing the calm, expressionless face of the young man who sat across from them looking blankly ahead as if he didn't care whether the poor old man beside him lived or died. Sarah lifted her Scotch again and attempted to relax as she escaped into its aroma and the burning sensation it left in her throat. She glanced down at the hard thigh inches from hers; she could almost feel the power in it as it tried to burst through the restraining fabric of Peter's suit.

"Hey," she said impulsively, grabbing his arm, "why don't we go to St. Tropez tonight. A little dancing, some drinking—I'm in the mood to be mad. How about it? Sort of a preview of tomorrow's dinner?"

"Tomorrow . . . ?" he repeated in apparent surprise, turning sharply to look at her.

"Yes, tomorrow." Sarah laughed back, slightly puzzled by his tone and the funny look in his eyes. "Dinner. Intimate little restaurant. You and me. Remember?" she teased, taking his right hand.

Peter had not anticipated the intimate trend of his original's earlier conversation with Sarah Dilworth and was saved momentarily by the stewardess who came to take their drink glasses and request that they fasten their seat belts for landing. He was composed when he began his apology.

"I really am sorry, honestly. But I'm afraid I've been letting what I *want* to do get in the way with what I *have* to do. I can't have dinner tomorrow. I'm stupid and I'm sorry. I've got to go on to Rome tonight; I have an assignment there."

"Rome?" Sarah almost shrieked.

"I've got to cover the rumored cabinet changes," he said quickly. "The government may fall again and . . ."

"What about your assignment in Cannes—the auction?" she demanded.

"Auction?"

Sarah looked at him suspiciously. "Your art auction, remember? I thought you were going to cover it for your paper." Her surprise at Peter Kent's about-face began to turn to anger. "Or have you been lying through your teeth all along?"

"No, of course not," Peter said, trying to salvage the conversation and his identity. "The paper can easily send another man from Rome."

There was no point in arguing; Sarah sat tight-lipped, staring out the window at the lights of Nice below. She was furious at him and at herself for having been taken in by another smooth operator. She knew a brush-off when she heard one. The plane's none-too-gentle landing at the seaside airport diverted her attention briefly but failed to cool her temper.

As the plane came to a halt, Sarah stood to retrieve her things from the overhead rack. "Well, Mr. Kent, it was nice while it lasted." He rose to help her on with her light jacket but she pulled it out of his hands. "Don't call me, I'll call you," she flashed out sarcastically. With these parting words, Sarah left him standing with a worried expression on his face and joined the impatient passengers inching down the aisle, their progress hindered by a sick old gentleman being eased down the steps into a wheelchair by his son and a very solicitous stewardess.

The delay in the arrival of her luggage seemed doubly long thanks to the insistent questions of Mrs. Van Schuyler, who had swooped down upon her as soon as she entered the baggage claim area demanding to know all about "that nice-looking young man" Sarah seemed to be having such a good time with. After a thorough grilling on Peter Kent as well as Sarah's life during the past few years, and after a gushing kiss, Mrs. Van Schuyler finally and reluctantly was led away by what Sarah considered to be a very nautical-looking chauffeur. Sarah, in turn, pointed out her bags to the chauffeur sent from the Bardoff clinic and accompanied him the short distance to the large black limousine bearing the elaborate gold H.B. crest on the door.

She flopped into a corner of the back seat, still brooding over Peter Kent's lies and ridiculous about-face on their dinner date; he obviously had had no intention of leaving the plane at Nice from the very start. It was not until they were well out of Nice that she noticed the chauffeur had taken the coast road to St. Tropez.

"Charles, why aren't we going to the clinic by the inland highway? It's much shorter and faster, you know."

"*Mais oui,* Mademoiselle Sarah, but Madame, she thought you would enjoy coming this way. It is much more beautiful and relaxing, is it not? She said to me, 'Charles, do not rush Mademoiselle, and stop at any club along the way that amuses her.' "

Sarah smiled to herself. How typical of Ava—always second-guessing people, and usually right. Ava Bardoff had taken over and filled Sarah's life when her father had grown so suddenly cool toward her and sent her away to a series of one boarding school after another. Now that both parents were dead, Ava was the only piece of security Sarah dared hang on to, even though she sometimes puzzled over the fact that she didn't really know or understand this woman. Men weren't to be relied upon; get too close to a man and sooner or later he'd let you down—besides, none of the men she knew could hope to measure up to her late father. They were okay for dating and sleeping with, and some were amusing, yet she wouldn't get involved with any of them; too dangerous. But Ava was always there.

"Yes, Charles," she said. "You and I are very lucky to have Madame."

"*Oui*, Mademoiselle, very lucky."

Even at night the Riviera had a magic all its own. The car moved smoothly along the coast road, sometimes winding high through rocky and verdant hills, sometimes dipping low to follow the Mediterranean rippling with the reflections of lights from the hundreds of pleasure yachts moored offshore or in small crowded harbors. They passed through Antibes, Juan-les-Pins, and continued west. Substantial old summer houses in the styles of various fashionable periods ranged side by side up the hills to the right, their solidity broken occasionally by brash glass villas out of *House Beautiful*. Now and then the dim shape of an elegant château could be seen through the iron fence containing its overgrown, semitropical garden.

Thirty kilometers later they turned onto the Croisette separating the imposing old white-faced hotels, expensive shops, and apartment buildings of Cannes from the long expanse of carefully raked beaches. The elegant resort city had not changed in all the years Sarah and her family had visited it. Tall palm trees lined the boulevard, and bushes of flaming bougainvillea, geraniums, and a vast assortment of other colorful vegetation gave it an almost unreal, plastic effect. She noted the familiar casino at the edge of the port ablaze with activity and with difficulty stifled her impulse to ask Charles to stop.

An hour later the limousine edged its way through the narrow, laughing streets of St. Tropez and Sarah abandoned herself to the urge to be gay. Not a single high-rise building marred this fishing village, which retained its unique, Old World charm with a thick overlay of modern sophistication. The open-air cafés lining the main square around the harbor were the official after-dinner meeting places for sun worshipers from all over the world. Although long past midnight, they were jammed, pouring forth a disarray of the current pop music into the lighted square as people strolled leisurely, shoulder to shoulder, back and forth, to see and be seen in the latest trend-setting fashions from Dior to army surplus. Late coffee and Cognac were being sipped hedonistically on the afterdecks of an incredible variety of motor yachts and sailboats, packed side by side into the harbor like sardines. In St. Tropez, night was day.

Sarah left the car and worked her way through the milling crowd toward the Citadelle, intent on making the rounds of several of the more insane discotheques to see who was in town and what parties were in the works for the next few weeks. As a reaction, to Peter Kent's rebuff, she felt a need to reassure herself of her popularity by throwing Sarah Dilworth into a mad social whirl. She fell, exhausted, back into the limousine at about 2:00 A.M. "Charles, take me home. I've only been in France for four hours and already I've drunk too much and danced until my feet are numb." Sarah smiled happily. "And Madame made me come to St. Tropez early for a rest. Ha!"

She was asleep long before the car started its tortuous climb into the hills far behind the resort town. It slowly navigated the narrow, twisting roads, finally reaching the grounds of the palatial seventeenth-century château that Madame Bardoff had restored and converted into her "clinic," a fountain of youth for those lucky women and men invited to partake of Madame's hospitality at exorbitant prices. While the steel and glass needle on Fifth Avenue symbolized the financial power of the House of Bardoff, this magnificent château filled with priceless works of art represented the very soul, the guiding spirit of Madame's empire.

Charles flashed the car lights in a silent code and a set of imposing iron gates set into the high ten-foot wall that surrounded the château grounds swung slowly open. After a mile-long drive through a beautifully landscaped park, the limousine at last pulled to a stop before the main entrance of the great three-and-a-half-story, mansard-roofed stone building that had stood the trials of history for over three hundred years.

As Sarah walked drowsily up the wide steps and into the vast, forty-foot-high marble entrance hall, she could not have guessed she was about to begin the most terrifying adventure of her life—perhaps the final adventure of her life.

Nodding to those members of the night staff lingering in the corridors, she followed the personal maid assigned to her to the small suite of rooms she usually occupied on the east side of the château.

"Madame has retired for the night, Mademoiselle Sarah," the maid informed her. "She will look in on you tomorrow after breakfast."

While her bags were being unpacked, Sarah wandered contentedly around the familiar, flower-filled room. She ran her fingers lovingly over the surface of the Louis XV writing desk, the delicate gold inkstand, and her favorite porcelain figurines on the mantel. How very good it is to be back, she thought. Dropping down on the edge of the bed, she watched impatiently as the maid finished hanging up her things, and then Sarah tactfully wished her good night. Alone at last. She smiled down at the tranquilizers that Ava's doctor had prescribed resting in a small saucer beside a glass of warm milk on her bedside table; there was certainly no need for them tonight. She rose with a yawn to dispatch the pills and milk down the bathroom sink and, coming back, stepped dreamily out of her clothes, tossing them casually over the back of a chair along with her nightgown that had been so artistically draped across her bed. Sarah switched off the lights and slipped between the fresh sheets, relishing their cool touch on her skin. She stretched luxuriously and drifted into a happy sleep filled with memories of her father and their good times together in this beautiful place.

At some point during the night running feet in the corridor outside the bedroom awakened her. Pushing herself up on one elbow, she squinted across the dark room at the window; the park outside was bright with floodlights and she heard the dogs barking. Her groggy brain absorbed the sights and sounds slowly before coming to its conclusion—another prowler like the harmless burglar they'd caught last year and held for the local police. The château was certainly good hunting grounds for every jewel and art thief in Europe. At least that was the reason Madame Bardoff gave for maintaining her own elite security corps.

It took the rustling of shrubbery outside her window to snap Sarah's brain fully awake. In panic she reached for the telephone beside her bed to call for help. A dark figure straightened up, turned, and tried to force her window. Sarah froze, not daring to move, her hand poised impotently above the receiver. Then her body relaxed and she released the breath that had been caught in her throat with a sigh of relief. In the dim light she recognized Peter Kent's disheveled face. She moved to get out of bed and call to him, but before she could, the figure disappeared.

That crazy fool, she laughed to herself. He was putting me on all the time; that garbage about going on to Rome was just to tease me and set me up for his dramatic surprise of sneaking out here. Well, I bet he's getting the surprise of his life right now. Sarah picked up the house phone and dialed the clinic switchboard. "This is Miss Dilworth. Can you tell me what's going on outside?"

"Just a prowler, Mademoiselle Dilworth. He will be caught soon and turned over to the police. There is absolutely no cause for alarm."

"Thanks very much." She hung up, smiling. Sarah decided not to interfere in the execution of justice; a night in the local village jail would serve him right. She'd phone him in Cannes later that morning, that is, if he'd got himself free of the police by then. He'll be madder than a wet hen, she thought, giggling mischievously. Sarah curled up and, after another fit of giggles, fell back to sleep anticipating their dinner date that night.

Peter Kent lay face down under one of the limousines parked by the side of the château. He wore the black T-shirt and trouser uniform of the security guard he'd overpowered; his feet were bare. His mind whirled in pained confusion; the summons to Washington, the trip from New York, the long legs of Sarah Dilworth he'd followed in Paris, the sick old man, the last few hours—everything flashed back and forth in front of his eyes in frightening disarray. His limbs were leaden and responded sluggishly to the commands of his brain. He felt strangely trapped within his own body. Peter had never experienced real terror before; if he should escape tonight, what he had just witnessed would torment him for the rest of his life. But in the back of his mind Peter knew he'd be spared this mental anguish . . . his chances of escape were zero.

Dragging himself out from under the car, he crouched behind it to avoid the circling beams of light and looked to the right and left. Then, in a last desperate attempt, he launched himself forward to run in agonizing slow motion toward the distant wall that, as in a nightmare, never seemed to get closer. Behind he heard the quiet calls of the dark figures closing in. Trees, palms, grass—the whole park spun before his eyes as he ran. Finally, Peter slowed to a stagger, he urged himself a few more yards, and collapsed. He tried again and again to lift himself but could only lie on the cold grass. Peter rolled over on his back and looked up helplessly. A circle of faces gathered above him, smiling down, gloating. They were incredibly handsome faces . . . and they were all the same.

Lying at their feet, Peter Kent curled up like a small, frightened child and began to cry. "Please," he whimpered, "kill me."

2

Morning broke in a pink haze so typical to the south of France. The streets of Cannes were quiet and cool, the metal shutters of shops not yet rolled up for business. Gardens and walks around the elegant hotels were wet from the hoses of an army of gardeners, and lounges and umbrellas were being set up around swimming pools. Across the Croisette, beach attendants flexed their tanned bodies in the fresh air as they raked up seaweed from the water's edge, pausing occasionally to look out at the magnificent yacht anchored offshore and dream of sailing in it to all the magic places of the world.

The streamlined *Krait* was one of the largest privately owned power ships on the Mediterranean and was acknowledged the most beautiful. Aside from its large, exquisitely decorated salon and dining room, one wall of which was entirely covered by a Gobelin tapestry, the *Krait* carried luxurious accommodations for its owner and ten guests, not to mention the crew of eighteen who catered to each and every whim of those guests. Picassos, Renoirs, Cézannes, and the works of other fine artists hung throughout this floating treasure house. The fore and aft decks were long enough to afford plenty of space for sunbathing and sipping cocktails. The top deck was usually kept under canvas for outdoor dining except during large evening parties, when it was removed to enable the stars to shine down on the dance floor.

Hugo Krait Montclair sat on the top deck at the head of the long-deserted breakfast table, opening mail and nursing a cold while sipping freshly squeezed orange juice. His chief steward stood at attention slightly behind his chair. As the multimillionaire owner and part designer of the *Krait,* Hugo enjoyed considerable respect not only among the yachting world, but the art and social worlds as well. He had spent his sixty-two years assembling one of the world's greatest private art collections, while at the same time collecting literally thousands of friends, business associates, and surprisingly few enemies from one end of the earth to the other. Through wise investments in art and property, he had managed to build his inherited wealth into a great fortune.

Hugo had a slight but firm build, close-cropped white hair, an aquiline nose, and intense, pale blue eyes. Now a widower, he had weathered two serious heart attacks that forced him to abandon his past physically active life. He was both praised and criticized for his best known trait, being just plain nice. Hugo Montclair was a pushover for a good sob story and generous to a fault, having probably loaned more money (not expecting its return) than any other person in his position. He backed faltering dance companies, theatres, playwrights, orchestras, and artists—all in the belief that those with talent should be encouraged in the hope that a few of them might flower into something worthwhile. As a result, people generally regarded Hugo as intelligent but weak willed and somewhat frivolous—a public image he took great pains to foster. But at this hour in the morning, Hugo was alone and far from frivolous.

"Have we no word yet on our friend?" he asked his barlike chief steward, Petras Furman, a man who had been in his employ for as long as anyone could remember. Although he had a heavy build, Petras walked with the light spring of a prizefighter, which led some to speculate that he might double as Hugo's bodyguard, a seemingly unnecessary precaution for one so universally liked.

"None whatsoever, sir. He didn't get off the plane last night. I checked with a friend at the reservation desk; their records show he changed his ticket in Paris."

Hugo shook his head from side to side. "I just don't understand; it makes absolutely no sense at all. Did you notice anything unusual at the airport? Tell me everything you saw." He buttered a piece of toast absently, devoting his full attention to the steward's words.

"Well, there was a lot of security all over the place, and they were trying to keep it secret. There were a lot of gendarmes in the parking area outside the terminal, and there must have been fifty or so plainclothesmen hidden around the building and field. And there was something funny going on in the first-class section of Flight 404. While I was waiting for Mrs. Van Schuyler, several limousines with drawn shades drove out on the tarmac and took off the first-class passengers. It was too dark out there to see much, but there were only a few passengers in the entire section."

"Knowing you, you didn't stop with that simple observation. What else did you learn about them?"

"All I could get out of my friend—I had to be casual about it—was that the airport was told they were just a bunch of VIPs on holiday."

"Highly unlikely," Hugo scoffed. "VIPs usually enjoy being seen and the French police don't mobilize that degree of security unless something very important and political is going on. Besides, I'd be one of the first to be told of an invasion of so-called VIPs in the vicinity; my hospitality is too well known not to be given the chance of including them."

"The shah flew in just before they landed; his private jet was being towed into the small hangar on the left. Do you think he's connected in any way with the arrival of the others?"

"I don't know, Petras, I just don't know," Hugo mused almost to himself while delicately slicing a ripe fig. "It's all quite baffling—the shah, security police,

mysterious VIPs, limousines with drawn shades. Our
friend was right in the middle of it and for some reason decided to fly on to Rome. Now why would he do
that? He must have received our anonymous invitation
to the auction at the gallery tomorrow and have known
he was supposed to attend. It would have been so simple; contact could have been made with him there
without anyone suspecting. But now?" Hugo finished
his fruit in puzzled silence.

"Why don't I do some discreet sniffing around at the
pied-à-terre he keeps in Cannes?" the steward suggested.

Hugo shook his head. "I think we'd better leave this
alone for the time being. We can't afford to be connected with him or his organization in any way—it
would be most embarrassing if not fatal." Pushing his
plate away, he looked up at his steward. "If I don't
see him tomorrow at the gallery, I'll call Washington.
Did you see anything else last night that may or
may not be significant?"

"A limousine was there from the Bardoff clinic to
pick up a young lady."

"Yes, I've heard that Ava Bardoff is due back momentarily. That was a nasty bit of work at her reception—probably the most public 'suicide' of the decade.
Who was the girl? Anyone we know?"

"I've seen her somewhere, but can't fit a name to the
face—plain but pretty, long dark hair. She was talking to Mrs. Van Schuyler."

"Ah, yes, dear Susy," Hugo smiled. "Well I think we
can rely upon her to unravel that mystery for us. Susy
Van Schuyler is one of our most unsuspecting and
valuable . . ."

"Do I hear my name being bandied about?" Susan
Van Schuyler called out as she mounted the steps to
the top deck and swept down on them, wearing some
fashionable summer garment far too youthful for her
advancing years and a bit too small for her ample
figure. "Darling Hugo," she said, beginning one of her
typical nonstop monologues that often left her gasping
for air, "you look absolutely divine this morning—

that foulard is perfect. Why more men don't wear white trousers and blue blazers, I'll never know; they're always in fashion. What a beautiful morning. I just couldn't sleep another second longer with all this lovely sun. How wonderful to be here with you; these next few weeks will be such fun. I just . . ."

"Susy," Hugo prodded gently, "what would you like for breakfast? Some of your favorite guava jelly is on the sideboard, and there are kippers just the way you like them. Please help yourself."

As Susan Van Schuyler greedily perused the sideboard, he turned to Petras. "That will be all for now. Will you send up the rest of the things—the other guests should be here soon. And Petras, remember, no discreet sniffing around."

The steward bowed slightly and left Hugo to Susy's stream of consciousness. After sitting through several minutes of it, Hugo asked, "Susy, how was your flight? Anyone interesting on it?"

Her eyes lit up with anticipation, and she took a quick swallow of coffee before lowering her cup. "Hugo, you've got to promise me you'll carry what I'm about to say to your grave. I'm only telling you because I know I can trust you—you never fail to keep a secret."

"That's very flattering, Susy, but I don't think you should break another trust by telling me anything you shouldn't."

"You see—you see how good you are?" Not to be deprived of the joy of betraying a confidence, Susan Van Schuyler persisted. "Hugo, guess who I had dinner with the day before yesterday, just the night before I flew over here. Go on, guess."

"I couldn't possibly—you know everyone in New York."

"*And* Washington," she added for the record. "I dined with the wife of the secretary of state—just the two of us. I contribute very heavily to her charities, you know. Well, she let slip that she'd cancelled all her engagements for the next three weeks, and guess why. You couldn't possibly. She's taking a holiday in

France. She was *so* upset about spilling the beans and wouldn't say a word more—swore me to secrecy. Well, I didn't say a word, not one, although I almost died of curiosity. And then, do you know, when I got to Kennedy Airport yesterday morning, my first-class reservation had been cancelled and I was put in tourist. Can you imagine? Me? In tourist?" Susan Van Schuyler bit firmly into a piece of toast and leaned forward. "I was furious, but they wouldn't do a thing about it. And later they wouldn't even let me peep into the first-class section. And I know she was there the whole time—I'm as certain of it as. . . . She has a terrible little poodle that yaps incessantly and I'm sure I recognized it barking up there. They don't let just anyone take dogs on board, you know. I wouldn't be at all surprised if they gave that nasty little dog my seat. Can you imagine?" she said indignantly. "I wonder who else was up there. I tried to pump the stewardess, but she was such a fool—didn't know a thing."

Susan Van Schuyler paused only long enough to take another large bite of toast heavily laden with butter and guava jelly. "Mark you, I'm sure something very important is going on. I've never in my life known her to be so mysterious about a trip before—her husband's trips, yes, but never hers. She wouldn't say where she was going in France, but I'll bet she's right around here someplace. We had to change planes in Paris and the first-class section on Flight 404 from Paris to Nice was treated in just the same way. They didn't have room for me up there either, but they had room for that horrible little dog; you could hear him yapping all the way down to Nice. Now what do you make of all that?"

Before Hugo had the chance to make anything out of it she continued. "Today I want to check all the hotels on shore to see if she's registered. Won't she be surprised when I come bounding in?" Susan Van Schuyler got up to replenish her empty plate. "Can I have a small party on the *Krait* for her—that is, if I find her?"

"Certainly, Susy, but if you do find her, why not invite her to my costume party tomorrow after the

auction? Several hundred people will be aboard and
she might find it amusing. We haven't seen each other
in years, so it will be a treat for me as well."

"Oh, Hugo, you *are* a dear. Just wait until you see
my costume for Thursday night—I had it made
by . . ."

Before she had a chance to launch into an unin-
formative monologue, Hugo asked casually, "Was
there anyone else on the flight you knew?"

Susan Van Schuyler thought for a minute and then
answered, laughing, "Oh, yes, that naughty but charming Sarah Dilworth. You remember her, don't you?
Her father and mother were killed in that awful avalanche five or six years ago in Switzerland while staying
with Ava Bardoff." Hugo's eyes narrowed at the sound
of that name. "She's spending a month or so at the
Bardoff clinic. I must say, I wish I could get in there—
Ava Bardoff works wonders. She's Sarah's godmother,
you know."

"No, I didn't know," Hugo said, feigning little interest while his mind raced, trying to absorb and cat-
alogue all the information Susy was throwing at him
over her second helping of kippers.

In an attempt to win back his attention, which she
considered to be waning, Susy decided to add a bit of
spice to her story. "Never let it be said that I'd say
anything against that dear child, but I'm sure her morals leave something to be desired. You should have
seen the way she was flirting on the plane with that
young man—outrageous! And drink? Why the two
were like fish in a bowl. I know what was on his mind,
but I don't want to start any rumors. Anyhow, he
never got a chance to do a thing, thank heavens—they
had some sort of quarrel and he went on to
Rome."

Hugo's delicate heart took a jump. "Oh? Was her
charmer a hot-blooded Italian?" he asked innocently.

"I wish he had been—then there might have been
some excuse for his behavior. No, I'm afraid he was
American—you know, with his hair the sloppy way
our young men wear it these days, falling all over his
face. Let's see, she told me his name. What was it?"

Susan Van Schuyler looked out across the shimmering water as she searched the filing cabinets and social registers of her mind. "Dent, or Pent, or . . ."

"Kent?" Hugo offered.

"Yes, Kent. It was Kent. How clever of you—do you know him?"

"Susy, darling, I don't know him; I just guessed. Kent is a very common name."

"It *is* common, isn't it?" she replied and then continued.

Hugo sat at the head of the table lost in thought while Susan Van Schuyler prattled on. He interrupted her only once—to suggest she telephone Sarah Dilworth at the clinic and insist she come to his masquerade party. Hugo stated he'd invite Ava Bardoff personally if she were back in residence.

One by one his other guests made their appearance on deck to join them for breakfast, and outwardly he became the gracious and concerned host for which he was famed, absorbed in their tales of adventure ashore the previous evening, helping them with their minor problems for the upcoming day, and issuing elaborate orders to his crew for that day's small champagne luncheon for twenty-four.

Hugo also looked forward to the arrival of his valued friend, Paul Mytilini, a brilliant Greek art expert who had promised to come early to consult with him about the next day's auction. Mytilini would bring behind-the-scenes gossip and the expected prices at which the major masterpieces would be sold. Hugo needed this information in advance to plan his strategy for obtaining a fine Monet for himself and two Renoirs for a U.S. gallery he had agreed to represent. Yes, the host, crew, and guests of the *Krait* had a very busy day ahead of them.

Some fifty kilometers away in the hills behind St. Tropez, Madame Ava Bardoff's first day back in the south of France had also begun. The beautiful and envied woman luxuriated in a shallow, pink marble pool eight feet square in the center of her vast, high-ceilinged room in the northeast corner of the château. This one great room served not only as her private bath, but as her living room and office.

The walls were covered in deep blue felt and crowded with gilt-framed, early Italian religious paintings. Three immense crystal chandeliers, the middle one hanging directly over her bath, illuminated the magnificent painted ceiling that was almost a replica of the one in the Sistine Chapel. Father, son, and the many guardians of Christianity swirled overhead in their kingdom of heaven. Rich blue and gold Fortuny draperies framed the six floor-length windows overlooking the hills and Mediterranean sea in the far distance. In contrast to the opulence of the walls, ceiling, and draperies, the furnishings of the room were simple and contemporary. A lush, deep-pile white carpet covered the floor from wall to wall, broken only in the center by the marble bath, which became an elegant reflecting pool filled with long-finned goldfish when not in use by its owner. The pool separated a mammoth, fur-covered bed in the sleeping end of the room from the living and office area that was dominated by a large stainless steel and glass desk facing a formal arrangement of plain but luxurious couches and chairs covered in white raw silk. The room contained numerous small glass-topped tables on which rested exquisite porcelain vases and objets d'arts of priceless value. Tall palms filled several corners and clustered around the pool and bed to form sybaritic oases for Madame's whims. The room was a mirror of its owner—a combination of sensual beauty and austere business acumen, passion and steel.

This morning a large Art Deco metal screen masked the pool from the office area. Two top gentlemen in the Bardoff French organization stood rigidly facing the screen. They only heard Ava Bardoff's voice in response to their reports, and waited patiently for her orders.

Ava lay back against soft leather cushions in the warm water billowing with scented foams and oils while she concentrated on the details of what her underlings told her, paying particular attention to the varying inflections in their voices. Her hand toyed unconsciously between the thighs of the young, blond Adonis who knelt naked beside her in the pool, gently massaging her face, shoulders, and breasts with rich, intoxicating creams. His lithe body glistened above her as he worked her pliant skin. A second, darker young god lay facing her on the far edge of the pool playing dreamily with himself as he studied her through half-closed eyes. The eyes of the countless Madonnas and holy men could not close nor be averted in modesty; they stared down in outrage from the walls and ceilings at the voluptuous scene below.

"I hope our guests spent a comfortable night after their trip," Madame Bardoff said. "Did we have any questions about the disturbance in the grounds?"

Stanislau Beel, the handsome number-two man in the House of Bardoff organization, directed his replies to the screen. "The Americans seem to be suffering from time disorientation and are still sleeping, but the others are up and in the massage rooms. Only one was wakened last night; we explained that a prowler had been apprehended and turned over to the police. She seemed perfectly satisfied with the explanation." He turned to the man beside him who very much looked his part as the head researcher and cosmetic surgeon of the House of Bardoff. "I have made a note, Dr. Mulciber, that she will require increased sedation during her stay here."

Dr. Mulciber nodded his thanks. He was a thin, distinguished man in his early fifties with a full head of dark hair graying slightly at the temples and a well-trimmed moustache and Vandyke beard. He wore a long white laboratory coat over his traditional pin-striped suit, while Beel appeared more relaxed in a white turtleneck sweater and light gray suit trimmed in black from the Bardoff men's collection. It was suitable to the smooth, muscled body of this thirty-year-old athlete. His dazzling smile and administrative ability made Beel a social, as well as a business, asset to Madame.

Ava Bardoff continued. "While our distinguished guests are with us for treatment, all their phone calls are to be intercepted by the switchboard. Only calls from their governments are to be put through to their rooms and, of course, taped. There should be no other calls as no one else knows they are here. Are the observation studios, tape machines, and cameras ready? And the briefing of the 'neuts'—it has been completed?"

"Yes," Beel replied. "They have been drilled letter perfect on all the information in the files; we can begin the fine tuning at once. You can be assured everything will go off without a wrinkle." He smiled at his choice of words.

"Beel, your humor is misplaced," Madame stated flatly. He sobered and stiffened at the rebuke. "This is our most ambitious project to date, essential if our overall plan is to succeed." Ava Bardoff's nails bit painfully into the wet flesh of the thigh beside her. "I assume only success. Is that clear?" she demanded.

Both men mumbled assurances.

"Speak up, gentlemen."

"It will be successful, Madame," Dr. Mulciber said clearly.

"A complete success," Beel echoed.

"Thank you," she said with emphasis, accepting their commitment. Ava relaxed her grasp on her young lover. "Doctor, you will explain our procedures to our female guests this afternoon and discuss with them exactly what changes they can expect. We need their complete and relaxed cooperation. Perhaps it would be wise to show them more of the before and after photographs to reassure them. Your staff will be ready for the operations in two weeks time?"

"Yes, Madame, all has been made ready. Whatever parts we needed have been obtained and are being prepared in the laboratory."

Ava smiled. "They will certainly get a surprise, eh, doctor?" She chuckled to herself and then sobered. "It will be more difficult with the men. They are here for business, not egocentric pleasure. Most of our work must be done with them at night, and we don't have much time."

"Will you be with me during the preliminary discussions with the women?" Dr. Mulciber asked.

"No, unfortunately I have a luncheon appointment, but I will introduce you this morning before I leave. Beel, you will accompany us and use your famous charm to make all our guests feel at home—even the interpreters. Arrange a welcome dinner this evening—our special foods, of course."

"Yes, Madame."

"Good, everything on *this* front appears to be covered." A silence fell over the room, broken only by the movement of water in the bathing pool. Ava Bardoff stood up slowly with her arms outstretched like Venus rising from a foamy sea and allowed herself to be gently toweled by her young men. As they helped her into a long blue silk robe she said, "Doctor, you will leave us. We meet again in exactly two hours." Then, turning to her attendants, "Ash, Peor, go as well." The two young men wrapped small towels around their waists, crossed the room, and left obediently by a door beside the fur-covered bed. Ava Bardoff strode from behind the screen to confront Beel. The muscles of her face began to harden into an iron mask; her voice was cold.

"And now the Kent affair. Is Moloch waiting outside?"

"Yes, Madame."

"Bring him in." She moved behind her large steel and glass desk on which rested a series of files and, among other objects, two large Ming horses.

Beel opened the heavy door and summoned a squat, piglike man with a shaved head. His appearance was in sharp contrast to all the other members of the Bardoff entourage. They were handsome, fit specimens of manhood; Moloch was none of these. He stood at attention, heels together, arms stiffly by his side and faced the desk.

Ava Bardoff stared at him for a full minute, her eyes moving over his black uniformed body. Finally she spoke sharply. "Moloch, you are responsible for the security of the House of Bardoff in Europe. I tolerate your appearance, an appearance that is abhorrent to me, because it is essential to your role and, Moloch, because it acts as a constant reminder to us all of the brutish instincts in man that lie under the veneer of beauty I create. You remind us, Moloch, to what depths we will have to sink to protect ourselves from the spies who would steal my secrets and the enemies who would destroy all we have worked so long to achieve. My empire must be protected. Are you able to perform this duty?" she demanded. Her eyes cut through the miserable man.

"Yes, Madame," he said, staring straight ahead. "The problem last night was . . ."

"Was *your* problem, Moloch," she interrupted angrily. "I do not wish to know the details other than that appropriate punishment has been administered. Mr. Martin had a problem; he could not solve it. Mr. Martin's lease on life was not renewed. I hope the lesson is clear to you and the others?"

"Yes, Madame, perfectly clear."

Ava leaned back into her chair, picking up a silver letter opener in the shape of a cross. She turned it over and over in her hands, her fingers absently exploring the ornate design as her anger subsided. A cool, dispassionate tone returned to her voice. "Did the operation on the plane go smoothly? There was no suspicion?"

"Very smoothly. I am sure no one suspected—even the cabin crew did not really understand what had happened. We picked up his suitcase without any trouble. As far as anyone is concerned, Mr. Kent went on to Rome and will disappear there. The matter has been concluded."

Ava stared at him, turning his words over in her mind as she turned the cross in her hands. She visualized the incidents on the plane the previous evening and spoke thoughtfully, more to herself than to those in the room. "It may or may not have been just a coincidence that Kent involved himself with my goddaughter, but I find that hard to accept. The CIA may have arranged it. I distrust the situation. It was a most unfortunate meeting either way, one which I hope will not haunt us." Ava Bardoff's mind snapped back to focus on the man standing before her, and she leaned forward eagerly, anticipating his words with relish. "Now, Moloch, for the good news. What did you learn from Mr. Kent?"

"I regret we learned nothing we already did not know."

Madame looked at him in stunned silence. Then her fist smashed down on the desk top. "That, Moloch, is impossible," she flashed out. "We did not go to all this effort to learn nothing."

The sweating man spoke quickly. "We found the microfilm of the file. As we had hoped, it was clean —there was nothing in it to implicate the House of Bardoff, nor did it even hint at our technology or purpose. Most of the information could be readily obtained from standard published sources. Martin and the others did a good job in this respect."

"And the name, Moloch, the name of the person to whom this information was being delivered?"

"He does not know."

Again Madame Bardoff slammed her fist on the glass top of her desk in rage and frustration.

"We used the complete range of drugs," Moloch went on to assure her. "He is a very strong-willed man, but he could not have resisted. He revealed only the method by which the film was to be passed on—inserted between the front and back of a postcard. He had not yet been contacted with the location of delivery. That is all we were able to get out of him; he wasn't even sure of the content of the file. Of course we already knew about his flat in Cannes, his cover in the news service, and Martin had informed us of all his activities in the department except this special assignment and the one last year in Piraeus."

Ava fixed him once again in her icy stare, taking note of his slightest reaction as she spoke. "Moloch, you are a thorough man and have had a great deal of experience in matters of this kind. Do you honestly believe Kent does not know who asked for the file?"

He replied without hesitation. "Yes, Madame, I do.

He was to be contacted in the next week, but by whom
—that remains a mystery. He does not even know
who sent him on this and the Piraeus mission. In both
cases he was sent for by an underling in the justice
department, isolated in a Washington hotel room for
one week, and then given the microfilm and a plane
ticket. After he arrived at his destination, he was to
wait for further direction. Everything was done in
great secrecy. Martin was never consulted by the justice department about the use of his own agent. If he
hadn't managed to find and put an electronic listening
device in Kent's hotel room in Washington, we would
not have even known he was coming to Cannes."

"We have lost a year," Ava snapped angrily. "One
entire year. I should never have relied upon Martin—
the assignment was too big for him. Had he done his
job, had he found out the method of delivery, we
would not be in this position—we would not have
picked up Kent in Nice but would have waited, followed him to his contact. Now it is too late, he can lead
us nowhere." She looked at the man before her with
annoyance.

"Do not just stand there like an idiot," Ava said with
an impatient wave of her hand, "sit down, Moloch."
He turned sharply on his heels and sat stiffly at the
opposite end of the couch from Beel.

Ava rose from behind her desk and began to pace
back and forth in front of them in frustration. "Gentlemen, I am being spied upon and I do not like it. I
am being spied upon by someone or some group I do
not know—and that I dislike even more. During the
last ten years I have become gradually aware of this
surveillance, but in all that time we have not been
able to find out by whom and why. We know it is
none of the established surveillance groups of the major countries and yet it apparently has free access to
their security files. The mere fact that it has been able
to remain anonymous for so long while gathering who
knows what information about us makes it all the more
dangerous. We cannot effectively move against what
we cannot see." She stopped and looked deliberately at
one man and then the other. "I have not worked for

over thirty years to risk having our operation exposed
at this crucial point. We are approaching the final stage
of our plan and so, too, we are approaching what must
be a direct confrontation with this unknown group. We
must attack first. We must uncover it *now,* and then
you, Moloch, will eliminate it completely."

Madame Bardoff returned behind her desk and took
up the silver cross. "I gave Martin one year to find
out to whom his own agency was sending reports on us.
His own agent twice a courier and yet he could not find
out." She threw the cross clattering down on the desk
in disgust. "It took us three years to prepare Martin—
three years wasted in his death. This man Kent represented our best chance. We prepared his replacement,
kept him ready for a year waiting for Kent's next special mission only to find out Kent knows nothing. Another waste."

Ava Bardoff sat silently, her face working with internal rage. Her anger and frustration centered on the
hapless agent. She looked up, a thin smile on her lips.
"I am a compassionate woman, gentlemen, and so as
he personally meant us no harm, I mean no harm to
the unfortunate Mr. Kent. Instead, turn him over to
Dr. Mulciber; I am sure the good doctor will be able to
use an intelligent, sturdy man like Mr. Kent in his
work. Who knows, he may be of some help to us yet."
Ava burst into a short, mean laugh. Her dubious kind-
ness toward Peter Kent helped somewhat to reduce her
anger and she leaned back into her chair. "Mr. Kent
may not lead us to our answer, but he may have un-
wittingly handed us another tool—Sarah. Tell me all
you know about my goddaughter's brief encounter
with him."

Moloch began the recitation of events from Sarah's
first meeting with Peter Kent at Orly to her phone call
to his flat in Cannes an hour ago. "We don't think she
knew him before he approached her on the Paris-Nice
flight. From what was observed, they got along very
well. Our neut reports she was expecting to dine with
him this evening and that their relationship promised
to be—" he hesitated—"to be intimate."

"You may speak about sex in front of me, Moloch,"

Ava interrupted with a cruel smile, "or does the subject still frighten you?"

His face reddened at her jab into his emotional problem. "Apparently Kent told her he was in Cannes to cover an art auction for his paper."

"Stop," Ava commanded abruptly. "The art auction —that is interesting. The auction is very small and has received no publicity outside of the trade for fear the rooms will be cluttered with curiosity-seeking tourists. Only galleries, dealers, and interested private collectors would be aware of it. Why should our Mr. Kent mention the auction? To impress Sarah? Or for that matter, why would he even know about it? He does not appear to be an art connoisseur, does he, Moloch?"

"No, Madame."

She thought for several minutes, picking up the silver cross once more and tapping it on her desk. "They sell art postcards at the gallery, don't they? A public but not-too-crowded place in which to make a contact. Perhaps Kent's subconscious has given us the information your drugs could not," she said with a small smile of triumph. "Add the gallery, the auction, and art to the facts we already have in the dossier on our mystery group. I want several of our men at the auction tomorrow—they will keep their eyes open and make a list of everyone who is there. Continue, Moloch."

"Kent gave Miss Dilworth his phone number in Cannes—it was the number she called this morning. I do not believe he would have given his correct number to an associate of yours if he felt a need to keep his presence secret from you. This substantiates my belief that Kent acts merely as a messenger boy in this instance and knows little or nothing of the potential importance of the file he carried."

"Perhaps you are right," Ava conceded, "but I never accept the logical at face value; that is why I and the House of Bardoff are here today. Now repeat Sarah's exact words on the telephone this morning."

Moloch stood up while taking the report from the clinic switchboard out of his uniform pocket. "Miss Dilworth started talking as soon as Kent's concierge picked up the phone. She said, 'Did the police give you a rough time?' and then began to laugh, saying, 'Serves you right, you fool.' Getting no reaction, Miss Dilworth asked 'Peter? Hello?' Then she must have realized she had the old woman instead of Kent, asked if he were there, and said she'd call back later in the day."

Ava Bardoff motioned impatiently to Moloch and took the paper from him, reading it through several times. "This definitely establishes she saw him here last night and also that she accepts the switchboard's explanation of the intruder who was turned over to the police in the village. Moloch, you will make sure that if she or anyone else questions them, the local police will admit to the arrest and subsequent release of a Mr. Palot, a curious tourist from Paris who got into my park by mistake. I do not want Kent's name connected in any way with the clinic. I am sure our influence in the village will guarantee police cooperation.

"As for Sarah?" Ava smiled sympathetically. "The poor, disturbed child did not see Kent here at all last night—she only *thinks* she saw him. Just as we confused her about what she thinks she did or did not see and hear on the terrace when Martin died, so she will also have to be made to believe she was tired and under the influence of medications when she saw our Mr. Palot of Paris and mistook him for Kent."

Ava Bardoff thought for a minute or two in silence. "Sarah is becoming more and more dangerous," she said at last, "but we need her for the time being. She is now our only possible link to Kent's mysterious contact. Moloch, you will use her as bait to flush him out. Make sure anyone interested will know of her association with Kent. I want our enemy to come after Sarah to learn about Kent's disappearance, and you, in turn, will come after him and eliminate him. I leave the details to you, but make the bait irresistible—this may be our last chance. Report to me this evening."

Ava Bardoff opened her desk diary and reviewed her appointments for the day. "Beel, when I return from lunch I want to go over the factory production figures for the last three months and tour Pandemonium, particularly Mulciber's labs. Also be present when I meet with our neuts from OPEC and the Ruhr group. I will see our Iranian neut alone at five-thirty. Make some excuse to break him away from our other guests."

Beel and Moloch rose, bowed to Ava Bardoff, and left. A minute later, as if summoned by an unseen command, the beautiful blond Ash and darker Peor appeared silently on either side of her chair; they still wore only towels. Without looking up, Ava's hand circled Peor's waist to the knot of soft cotton. Releasing it, she pulled him closer and pressed her cheek to his firm, warm belly. "Madame has had a difficult morning," she said in a low, teasing voice. "She needs a little love."

The dark youth closed his eyes; his lips parted in a half-smile of pleasure.

The sky was clear blue and the day had turned hot when shortly before noon the *Krait*'s power launch pulled alongside the yacht transporting Paul Mytilini to Hugo's luncheon party. He sprang lightly up the steps to embrace his host. "My dear Hugo, it seems like years rather than months. How wonderful to see you again. I called as soon as I got in from Athens."

"Paul, you never change. If anything you look even younger than when we last met." Hugo knew this compliment would please his overgroomed guest. "You must give me your recipe for vitality." As the two men walked back to the afterdeck, Hugo asked, "I hope your Spartan diet will allow you to join me in a champagne cocktail?"

"Ah, but my diet is also Athenian," he laughed, "it allows me to enjoy whatever is beautiful in life, and at this very minute a champagne cocktail is about the most beautiful thing I can think of."

Physically, Paul Mytilini was not appealing. He looked about forty, was slightly less than average in height, and had a nondescript build. His beardless, smooth complexion emphasized large dark eyes and immaculately shaped eyebrows. Thinning black hair was combed cleverly across his skull to conceal approaching baldness. Despite the heat of the day, he wore a business suit and his shirt buttoned up tightly under a pale silk tie. Several gold rings set with garnets glittered on his fingers. Hugo had never seen Paul Mytilini in a bathing suit—even at beach parties he remained completely clothed—and thought that perhaps his Greek friend was embarrassed to show his body publicly because of some real or imagined disfigurement. Although his physical appearance did not command respect, Paul's intelligence and wit most certainly did.

He had surfaced in the mid-1940s and soon became renowned for tracking down masterpieces looted by the Nazis during World War II. As an undisputed expert, he was employed to authenticate works of art for a growing number of the world's museums and galleries. In addition to this work, Mytilini had personally procured for Hugo many of the best works in his large collection—for sizable commissions, of course. Paul had little trouble holding the center of attention at my gathering thanks to his amusing, if somewhat acid, wit, which he took pleasure in using against any woman who shunned or slighted him in any way. His rapierlike thrusts at various grande dames were repeated along the Riviera, where he maintained a tiny villa in the summer. Needless to say, he was in great demand for spicing up what might otherwise have been dull parties.

Before Hugo could even broach the subject, Mytilini jumped to what was on both their minds. "Now about the auction tomorrow, here is a list of the hold prices on the eight best paintings. They are absolutely first-rate, and although not the most known, are certainly among each artist's best works."

"And the Monet?" Hugo inquired, producing a postcard reproduction of the painting which hung in the gallery.

Paul Mytilini took the card and looked thoughtfully at it and then at Hugo. "Ah, the Monet," he sighed. "It is perfection, absolute perfection. Unfortunately, everyone knows of your interest in this painting, which, of course, you must have for your collection. The dealers will be out to push you up and so push up the value of their own Monets. Make a show of dropping out of the bidding at the $200,000 level. Let one of your friends take over from there; he should get it for—" he paused to think—"for, say, $280,000. Now about the other two . . ."

As the two men discussed the tactics of the art world over champagne, Sarah Dilworth was about to sample the tactics of a far different and more cruel world. She piloted her small white Mercedes sports car through the hot, crowded back streets of one of the less fashionable districts in Cannes looking for number 19 Rue St. Denis. Sarah smiled to herself, thinking how the small bistros, cafés, and crumbling buildings of this Bohemian section suited the stereotyped image of a young reporter writing his first great novel.

Earlier that morning, while she had been talking on the phone with Mrs. Van Schuyler about Hugo's invitation to his costume party, she had received another invitation. Peter Kent had called and left a message with the clinic switchboard saying he'd returned from Rome and asking her to come to his flat for lunch to be followed by a swim somewhere up the coast. Flattered by his obvious change in plans on her behalf, Sarah had jumped into a simple off-the-shoulder cotton sundress and now found herself parking outside a decaying, narrow, four-story apartment building on the steep, tourist-filled street that ran crookedly up toward the old chapel of St. Denis.

She pulled the strap of the bulging beachbag over her shoulder and smoothed her dress as she crossed the street to the small door set into a larger courtyard gate. It was off the latch and opened easily to her push. Sarah rang the bell to the left of the shabby door of the ground-floor flat occupied by the concierge, but there was no answer. Then her eye caught sight of a row of rusting letter-boxes, and her finger traced the names until it came to a newly printed "Kent, No. 9." Straightening up, she looked about for the stairway and saw it on the far side of the courtyard. As she crossed the cobblestones, Sarah smiled at the pathetic attempts of unknown gardeners trying to raise herbs and a few thin geraniums in cracked pots on their window ledges. Several feeble vines crawled up the sides of the peeling building, their efforts too spent for blossoms.

She pushed the light button at the foot of the stairway. It was out of order. Shrugging in resignation, Sarah took a firm hold on the circular iron railing and climbed unsteadily upward to the gloomy third-floor landing. She found the door of No. 9 by the faint light that managed to filter through a small, dirty window and knock lightly. Her knock went unanswered. She tried again, louder. "Peter," she called. Still no reply. "Do stop playing games and let me in."

Sarah grabbed the doorknob in frustration and shook it. The knob turned easily in her hand and the door swung open to a small, distinctly masculine living room. The windows were wide open to let in the light and warmth of the noon sun. Typical, she thought, looking at the dried remains of an avocado stalk in a pot on the coffee table. A battered couch, two overstuffed chairs, a desk littered with papers, and a few wall posters completed the contents of the room.

She assumed that Peter, like every other bachelor she'd known, had run out at the last minute to do the shopping for lunch. Setting down her bag, she occupied herself looking at the posters stuck with tape on the whitewashed walls and finally sat down on the windowsill to watch the colorful stream of human traffic moving in the narrow street below. He really does have a colossal nerve, she thought after ten boring minutes passed without his return. Stubbing out her cigarette in a brass bowl, Sarah got up to kill time by a further investigation of the tiny apartment. The magazines on the desk were several months old and not really meant for female reading. She opened a pair of double doors to the minuscule kitchenette sandwiched into an area two feet deep by five feet wide; it was covered with dust, and a dead cockroach lay on its back in the sink. My God, she wailed to herself, we'll both be poisoned. Obviously Peter was neither a housekeeper nor a cordon bleu chef.

The only other door in the room must lead to the bedroom, Sarah reasoned, and curiosity about where she and Peter might end after lunch drove her to it. The door opened to a sunny room with a large double bed on which. . . . It took Sarah's brain a second or two to register on what she saw lying on the bed. She went cold, her stomach retched into a knot. Sarah stood rigid, staring with eyes wide open, screaming again and again and again. She didn't stop until a sharp slap across her face brought her out of shock. Then she began to cry, only vaguely aware of the people in the room and the door being shut against others crowding the landing.

"Mademoiselle," a policeman said to her softly as she wept against his chest, "Mademoiselle, please. Everything will be all right. Do not think about it."

"Don't think about it?" Sarah almost shrieked, backing away from him. "Don't think about it? Blood all over the walls," she gasped, "and that thing—that, that old woman." Sarah looked at the policeman trying to make him understand. "Didn't you see it?" she cried. "It didn't have any hands—or a head. They . . . cut . . . off . . . her . . . head!"

The news of the horror on Rue St. Denis spread quickly through Cannes and across the water to the *Krait,* where Hugo Montclair and his guests were finishing their elegant champagne luncheon. Every time the launch returned from shore after delivering a departing guest, it was accompanied by more rumors about the murder. The gossip surrounding the surprise visit to Cannes of the shah was completely overshadowed by speculation over the dismemberment of the corpse of what the police assumed to be the concierge of 9 Rue St. Denis. Susan Van Schuyler played the dominant role in the conversation aboard the *Krait,* since she not only knew Sarah Dilworth, who had discovered the body, but had seen her on the plane with the American in whose apartment the heinous act had been committed. Hugo sat looking sick to his stomach while quietly listening to the gory details of the tragedy. Paul Mytilini departed shortly after the news first came aboard the yacht, promising to meet Hugo at the auction the next afternoon. His going signaled the departure of the other luncheon guests from shore and left Hugo surrounded only by those holidaying on board the *Krait*. He consoled several of the more distressed and timid ones, assuring them that their night aboard the *Krait* would be safe from the "mad rapist," as Susan Van Schuyler had christened the murderer. "After all," Hugo explained in a vain and weak attempt to be cheerful, "any mad rapist I've ever had the pleasure of knowing would have long since lost his passion by the time he swam way out here through all that cold water."

By 3:30 Hugo managed to convince his guests that a nice drive ashore through the village of Grasse and the hills beyond would not only be a beautiful idea, but a diverting and soothing one as well. He had phoned a titled friend owning a magnificent villa overlooking Cannes to obtain the desired cocktail invitation to occupy his guests later that afternoon and limousines waited on the quay. He explained that of course he would be forced to remain aboard the *Krait* for the nap that his cardiac specialists insisted follow lunch every day.

Hugo Montclair stood at the top of the steps, waving a cheery goodbye to the launch as it cut away through the shimmering water toward Cannes harbor. As it faded into the distance, so too did his smile. He looked up at the clear blue sky, remembering how sixteen years ago a hot, sunny day like today would have found him and his beloved wife, Eleanor, basking on a deserted beach with a few select friends, laughing gaily over some amusing literary event or trivial social misstep of the previous evening. Those were happy days—never lonely, always carefree, and filled with great love. And now? Hugo shook himself away from beautiful dreams of the past. Now he had practical decisions to make. Now might just be the time he would be forced to gamble his life.

Hugo gave a slight nod of his head to Petras Furman and walked to the foredeck, where there was no risk of the two of them being overheard. They leaned together over the rail, looking down at the dark water in the shadow of the ship. Without shifting his gaze, Hugo said, "I'm glad you didn't take the discreet sniff around this morning; a fine mess to get tied in with."

Both men continued to stare down at the water lapping hypnotically against the bow. After some minutes of deep thought Hugo continued. "That murder was most brutal, Petras—it had none of the finesse we've become accustomed to expect. And yet I'm as sure as if I'd been there myself that it's tied to Madame B. Peter Kent was bringing us the Bardoff file but instead he flies on to Rome and vanishes without a trace. The next day a harmless old woman is hacked to death without apparent reason in his flat and it's somehow arranged that the body is found by Madame's own goddaughter. Why? Why draw attention to the connection between Kent and Sarah Dilworth unless you want that connection known to someone. Known to whom, Petras? To us. We are the people to whom Kent was bringing the file. We are the people who would be most interested in that connection.

"I'm forced to assume that Ava Bardoff knew the purpose of Kent's trip here, and the late George Martin was therefore involved somehow in her organization. She knows we exist, my friend, but I doubt she knows who we are—yet. I believe that disgusting murder is an invitation. Madame is inviting us into her parlor—she wants us out in the open. Petras," Hugo said, almost savoring the danger he knew lay ahead, "Madame has lost her patience with us."

The millionaire, the art collector, the glib host stood up from the rail. "My old friend," Hugo asked, "are you and the others with me on this? You know what she is capable of."

"We know."

He put both hands on his steward's shoulders, his look of gratitude much more eloquent than words. "Then it's time to commit ourselves, to start putting things in motion. Once we start, we can't stop," he cautioned. "It's all or nothing."

Petras Furman nodded his head grimly. "What do we do now?" the steward asked.

"She will have her eyes everywhere, so we must appear to do nothing while at the same time we prepare for battle. It will be a race against time. I'm certain we'll never see Kent or that file, and I certainly don't want to risk asking for a copy to be sent. Miss Dilworth is a possible key to the House of Bardoff, but a key turns both ways. We must be careful or she will unlock our door before we can unlock Madame's to find out what happens in her so very secret parlor. Let's observe Miss Dilworth carefully tomorrow night."

"But surely she won't come to your party now, not after the shock she must have got today."

"Petras, unless I miss my guess, she will most certainly be here. Madame won't want her bait locked away out of reach. Besides, young people like to forget unpleasantness—they cover it up with gaiety and, in this case, probably a great deal of alcohol and loving. Yes, Sarah Dilworth is a possible key and now we need the right person to turn it.

"Petras, bring me Michael dePasse—he will probably be on the beach beyond St. Tropez about now." As Hugo issued his orders his voice hardened and the two once more resumed their roles of captain and crew. "Bring him on water skis and use the underwater entrance. I'll wait for him in the study." As the steward turned to go, Hugo reminded him, "And Petras, we don't have much time. He must be off the ship before my guests return."

Petras Furman gave a small salute and hurried to the top deck where he ordered the crew to lower a powerful motorboat. As it swung over the side, he jumped in with the skis and rode it down to the water to cast off. A few minutes later, from the bow of the *Krait*, Hugo Montclair watched the small red and white boat disappearing west at full throttle, a spray of saltwater tossed high in its wake. His fragile heart beat fast. After years of painstaking preparation it was exhilarating to know that at last they were on the move.

3

The Palms Beach Club was the best of the many
"clubs" that ran the length of the wide, sandy beach
just west of St. Tropez. It consisted of a weather-worn
shack that offered changing facilities (which few bothered to use), a tiny bar with six stools, a hidden kitchen
famed for its superb grilled sardines, and half a dozen
picnic tables and benches scattered outside in the sand
well back from the water. Humble though it might
look, the Palms served the best chilled Dom Perignon
to an assortment of young socialites, models, film di-
rectors, and all their various hangers-on. Nude sunbathing was permitted on only one area of the club's
beach, but the restriction was only a formality; besides,
the size of the ultrabrief bathing costumes worn by
both men and women at the club left absolutely nothing
to the imagination of the French police who occasionally swooped low in helicopters to guard the morals, or
perhaps it would be more accurate to say guard *against*
the morals, of the bathers.

Afternoon siesta time was in full swing. The elon-
gated, oil-covered bodies of high-fashion models dozed
next to the more voluptuous ones of hopeful starlets.
Only a few energetic young men and women, their
bodies burned black by the sun, kicked a soccer ball
about by the water's edge in a mock game designed to
encourage bodily contact; they fell laughing over each
other and rolled happily in the warm water.

Michael dePasse lazily stretched his naked six-foot, two-inch frame, flexed his smooth muscled body, and rolled over on his back to soak up more sun. He was proud of his body, the body of a champion athlete, and spent an hour every morning exercising to keep it limber and well toned. Michael held out his empty champagne glass without bothering to say a word; it was filled with icy wine by his latest love interest who sat beside him reading a copy of *Playgirl* through dark glasses with lenses the size of hub caps. Her long, streaked-blonde hair fell loosely over her face and bare breasts. Michael liked only those women who were very beautiful or hard to get, because winning either was a boost to his male ego. She leaned over and kissed his champagne-wet lips and tousled his thick, black hair affectionately before returning to her magazine; he didn't respond. He did respond, however, when several minutes later he felt a cool shadow across his face, and he slowly opened his eyes, annoyed at the inconsiderate interruption of the sun in its tanning process. To his surprise he saw Petras Furman in white T-shirt and trousers standing above him.

"Hi, Petras," he said raising up on one elbow, "What brings you here?"

"I've brought the boat and skis you ordered, sir. Sorry to be late."

A puzzled frown spread across the strong features of Michael dePasse's handsome face as he saw the look of command in the other's eyes, and then he smiled. He had come to expect the unusual from this man and his wealthy and eccentric employer; if they wanted him to water-ski, then water-ski he would—there had to be some happy reason for it. "Right, let's go," he said and leaped up, pulling on his white bathing shorts. Leaning down, Michael kissed his girl friend's nose. "Be back soon."

"Okay, love," she mumbled, not looking up from her picture book. She waved vaguely after the two men while turning a page to the centerfold.

"What's all this about?" Michael asked from the side of his mouth as he took the skis from the boat and waded out into the water.

"It's very important, sir—that's all I can say. Mr. Montclair wants to see you." Petras started the motor and moved out from the beach until the tow rope was taut. Waving his hand, the steward threw the powerful twin engines into high gear; they jumped ahead, pulling Michael up behind them. After making a ritual circle in front of the beach club, the boat and skier skimmed east for a long run along the coast.

Once out of sight of the club, the boat stopped and Michael hoisted himself aboard. As Cannes came into view, he was back on his skis executing a few of the maneuvers that had won him several championships in the sport. The boat pulled him between Cannes harbor and the *Krait,* made a wide turn, and swung back on the far side of the yacht; it emerged from behind, towing its skier, but the skier was not Michael de-Passe.

Hugo got up from his desk when he heard the sounds of splashing water coming from the next room. Opening a panel in the wall of his study, he stepped through into a small tiled room with what appeared to be a pool containing the whirlpool equipment needed to massage the aching muscles and joints of an elderly, arthritic gentleman. Michael dePasse surfaced and climbed out of the pool, shaking water from his body. He took the large towel Hugo held out to him.

Looking at the older man, Michael began to laugh. "Hugo, have you gone completely mad? What are you up to this time—filming spy pictures?"

Hugo stood looking back at him with only a trace of a smile on his lips. He said nothing, feeling it best to let Michael get it all out of his system; after all, he had been given quite a few surprises in the last few minutes.

"I'm used to your doing some pretty weird things, but this has to take the prize. Secret underwater entrances and that waterskiing switch—it was inspired. How long is that poor guy out there supposed to go sailing over the waves?"

"Until we're finished," Hugo replied calmly.

Michael looked at him for a few seconds. "Are you

sending me up? You're not really serious about all this hocus-pocus, are you?"

Hugo returned his gaze without answering.

"This underwater entrance—what in hell do you need it for? You haven't been smuggling young virgins in here under the very noses of your grand guests, have you?" He laughed.

"I thought it safer for you to come this way," Hugo answered smoothly, not reacting to Michael's suggestion, which he found in poor taste.

"Safer? Safer for me? Hugo, you've got to be kidding." Michael dePasse still grinned from ear to ear. He had known Hugo ever since he was a child. This kind, gentle man was closer to him than his own father. He couldn't reconcile the almost James Bond manner in which he'd just been smuggled aboard the *Krait* with his image of good old Hugo Montclair. But as the surprise began to wear off and Hugo didn't seem to be joining into the humor of the situation, Michael started to feel uneasy. His smile faded. "Well, are you going to explain all this, or—or what? Why am I here anyway?"

"I assume you've got over your fit of giggles, young man, and are ready to talk sensibly?"

Hugo's question came like a sobering rebuke to Michael, who had not been talked to in that tone for many years. It reminded him of his wilder school days in America when he had often gone to Hugo to obtain his help against the wrath of the Deerfield Academy faculty who had tried to expel him periodically for his more unorthodox activities with the young ladies of the town. Now at age thirty-one and a recognized international sportsman, Michael once again felt what it was like to be put down firmly by this man.

"Okay, okay, I'm sorry. But you have to admit this is all pretty far out," he said defensively.

Hugo led him through the panel into his study and indicated a large, overstuffed leather armchair into which Michael collapsed. Without asking, the older man picked up a crystal decanter and poured two bubble glasses with Cognac. "I think you may want this at some time during our discussion," he said, placing the glass at Michael's elbow.

He returned to sit behind his desk, littered with books and papers, and stared at Michael in silence for a long time, trying to decide how to begin. Finally he asked, "How long have we known each other, Michael?"

"Why, for as long as I can remember," the other answered. "Hugo, you've always been like a father to me. You aren't ill are you?"

Hugo shook his head no and said quietly, "Michael, what I'm about to tell you will surprise and may even shock you. In a few minutes you will know more about me than perhaps anyone else on the face of the earth. And, Michael, I am going to ask for your help. If you agree, you will most certainly be risking your life, just as I am risking mine. If you don't feel you can help then for your own protection *and* mine, we shall never again be able to see each other. Do you understand?"

Michael stared at Hugo. This was not the funny, lovable, and generous little man who had helped him laugh his way through life; in his place sat a very different person, a very grim and surprisingly forceful man. "I understand what you've just said, but . . ." He paused and then began to smile again. "Hugo, you *are* setting me up for something, aren't you? It's all a joke—a joke, isn't it?" Even while he was saying these words in a vaguely conscious attempt to wish away the man sitting in front of him and bring back the Hugo he knew and loved, Michael realized it was no joke. Hugo's silence and the look in his eyes confirmed it. Lowering his voice, he asked the unthinkable, "You're not in trouble, are you?"

"I'm afraid we may *all* be in trouble, and I'm also afraid you and I may be the only ones who can do something about it." He held up his hand to forestall questions. "Michael, we lead very comfortable lives, you and I. We have all the money we need—we come and go and do just about anything we please. We are what others might call the 'privileged few.' But,

Michael, with that privilege goes responsibility. If you were to ask, I don't think I could honestly tell you to whom we owe that responsibility—perhaps to some supreme being, to the world in general, our friends, or maybe just to ourselves. Perhaps it is more accurate simply to say we have a responsibility to what's good in the world. If, because of our position, we become aware of something vile, some evil, corrupting force growing among us, then we above others have the obligation to fight it, to destroy it." His fists clenched.

Michael shook his head. "Evil? Vile? Those are strange words to use these days—they sound old-fashioned. It sounds as if you were talking about hell."

Hugo smiled thinly. "I think perhaps I am. Make no mistake, Michael, hell is not an outdated concept. Moral depravity exists all around us today just as it has throughout the centuries, but today our great technological advances make the consequences of depravity a hundred times more horrible to contemplate."

"Aren't you exaggerating a bit? I admit there are an awful lot of lousy people around—the Mafia, murderers, even white-collar thieves—but we have the police and I don't know how many security organizations to keep it under control."

"Yes, we have the police, but sometimes the police and those other organizations you talk about can't cope for one reason or another. Sometimes they can't reach into hell until it's too late." Hugo Montclair leaned forward on his desk. "Michael, enough philosophy—I brought you here today to tell you a story, a story of depravity in which you have already played a small role." The young man looked at him quizzically.

"Thirty-four years ago a very dear friend and classmate of my late wife married a very distinguished politician and art connoisseur, the Count Jean Claude Henri dePasse, in a wedding ceremony the likes of which Paris will never see again. The four of us became the closest of friends, vacationing together, climbing mountains, sailing anywhere and everywhere around the world. Your arrival in our midst was a joy, not only to your wonderful parents, but to Eleanor and me, who were never able to have children of our own."

Michael looked at the carpet. "Poor Mother—I'm still not allowed to see her," he said sadly. "She was very beautiful, wasn't she?"

Hugo continued as if Michael had not spoken. "Fifteen years ago your mother became strangely ill—her mind became vague and she was often violent."

"I remember it so well," Michael went on, reliving Hugo's words. "Father changed, too. I almost think he started hating me. I never understood why—we had been very close until then. He kept the house closed—no friends were allowed to visit. It was terrible. Then he sent me away to school in America to get rid of me." Michael would never repeat to anyone the words of his father, the taunt that still burned in his brain: "You're a sissy. I've got to get you away from your mother—make a man out of you."

"It was shortly after you left that your mother tried to harm herself, and the Count dePasse committed her to a hospital outside Paris." Hugo paused and then asked, "You don't see very much of your father, do you?"

Michael gave a sneering laugh. He'd been trying subconsciously to win his father's respect and acceptance of him as a man ever since the taunt was thrown. In his mind he equated masculinity in terms of sports and women and so had driven himself to excel in both, but to no avail—the count remained aloof. "I haven't seen him for more than a few minutes in the last fifteen years. After those four years in Deerfield in the States, he enrolled me in the École Polytechnique to 'build my character' and after that suggested I move out on my own to continue building my character—in other words, get lost. Father never used the Neuilly house while I was there and I've hardly seen him since graduation. You've been more my father than he."

"Your father continues to be one of the most powerful politicians in the French government as well as being a brilliant financier—not to mention his art expertise. You know it was he who introduced me to Paul Mytilini; the two met just after the war while tracing looted art, and . . ." Hugo caught himself.

"But that is beside the point. At the time of your mother's illness your father also seemed different to Eleanor and me—more cool, more distant. He didn't remember our little 'in' jokes and games. At the time we put it down to worry and then, as you said, he began to isolate himself from all social contacts. We were no longer welcome at Neuilly. But you were mistaken when you said no friend ever came to visit—Eleanor used to see your mother secretly, helped by her maid. Unfortunately those little visits came to a halt when the complete household staff was changed. Michael, during those last days your mother said things to Eleanor that puzzled us. She said we'd never see her again, that she was frightened, and begged my wife to protect and care for you. We thought that very strange as you had a devoted father to care for you. And then on Eleanor's final visit, your mother claimed the Count dePasse was not your father."

Michael sat bolt upright in his chair. "Not my father, but then who . . ."

"My young friend," Hugo interrupted, "don't alarm yourself on that score; I can vouch for the fact that you are the legitimate son and heir of the Count Jean Claude Henri dePasse. What I cannot vouch for is that the Count dePasse *is* the Count dePasse."

Michael stared across the desk at him. "That's impossible—I know my father when I see him."

"Ah ha, 'when you see him' and how often did you say you see him? 'A few minutes in the last fifteen years'? And didn't you just say he changed toward you—almost as if he hated you? How do you really know that the man who looks like your father is your father?"

"Hugo, you're mad. I . . ."

Hugo held up his hand to stem Michael's protests. He drew two photographs from a file and pushed them across his desk. "Look at these. Who do you see?"

Michael took the photographs and glanced at them briefly. "You know damn well who that is. It's my father."

"Look carefully once again, Michael. The photo in

your left hand is that of my dear friend taken in 1959. The one in your right hand . . ."

"Is the same man—they are identical."

"Exactly, for all practical purposes they are identical. But the one in your right hand was taken last year, 1974. Michael, a man ages more than that in fifteen years. Either your father made a pact with the devil fifteen years ago, or he has an eternally young double."

The young man sat looking from one photograph to the other, trying to absorb what he had just heard. Finally he looked up. "Exactly what are you saying?"

"Michael, I don't have the answers to give you, only the questions. I want you to help me find the answers. I started looking for them fifteen years ago when Eleanor and I became puzzled about the situation in your household. We wanted to find out what was behind it. And that brought us to Madame Ava Bardoff."

"The one who makes cosmetics?"

"Yes. A little over fifteen years ago your father became the financial adviser to the then small House of Bardoff in Paris. He still holds that position today."

"So what? I don't understand what possible connection she could have with my mother's illness or with my father, who's not supposed to be my father anymore."

"I think you will. You see, I believe she holds all the answers. Ava Bardoff leaves a confusing and well-covered trail. I've had years to think about it—you've only had minutes. I started my story with your father only because he led me to her and because I wanted you to be aware from the beginning how this woman may already have touched your life. There's a lot more to tell."

"Oh, brother," Michael moaned as he reached for his glass of Cognac, "I have a feeling I'm going to need this."

Hugo smiled and raised his own glass. "My doctors will kill me for this but, after all, I can only die once." He reflected wryly on those words for a minute and then continued. "Before I tell you about Ava Bardoff, I want you to realize that what I say is not imagination or the speculation of an eccentric old man. I want you to understand once and for all that I am deadly serious *and* I am no fool, regardless of the image I've built for myself. Collecting information has been one of my great abilities for years—a talent which I have used not only for my own ends but to help intelligence organizations around the world." As he was speaking, Hugo moved about his nautical study opening one wooden wall panel after another. Michael's eyes bulged as he recognized highly sophisticated radio transmitters, phones, closed-circuit television screens, tape machines, and various other types of complicated electronic equipment.

"Hugo," he gasped, "you belong to the FBI or the CIA or something."

The older man smiled. "I am the 'or something.' I belong to no national organization although I do have access to much of their information—and that includes East as well as West. I run a very small, very effective, and very unusual group, and today I am asking you to join it."

Michael dePasse sat dumbfounded.

Hugo continued. "Because of my wealth and 'privileged' position, I am expected to know important people all over the world. I do. And many of them are the heads of their countries. I encourage outsiders to regard my connections with these people as merely frivolous social friendships, but while appearing to laugh over a glass of champagne we can pass a great deal of information or our requests for information to each other. Aside from ourselves, these heads of state are the only men who know of my group's existence. They cooperate because they know I will not meddle in the internal and external affairs of their countries and that I concern myself only with, as you said earlier, matters of hell—drug traffic, slavery, and similar things that are an abomination on this earth. No major state really wants these practices to continue because they sap a country's strength and moral fiber. The material I gather is passed on to the appropriate authorities anonymously, and when I need information from them an executive order from the president, prime minister, or party chairman assures that it will be delivered, and not even the delivery boys know to whom."

"But aside from tapping the existing surveillance organizations, how do you gather your private information?" Michael asked.

"Simple. I ask questions and I listen. Who would expect an eccentric old man, one who has a weak heart, who surrounds himself with freeloaders and gossips, who's a soft touch for con artists, who cares for nothing other than art and parties—who would expect a man like that to have the interests and organization about which I have just told you? No one. So I sail gaily around the world throwing parties for the great and not so great—the politicians, the military heads of industry, and the jet setters who circulate freely and talk incessantly. My machines, my crew, and I listen. When you combine the casual remarks with many different sources you often come up with fascinating pictures. Three years ago we were able to trace two drug-processing centers in North Africa. I'm afraid that several of my most popular and respected party guests now find themselves in prison. I have quite a file on you, my young friend. Would you care to read it?"

"My God," Michael said. "I blush to think. Don't."

Hugo opened it. "You do yourself an injustice. Although you hate to admit it, you are a man of honor and you are highly intelligent, facts which you have fortunately chosen to hide. Your athletic prowess is well known and, I assume, represents your way of channeling your energies. Let me see . . ." Hugo thumbed through several papers. "Yes, here we are. Olympic ski champion, gold medal in the Giant Slalom, silver in the Downhill—never took up jumping, did you?" Before Michael could answer, Hugo went on. "Bobsled mishap in St. Moritz two years ago—nothing serious; French water-skiing champion last year; top boxer in your regiment during your national service; pole vaulting, tennis and—shall I continue?"

"No." Michael smiled. "You've made your point."

"Oh, and Michael—" Hugo smiled wickedly— "about your prowess in affairs of the heart—you have only rave reviews here." He patted the file.

"You mentioned that your crew listens, too," Michael said, trying to change the subject. "Do they know what you're doing?"

"I have sixteen excellent men and two women crewing this ship. Most of them have been with me for ten years or more—some served under me in the war, others came to my attention and joined in what we call our twentieth-century crusade. Don't be fooled by their appearance—we're all actors on the *Krait*."

"And your steward, Petras?"

"Petras Furman is my right hand. He and the others are brilliant men, speak many languages, and are highly trained in self-defense—and all are experts in some field ranging from demolition to electronics. We are bound together by the need for absolute secrecy and have dedicated our lives to the security and cause of the group. These men are my closest friends."

Hugo sat back in his chair and studied Michael de-Passe; his pale blue eyes were like steel. "I've taken a gamble today, bringing you here and exposing our operation to you without first probing to determine if you really are the person I've judged you to be. One thing worries me—you are a loner, you've never played team sports, always relied solely upon yourself. My operation can exist only as a team effort. I took the gamble on your fitting in because our time may be running out. We may have to risk our entire organization in an attempt to destroy what I believe to be the most evil and dangerous force we've ever faced—the House of Bardoff."

"A cosmetic company dangerous and evil?" Michael almost laughed. "How can . . ."

Hugo held up his hand again. "We'll come to that in a moment, but first I want to impress upon you that my life and the lives of all my crew now depend on your being able to keep our secret." Michael started to protest but Hugo again silenced him with a gesture. "Of course, it's easy to promise secrecy and mean it, but actually doing it is nearly impossible today. Drugs can loosen your tongue within minutes. Once someone knows you have the information they want, they can get it. That's why the water-skiing ruse and the underwater entrance on the *Krait*—I couldn't afford to let curious eyes see you here without the trappings of a party. I couldn't afford to expose our possible connection until I was, shall we say, in a position to offer you some measure of protection. That's also why if you feel you can't join us, I must not see you again except, of course, accidentally at some social gathering or other. You now know far too much to risk it."

Michael shook his head in appreciation of all he'd heard. "I admit it, Hugo, I'm impressed and flabbergasted. I'd never in a million years have associated you with anything like this. It's a fantastic setup. And to think you've been able to keep it secret for—for how long?"

"For thirteen years, ever since Eleanor's death."

Michael whistled in appreciation. "And the project in which you want me to join—it has something to do with my family and Madame Bardoff?"

"I'm not really interested that much in the Count dePasse any more—he's secondary to Ava Bardoff. It's what she may be doing that has us frightened."

"Okay, Hugo, tell me what you suspect. I'd like to know what you want me to get involved in."

Hugo opened the fat file on the Bardoff history and briefly rearranged some of the documents in it before looking up. "In many ways, Ava Bardoff doesn't make sense, Michael—she's a mystery woman. The Ava Bardoff we know today first came to light in 1949, running a small cosmetic house in Paris. Neither I nor any of the other surveillance organizations have been able to trace her back beyond the year 1945 at the end of the Second World War. For all practical purposes, Ava Bardoff has no background. She claims to be a Hungarian refugee, but her Hungarian family, home, friends, school—everyone and every record connected with her—appear to have been destroyed in the war. Convenient, isn't it?

"Her salon in Paris was an instant success, a success based on a line of cosmetic preparations that claimed to do all the things women wanted. They removed wrinkles, improved skin texture and tone—a veritable fountain of youth in little jars. There's nothing exceptional in this—many cosmetic and fashion houses started after the war—but it takes a great deal of money to develop and package preparations of this type and set up a salon, small though it might have been. Yet I have not been able to track down the source of Madame Bardoff's money. How did a penniless refugee get all that money? And if she had backers, why their reluctance to come forward and be counted? It raises many questions.

"The Bardoff salon blossomed and expanded at a phenomenal rate in the late fifties. All this took money, but again, not a hint of its source. And, Michael, the tax and other official records in France and the United States are strangely vague and sketchy on her financial status and other activities. Ten years ago the Paris police actually called off an investigation of her possible involvement in a not so minor financial scandal. The Internal Revenue Service seems to have more information on the average John Doe than on the great Madame Bardoff. Why, Michael?" Hugo paused dramatically before continuing.

"I believe the answer is that along with the founding and expansion of the House of Bardoff, Madame B. began to circulate more and more in political and diplomatic circles. Today she has political connections all over the world. Connections mean power—we both know that—and political power when combined with the vast wealth of the House of Bardoff bears watching, particularly when it's in the hands of a shrewd and ambitious woman about whom nothing is known.

"Your very political and well-connected father met her in 1959 and was fascinated by her—oh, not sexually, but with her charisma. Soon he became her financial adviser and, thanks to his great ability, her wealth in France mushroomed. I still haven't been able to trace the extent of that wealth due to the labyrinth of holding companies and subholding companies he's set up for her here, but you can be sure it is immense. It was not long after their meeting that your mother became ill and the family estrangement from friends began. Ever since that time I have befriended Ava

Bardoff's acquaintances and kept a close watch on all those around her."

Hugo Montclair's pale blue eyes narrowed. "Michael, very strange things seem to happen to all those closely associated with her. Like your father, their personalities often change, divorces occur, and far too many fatal accidents happen. You may have read about George Martin's apparent suicide in New York." Michael nodded. "I find it hard to believe that it was suicide no matter what the police claim and the autopsy report states. A top Iranian member of OPEC was a friend of hers—he died in a private plane crash with two other members of that association and shortly after that OPEC began its confrontation with the Western states. Ambassador Dilworth and his wife were killed in an avalanche while staying with Ava Bardoff in Switzerland—it was rumored that he was under investigation by the CIA at the time. I could go on ad infinitum. Now look at some of her intimates: several U.S. senators, two recently divorced; one member of the British Cabinet whose wife recently died in a car crash. In France we have not only your unhappy family but members of the Assembly and police involved with divorces, cerebral hemorrhages, and fatal accidents. The shah, who now happens to be in Cannes, is another friend of Madame's and their friendship coincides within a month to his divorce and remarriage to the present queen. Each of these isolated incidents in itself would seem innocent enough and doesn't attract much attention, but if anyone had bothered to do what I have done—to look for and find the common denominator in all the incidents and so link them together—he, too, would have found this modern horror story."

"Hugo, what you're saying . . . you're accusing her of murder and . . ." Michael broke off in mid-sentence, unable to grasp all the implications of Hugo's words.

"Since 1949—" Hugo looked down at his file and then back at Michael—"seventy-one certain murders. I don't know how many others I've failed to consider because I've not yet found a direct association between the victims and the House of Bardoff. And, of course, I'm sure we can add the mutilation death in Cannes today to our list."

"Not that concierge?" Michael asked in shocked surprise. "Ava Bardoff had something to do with that ghastly thing?"

"I'm almost positive, but I'll go into that later. Finally, there is one more piece to the picture—perhaps the most ·frightening of all." Again Hugo paused and then he spoke with added intensity. "In some horrible way I believe Ava Bardoff may actually have discovered a very real form of what men have been searching for since the beginning of recorded time—the fountain of youth. If she has, do you realize what this means? It means she controls the most powerful weapon ever put into the hands of man." Hugo saw a thin trace of a smile begin to form on Michael's lips and cut it off with his next words. "You think I'm talking science fiction? You want proof? Then just look at Ava Bardoff. She looks thirty years younger than her age, and you've seen those photographs of the supposed Count dePasse. Too many of her associates—both women *and* men—look too young for their years, as if time has stood still for them."

"But plastic surgery can work miracles," Michael protested logically.

"True, but not these miracles. Look closely at those youthful-looking people. Study the skin around their eyes, hairlines—you don't see even the hint of a surgical scar. Look at their bodies—where are the wrinkles, the bulges, the sagging muscles? No, she has something going on in those clinics of hers scattered around the world, or else why would she keep them so closely guarded for 'security' reasons."

"Well, what's wrong, or even dangerous, about having developed some preparation or regimen for keeping people young?" Michael asked. "I don't look at it as a horrible weapon—I think it's great."

"In itself, there may be nothing wrong with it, but only if everyone has access to it. Don't you see that Madame's discovery becomes dangerous when she restricts its use, barters it for—for what, Michael? That we must find out. Remember, not just anyone can go to her clinics—one is invited to attend, and Madame is very selective. Ava Bardoff wields far too much power—you can sense it exuding from her every pore. She takes her right to have it for granted and, I fear, wants even more—and I'm convinced she doesn't care in the least how she gets it. When I think of her, I am reminded of Milton's lines from *Paradise Lost*: 'To reign is worth ambition though in hell:/Better to reign in hell than serve in heav'n.' "

"You're back to your hell philosophy again," Michael complained.

"Yes, I am—the analogy fits. Tell me, Michael, would you sell your soul to the devil—or to Ava Bardoff—for eternal youth?"

Silence fell over the two men as they stared intently at each other. Through the closed portholes, sounds of harbor activity were only vaguely heard. After a minute or two, Michael drained his Cognac and said, "Hugo, I honestly don't know. It's a hypothetical question. I don't believe a fountain of youth exists. If it did, I guess my answer would depend upon what I had to do in return for 'eternal youth.' "

"A straightforward answer to a dilemma I hope you'll never have to face. But if the offer were made, you can rest assured the price you'd have to pay would be high. Michael, I can't offer you anthing as tempting as that, but the price you may have to pay is just as great. I'm asking you to risk your life for nothing more than honor and self-respect, but if you're the man I think you are, you regard these attributes as highly as I do. Michael, we need you. Something terrible is about to be done by the Bardoff organization—I can feel it in my bones. Too many things are happening too fast. First we have Martin's death, then the disappearance of his man bringing me information on Ava. Madame arrives on the day of the disappearance as does a plane from Paris whose first-class section has a veil of secrecy dropped over it and a mass of security guards to assure that no one lifts that veil. I'm sure the wife of the American secretary of state and other important people were aboard, but who are the others and where are they? At the Bardoff clinic? Why is the shah here—he unexpectedly cancelled two diplomatic trips scheduled months ago. And now we have the murder and mutilation of the concierge, a murder which I believe was done to lure my group out into the open where Ava Bardoff can dispose of us before we can put a spike in her plans. They are up to something, and whatever it is, it must be stopped."

Michael sat back in his chair. "Whew," he said, shaking his head and pursing his lips in a low whistle. He stared at his empty glass while considering all Hugo had just said and then looked up. "I'm not sure I understand all this and even if I did, what can I do about it? I'm no super spy—or detective, for that matter."

"You can do a great deal more than you think. First, I want you to get inside the Bardoff clinic and find out all you can about what's going on there."

"From what you say it's not very likely I'll get an invitation to visit the clinic. I've only met Madame Bardoff at a few parties connected with the Olympics," Michael said, looking for a graceful way to avoid an ugly situation he did not want to admit might really exist.

"Not from Ava Bardoff—but you'll get one from Sarah Dilworth. I believe you two have met."

Michael looked at Hugo, surprised at the mention of the name and at the detailed knowledge his host had of his life. "Yes, Sarah and I once knew each other very well, but how can she get me in?" He began to feel as if he were being backed into a corner.

"She's Madame Bardoff's goddaughter and current houseguest. What's more natural than that she should invite a handsome friend to spend some time up in the hills with her in that vast château? They certainly have enough bedrooms, although with you I'm sure an extra one may not be needed." Hugo added his last flippancy to relieve some of the tenseness that had built up in the room. "Sarah will be at a party I'm giving tomorrow and, if you throw in with us, so will you."

"Wow! You don't believe in letting a guy adjust to things gradually, do you? From beach bum to secret agent X in—" Michael looked at his watch— "in thirty-seven minutes."

"I think you can make the adjustment very well. Will you join us?" Hugo asked calmly.

"I don't know, Hugo. I'm not at all sure I'm cut out for this sort of thing." The young playboy saw his happy, relaxed days on the beaches, his sports activities, his girls slipping away when he thought of Hugo's little band of dedicated men. He also thought of the danger. "Do you really believe that woman did something to my mother and father?" he asked, dreading Hugo's answer.

"I believe your father is dead." He paused to let his statement about the real Count dePasse sink in and then continued. "And right now, Michael, your mother is in the Hospital Ste. Anne. The Hospital Ste. Anne is owned by the Bardoff Foundation."

Michael's jaw tightened and his back straightened imperceptibly. "Hugo, let's go over this whole thing again."

The owner of the *Krait* smiled. "Certainly. Let me start at the beginning, and here's a file and aerial photographs of the château and nearby factory that we should review. There are some very intriguing discrepancies about their construction which we want you to check out if possible."

An hour later the head of Michael dePasse bobbed up some thirty feet from the far side of the yacht, shielded from any interested eyes on shore. As the motorboat turned to tow its weary skier close in by the ship, a second, shorter rope was dropped from behind. Grabbing it, Michael's body was pulled roughly up from the water as the second skier released his line and sank from sight. To even the most watchful eyes, Michael dePasse had about finished practicing his routine and was now heading back toward the beach just west of St. Tropez.

4

On Thursday night the quay in Cannes' harbor looked like the film set for a psychedelic motion picture. All the creative energies of the Riviera's bored summer colony had been poured into the wild and imaginative costumes that each hoped would outshine the others. Kings, queens, and jewel-draped Lady Godivas hobnobbed with rabbits, dragons, and devils. Nymphs and satyrs pranced about laughing while plumed eunuchs stood silently behind their mistresses protecting their elaborate hairdos from the stars with peacock parasols. Launches arrived and departed, ferrying this exotic collection of celebrities to the *Krait* which tonight reflected on the Mediterranean like a series of giant Christmas trees. Thousands of lights outlined its smooth lines and lifted like a circus canopy over the dance floor on the top deck where a large orchestra played. The latest pop music flowed across the water, over the quay, and beat against the windows of the city, proclaiming to all that the elite were having a party tonight.

Hugo Montclair stood at the top of the steps greeting his many guests as they were helped from the launches and mounted the stairway with varying degrees of ease. He was dressed as Charlie Chaplin's pathetic tramp—bowler hat, small cane over his arm, and outrageous, floppy shoes. As Chaplin he did not cut a very impressive figure in relation to the more im-

64

posing characters swirling around him, but Hugo wanted to reassert his ineffectual public image and maintain a subtle form of anonymity tonight—he did not want to call Ava Bardoff's attention to himself as anything more than a wealthy eccentric.

Paul Mytilini, dressed as a harlequin from Picasso's blue period, stood beside the Monet painting of lilies that now hung over the fireplace in the main salon. He took pride in answering the questions of the guests, who had all heard by now that Hugo had paid a quarter of a million dollars for it that afternoon. The salon was not nearly as crowded as the auction gallery had been, but then the night was still young. Paul threw out a few witticisms to assure he'd be quoted widely the next day and prepared to leave for a pressing engagement, but not before being caught in the clutches of a most unbelievable Scarlett O'Hara in the buxom form of Susan Van Schuyler. She pulled him, protesting, to the buffet to inquire discreetly about the Monet and the value of some of Hugo's other paintings.

A knight in full armor fell down the stairs leading from the top deck with such a clatter that the music was briefly drowned out. A laughing cancan dancer and the Duchess of Alba dragged him to a couch on the afterdeck, where they poured champagne through the visor of his helmet in an unnecessary attempt to revive the struggling Sir Lancelot. Two well-known theatrical lesbians from Antibes dressed as Gertrude Stein and Alice B. Toklas held forth about the success of a new BBC television series they'd written. Alice B. was finally coaxed to the dance floor by a rather effeminate kangaroo, commenting wryly that she'd never seen a larger phallus in her life, but it was sticking out the wrong end.

Sarah Dilworth arrived with Ash, the two dressed as apache dancers. They both wore red-and-black horizontally striped jerseys, handkerchiefs knotted around their necks, and black caps. Sarah's narrow skirt was slit high up her leg to show an abundance of black mesh stocking. She was well on the way through her first bottle of champagne in contrast to Ash, who stood alert by her side, smiling and watchful. Sarah was beginning to think coming tonight had been a great mistake, but Ava had encouraged her to get out and forget the grim details in Peter Kent's flat and the long police interrogation. Instead of forgetting, too many inquisitive guests kept pumping her about the ugly event. Oh, well, she thought, after another bottle of bubbly, I won't give a damn about anything. She handed Ash her empty glass with the simple demand: "Please."

While standing in the middle of her questioning group, she saw Michael dePasse go up to the dance floor, leading what Sarah could only describe as a sex kitten. He was wearing a beachcomber's outfit—tattered tennis sneakers, white trousers frayed at the knees and held up with rope, a torn shirt open to expose his tanned chest, and a necklace of shells. His mate wore an almost identical costume, but much, much less of it. Michael was better looking than she remembered. He had distinctive features and the confident virility of an athlete as opposed to the classic male beauty of Ash, who she felt could have posed for the impassive statue of Michaelangelo's David.

Watching the sex kitten, Sarah felt a twinge of jealousy. She had been very attracted to Michael and he had flirted with her a few times, but nothing had ever come of it. I wonder what she's got that I haven't, Sarah thought, and then answered her own question, besides big breasts and a butt that wiggles like a snake. She felt decidedly overdressed as another Lady Godiva walked by.

"But darling, how absolutely marvelous, we'd love to come," Edith Piaf said to Don Quixote. "Who else will be there?"

Stewards dashed to and fro with trays of tinkling crystal and bottles of champagne, topping up every glass they could find. Long buffet tables on both the fore- and afterdecks displayed ice-filled bowls of crayfish, glazed hams, simmering meatballs, pastries, vast piles of caviar, steak tartar, fruit, canapés of every size and description, and every other delicacy anyone could possibly want.

Ondine stood on the port rail stuffing her seaweed bra with hundred-franc notes before she leaped laughing into the Mediterranean to win her bet and the applause of the men lining the rail. A launch from the *Krait* moved slowly around and around the yacht to pick up the assorted guests who would eventually decide to pay a visit to King Neptune during the evening.

Tiring of his position at the head of the steps, Hugo walked down the companionway to check his study. Unlocking the door after giving a coded knock, he quickly reviewed the effectiveness of all the bugging devices on the ship with his electronics expert, Tim Carpenter. "Everything's going smoothly, particularly the hidden cameras," Carpenter reported. "That damn fool knight who fell downstairs almost broke my eardrums. Why don't you ban that sort of costume from these nutty parties?"

"You shouldn't talk about the British ambassador that way, old chap," Hugo retorted with a smile. "Ava Bardoff hasn't arrived yet—pay special attention to any conversation she might get into with Dr. Chandler. Although he's retired, he is one of the world's top plastic surgeons, and I'm particularly interested in his reactions to Madame B. and any trade talk they might engage in."

"Right on," Carpenter replied. Then looking at Hugo in his silly costume, he laughed. "Boy, if the guys in the old squad could see their leader now."

"It serves the purpose very well," Hugo said with offended dignity and tapped the microphone hidden in the tip of his bent cane. After checking the TV monitor to make sure the corridor outside was deserted, he left, giving Carpenter the V-for-victory sign.

From the dance floor Michael could look down on the afterdeck to where Sarah stood with her apache partner. He recognized Ash from photos Hugo had shown him of Ava Bardoff and her friends at various functions in Europe and the United States. Sarah was surrounded by guests and looked miserable as Susan Van Schuyler held her arm, apparently giving her the fifth degree. Michael kissed his "sex kitten" on the ear and with a deft movement swung her into the arms of a Mexican bandit who stood alone. "May I present Miss Andrea Hunter," Michael said to the startled and delighted bandit. "She's been dying to do a hat dance with you all evening."

"Hi," Miss Andrea Hunter said in a dreamy voice softened by marijuana. Michael left.

"But how ghastly," Susan Van Schuyler said. "Was the head really missing as the papers reported?"

Views of the blood-spattered room rushed through Sarah's mind like a series of slides flashing on a screen. Her stomach began to tighten and she fought not to be sick. "I'd really rather not talk about it, Mrs. Van . . ."

"And in Peter Kent's apartment, wasn't it? He's the man you were with on the plane, wasn't he? Do you think he killed her? Goodness! How lucky you were to have escaped him. But as I said at the airport, he didn't look the kind of person you should be with. You poor dear, how terrible for you . . . and her hands had been cut off, too?"

Before Sarah could say a word, an arm slid around her waist and Michael dePasse's voice asked, "May I tear this ravishing creature away?" Without waiting for an answer, Sarah found herself whisked quickly across the deck and up to the dance floor. She caught a glimpse of Ash's startled and angry face as she disappeared through the crowd. Susan Van Schuyler now held him captive, her interrogation shifted to his supposed intimacies with Sarah.

"Surprise," Michael said, looking down at Sarah in his arms. "I didn't know you were on the Riviera. When did you get here?"

"Tuesday, and if you didn't know I was here, you're about the only one in the entire world. Didn't you read the papers about the 'mangled corpse found by late diplomat's daughter'?"

"I don't read anything but the sports sections."

"I wish the same thing could be said for all the ghoulish, curious characters here tonight. I should never have come."

"I'm glad you did."

"I don't see why. You seemed pretty content with Miss Hot Pants of 1974."

Michael laughed. "Do I detect a bit of your old bitchiness coming to the fore? Jealous?"

"Don't flatter yourself." Sarah looked up into his teasing eyes and smiled back, feeling more relaxed than she had all evening. "Well, I will admit to a certain envy of a few of her more ostentatious curves."

"Your body always looked pretty good to me."

"Thanks for the compliment—better late than never. You never did anything about it."

"Shy."

"That will be the day."

Michael saw Ash weaving through the mob at the foot of the stairs to the dance floor. "Hey, let's shake the crowd for a while. I know a nice little spot where two people can have a drink in peace and get caught up."

Without waiting for her reply, he took Sarah's hand and pulled her around behind the orchestra to a flight of internal stairs that led down to the foredeck. Grabbing a bottle of champagne and two glasses from a passing steward, they moved across the less-crowded deck and climbed under the forward railing to sit with feet dangling over the bow, sheltered from view by a hatch cover. Michael put his arm around Sarah to steady her and protect her from the mild offshore breeze. "Cheers," he said, raising his glass.

Madame Ava Bardoff was one of the last to board the *Krait,* but her arrival did not go unnoticed. Dressed as a most beautiful Marie Antoinette and accompanied by Peor in the livery of Versailles, she was immediately surrounded by admirers and those hoping to be introduced. "You all look absolutely divine," Ava said graciously to those around her. "You, my dear Sophia, are radiant tonight, and you, too, Helen." Her eyes darted about the afterdeck as she stood by the sliding glass doors leading into the salon. "Marvelous. Everyone is here tonight. How wonderful to be back in France."

Hugo approached in his comic Chaplin walk. "Ava, how beautiful." He took her hand and brought it to his lips. "Welcome to my home away from home. This is the first time I've had the pleasure of your company here."

"Yes, Hugo, and I hope you will give me the complete tour. I had no idea your ship was so large. Is that the Monet I've heard so much about? It's exquisite."

"I am very proud to have it but must give most of the credit for its being here to my good friend Paul Mytilini —you must know him."

"We are acquainted."

"I understand you, too, have quite a magnificent art collection. I'd love to see it sometime."

Ava did not reply to Hugo's request, asking instead, "Have you seen my dear little Sarah? Such a terrible thing to have happened to her. I was worried about her coming this evening, but thought champagne might be the best cure for getting over her affair with Peter Kent and that mess."

"I greeted her when she arrived, but haven't seen her since," Hugo replied. "Oh, dear, please excuse me. I forbade the orchestra to play that tune—I do so hate it." Hugo waddled off on his contrived errand, having played the fool for her.

Ava smiled condescendingly after her strange, effete host and then turned her attention to the president of one of Switzerland's large ethical drug complexes after ordering Peor to bring Ash and Sarah to her. A few minutes later she saw the two beautiful young men standing alone to one side. Extricating herself from her admirers, she joined them and moved into an empty corner of the now stifling salon.

"What do you mean you do not know where she is?" Ava snapped at Ash. "You were assigned to keep an eye on her all evening and note everyone who talked with her and precisely what they said. What earthly good does it do to read the lips of someone you cannot see?" she rasped through clenched teeth while maintaining a smile for the benefit of those who might be watching. "I would hate to lose you to Dr. Mulciber, my young beauty, so do not try my patience."

Although Ash, too, was trying to maintain a calm outward appearance, he was on the verge of fainting. "Yes, Madame, I'm sorry. Someone dragged her off to dance before . . ."

"I do not expect excuses—excuses are needed only by those who make mistakes. Peor, help him. I hope Moloch has done a better job with your training."

Ava Bardoff turned abruptly away with a radiant smile, moving smoothly toward an elderly French banker dressed in silk rags. "My dear Leon, what a charming and amusing costume for you of all people to wear. I hope you are not trying to tell us something." She took his arm with a gay laugh and guided him to the buffet. A young Apollo and Venus ran laughing in front of them and dived over the rail of the yacht to more applause from a group of bacchantes.

"How about it? Shall we take a swim, too?" Michael asked as they watched the two gods frolicking in the water below them.

"That's more your scene than it is mine," Sarah replied. Their conversation, which had started in a frivolous vein, had become more serious as they talked about their separate lives over the past few years. She looked down at the laughing pair who were now treading water in a passionate embrace. The champagne gave her the courage to ask, "Michael, why didn't we ever make it together? Two years ago I thought you liked me a lot. What happened?"

"Nothing, really, I *did* like you, liked you very much, but then . . ." he paused.

"Then what?"

"Well, I guess I thought any girl who had your looks and brains shouldn't . . . well, shouldn't settle for giving her body to any horny bastard that came along. Christ, the beach out there is loaded with easy tramps who can do that."

"You should know," Sarah snapped bitterly.

"Yeah, I know. Do you care?"

"You've got your life, I've got mine," she countered.

"And never the twain shall meet?" he asked, looking directly into her eyes.

Sarah averted hers. "You don't want any ties, why should I?" She looked down at his sneakered feet and then irresistibly her gaze moved up the tanned legs to the bulge at his crotch. Her throat tightened; she felt his arm around her shoulders protectively and his warmth beside her. What had attracted Sarah to him two years ago was still there. He had tremendous physical appeal, but more, he was a champion like her father, self-reliant and sure of himself. She had given her life to her father, sublimated her personality to his. She had always been "his little girl," never Sarah. And he had left her. Without him she now had no identity; she was no one. So Sarah drifted aimlessly, without purpose, buying affection with her body, not her emotions. She would never again give herself as completely as she had to her father; it would mean being hurt sooner or later—and Michael had already shown he could hurt her.

"You haven't answered my question. Do you care?" Michael repeated.

"No," she whispered, and then she turned on him. "God damn it," she almost shouted in anger, "you are about the most egotistical, rotten . . ."

Michael put his finger to her lips to silence her. "Before you go shouting your head off, *I* care—I always have. I just didn't want to be another one-night stand and then watch the butterfly flit off to the next stud. I don't want one-night stands with women I really like and, corny as it may seem these days, with women I respect. You don't seem to have much respect for yourself, but I do."

"But . . ." Sarah started.

"Shut up," Michael said quietly. "Two years ago you were a pretty 'I don't give a damn about anything' girl. You had a hate on about the world. Eat, drink, and be merry—with anyone who gave you the nod. I thought if you didn't give a damn about yourself, you certainly couldn't give a damn, let alone care, about anyone else. I didn't want to take the gamble, so I up and grabbed the first beach bunny that hopped my way and goodbye sweet Sarah."

They sat quietly for a few minutes. "I haven't changed much since then," she said quietly.

"Do you want to?" he asked. "With me?"

She stared back down, watching the reflections of the harbor lights dancing on the water. She distrusted men, and this playboy type sitting next to her, the man known as the stud of The Palms, was about the last man on earth she should trust. But she wanted to. Maybe, she thought, we're more alike than we suspect. Underneath all that infuriating bravado, maybe he's just as vulnerable as I am.

"We could try," she said tentatively. "Where do we start?" Even this partial commitment made her feel a little more secure. He tightened his arm around her. Suddenly Sarah began to giggle.

"What's so funny?" he asked.

"I was just thinking—after all this, if you throw me in the sack now, I'll scratch your eyes out." They both burst into laughter.

"No, tempting as that may be, I think we'd better get to know each other first—then the sack," he added with a mischievous wink. "To start with, you're going to spend the next few days with me, and only me. We'll swim, tennis, eat, drink, and talk each other's heads off. How does that sound?"

"You're on," she said gaily, and then frowned. "Oh, damn, I promised Ava I'd have lunch with her to-morrow at the yacht club and—well, after all the curious thrill-seeking people I've run into tonight, I think lunch is about as public as I want to be for a while. Every time I remember . . ."

"Okay," he butted in, "I'll stay out of circulation with you. Where shall we do it?"

"I'm staying at the château, but I don't think Ava'd . . ."

"Does it have a swimming pool and tennis courts?"

"Yes."

"Perfect—we'll do our noncirculating together at the

château. She can't object—after all, she and my father *are* friends, and that should vouch for my social and moral standing."

Sarah hesitated, and then her newfound confidence asserted itself. "Oh, what the hell, of course she won't mind," Sarah blurted out. "And if she does? Well that's just too bad. I don't see why my friends shouldn't be welcome. That old building certainly has plenty of bedrooms." She looked at Michael strangely. "Why are you smiling?"

"Oh, no reason—you just reminded me of something someone else said recently."

"Come for dinner tomorrow night and spend the weekend, or more if you'd like." In her mind, Sarah began to plan the next few days. She was really enthusiastic about something for the first time in months. She scrambled to her feet. "Come on, let's find Ava; she should be here by now." Michael stood up beside her. "Do you want to kiss me?" she asked.

"Yes, but I'm not going to."

"Beast." She aimed a jab at his ribs and smiled up happily at him.

Looking down at her, he didn't know quite what he felt aside from feeling, as his locker room pals would say, like a shit.

Dancing had now spread to the foredeck and many of the more weighty costumes had been shed in favor of comfort. Animal heads, shields, cloaks, and elaborate headdresses adorned the *Krait*'s ventilator shafts, hatches, and railings. Hugo waddled about in his flopping shoes, tipping his bowler hat to the guests and signaling stewards to fill empty glasses. Whenever the opportunity presented itself, he subtly inserted Air France Flight 404 into his conversations and waited to see what information these fishing expeditions might turn up. Out of the corner of his eye he saw Ava Bardoff in conversation with Fred Chandler on the sofa by the port rail.

"Your work has fascinated me for years," Dr. Chandler continued. "The results are only partially attributable to surgical techniques, I assume."

"We have added a few new techniques to traditional methods," Ava conceded, "but as you most certainly know, reshaping bone structure is an underlying necessity to achieve truly dramatic results."

"But I refer to your apparent restoration of skin texture and the rejuvenation, if I may call it that, of the underlying collagen fibers that keep it flexible and taut. Your muscle-tone results are excellent. Surely this must be the result of some new treatment involving both the epidermis and underlying dermis of which we in the profession know nothing."

"Now, Doctor, you are prying into the secrets of the House of Bardoff." Ava smiled enticingly. "You would not expect me to give away my secrets, would you?"

"Certainly not, Madame Bardoff—not as the founder of a commercial enterprise. But on the other hand, as an ex-member of the medical profession, you can surely understand my great curiosity about your treatments. You must have been lucky, very lucky indeed, to have made such dramatic discoveries in such a short time. In only twenty years . . ."

"You do not flatter me, Doctor," Ava flashed angrily. "Twice twenty would be more accurate, and luck played no part in it. I have worked hard and long for this knowledge, sacrificing everything to . . ." She stopped herself and once again the charming Bardoff smile spread across her face. "Perhaps I shall publish our research one day, but until then shall we talk about something more suitable to this lovely and amusing occasion?"

"I am sure the wait will be worth it," Dr. Chandler said, "and I must apologize if I have offended you."

"You have not. Ah, here comes my lovely goddaughter. You must meet her, Doctor—I am very proud of her."

Pushing her way through the crowd, Sarah pulled Michael after her, closely followed by Ash and Peor. Ava noted the relaxed and happy look on Sarah's face and her eyes took in the man who must be responsible for it.

"Ava," Sarah burst out before the doctor could be introduced, "I've invited Michael to the château for the weekend. You know his father, the Count dePasse."

"But of course, the Count is an old friend, and if I am not mistaken we, too, have met," she replied, looking hard at Michael.

"Yes, at several Olympic affairs. I hope my visit this weekend won't be an inconvenience."

Still looking at Michael, Ava addressed Sarah. "Darling, I do think you should rest this weekend—after all, you had quite a nasty shock yesterday and . . ."

"I don't need any more rest. Besides, it was you who encouraged me to come this evening, so you couldn't have felt I was in that desperate need of rest. Michael and I can relax at the château. He's an old friend and —honestly, Ava, I don't see why . . ."

Madame Bardoff held up her hand and laughed. "All right, darling, all right. I was only thinking of you. Of course Monsieur dePasse is welcome." Although she was smiling, Michael sensed an underlying hostility to him and the idea of his spending several days at the château. He was sure she'd relented and bowed to Sarah's wishes only to save a scene in public.

"Thank you, Madame," Michael said with a slight bow, pressing his advantage. He turned to Sarah. "How about a dance?"

Ash practically jumped between the two. "The evening is almost over. I hope you will give me the chance before we have to leave," he said, smiling at her.

Sarah laughed. "Michael, don't be selfish. Of course, Ash, I'd love it." As she walked toward the dance floor with her blond escort, she looked back over her shoulder and winked at Michael.

"Until this weekend, then," Ava said, dismissing Michael. She took Dr. Chandler's arm and guided him toward the salon. "My dear doctor, you are staying aboard the yacht for several weeks, I understand. Would you give me the pleasure of a little tour—it is quite breathtaking, is it not?"

"Most certainly," he replied, "but wouldn't you prefer Hugo to do the honors? He'd be able to tell you much more about it."

"Poor Mr. Montclair is so busy with all his guests, I would feel guilty dragging him away. Let us have another glass of champagne to take with us on our tour. Peor, you come, too. Peor is quite an expert on ships," she confided to the doctor.

The three continued through the salon and started down a long corridor leading to the heart of the yacht. Seeing them go, Hugo moved casually to one of the salon's built-in bookcases and pushed a small warning button hidden under a shelf.

Late the following morning found the two opposing forces pondering the events of the previous night. Michael had taken another spin on water skis and now sat in the *Krait*'s study with Hugo, Petras, and Carpenter, listening to a compilation of the tapes relating to the House of Bardoff and watching replays on the TV monitors. Ava sat behind her desk at the château, listening to the reports of Ash and Peor and discussing them with Beel and Moloch.

"I found last evening disappointing," she sighed. "With the exception of what young dePasse may have said to Sarah while she was lost from your sight, Ash—" the young man seemed to shrink in his chair —"no one other than curious idiots seems to have tried to contact her about Kent's disappearance. But we have established one thing about Sarah and Kent. Sarah's meeting with him on the plane may already have been known to his contact here on the Riviera, thanks to the very big mouth of Susan Van Schuyler. Therefore Sarah's invitation to the party on board the *Krait,* even though it arrived before the unfortunate demise of Kent's concierge, might be connected in some way with Kent's disappearance. Although Susan Van Schuyler asked her, any one of the guests staying on the *Krait* or a close friend of Hugo Montclair's could have put her up to it. Moloch, here is a list of those staying on the *Krait*—check them out."

Moloch rose and took the list from Ava's hand, quickly scanning the names. "None of them look promising, but I'll run them through our computers."

"Here, too, are the names of the people Ash saw talking to her. Note that those with an asterisk asked about the murder, but he feels they asked only through morbid curiosity, not for ulterior motives. None, with the exception of Susan Van Schuyler, tied Kent's name to the affair. But check them anyhow. Let us hope we fare better when I take Sarah to the club today. Last evening I publicized our intended visit there for luncheon. I will leave her alone as much as possible. Moloch, have one of our men working there keep an eye on all who approach her."

Moloch took Ash's list. "What of the Dr. Chandler you mentioned?"

"Ah, yes, the prying doctor. Instinct tells me he is not our man. All his questions about our work here centered strictly around techniques—things that would obviously interest a top man in his field. He did not even have the chance to be introduced to Sarah and made no attempt to talk with her." She paused to consider Dr. Chandler again. "Although, now that I think of it, he seemed rather out of place in that crowd last night—he is not the mad, party-going type. I do not understand why Hugo Montclair would mix him in with that group of insatiable socialites he has staying aboard the *Krait* for the next three weeks."

"Unless it was to study you," Beel said quietly.

Madame Bardoff's eyes shot to him. "A very astute observation, my dear Beel. I wonder if Hugo is equally astute in matters of this sort." She pondered the thought, toying with it as she reviewed the many-faceted life of Hugo Montclair. "I have always considered him a vain, silly man who has far more money than he knows what to do with. He would have to be an excellent actor to be the one we are looking for. Yet he does fit in with some of the suppositions we have made about our mystery man, *and,* as we learned last night, that ship of his is far more sophisticated than I had originally suspected."

"I thought last night was your first visit to the *Krait,*" Peor said.

"It was," Ava said quickly, "but agents of mine

have been aboard at various times." Moloch's and her eyes met briefly in a silent understanding. "The ship is much larger under the waterline than one would suspect and much more of it is devoted to quarters for the crew and machinery than I would have thought necessary. Was that not your opinion, too, Peor?"

"Precisely—a private yacht should not require that amount of equipment space."

Ava Bardoff continued. "Dr. Chandler and I were not allowed entrance into the crew area, but I did catch one glimpse that makes me think our Mr. Montclair spoils his men—something we cannot be accused of, eh, Moloch?" She chuckled. "I understand Hugo had a hand in the design and that is probably why it is so strangely built." Ava thought of his costume and laughed condescendingly. "You should have seen him waddling about like a duck last night. He . . ." Madame's laugh faded. She looked soberly at each of the faces in front of her while her mind worked. "He is such an unlikely prospect that I want a twenty-four-hour watch put on that ship. Beel, you may be right. We cannot afford to overlook anyone. He may be a long shot, but he is the most interesting suspect we've had to date. Moloch, run Hugo Montclair through your computers and use our contacts at the CIA and the Sûreté—I want a thorough check made on him."

"Now, gentlemen, Michael dePasse. Everything we know about him suggests he is nothing more than an athletic young playboy, and Sarah confessed last evening on the way here that she had been infatuated with him when they met two years ago. Although I find it hard to believe he has anything to do with our current problem, through his family he has known Hugo Montclair all his life, and so if Montclair is to be watched, so, too, should young dePasse. Also, I want to make sure he does not get in the way or see things here that might cause him to talk or ask embarrassing questions once he leaves. Ash, you will escort one of the girls from Pandemonium for the weekend and both of you will keep our two lovers in sight at all times. I hope that is understood, Ash—at all times."

He reddened and nodded agreement. "Make sure the security guards maintain a low profile; I do not want him telling people we have an armed camp here. I will invite two other couples, friends of Sarah's, to dinner Friday night and include several of our token guests from the clinic. I want the château to be gay for Michael dePasse."

She nodded abruptly, signaling the end of the meeting, and turned her attention to the papers on her desk. Just before the men left the room, and without bothering to look up from the reports before her, Ava said, "Moloch, put that watch on the *Krait* at once, is that clear?"

"Perfectly, Madame."

"I found last evening very enlightening in several respects," Hugo told those sitting around him, "—enlightening as well as confusing. First, we've established clearly that Peter Kent's disappearance can be linked directly to Ava Bardoff."

"Yes," Michael continued, "Sarah told me she thought she saw him at the clinic the night before the murder, although the Bardoff people claim she was mistaken and confused. She didn't mention her supposed vision to the Cannes police because of Ava's counterclaims and the fact they were confirmed by the message Kent left at the switchboard saying he'd just returned from Rome."

"He's probably being held somewhere in the clinic if he's still alive," Hugo concluded. "Next, we can be certain that Sarah is being used as bait to uncover the group to whom Kent was to have delivered his file. We are, therefore, still anonymous, but I fear not for long. Obviously Madame has intensive and very subtle investigative powers at her disposal. Her young paramours are certainly more than we thought. To use her own words, they're highly 'trained' and, besides being her bodyguards, act as extra eyes and ears as well. That lip-reading stunt of Ash's is a brilliant asset in situations like last evening—almost like bringing your own electronic bug with you. Michael," he said, turning to the younger man, "be very careful what you say within anyone's sight at the château and also check your room for listening devices this weekend. I'm sure we're not the only ones on the Riviera this summer with electronic capabilities."

Michael nodded. "You'll have to show me what to look for."

"Don't worry—we've got the entire range here for you to see," Carpenter replied.

"And now for Madame B. herself. At breakfast this morning I casually asked Fred Chandler what he thought of her. He was fascinated. Aside from possible bone work, absolutely no cosmetic skin surgery has been done on her face, or at least no type of surgery known to Chandler. Although she's at least sixty, he says her skin has the texture and elasticity of a very young woman. As he explains it, the outer skin, the epidermis, constantly sheds dead cells that have to be replaced with new ones if the skin is to stay youthful-looking. As people age, their body's ability to make and replace lost skin cells decreases as does the ability of its glands to produce oil, and so their skin texture suffers—it gets dry and coarse. Apparently Madame B. has found some treatment that will stimulate both rapid cell replacement and oil production. But of even greater importance, she seems to have found a way to stop the underlying network of fibers that keep the skin firm—I believe he called them collagen fibers—from losing their elasticity and deteriorating with age, so the skin continues to stay taut without wrinkling or sagging. Chandler says she or her scientists must be geniuses. For all practical purposes Ava Bardoff has found a successful way to stop skin from aging, and so she can keep a person looking young all of his life. What do you think of that?"

"Where do we sign up?" Michael said, half-joking.

"Ready to sell your soul so soon?" Hugo asked. The younger man sobered instantly, remembering their conversation Wednesday afternoon.

Hugo continued, covering his smile. "Chandler also points out that she wears the most natural wig he's ever seen, one that is almost impossible to detect, and that her hands and feet are very slightly out of proportion to the body of a woman her size. There's nothing unusual about wearing a wig these days, but the hands and feet indicate extensive bone surgery may have been performed on the rest of her body at some time in the past. Obviously we have a woman who practices what she preaches."

Petras Furman spoke up. "She let slip to Chandler that she personally has been doing research work in this field for about forty years. That means she must have started sometime around 1934, but where? We would certainly have been able to trace a researcher of her obvious caliber to some laboratory or university, no matter what happened to her records and those of her family during the war."

Hugo nodded agreement. "She must have continued her research during the war. If she were trapped in Europe as she claims, I'm sure the Nazis would have put a skilled technician like her to work for the greater glory of the fatherland—they stole every specialist they could lay their hands on. That could account for her dropping from sight. I'm positive the missing part of her life is the key to understanding what she's up to now."

"Exactly what would her field have been?" Michael asked.

"Biology, genetics—it could be in several areas—dermatology or even medical research," Carpenter said.

"Well, then, perhaps she worked in the hospitals with the wounded. Didn't plastic surgery, skin grafting, and all that sort of thing really come of age during the war? They must have had a lot of experimenting and . . ."

"Genetics, experimentation, skin grafts," Petras exclaimed, his mind putting together Carpenter's and Michael's words. "My God, that smacks of the Nazi death camps." The other three men looked at him in surprise. "And it fits," he continued. "Last night she mentioned the name Moloch, didn't she? Doesn't that ring a bell?" The others shook their heads. "Hugo, remember several years ago when we were investigating suspects in the North African slave trade, those we thought might have been S.S. men? Well, the name Moloch came up then."

"You're right," Hugo said, getting up quickly from his desk and opening one of the many filing cabinets hidden in the wall. He produced a thick file and after minutes of mounting tension extracted from it a sheet of paper. "Here it is. 'Moloch,' spelled Molokh in Hebrew. It was the nickname the prisoners in Auschwitz gave to one of the top S.S. men running the death camp. Molokh was the name of the Phoenician god to whom children were sacrificed by burning." Carpenter pressed his face into his hands in disgust. "The file states his body was found by the Russians in January 1945 when they reached Auschwitz and it was identified by many of those in the camp. We stopped further investigation of him." Hugo studied several other pages in the file. "This may all be just a coincidence. There is no record here of a woman researcher or doctor or, for that matter, of a woman connected in any significant way with the camp."

"Play the tape of Madame Bardoff's conversation with her bodyguards again, Tim," Petras asked.

Carpenter spun the tape through the machine until he came to the appropriate section. The four men heard Ava Bardoff repeat her threat to Ash. "Excuses are needed only by those who make mistakes. Peor, help him. I hope Moloch has done a better job with your training." All eyes in the room went to Hugo.

"You may be right," he said. "If you are, it would explain a great deal. If Ava's Moloch is the same man who helped run Auschwitz, she might have been mixed up somehow in the biological experiments carried out on the human guinea pigs at the camp." He smiled grimly. "Can you imagine the terrible irony of it—that the foundations of the greatest beauty empire today might rest on the disfigured, violated bodies of the death camps."

Petras Furman continued his line of thought. "If Bardoff is such an expert, so advanced on skin, plastic surgery, and the rest of that stuff, wouldn't it have been easy for her to have faked a body to resemble the Moloch of Auschwitz? After all, during those chaotic days toward the end of the war identification of many of the war criminals was pretty haphazard, and many slipped through the Allied nets."

"It might easily have been done, Petras. There are several supposed deaths right here in this file that we don't believe," Hugo replied. "Let me read a little of the background information as long as we are pursuing this area."

He turned back through several pages of notes and began to read, "The Nazi Party came to power in 1933 and the elite S.S. Corps was founded under Himmler. In 1935 they passed the Nürnberg Laws to guarantee a pure Aryan race—there were to be no marriages between the pure race and the other 'dirty' ones. They developed a Neo-Darwinian philosophy, believing in the survival of the fittest, and began their attempts to breed a superior race—they were after pedigreed humans. In that period the S.S. began opening the camps— Dachau was one of the first—and in 1938 they began rounding up the Jews for mass extermination. Moloch's name also appears on the list of early S.S. men connected with Dachau."

"Madame Bardoff couldn't be planning to breed a superrace, could she?" Michael asked.

"An interesting thought," Hugo mused, "but it seems highly unlikely and impractical. Actually breeding a Nazi-styled superrace genetically would take too long, but she might be trying to create and maintain one artificially through science—it would certainly explain the continued youth and good looks of all those in her organization."

"You think that's possible?" Michael persisted. "I didn't really take you seriously Wednesday."

"I sincerely hope it's not possible, my friend, but you've heard what Dr. Chandler said, and when I look at those photographs of your supposed father taken fifteen years apart and the photographs of others in her organization, I have my doubts. Organ transplants are common enough today and if she was able to experiment on humans during all the war years, who knows what advanced discoveries she may have made. Apparently she is able to rejuvenate skin—perhaps she has found ways to actually rejuvenate the other glands and organs of the body and so extend their life."

Hugo shook his head. "As I explained to you, Michael, what really bothers me is that I think Ava Bardoff plans to use her discoveries not to benefit mankind but as weapons. Ask yourself why, if she has come close to or has actually achieved the ability to prolong life and youth—why not announce it and become the richest and most famous woman in the world? Why keep it a carefully guarded secret? Why, indeed, unless she has some far greater goal in mind. But what?" Hugo paced back and forth across the study in frustration. "We have already traced seventy-one deaths around the world to her—deaths that have nothing to do with the running of a cosmetic and fashion house. What is she planning? Whatever it is, it must be vast in scope and, I fear, a terrifying threat to us all." He looked through the porthole at the bustling city of Cannes across the shimmering blue water. "A threat to the entire world."

"What about the other information we picked up on the wife of the secretary of state?" Petras asked. "Do you think this gives us any clues to Ava's plans?"

"What information is that?" Michael asked.

"From piecing together comments made by many of the most prominent people here last night," Hugo replied, "it appears that all public and social engagements involving the wife of the American secretary of state and, indeed, the secretary himself, have been cancelled without explanation for precisely three weeks, and they have dropped from sight. Based upon Susan Van Schuyler's report, it's most probable that the wife and other Americans, probably the secretary as well, were passengers on the very hush-hush and well-guarded Flight 404 from Paris. We don't know if they or their movements can be tied to the House of Bardoff. While you are at the clinic this weekend, Michael, you must try to find out exactly who is there."

"But what's wrong if they are there? Women are always going off to retreats and ranches to lose weight or have beauty treatments—so what if she's brought her husband along for a health cure?"

"Nothing is wrong unless Madame B. has other plans in store for them besides a simple beauty and health treatment. Remember, her husband is a very important statesman and so may be her other co-passengers, and as we don't yet know Madame's long-range plans, it's wiser to suspect and prepare for the worst than hope for the best."

"I guess that makes pretty good sense," he admitted.

"Now let's discuss your visit to the château," Hugo said. "Regard it purely as a reconnaissance mission— get as much information as you can without attracting suspicion. Don't try to be a hero—remember, you're on a team now, and we can't afford to have our hand forced until we're in a position to act. If you're caught and questioned, the House of Bardoff will be after us like a pack of dogs."

"Right."

Hugo spread out several aerial photographs of the château and a small, modern factory on the other side of a hill from it. "Familiarize yourself with these pictures and the terrain. We want to know as much as possible about the layouts of these buildings and what goes on in them. We do know the factory manufactures two cosmetic preparations which Madame exports only to her own beauty salons. They aren't sold publicly. From discreet observation, we think more materials are trucked into that factory than come out. What happens to the rest?" Next he pointed to two dark squares on the buildings. "Notice these large openings—one in the tower at the center of the factory roof and the other in the roof of the northwest corner of the château. What are they for? Also try to find out from Sarah all you can about Kent and Ava Bardoff's recent and future movements—but for Christ's sake, be subtle. You're new at this game, so don't push it and don't try to be too clever."

"I understand," Michael said. "I'll be as casual as I can."

"And be careful not to talk much about the *Krait* and me. Remember that I am just a friend of your family—that's all." Hugo stood up and smiled. "Now, Tim, if you'll take Michael below and give him a few tools to help him on his first mission, I'll go and charm my guests at luncheon. I'm sure Susan Van Schuyler has a great deal to tell me about what went on at my own party last night."

The three men laughed as Hugo walked to the door. Before leaving, he looked back at Michael. "Good luck. I'll see you back here Sunday evening."

5

At 7:00 P.M. that evening, Michael's silver Porsche sped up the winding roads toward the château twenty-five kilometers beyond St. Tropez. He'd spent the early afternoon with Carpenter, Petras, and others of the crew before skiing back to the beach club for a volleyball match and drinks with his beach bunny. Now dressed in a black dinner jacket and with an overnight bag and two tennis rackets on the seat beside him, he looked forward to his weekend with mixed emotion.

He felt exhilarated by the foreign and challenging task Hugo had set for him, and his mind raced through the scenes of espionage and dramatic confrontation he'd seen in so many films. Exhilarated, yes, but in the pit of his stomach Michael was frightened out of his wits. Strangely enough, he now looked upon Sarah, defenseless as she might be, as a source of security—his sole link with the world he knew outside the walls of the Bardoff estate. The thought of Hugo and his small band of men floating so far away on the clear blue Mediterranean outside Cannes harbor did little to restore the confidence he'd felt while talking with them that afternoon. Whenever his resolve began to fade, he bolstered it with thoughts of his mother and father and the life that Ava Bardoff had stolen from him. You're on your own, old man, he told himself, just play it cool—real cool.

Michael swung the Porsche left onto the branch road leading first through a small village and then on to the clinic, a narrow and winding road with blind curves and steep inclines that took all his concentration. It was obviously not suited to the speed at which he was traveling, but this was the type of danger he was used to and enjoyed; the cliffs and sheer drops on his left thrilled and challenged him. The road wound through a thick forest that finally opened onto a meadow across which Michael saw the large château sitting well-protected behind the high wall that enclosed the several square miles of its park. His shiny little sports car seemed out of time and place to him—instead he should have been bouncing about in a gilt carriage pulled by galloping white horses toward the summer palace of Louis XIV.

He crossed the meadow and braked sharply before the ornate black-and-gold gates. Michael gave his name to the guard, who smiled in recognition and pushed the electric button; the gates swung open as easily and silently as if they'd been constructed of black lace rather than heavy iron. The drive ran straight to the main southern façade of the château a mile distant through two rows of poplar trees and the beautifully landscaped park filled with formal gardens in various geometric shapes that stretched out on both sides. To the right he caught a glimpse of a series of elaborate fountains and a large pool. It certainly was impressive, he thought—a sort of mini Versailles. And then he remembered Hugo's words, "the foundations of the greatest beauty empire today set on the violated bodies of the death camps." The geometric beauty of the estate suddenly looked regimented and sinister to him.

The château that housed the famous Bardoff clinic was a vast, rectangular building constructed around a central court. The façades of the four sides of the gray stone building were symmetrical in design, each with a central door flanked by rows of tall windows. They were two stories high, but a steep, moss-colored mansard roof added another story and a half. The corners of the château extended out from the main walls several feet and were higher to give the effect of blunted towers, three windows in width, connecting the symmetrical faces of the building. Tall, flat columns were carved from the walls between the windows and appeared to support the heavy-leaded roof with their elaborately designed caps of entwined leaves and faces. No expense had been spared by the original architect in the construction of this magnificant edifice, and no expense had been spared by Madame Ava Bardoff in its restoration after the war.

Michael pulled his car to a halt in the wide gravel area before the broad steps that led up to the main south entrance. As he slid out, he heard Sarah call to him. She disengaged herself from a group of people sitting in a cluster of white wicker lawn furniture in a grove of trees to the left of the château and ran toward him. He walked forward to meet her at the edge of the lawn and gave her a light hello kiss on each cheek.

"Leave your bags in the car," she said. "Your valet will take them to your room. Now come and meet some friends. Isn't Ava a mystery?" Sarah laughed gaily. "I was afraid I'd upset her by inviting you here and instead she does a complete turn about and throws a dinner party for us tonight as a welcome home to me and a just plain welcome to you."

Sarah wore an ankle-length floral skirt and long-sleeved, pale green blouse with a wide collar opened almost to her navel. Several long strands of pearls glowed against her tanned skin. Her hair fell loosely behind. "Did you miss me?" she asked, taking his arm and leading him to the grove.

Michael looked down into her green eyes. "You did cross my mind once or twice today," he said, smiling.

As usual Madame Bardoff was in command and looking beautiful, tonight wearing a gold kaftan. She sat in a large wicker armchair behind which stood Stanislau Beel and held up her hand to receive Michael's kiss. Sarah introduced the other attractive members of the group. Ash sat beside his date for the weekend, a ravishing cat-woman type named Iris something-or-other—Michael hadn't caught the last name, his brain completely absorbed in cataloguing her physical charms. Next was Andrea Fouchon, an old school chum of Sarah's, and her fiancé, Simon Gaillard, a hotel owner from Geneva. Two older women, Harriet Granville and Patricia Hall, were staying at the clinic as guests of Madame for a series of beauty treatments. Again Michael failed to register the mumbled names of their escorts, whom Madame Bardoff had obviously supplied for the occasion. A uniformed waiter took his drink order, and while it was being prepared at a small portable bar, they were joined by two more couples from Cannes, who were spending a few weeks traveling between roulette tables, James and Lydia Hutton of Palm Springs and Walter and Sheila Carrington from London.

The group sat in the warm early evening watching the sun sink slowly behind the hills to the west while carrying on bright and witty conversations filled not only with the gossip of the Riviera's summer colony, but the troubles of the Common Market and the forthcoming meeting of the OPEC countries. The men were very concerned over the possibility of another oil boycott of the West and speculated over its disastrous effects on Wall Street. Michael sat close beside Sarah, answering the questions of several of the younger members of the group about the Olympic games. Suddenly one of the women screamed; she put her hands over her head to protect her hair from the wings of a small, black, screeching missile that shot past her through the air.

"Do not worry, my dear—" Ava laughed over this typical female reaction—"it is just a harmless little bat. They are far more interested in staying out of your way than getting in it."

As Ava Bardoff tried to calm her uneasy guests about their safety from attack, Michael looked up at the château. It seemed to him that the bats were coming from the building itself, or at least appeared to be concentrated above the roof of the northwest corner, the corner with the puzzling opening Hugo had asked him to investigate.

"There are a great many bats in these hills," Beel commented. "Their one great advantage is keeping us relatively bug free."

"If it worries you, why do we not go in," Ava suggested. "It is almost time for dinner."

The older women quickly accepted the chance for escape and headed for the château, while the younger members of the party straggled along behind with fresh drinks in their hands, admiring the gardens along their route. Andrea Fouchon knelt from time to time to examine various blossoms and exclaim with delight over varieties she'd never before seen.

"Ava's hobby is developing new strains of plants," Sarah explained. "Wait until you see her conservatory —the entire center court of the château has been turned into a huge glass-domed garden."

"They're beautiful," Andrea said, touching a delicate rose of an unusual color.

"Oh, these are what Ava calls her mutants—she exiles them to the outdoor gardens, where the bees can do their worst. Inside are her real triumphs, they're pure species bred for size and strength. Some of them are enormous."

"I take it Madame Bardoff doesn't believe in mixed marriages," Michael commented innocently.

Sarah looked at him strangely. "That's a funny thing to say, but if it's flowers you're talking about, I guess you're right. She has a fit if a bee gets into the conservatory, does all the pollinating herself by hand."

"Pollinating by hand is a pretty boring way to do it, don't you think? I know many more interesting ways."

Sarah laughed. "I just bet you do, you lecher. Come on." She took Michael's arm and pulled him toward the château. "And behave yourself. Ava's not very fond of puns and wisecracks, and you'll be sitting on her right. She wants to know all about the men her goddaughter shows an interest in."

"Oh, so you're showing an interest, are you?" Michael's flip comment covered a tightening in his stomach as he remembered once again why he was there and realized he was about to face his first interrogation by the head of the House of Bardoff.

"That's right, and don't get smart about it," Sarah warned.

"I won't—I'm flattered." He put his arm around her waist and pulled her close as they walked.

Although the dining room, the table, and the guests were dressed for a formal dinner, Ava Bardoff made sure that a mood of casual gaiety filled the room. Laughter and amusing anecdotes fluttered back and forth across the crystal and china, while superb wines flowed endlessly into the various-sized glasses surrounding course after course of brilliantly prepared dishes. Ava maintained a light and witty conversation with Michael and those close by while occasionally hurling a clever verbal challenge to others at the far end of the table.

Michael was keenly aware that he was not being pumped by his hostess—she asked only those questions appropriate to his position and interests in life and those that one would expect from a woman concerned about the welfare of her goddaughter. The evil suspicions voiced earlier that day by Hugo and his men seemed utterly preposterous in this atmosphere; Michael had to pinch himself occasionally as a reminder not to let down his guard, that he was more than a guest this weekend.

"You do not see your father very often, do you?" Ava asked. "I only bring up the subject because I have seldom heard him mention you. Do not the two of you get on well?"

This was the first question he'd been asked that made Michael sit up and think. "I'm afraid we've grown rather far apart since my mother's illness," he replied vaguely. "Father was terribly upset. We correspond occasionally—" he laughed—"particularly when I'm strapped for cash."

She smiled. "Well, I suppose all fathers and sons maintain that sort of relationship no matter how far apart they drift. Blood *is* thicker than water or an ailing bank balance. And Hugo Montclair? Do you go to many of his parties?"

"Not too many—he's more my parents' friend than mine."

"Oh? I had the impression you two were very close when you were a student at the Deerfield Academy in Massachusetts." Before Michael could recover from this surprise bit of intelligence so casually dropped, Ava continued. "He seemed to have a great many young people on the yacht last evening. I wondered if they were all friends of his or just attractive background fillers to brighten things up."

"I'm not really sure. I think he knows most of them," he replied lamely. "They're mostly in the arts and everyone knows how much he likes artists, dancers, and people like that." What's she getting at? he wondered.

"Sarah said she did not know him, and so I thought it strange that he would invite her."

There it was, a real hot potato. She knew very well Susan Van Schuyler had issued Sarah's invitation. Michael reasoned the best defense was no defense at all. "Oh, I didn't know they'd never met before, I just assumed . . ." He let his answer trail off. He'd seen the first trap, would there be more on their way?

"What do you think of Hugo?" Ava asked.

"Mr. Montclair? I've never really thought much about him. I guess he's sort of an eccentric, always fooling about. Mother and Father used to go all over the world with him doing nutty things. Probably he's the same now as he was then."

Ava smiled while searching his face. Having found what she was looking for there, she said gaily, "Well, I think you gentlemen would like to be free of us ladies for a few minutes. Do not be too long."

Madame Bardoff stood up, a signal for the women to leave the dining room to the risqué jokes of the men while the ladies enjoyed a good gossip over coffee in the conservatory. Rising gallantly, the men waited until the women left and then gathered at the far end of the table around Stanislau Beel to sip Cognac or port and smoke cigars while discussing either women or business affairs.

"How long have you known Sarah?" Beel asked Michael while the others were engrossed in the current maneuvers of the bourse.

"Two or three years. She's quite a girl."

"Have you seen much of her recently?"

"No, not for a year or two. It was a happy surprise running into her at the party on the *Krait*." Before Beel could pursue his line of questioning further, Michael jumped into the discussion of the securities markets with the others. You and Madame have had your quota of questions for the evening, he thought.

Shortly after that the men abandoned their solitude to seek out more enjoyable feminine companionship. Some of the ladies still sat with their coffee, others were in the billiard room that opened off the conservatory. Michael moved up behind Sarah, who stood there watching Andrea as she stretched across the green felt trying to make a difficult cushion shot.

"How about showing me where my room is?" he asked quietly. "We can slip away for a few minutes without anyone missing us."

She nodded agreement and walked casually to the door with him. This seemed like the ideal and logical time to Michael for his first cursory investigation of the château; later, after he'd got the feel of the place, he'd strike out on his own. Madame Bardoff and Stanislau Beel were now occupied with their other guests, but Ash watched in frustration as Michael and Sarah left the room; to follow them would have been much too obvious.

As this was the first time he'd been alone with Sarah since his arrival, it took only a little coaxing to get her to extend the proposed visit to his room into a brief tour of the château. The large and elegant public rooms, the entrance hall, salons, library, billiard room, and main dining room ran pretty much into each other along the ground floors of the southern and western sides of the rectangular building. The eastern side contained four or five large suites of rooms, two of which had been assigned to Sarah and Michael. Above, on the second floors of the three sides, long, beautifully paneled corridors ran past the smaller suites of the guests staying at the clinic for treatment. Each contained a small sitting room, bedroom, and bath. Sarah told Michael that the servants' and attendants' quarters and social rooms were above them cramped under the steep mansard roof.

"What's in the north wing of this hulk?" he asked, coming to a closed door leading to that side of the château from the end of the second floor corridor in the east wing.

"More guest suites and Ava's private rooms—her main room is fantastic."

"And below?"

"Public rooms for the guests. The entire cellar is full of super massage and therapy rooms. I'll take you down tomorrow for a sauna and rubdown. There's also an operating theatre down there where they do bone corrections and other types of plastic surgery, but I don't think even your colossal ego could be interested in that stuff yet." She stuck out her tongue at him and laughed.

Michael tried the door. "It's locked."

"Ava always keeps her rooms locked and, as there aren't any guests staying in that wing now, it's been closed off."

"I liked the two women I met tonight who are staying here. Are there any others?" he asked as they walked slowly back down the long corridor.

"Only two," Sarah replied. "You'll probably meet them tomorrow at the pool." She stopped and corrected herself. "Oh, no you won't. I forgot. They had surgery this morning and will have to stay in bed for a few days. Why? You aren't getting bored with me already, are you? I guarantee none of them is your type."

He smiled. "Just my natural curiosity about the mysteries of what goes on behind the scenes at a woman's beauty store."

"Ava'd kill you if she ever heard you refer to her clinic as a 'store.' " As Sarah talked, Michael was sure he heard the faint yapping of a small dog coming from somewhere behind them down the corridor.

They went on to his rooms, where he checked to make sure his clothes had been unpacked to his satisfaction and washed his hands, making a great deal of unnecessary noise. After chatting about nothing in particular for several minutes, he extended his elbow in a pseudoaristocratic gesture and asked, "Shall we join the others?" She took his arm and, as they left the room, he thought to himself, well done, old man. You've cased the joint, as they say, *and* established an alibi at the same time. Hugo would be proud of you.

They entered the conservatory through the library doors and sat behind a cluster of palms that must have been at least thirty feet tall, extending up almost to the lacy construction of decorative iron arches supporting the glass dome of the room. Canaries fluttered overhead, confused by the artificial sun shining so late in the evening.

"This place is amazing," Michael commented as he scanned the dome and the interior windows that faced inward onto it from all four wings. He noted one on the second floor of the north wing was slightly ajar. "But don't the guests get a feeling of insecurity—after all, anyone in here can look right up into their rooms."

"Look again," Sarah said. "Notice how they reflect the plants?"

"Yes, clever lighting," Michael replied.

"Not at all—those windows are one-way glass. The guests can look into the conservatory, but we can't look back at them. They reflect like mirrors from this side and so they not only give privacy, they make the conservatory look almost twice as large and green as it really is."

"Very clever indeed," he conceded while trying to determine how he might gain access to that north-wing window. It looks like I'm going to end up having to do a Tarzan act, he thought. Although Sarah had said the wing was deserted, he very much doubted it —at least there was a nasty little dog in there somewhere.

"There you are," Iris said as she and Ash joined them. "Where on earth have you two been?"

"I took Michael on a little . . ." Sarah began.

"Trip to my room," Michael interrupted, and finished, giving a wicked wink to Ash. "This is certainly a beautiful place, isn't it?"

Before Ash could really answer or ask any more questions, Andrea and Simon joined them. "Sarah, I'm afraid that, like the Arabs, we must fold our tents and silently steal away. It's been marvelous to see you again and—" As Andrea went forward to kiss Sarah's cheek good night she threw a quick glance at Michael and whispered, "Hang on to this one, he's a dream."

"I may just do that," Sarah answered under her breath and then, laughing, the two girls hugged each other. "But won't you please stay for just one more drink?"

Simon looked at his watch. "Well, Harriet Granville and Pat Hall have gone off to bed to follow the strict regimen your godmother has set for their rejuvenation and their escorts have vanished into the night. The Huttons and Carringtons have pawned the family jewels and are in a rather expensive and exclusive battle royal at the billiard table, and so—and so—" He looked at the tall, cool drink in Michael's hand, then warily at Andrea, and then back at the frosted glass. Simon capitulated. "And so I think we might just squeak in one little drinky for the road."

"Oh, Simon," Andrea wailed as she sank into a chair, resigned to another late, alcoholic evening.

The party finally broke up about 1:00 A.M. as Sarah, Michael, and Ava Bardoff stood at the top of the wide front steps waving good night. Ava looked up at the moonless sky and said, "I am afraid you two are going to be in for a little rain tomorrow. It is a pity, but it cannot be helped." Halfway across the entrance hall she stopped to give Sarah a goodnight kiss and gave a brief one to Michael as well. "Now do not stay up all night, and please, no wandering about outside. Stanislau has ordered the dogs set loose." Looking directly at Michael, she said, "You cannot imagine what lengths I must go to in order to protect my home from prowl-

ers." Leaving him with what may or may not have
been intended as a warning, Ava gracefully ascended
the great spiral staircase and continued down the long
corridors to her private chamber in the north wing.

"Well, I guess we'd better turn in, too," Michael said.
He noticed the look of disappointment in Sarah's eyes
and added, "I don't want to blot my copybook with
your godmother on the very first night. Besides, we'll
be nice and fresh for anything that comes along tomorrow night."

Sarah sighed. "I guess you're right. I must admit I
haven't completely recovered yet from Hugo Montclair's champagne. We didn't get back here until almost three-thirty this morning, and Ava had me up
bright and early for shopping and lunch in Cannes."

They paused outside her door. "Good night," he
said, pressing her close for a second. Then, holding her
back at arm's length, he bent slowly forward and kissed
her gently, almost paternally. Their eyes met and
held. A puzzled look crossed Sarah's face; Michael
released her and walked quickly down the corridor to
his room.

She looked after him, or where he had been, for
several minutes and then slowly entered her room. Sarah dropped her clothes in a heap on the floor, picked
up the glass of warm milk beside her bed, and stood
by the window looking out over the dark park. A picture of Peter Kent popped into her mind, but she forced
it out, remembering that she'd made a mistake thinking
she'd seen him here two night ago. She concentrated
her thoughts on Michael. He'd certainly seemed different tonight—more intense, less cocky than usual. She
visualized him slowly undressing and wondered if
he slept nude. Suppressing the desire to slip into his
room, she swallowed the last of the milk and slid into
her own bed feeling content and at peace with the
world.

Michael pulled the draperies in his room and began
searching systematically for hidden microphones. His
efforts were rewarded. As Carpenter had suggested, one
was hidden in the telephone beside his bed and one in
the phone on the desk in his sitting room. He left

them where they had been planted. Next he poured the milk that had been so thoughtfully left beside his bed by the valet down the bathroom sink and turned off the lights. Still dressed, he drew back the draperies several inches and opened the window, looking across the park and listening. He heard an occasional bark from one of Madame's watchdogs who, he was sure, were also killers.

There were three objectives in his mind: the factory, the north wing, and the northwest tower roof. It would be foolish to try for the factory tonight—he'd have about a mile and a half of park to clear with those dogs running loose, a wall to scale, and who knows what on the other side. He'd have to find a legitimate way to investigate the factory tomorrow in broad daylight. Why not, he thought, I'll just ask for a tour. The simplicity of this scheme amused him, and he crossed the room confidently to start toward his other two objectives. But when Michael opened his door and peered cautiously out, he quickly abandoned his plan of sneaking through the deserted château to the northwest tower and the north wing. His valet sat reading a book in a straight-backed chair at the far end of the dimly lit corridor, where any movement to or from Michael's room was clearly visible. He's not there just to chaperon Sarah and me, he thought angrily.

That settled his investigative activities for the night. Michael undressed slowly, kicking himself for his initial naïveté in underestimating Ava Bardoff and thinking all he had to do to get around the château was to slip invisibly from one shadow to the next the way they did it in films. Figuring out a way to escape from his plush cell was not going to be easy and would call for a great deal of imagination. He remembered houseguesting in some of the stately old homes in England; God, the halls were virtually superhighways at night, clogged with people on their way to each other's beds. At the crack of dawn everyone was back in their respective rooms ready to be wakened by the butler for breakfast. Right now he wished he were in jolly old Angleterre.

"Where there's a will, there's a way," he said aloud to the dark room, suddenly clamping a hand over his mouth as he remembered the tiny microphone not three feet from his head. Some supersleuth, he thought wryly. I wonder what, if anything, was in that milk—or am I becoming paranoid?

Michael awoke Saturday morning to the sound of rain falling on the leaves of the trees in the park. He stretched lazily and was about to curl up and go back to sleep when he realized with a bang where he was and why he was there. Whatever happy thoughts he might have had drained away as pictures of Ava Bardoff, her mutant flowers, and the mysterious north wing passed through his brain. He lay staring up at the ornate ceiling some sixteen feet above his head. "Boy, they sure knew how to build 'em," he mumbled aloud. The sound of his voice reminded him again of the microphone nearby. Michael remained staring at the ceiling, making and discarding one plan after another until his wristwatch read 9:30. Well, he thought, here we go. Reaching for the phone, he asked the clinic switchboard to connect him with Miss Dilworth's room.

"Good morning, you lovely creature," he said to the sleepy voice that answered his call. "I trust that visions of sugarplums danced through your head all night and you're ready to greet this lovely wet day refreshed and ready for action."

Sarah resisted the temptation to tell him to drop dead; she detested overly cheerful and bright people in the morning. She was a night person, would always be a night person, and was proud of being a night person. But on this occasion Sarah summoned as much enthusiasm as she could muster from her groggy brain and tried at least to sound intelligent. They arranged to meet for breakfast in an hour and develop some "mischief" to occupy the rainy day. She was almost thankful that the rain would postpone her inevitable defeat on the tennis court and the overexuberant play in the swimming pool.

While Michael chatted with Sarah, a light knock on

his door announced the arrival of his valet, who nodded a silent good morning and proceeded to open the heavy draperies and draw his bath. He was handed a glass of fresh orange juice and a silver thermos of hot coffee was placed carefully on a table across the room; the valet smiled and left.

Between sips of the steaming coffee, Michael showered, shaved, and reviewed his plans for investigating the factory and estate. His major problem would be accomplishing all he had to do under the watchful eyes of Ash, who he was certain would dog his every step this weekend. He wondered if Iris, too, was in the pay of Madame Bardoff and what talents she might possess to make his mission more difficult.

Sure enough, at 10:30 that morning when he and Sarah entered the dining room for breakfast, Iris and Ash were coincidentally just sitting down to eat. Ava Bardoff joined them a few minutes later. The happy family had all been conveniently assembled. Ava wore another one of her many beautifully worked kaftans and looked radiantly alive sitting at the head of the table.

This morning she was very much at ease with Michael dePasse. His earlier phone conversation with Sarah and those other conversations Ash had reported last evening seemed perfectly innocent to her. His explanation of his brief disappearance from the party last evening had been verified by the microphones in his rooms and if he and Sarah had taken longer than necessary to make the round trip to his suite through the large château, Madame Bardoff put it down to a bit of understandable and natural sex play.

As they were finishing their last cup of coffee, Michael put his first plan into action. "Madame Bardoff," he said, "may I ask a great favor of you?"

"Certainly, Michael," she replied amiably, "what can I do for you?"

"As nature seems to have conspired against tennis or a sunny swim this morning, I wonder if you would permit Sarah to take me on a small tour of your factory. I'd like to see how you make all those creams and lotions and perfumes that turn the women of the world into great beauties. I've never been inside a place like that before, and I should think it would be fascinating."

"Well, I am not sure that . . ." she hedged.

"Ah ha!" He laughed. "So you're afraid to let me see what actually goes into all those little jars. I'll bet it's witchcraft of some kind—eyes of newt, wing of bat, and all that sort of thing."

"My dear young man," Ava protested in amusement, "you are just as impossible as all the others of your sex—nonbelievers. We women are perfectly capable of using science, not a witch's cauldron, to achieve our ends." She sobered. "But I am afraid you would be terribly disappointed. The 'factory' as you call it, is really an experimental laboratory. We manufacture only two types of creams there and both are packaged in rather plain jars, not the fancy things you think of. And unfortunately it is shut on weekends; I do not think any of the workers will be there, and certainly the lines will not be in operation."

"It would still be interesting just to see what it looks like, wouldn't it," Michael said turning to Sarah. He was obviously waiting for her support.

"I've never been over there," Sarah said without enthusiasm. "Would it be all right, Ava. It really is a terrible day."

"Very well," Ava Bardoff replied after a few seconds of thought. "Ash can take you through; he is familiar with everything there. Would you not like to go, too, Iris?" she asked.

The young woman nodded enthusiastically. "Oh, yes, Madame. I've heard so much about your wonderful products—I'd love to see where they're made."

"Great," Michael said happily. "Let's go." He stood up, offering his arm to Sarah and bowing the way to Ash. "I guarantee, Madame, that I won't steal a single secret and won't touch a single newt's eye or bat's wing." The young people departed, leaving Ava Bardoff at the table in deep thought.

"Bring the telephone here at once," she directed a

handsome young servant standing nearby in a white, military-looking uniform. Her mind raced quickly through the small factory, picturing each of the rooms to determine if anything the touring group might see could embarrass the organization. The stocking of Pandemonium would, of course, have to be halted for an hour or so, but that should cause little trouble, and she knew the plant and labs were always kept up for outside inspection. She dialed the number of the factory to warn them of the imminent visit.

Michael, Sarah, and Iris clambered into the Mercedes that Ash drove up to the west side of the château. At his insistence both girls had gone back to their rooms for sweaters, and Iris had spent a ridiculously long time trying to find an umbrella. Michael attributed all this time-wasting activity more to Ash's desire to delay their arrival at the factory than to concern over his companions' comfort and health.

The black car moved slowly through the park behind the château and paused while the high iron gates in the north wall were opened to enable them to continue their short trip. They drove through a small wood at the base of a hill that completely shielded the factory from the château and emerged a few hundred yards from the small, one-story, modern building that housed Ava Bardoff's laboratory and two manufacturing lines. Although the trip had taken some ten minutes, Michael estimated the actual distance to be less than a mile as the crow flies.

From the outside, the factory looked much like a flat rectangular box, three sides constructed of gray brick and the fourth of opaque glass reinforced with steel bars. A twenty-foot-square brick tower rose about eighteen feet from the center of the flat roof. Ivy covered much of the walls, softening them, and rhododendrons and azaleas grew wild about the sides to help blend the building inconspicuously into the landscape.

The Mercedes pulled into a parking lot much larger than the size of the small factory seemed to justify. Ash explained that although most of the workers bi-

cycled from the local village, a sizable lot was necessary to provide big delivery trucks room in which to
maneuver. There were only two entrances to the building: the main, thick glass door leading through a small
lobby into the plant proper, and a loading dock with
tightly sealed overhead steel doors. A large, unmarked
truck sat backed up before this dock.

As they walked from the car to the factory, Michael
detected the faint odor of chlorine hanging over the
area, almost as if a cholorinated swimming pool were
nearby. The party entered the lobby and signed in with
the young, white-uniformed security guard sitting at the
reception desk.

"Madame called to say you'd be coming. I'm afraid
there's nothing going on here today," he said regretfully. "This month's shipment went out yesterday."

"That's okay," Ash replied, faithful to his script,
"we'll just take a quick look around and then head
back."

The guard unlocked the door to the plant floor and
Michael and Sarah found themselves in the twenty-
first century. First they entered a small glass booth
through which a strong, steady blast of air rushed.
"It's a form of vacuum cleaner," Ash told them, "to
get rid of any loose dust, dirt, hair, or other alien
particles you might be carrying."

From the vacuum booth, they entered a changing
room, where they slipped into one-piece white coveralls
with hoods. Only their faces showed from these "moonsuits" as Michael called them with a laugh, commenting that he felt like a trick-or-treater on Halloween
night. Thus prepared, they entered onto the factory
floor itself. Pale acoustical tile covered the windowless
walls and soft rubber tiles cushioned the floor. The air
was cool and fresh, which surprised Michael; from the
chlorine odor he'd picked up outside, he had expected
the factory to be oppressive with the smell of chemicals. The ceiling twenty feet above them contained recessed neon lighting and a complex system of baffles
to deaden sound.

They made their way down the two lines of con-

veyor belts that began by large steel bins and vats and
ran the length of the building through a series of machines, one more complicated and mysterious than the
next. The factory seemed to be divided roughly in half:
one part for the actual manufacture and packaging of
the two creams Madame Bardoff had referred to that
morning, and the other part devoted to the laboratories
that Michael could just see through small windows set
into several steel doors in the dividing wall. That wall
was intersected in the center by the square tower he'd
seen rising through the roof; large sliding steel doors,
seven or eight feet wide, barred entrance to it.

Although none of the machinery was in operation,
Michael thought he could feel a faint vibration coming
up through the rubber floor tiles, but before he was
able to really pin it down, Ash started one of the conveyor belts for a "dry run" as he put it. While they
walked slowly down the line, he switched each machine on and off so they could follow the progress of
about a dozen empty plastic jars moving along the line.
Incredibly complicated pieces of equipment sprang to
life, first depositing the jars on the conveyor belt with
multihinged arms, then guiding them along where they
were lifted up and engulfed, presumably to be filled
with the potions of the House of Bardoff, then vibrated,
cooled, lids secured, labeled, and finally moved off to a
holding area for packing into the shipping containers
destined for Madame's salons all over the world. As
Ash turned the machines on and off and kept up a running commentary on their actions, he also kept his eyes
firmly riveted on Michael, who had absently fallen a
bit behind the others. "What do you think of it?" Ash
called to him over the hum of the machines. "These
are the most modern lines in the cosmetic industry.
It's too bad you can't actually see the creams being ex-
truded into the jars, but the vats are empty now."

"It's fascinating," Michael called back. "What's in
here?" he asked, pushing a button just to the right of
the doors leading into the tower block. They started to
slide slowly open.

Ash covered the distance to them in a flash, hitting

out at another button with his fist to reverse the direction of the doors. "Just a utility area," he said angrily. "Heating and cooling equipment, that's all. Please don't touch or open anything without asking me first —you might damage these sensitive machines and you must realize that much of this equipment is highly secret."

"Sorry," Michael lied, "I hadn't realized." He let Ash take his arm and physically lead him on to the next machine on the packaging line. He pretended to be absorbed in the mechanical robot Ash had set in motion, while pondering what he had barely glimpsed in the tower—not heating and cooling equipment, but two startled men in black uniforms leaning against stacks of boxes with the marking of a Swiss factory renowned for the manufacture of vitamins and food supplements and a folding iron gate that could have led to another room or to a freight elevator.

As they watched the last machine on the line, Michael asked Ash innocently, "This layout is so clean and simple, where do you store all the raw materials? Down below?"

"Below?" Ash retorted, almost jumping out of his skin.

"Yes, in the basement?"

A brief look of relief flashed across Ash's face. "That's right, in the basement," he said firmly. "The ingredients are measured there and brought up to be fed directly into those stainless steel vats at the beginning of the lines where the blending starts under controlled heat conditions. The special active ingredients used in all the House of Bardoff preparations are made in that laboratory," he indicated one of the doors in the dividing wall, "so that our chemists can test each blending before it goes into the packaging machines. It's a very tricky operation." His answer seemed casual and honest, but Michael felt Ash studying his face for some reaction other than that to his explanation.

He decided the situation called for discretion and so did not follow up with further questions about the basement or the purpose of the tower. Instead he asked eagerly, "Can we see the laboratory? Ever since I was a small boy laboratories have intrigued me, even though I know absolutely nothing about them."

"Oh, yes," Sarah agreed, looking through one of the small windows. "I've never seen so many test tubes and bottles. Do let's go in, Ash."

"I guess it will be all right, but please," he emphasized, "don't touch anything."

He led the way to one of the steel doors that had a combination lock instead of the regular keyhole and latch. Ash twisted the dial to the right and left a few times and swung the door inward. Sarah had not exaggerated—Michael was impressed with the elaborate equipment and scope of the laboratory. The entire far wall was of opaque glass that let in daylight but no prying eyes. Long marble-topped benches ran the length of the room in rows broken only by some of the larger pieces of equipment and a bank of computers. They wandered up and down the aisles, looking over the various experiments and tests in progress. Michael asked and received Ash's permission to look through several of the microscopes and acted with almost childish delight at the magnifications he saw on the slides beneath the lenses. While leaning over these microscopes, he took the opportunity to examine and sniff, unobserved, any open test tubes nearby.

Several things puzzled him during his trip around the lab. First, he noted a significant degree of evaporation had taken place in all the tubes he saw, and also, they gave off little or no aroma—they might have been colored water for all he could detect. Then, he was surprised that prepared slides had been left by those working there to dry under the microscopes. It seemed very sloppy procedure, particularly for the high caliber of chemists Madame Bardoff obviously employed. Finally, there were traces of fine dust on those slides. In a sterile environment like the one of this laboratory, Michael estimated, it would take considerable time to build up even this fine accumulation. The dust and evaporation suggested to him that the lab might not have been in use for many days. In fact, Michael, who had been a top chemistry student at the École Polytechnique, began to doubt that this elaborate laboratory and, perhaps, the adjacent packaging lines were more than elaborate frauds. But if research work were not done here, where was it done? And why the pretense? There had to be some very important reason for this expensive toy to have been constructed here in the hills of the south of France.

Raving about the facilities in the lab and the automated packaging lines, Michael and the others completed their tour, removed their "moonsuits," and left the building. It had stopped raining while they were inside and a low ground mist had formed in the cool air. Before getting into the Mercedes, Michael looked up at the tower and the factory roof. The mist formed by pools of water trapped on the warm, flat roof was rising in an unusual manner; it was being slowly swept toward the tower and then shot quickly up over it to dissipate as if being drawn in a great updraft of air. It might be a ventilating shaft of some sort, he reasoned, but why would such a large one be needed for a plant of that modest size, and why would it be expelling such a vast amount of air today when the factory was supposedly closed? The operation of a large ventilating fan might explain the minor vibration he'd felt under his feet when they'd first entered the plant, or perhaps there really was a basement beneath the factory in which some secret manufacturing process was going on. That would account for the men he'd seen in the tower and the possibility of an elevator. But why weren't they wearing the costumes Ash had made his party put on so they wouldn't contaminate the place? And what were they doing with that vast supply of vitamins? Maybe vitamins were one of the secret ingredients in Madame Bardoff's potions or in her beauty treatments.

He pondered all these questions in silence during the short trip back to the château while Sarah studied him curiously. By the time they'd got back, the sun had broken through the overcast and patches of blue sky headed in their direction.

"It's going to be a nice hot day after all," Ash said smoothly. "We'll be able to have lunch down by the pool. Come on, everyone, let's change and get down to the water bar."

Michael returned to his room to slip into bathing shorts and met Sarah as she emerged from her room. They headed across the lawn toward the pool, where Ash and Iris lay waiting for them.

"Well, do you care to tell me what you're up to?" Sarah asked very directly.

He looked down at her in surprise. "Up to? I don't understand what you mean." He hoped his innocent and slightly amused tone would cover the little shock she'd just given him.

"Oh, yes you do. I may not know you all *that* well, Michael dePasse," Sarah retorted seriously, "but I know you well enough to wonder why you'd be so interested in Ava's plant and laboratories—cosmetics and industry just don't fit into your image. You had a reason for wanting to go there." Her voice was guarded and filled with suspicion.

He smiled at her disarmingly and put his finger on her lips. "I was just curious, and besides, there really wasn't anything else to do in that mausoleum this morning, now was there?"

"Michael, don't put me off. I'm not a child—you can tell me."

Can I? he wondered. Can I tell you everything when you obviously feel the way you do about your godmother? Would you even stop to try to believe whatever I did tell you about her? "All right," he confessed, "it's nothing sinister, honestly. I've heard my father speak so often about the Bardoff operation that I thought it might give us something to talk about next time we meet instead of just arguing." He looked down at the grass in embarrassment.

"Oh, Michael, I'm so sorry—I didn't mean to . . ." Sarah wanted to bite off her tongue. She let the matter drop, fearing to pry further into what must be a sensitive family problem.

Michael's mind, on the other hand, raced ahead.

He wondered if it was only Sarah's familiarity with him that had made her question his motives or if he had done something that Ash, Iris, or Ava Bardoff might also find obvious or strange. He had tried to borrow a page out of Hugo's book, playing the fool to calm any suspicion about his real intent, but he was not as skilled an actor as Hugo. He also felt guilty about lying to Sarah, about using her like this, and was growing acutely aware that he might be putting her in great danger. Michael was slowly beginning to realize that the responsibility for keeping her safe in this nightmare now would fall squarely on his shoulders.

Sarah didn't bring up the subject again, although she threw several puzzled glances at him during lunch because of his strangely evasive answers to the seemingly innocent questions of Ash and Iris. The afternoon passed lazily around the pool and the four couldn't even muster enough energy to get to the tennis courts. Michael was keenly aware of the ever watchful eyes of Ash and his beautiful friend and fearful that some concealed mini-microphone might be carrying his every word to hostile ears listening somewhere in the depths of the château. As a result, he spoke little and relied on Sarah's innocent chatter to carry most of the conversational ball. Finally she said, "Hey, you, I thought we were supposed to get to know each other this weekend. All I've learned about you so far is that you probably descended from a clam."

He laughed and jumped up from his poolside chaise. "How about a walk?" He pulled her up and said to Ash, who pretended to be napping several feet away, "We're just going to take a look around the fountains over there—be back in a few minutes."

Ash rolled over on his stomach and rested his head on folded arms so he could keep his two charges in sight. As long as they kept to their stated plans, he'd have no trouble keeping track of them.

Sarah and Michael walked slowly across the manicured lawns toward the formal pools and the gushing fountains that fed them while he gave her a brief synopsis of his childhood, exile from the family, his moth-

er's illness, and his various activities since then. In no
way did he infer that his estrangement from the Count
dePasse had any sinister motivation and he left all
mention of Hugo and Ava Bardoff completely out of
his story.

"You and I could almost be twins," Sarah said sadly
as they sat on the edge of one of the reflecting pools.
"We're both orphans in a sense. You don't really have
a family anymore and both my parents are dead." She
had felt the rejection and loss of her father so much
that she'd never spoken of it to anyone before but Ava.
But knowing his problems, she felt Michael would understand. Sarah told him of the life in Washington and
London. "I can't tell you how wonderful my father
was. I loved him so very much—he was my entire
life. We were a team, always together. We rode horse-
back in Regent's Park, swam—everything. He even
helped pick out my clothes and dressed me up for his
friends. I was so spoiled—I must have been awful.
But mother encouraged it because, I guess, she loved
him as much as I did, and if it made him happy,
she wanted him to do it. They wouldn't hear of my
going away to school and we always traveled together,
the three of us. Oh, Michael, we spent wonderful weekends in Scotland, Ireland, and in all those beautiful
country estates outside of London. Father sometimes
let me come shooting with him, even though the other
men hated it." She giggled to herself, reliving some
silly incident on one of those occasions. "I was a princess then."

"You're a princess now," he said, running his hand
gently through her long hair.

She didn't feel his touch; Sarah was lost in her memories. "When I was sixteen, he and mother went off
alone on a holiday together—a three-week honeymoon,
they called it. I was so jealous I could have exploded.
I practically locked myself in the London house for the
first week and wouldn't go to any of the debutante
parties. Then—I guess it was spite—I began going to
the dances and flirting outrageously with all the boys
to make him jealous. Silly, wasn't it? Of course no one
ever told him so he never knew.

"Then they returned and everything went wrong. All of a sudden I was an outsider. Just like you, my father said it was time he untied the umbilical cord, that I was old enough to stand on my own two feet. He bundled me off to schools in Switzerland and Paris and we didn't see much of each other after that."

Sarah's voice fell almost to a whisper and Michael felt a tightness across his chest, knowing how she had felt, remembering how he had felt. He put his arm around her, silently communicating his understanding.

"They died in Switzerland several years ago. I was at the Sorbonne when it happened." She looked down at the water rippling around her ankles. "I didn't even get a chance to see them. Their bodies—their bodies were mangled so badly in the avalanche."

"Is that when you met Ava Bardoff?"

Sarah didn't seem to notice Michael's making the link between her parent's death and Ava Bardoff. "Oh, no—she came often to the embassy in London, and my father made her my honorary godmother at my last birthday party, just before they all went off on that 'honeymoon' trip. I really got to know her well when she brought me from college to her chalet after the accident. Ava knew I'd want to be there, particularly since there was still some hope my parents might be found alive. Ever since then she's been the only one I could talk to about it."

"You've got me, now," he said softly, smiling down at her. By this time they were wandering and splashing aimlessly through the spray of the fountains, letting the water cool their sunbaked bodies. "Where did your parents go with Madame Bardoff on that first trip?" Michael asked, his voice barely audible over the noise of the falling water.

"Why, here, of course. With all that embassy running around, my father needed a complete rest and so did Mother. Ava told them they'd be like new after three weeks in the south of France with her—and they certainly were," Sarah added bitterly.

Michael was silent for several minutes. Her phrase "they'd be like new after three weeks" rebounded around in his brain. The three-week time period seemed significant. Then it clicked. He remembered Hugo saying yesterday on the *Krait* that the secretary of state and his wife had cancelled all social engagements and vanished for three weeks. Like Sarah's parents and perhaps his, were these two here for three weeks of rest and treatment—a treatment that would make them "like new"? He had to get into that closed north wing tonight. Hugo had warned him about taking risks, but now the risk seemed justified.

"Hello," Sarah said, "have I lost you?"

Coming out of his thoughts, he kissed her gently on the nose. "I hope not." Michael stood studying the sad and vulnerable face before him, holding her arms in a grip she thought too tight. "Sarah, promise me one thing—that you'll trust me no matter what. I know I may be acting strangely, but trust me. Please. You'll be all right, I swear."

The urgency in his tone impressed and worried her. "Michael, if you're trying to frighten me, you are."

"Just bear with me for a few days and then—" He glanced over her shoulder and his grim mood suddenly changed. "—and then I'll buy you the biggest, best, bubbliest bottle of Dom Perignon on the entire Riviera." He laughed.

Sarah looked around to see Ash standing quietly nearby. A funny little chill ran down her spine. How long, she wondered, had he been there listening to them.

"C'mon," the intruder said gaily to them, "drink time approaches. Ava is on her way down to join us." The three walked together back toward the pool.

Ash's silent arrival at the fountain and Michael's strange plea for trust had raised a foreboding in Sarah that still lingered as she watched her lovely godmother approach, waving to them. Ava was followed by two servants bearing trays of hot hors d'oeuvres. Here I am, Sarah thought, living in this beautiful estate with its high, protective walls. What could possibly hurt me in this Garden of Eden? Nothing, absolutely nothing, she told herself, but why didn't she believe it? Sarah suddenly ran ahead to meet Ava and gave her a squeeze, the kind of squeeze she used to give her old teddy bear. "Everything's going to be wonderful, isn't it?" she cried.

"Of course, darling," Ava purred, wondering if Sarah were asking a question or making a declaration. "But why this sudden burst of emotion? Been having a little heart to heart with your charming young man?"

"Yes." Sarah smiled. "But he's changed so much, I'm having trouble figuring him out. He's so much more serious, more . . ."

"Later we will have a nice long chat, just we two, and you can tell me all about it, but right now we must not keep the others waiting."

Dinner that evening was a duplicate of the one the preceding evening except that the two gambling couples from Cannes had been replaced by a young princess and her current lover. As before, cocktails were served in the grove to the west of the château followed by dinner, coffee in the conservatory, and games in the billiard room.

Michael had flattered Ava on her laboratory and factory and felt sure she did not suspect he had any ulterior motive other than curiosity in visiting them. He also believed that Ash had not been able to report back anything from his conversations during the day to arouse her suspicions. He was not quite right.

Madame Bardoff had not been pleased about his interest in the tower at the factory and had delicately probed Michael to learn what, if anything, he'd seen. Also, based upon her "chat" with Sarah before dinner, Madame had been busy taking a new look at him to determine if he were more than just the athletic playboy he pretended. She'd ordered his car gone over with a fine-toothed comb that afternoon and during dinner his room had undergone a thorough search. Throughout the evening, Ava Bardoff and Michael dePasse had been at a standoff, eyeing each other like wrestlers circling in the ring waiting for the other to drop his guard while laughing gaily over sophisticated stories and cocktail-party gossip.

Before leaving Sarah that night, Michael joined her in her suite for a nightcap. He wanted his innocent conversation about the factory visit, the activities of the day, and the dinner party to be registered by the hidden microphones he was sure were also planted in Sarah's rooms, *and* he wanted them to pick up his suggestion that they both get up for an early breakfast the next day followed by a drive through the hills. "If the view of the sea is so beautiful from here," he said, "just think what it will be like higher up. Let's take a picnic lunch." Sarah agreed and put in an order with with the night operator. Thus, having prepared the way for a possible escape, Michael kissed her and once more retired alone to get a "good night's sleep."

But while Sarah slept the sleep of the innocent, he prepared for his nocturnal invasion of the north wing. He knew the danger of his plan to Hugo and the others should he be discovered, but they had to know what was going on. He had to be doing the right thing. Removing his dinner jacket and ruffled dress shirt, he wriggled into a dark blue pullover and dropped a roll of adhesive tape, his penknife, and several of his diamond studs into his pocket. Next he rubbed soot from the fireplace in the sitting room onto his tennis sneakers to darken them; fortunately his face was so brown from the sun that no further blacking was necessary.

He then quietly bolted the door from the inside and made the standard bathroom noises, yawning loudly several times for the benefit of the hidden telephone mikes. Throwing open the tall windows with a bang, he turned out the lights and lay back on his bed, reviewing his next moves while giving the château plenty of time to settle down for the night. At 3:00 A.M., Michael slipped quietly off the bed and placed several pillows in it to simulate his sleeping figure just as a precaution. He tiptoed to the open window and, drawing the draperies together behind him, stared out, studying the shadows in the park for a moving figure, a dog, the glow of a lighted cigarette. He found nothing. Leaning out, he looked up the side of the stone wall to the ledge of the window some twenty or so feet above— that was his goal.

One of Michael's activities that Hugo had apparently overlooked in compiling his thick dossier on the young man was his mountaineering skills acquired during his military service where he had learned how to traverse mountain faces, drive in pitons, and rappel down sheer cliffs. Now, years later, he found himself about to scale the face of a château constructed by one of the ministers in the court of Louis XIV. Fortunately the joints between the old stones were deep and the carving of the design bold enough to afford the handholds he needed for the climb.

Standing on his windowsill, his fingers felt over the stone and mortar surfaces in the dark for the first crevice deep enough to hold his weight. Michael pulled himself slowly upward, nine inches at a time, as his fingers and toes found their holds, one after the other. The fluting of the stone column carved from the wall on his right made the climb easier, although by the time his left hand reached out to grasp the sill of the upper window, his toe and leg muscles had just about exhausted themselves. He hung from the sill by his hands for a minute to let them regain some of their lost strength before continuing the climb. It took five more painful minutes to work himself up the wall another six feet to a position where he could put his left foot on the windowsill and then edge the rest of his body over to stand with his face pressed against the glass.

Well, he thought, the first lap of the trip is over without being discovered by patrolling guards and yelping dogs—let's hope they won't hear this. Michael took one of the diamond studs from his trouser pocket and scratched an eight-inch circle into the pane of glass by the window's elaborate old latch. This accomplished, he tore two strips of tape and stuck them over the scratch at the top of the circle. After one last look around the park below him, he gave the glass a sharp, hard tap with his knuckles. The circle of glass popped out and hung inside the window, held from falling by the tape. It took Michael only seconds to lift the latch, swing open one half of the window, and drop gently down inside.

Aware that microphones might inhabit this room just

as in his suite below, he pulled the window carefully shut behind him and moved silently across the dark room that he had made sure was empty on his brief tour with Sarah the previous evening. He smiled to himself, remembering how she had laughed at him for being so nosey when he popped his head into this room and the one across the way just to "take a peek at the fabulous decor." He inched open the door, his ears alert for any sound, and moved slowly forward to peer around the thick doorframe up and down the corridor that ran the entire length of the east wing. One of Madame's men sat reading a magazine in a chair tilted back against the door leading into the north wing. He wore the white uniform that could be interpreted either as a military uniform or the uniform of a male nurse, depending upon one's frame of mind; Michael's frame of mind was distinctly military at the moment. He waited until the guard had finished one page and was busy fumbling in the back pages for the remainder of the story before darting quickly across the corridor to the door of the room which faced onto the conservatory in the center of the château. He grasped the doorknob, praying it wouldn't be locked. It wasn't—with a sigh of relief, he let himself into the darkened room and leaned back against the closed door, waiting for his heart to stop hammering.

After a minute or two he tiptoed to the window and stared through the one-way glass into the space below. Only a few dim streaks of light from the ground-floor public rooms illuminated the shadowy conservatory, its vines, assorted plants, and palm trees reaching up toward the glass dome forty feet or more over the tile floor. He looked to the window on the far side in the north wing; thank God it was still open a crack. That was to be his next goal if his fingers and arms didn't fail him.

Michael's eyes traced his aerial route to that window. From the sill of the window where he now stood, he would have to jump up to reach one of the ornate and lacy iron beams that arched gracefully up to the top of the glass dome. He would have to follow this

beam, hand over hand, to that top intersection and
then work his way back down the beam leading to the
support over the open window in the north wall. Swinging his window open, he listened long and hard for any
indication that the guards were near or about to enter
the conservatory. It's now or never, he mumbled to
himself, and climbed out onto his window ledge, closing the window all but a crack behind him. He took a
deep breath, crouched, and than sprang up two feet
to grasp the base of the iron beam. Michael hung there
momentarily, looking down at the smooth, highly polished tiled floor beneath him; a fall meant far more
than painful broken bones, it meant almost certain
death at the hands of Ava Bardoff.

Swinging his body to gain the proper momentum,
he began to climb upward along the beam. Halfway
there, his feet brushed through the top of one of the
palms sending a startled flock of canaries chirping nois-
ily through the air around and around the vast room
before coming to rest on branches and perches elsewhere. Michael held his breath and hung partially ob-
scured by the fronds of the giant palm. He heard voices
coming closer, and two of Madame's guards entered
the conservatory. They looked around the room and
then up, playing the beams of their powerful flashlights
over the foliage. Closing his eyes, he waited for their
shouts of discovery. After what seemed hours, he
opened them to see the guards standing almost directly
under him, talking quietly; they lit cigarettes for each
other, reluctant to leave. The minutes ticked by and
his fingers grew numb and his arms ached from supporting the dead weight of his body, but he dared not
move a fraction of an inch for fear of rustling the palm.
The guards checked their watches and, after taking a
last cursory look about the conservatory, finally left.

In desperation, Michael pulled himself along another
ten feet of the beam to a place in which its design called
for a series of large holes. He put his arms through two
of the holes so that his weight now hung suspended by
his arm pits. Although terribly painful, this position
relieved the killing tension on his hand and arm mus-

cles, which he now slowly flexed to increase their circulation and restore some of their lost strength. He blessed all those hours and days spent hanging onto a tow rope practicing for the water-skiing championships —hours that had also prepared his muscles for this obstacle course he was now trying to get through.

After resting five or ten minutes, Michael was able to cover quickly the remaining distance to the top of the dome and climb back down the other side where he now dangled, his toes two feet above the sill of the northern window. As he hung there, he faced two risks: first, that he wouldn't be able to keep his balance on that narrow sill after dropping onto it, and second, that someone might be inside the room behind the window—someone who would scream bloody murder. Well, he thought stoically, no sense hanging around; if I fall, I won't have to worry about some phantom waiting for me in the room. He released his hold and dropped the two feet, swaying out from the window and then back. His knees trembled under his weight but held his body long enough for him to get a new hold on the ornate stone carving around the window frame. A quick glance and he realized the room was dark, and so, without hesitation, Michael swung the window out and slipped inside.

He stood motionless in the blackness, listening for the sound of breathing coming from some sleeping occupant; he heard none. Reaching into his pocket, he withdrew the gold cigarette lighter, and with one flick of the flint, the small gas flame showed him to be alone in a narrow, officelike room. He pulled the window tight behind him and switched on a flexible, gooseneck lamp sitting on a desk in front of a set of draperies some six feet wide. Looking slowly about him, Michael tried to memorize everything he saw. The room was covered in soundproofing material and divided in half lengthwise by a seven-foot-high partition, each side containing a simple desk, chair, and a small set of loudspeakers. On the desk to his right he saw an elaborate tape machine, a Polaroid camera, and a file marked with what was obviously a code number—21.19/19.5.3–19.20M/5.8.74.

An ashtray was filled with filtertips and the desk was a jumble of papers on which had been scribbled sentences and phrases of little apparent significance. The words were all marked with various symbols similar to those used in a dictionary to indicate proper pronunciation and inflection. He found a list of names, many of them familiar in world politics, with small notations of a personal nature next to each of them, such as, "lunched 3/7/74, escargots favorite, foul breath, mistress Dominique Martinez, against alliance, committed to Fahd," etc. Just like tiny, scandalous dossiers, Michael thought. He turned his attention to the piles of photographs by the camera; they were of the same man in various degrees of dress and undress, getting into bed, yawning, close-ups of him shaving— all unposed and relatively unflattering. But that face was certainly well known. Michael turned off the desk lamp and carefully parted the draperies to see exactly what was behind them. It was an interior window, another one-way mirror, he judged, from the strange color it gave to everything in the room beyond. The room was a beautifully, if not lavishly, decorated bedroom, and there, sleeping peacefully, lay the object of all those Polaroid photographs. The face was dimly illuminated by a night light. Michael found himself staring at the controversial American secretary of state. So Hugo's suspicions had been right all along.

Feeling like an intruder, he let the drapery fall back over the window and turned on the lamp to continue his investigation. He punched the play button on the recorder and listened fascinated for several minutes to the voice he'd heard many times on radio and French national television; but these weren't speeches, just miscellaneous bits of conversation with various people— a maid, a masseur, and, yes—that was Madame Bardoff's voice. Madame was laughing gaily with him over some little political scandal and asking for more of the details which were forthcoming in this congenial atmosphere.

Michael didn't have time to listen further. He turned off the machine and went to the desk in the other half of the office; it was bare, no dossier lay there. Probably no one in there, he thought as he almost casually parted the draperies on the one-way window. Much to his surprise, the room beyond was inhabited; he saw the very recognizable, handsome shah sleeping comfortably in an elaborate four-poster.

So these great men had got together at the Bardoff clinic for a health cure. At first he smiled to himself at their vanity, then he remembered Hugo's fears and began to think of the possible reasons for and the consequences of having these important men under one roof. It spurred him on.

Crossing the room, he listened at the door for noise in what he presumed must be the hall. He opened it a crack and encountered nothing but darkness. Using his lighter again, he found that the office in which he was now standing opened into the back of a phony broom closet; a slit of light showed under its door. Entering it, Michael put his ear against the door and was just inching it open, when the rattle of a metal cart of some kind stopped him. The sound grew louder, passed, and began to fade. He peered through the partially open door in time to catch sight of Stanislau Beel followed by a nurse pushing a white metal medical cart loaded with bottles and needles as they entered a room at the far end of the hall. Michael waited a few minutes and, when no further activity occurred, slipped out and moved silently down the corridor, stopping before a door one short of the one Beel had entered. He'd guessed right, it opened into another type of phony closet, this one a linen cupboard. After a very brief search he found the latch for the door in the back wall and let himself into another partitioned office. Michael didn't waste a minute, but went to the one-way window, pulled back the draperies, and settled back in the dark to watch Mr. Beel and the nurse with 21.19/19.5.3–19.20F/5.8.74, the wife of the U.S. secretary of state.

The nurse, in a slightly more feminine version of the guards' white uniforms, was just withdrawing a hypodermic needle from the drugged woman's arm. "She should be receptive in a minute or two. If you're going to be longer than an hour, she'll need another shot, and that can be dangerous."

"Just keep her mind alert for the next few weeks, and then the good doctor can have her," Stanislau Beel said with a cold voice.

"Remember," the nurse cautioned, "she's got to be in good enough condition to function normally during the day. Her neut has to study her under normal conditions."

Beel turned to the nurse and gave her a withering look. "Are you trying to tell me how to run this operation?"

"No, sir."

"Then be quiet." He indicated a chair on the other side of the bed. "Sit down and keep a watch on her vitals."

The nurse busied herself taping wires to the American's forehead, chest, and wrists, and plugged them into a dial-covered machine on the metal cart. Beel sat on the other side of the bed playing with a tape recorder and looking over his note pad. After fiddling with her machine for a minute or two, the nurse nodded to him and Beel turned on the recorder.

"Hello, how nice to see you again," he said to the woman lying in the bed. "Do you remember me? I'm your very good friend. Open your eyes and look at me. Open your eyes and look at me. That's right."

The woman's eyelids fluttered and slowly opened.

"Hello, how are you feeling now?"

After a long pause, she answered, "Fine," in a dreamlike voice.

"Good. Will you count to ten for me?" She lay looking up at him through glazed eyes. "Count ten—that's a good girl."

She slowly began to count while Beel smiled reassuringly down at her.

"That's very good. Now let's talk about your family again. Won't it be nice to talk about your husband? Where did you meet him—I bet it was somewhere nice." Beel's voice floated in a seesaw rhythm.

She replied, and with his urging began to speak

more and more freely and naturally about the details
of their courtship and home life together. She talked
about subjects ranging from his and her favorite foods
to how they made love together.

Michael felt nauseated, felt like a double intruder,
prying not only into the ugly acts being performed by
Beel but into the intimate life of a woman he respected.
He turned away and directed his attention to the other
window. Through it he saw another drugged woman
undergoing questioning by one of Madame's men. Her
face looked vaguely familiar but he couldn't place it.
The file on the desk before him read 21.19.19.18/
16.18F/5.8.74; the notes were in a language Michael
didn't understand. Was it Greek? He listened to the
voices in the next room for a few minutes and then
the pieces of the puzzle suddenly fell into place. It was
Russian and that was the wife of the chairman of
the Central Communist Party. "My God," Michael
whispered under his breath, "he must be here, too.
What in hell is going on?"

He'd learned all he needed to know and retreated
quietly into the linen cupboard. Michael was tempted
to return directly to the room through which he'd first
gained access to the north wing, but curiosity drove
him silently down the corridor to an elevator door at
the opposite end. He was about to investigate the elevator when its motors purred into action and a car
stopped on the other side. Michael jumped quickly into
an adjacent service room and pressed himself flat
against the wall behind a metal and cloth hospital
screen. From his position he could see out into the corridor perhaps six or seven feet. The elevator doors slid
open and Michael again heard the rattling of a metal
cart that was soon pushed into and out of his view by
another so-called nurse accompanied by a man in one
of the white uniforms to which he was now very accustomed. He heard a bedroom door open and close
somewhere down the hall, and then only silence.

He edged slowly around the service-room door, so
intent on being quiet that he almost upset a rack of
six breakfast trays, each with a neatly folded napkin

and a vase filled with one bright-red rose. The elevator doors were still open and it was deserted. Three fast steps and Michael was inside studying this very stream-lined piece of equipment. Aside from open, close, and emergency-stop buttons, the control panel contained four other buttons indicating the elevator opened at the basement, ground, second, and third, or servants' floor. He noticed the panel didn't seem to be lying completely flat against the steel wall of the elevator and, using his penknife, slipped the blade around the edge of the panel until he found a catch. One push and the panel snapped open on hinges to reveal an identical control panel underneath; identical, that is, with the exception of two more buttons running down vertically under the basement button. So, he mused, snapping the phony panel back into place, this old pile of stone has subbasements. Then Michael's eye caught the "in case of emergency" panel which opened without trouble to reveal several face masks and two canisters that at first appeared to be fire extinguishers, but upon examination proved to contain oxygen. How very strange, he thought as he reached for one of the masks, but his investigation was to be cut short. The elevator doors began to close slowly, obviously in answer to a button being pushed from above or below. He just had the time to slam shut the emergency panel and leap out before being trapped and presented to Madame's guards on a platter.

This near miss was enough to send Michael up the corridor as fast as he could make it; his tennis sneakers didn't make a sound as he sprinted over the thick-pile carpet past the beautifully paneled and carved walls of the VIP north wing. I wouldn't trade places with those VIPs for anything in the world, he thought as he moved inside the broom closet and on through into the office he'd first entered. He swung the window slowly out a few inches and studied the conservatory below for any sign of movement. His watch read 4:10; it would soon start getting light and he had one more job to do before slipping back into his own room. He had to investigate the roof at the northwest corner of the château—the corner that had looked so strange in Hugo's aerial photographs and over which the bats seemed to like to fly.

His path to the roof lay back up the lacy iron beams of the conservatory dome and out through one of several ventilating doors built into it. Michael had compared his size to these openings on his way over and thought that with a little squeezing he should just about be able to fit through. Once outside and on top of the dome, he would follow the more serviceable support beams to the château's inner wall and scale it to the mansard roof.

He dreaded climbing out again onto the windowsill and making that first jump up to the support beam, but there was no other way open to him. And this time he would be careful about brushing into the flora and sending its fauna chirping like little yellow demons about the place. Standing on the sill, he gently swung the window back in until it was just as open as he'd found it, then, taking another deep breath, he jumped up to grab the beam and once again began the disquieting hand-over-hand journey up the side of the dome. Halfway there his hand knocked into something soft and his heart stood still as a canary swooped by his head with a frightened cry. Michael continued upward, hoping that one isolated burst of chirping wouldn't alarm the guards sitting in the main entrance hall that opened directly off the conservatory. He could hear the dull murmur of their voices in conversation as he climbed.

At last he reached one of the glass ventilating doors. It was attached to a simple automated machine that turned a large worm screw to raise and lower it at the pushbutton command of a gardener below. Putting his left arm through one of the large decorative holes in the beam to support his weight, Michael used his right hand to slip the cotter pin out of a connecting hinge and so disconnect the door from the machine. His next problem was to remove the interior screen that Madame Bardoff had obviously installed to keep bees and other insects from cross-pollinating her precious pure-bred species in the gardens forty feet beneath his dangling body. Because he could only use one hand, it was with great difficulty and a running stream of muttered profanity that Michael finally managed to slide the screen up and out through its restraining slots. Once free, he pushed it out through the glass door onto the outside of the dome, praying it wouldn't slide down, banging over each of the hundreds of glass joints forming the dome. Luck was with him; the screen slipped only a foot before becoming caught on a horizontal metal joint.

The operation of freeing the door and screen had taken almost fifteen minutes, fifteen minutes of hanging by only one arm and then the other as he worked. Now he hoped he'd have the strength left to pull himself up through the opening. He gripped the frame of the door with both hands and, straining his arm muscles to the limit of their endurance, began lifting his body slowly up through the ventilator. His shoulders scraped painfully against the metal frame and he had to twist to jam them through. Then, reversing his hold one hand at a time, he managed to pull himself up the rest of the way until he could sit on the outside edge with his legs dangling down into the conservatory. Michael sat there for several minutes, gasping to catch his breath and rest before swinging his legs up and out and starting across the dome for the northwest corner.

Some forty feet below, a figure in a white uniform lay on one of the chaise longues behind a cluster of tall philodendrons. He had watched in quiet amusement as the intruder, dressed in black, moved hand over hand along the decorative beam above and struggled through the ventilator opening. His eyes followed Michael's delicate progress across the outside of the dome to the château wall, and then, smiling, he slowly stood up from the chaise and flexed his powerful body. Rimmon was one of Madame's most expert killers.

Reaching the château's interior wall, Michael found little difficulty in scaling it to the wide gutter of the mansard roof; old, unused drain pipes served as steps

most of the way. He pulled himself up to the gutter
and walked along it toward the corner tower until he
came to a ladder built into the arching roof to facilitate
repairs. Scampering up like a cat, he lay at last on the
wide, flat top of the roof. Although he couldn't see them
in the dark, he knew the trees in the park below would
look like toys and the wide drive like a narrow ribbon
from way up here. Running the rest of the way along
the roof in a crouch, he reached the final ladder that
took him up the last ten feet over the gray-green lead
roof of the northwest tower. At first he was confused;
as he looked around him, instead of the normal flat top,
Michael found the opening of a large square shaft cut
into the roof, leaving only nine feet or so of the green
lead around the edge. He lay on his stomach and
inched forward toward the hole, bracing himself against
a strong current of air sweeping over him and pulling
him toward the edge. Michael peered down into the
blackness of the shaft. It was deep—he could sense it
—but just how deep he couldn't tell. On the left he
barely made out the top of the elevator housing that
was built into the side of the shaft; it took up no more
than a quarter of the opening. Over the sound of the
air rushing past him, Michael heard the distant churn-
ing noise of some sort of machinery coming from far
below. His eyes strained into the darkness, but he could
see nothing.

Tearing a small strip of old lead from a roof seam,
he bent it into a crude ring about an inch in diameter
and tied his thin cotton handkerchief to it. His butane
gas lighter gave him a great deal of trouble because of
the wind roaring into the shaft, but after curling up to
shield it with his body, Michael was finally able to set
the cotton cloth on fire. As soon as the flames had a
good hold on the material, he dropped his fluttering
torch into the black void. The flames grew smaller and
smaller and vanished more from the distance it had
fallen than from being extinguished by the current
of air through which it fell. "That is some deep hole,"
he mumbled. It was a hell of a lot deeper than a few
subbasements would make it. Well, that's it for tonight,

he thought as he rolled over on his back to face the ladder leading down from the roof—and froze.

Floating above him against the black sky, Michael saw an incredibly evil face illuminated from below by the beam of a flashlight like the flames of hell. Its handsome features were contorted, nostrils flared, and lips twisted in the vicious, almost lustful smile of one exhilarated by the pure pleasure of destroying life, crushing it out with bare hands, savoring the terror of its victims before smearing itself with their blood. The shock paralyzed him. Michael lay there as the beam of light slowly moved down the bare arm of the powerful figure squatting on its haunches at the edge of the tower roof between him and the ladder. The light came to rest on the shiny object in Rimmon's hand.

"Do you see this gun?" he asked in a low, gloating voice. "It is a very special gun. You are going to die, dePasse, but not at the hands of Mulciber—I want you all for myself." A disgusting chuckle bubbled deep in his throat as he looked hungrily over the half-raised body before him.

Michael stared, hypnotized by the gun in the killer's hand. Every detail etched itself into his brain—the reflected light on the almost sensuous curves of the weapon resting in the strong hand, the smooth skin taut over thick veins, the perfectly manicured nails, the tiny blue dot by the right thumbnail. Behind in the blackness, two eyes glowed like red coals.

Again he heard the menacing chuckle and the gun slowly raised to point directly between his eyes; he saw the finger tighten slowly, very slowly, as if to tease him. The laugh began to rise in Rimmon's throat, and Michael knew that when it burst into the open, his life would end. His body tensed. The laugh, the snap of the gun, and Michael's sudden kick and lurch to the side all happened at exactly the same instant. His foot smashed into Rimmon's hand and he heard a "thunk" in the lead by his ear as a shiny missile flashed past; the flashlight and gun skittered across the roof. With a snarl of rage, Rimmon brought his knee crushing into Michael's groin and fell upon him, locking his hands around his victim's throat. Michael nearly fainted from the excruciating pain in his stomach; he couldn't breathe; powerful hands were slowly crushing his windpipe. He tried to pry Rimmon's face away, then struck out at him frantically with both fists—it was useless.

Through a red haze Michael saw the evil, devouring smile looming over him—its tongue licked across wet lips and came closer to kiss him at the instant of his death. Summoning his last ounce of strength Michael dug in his heels and, snapping his body like a spring, flipped Rimmon to the side. The two struggling men rolled over to the shaft edge, Michael near to unconsciousness, his throat still in the closing vise. As Rimmon's back hit the roof he gave a sudden gasp and his shoulders instinctively jerked up. His eyes bulged wide with terror and every muscle in his body tensed —Michael thought surely his neck must snap—and then Rimmon's hands loosened and fell lifelessly away. Michael collapsed on top of him gulping air into his starved lungs, and passed out.

He regained consciousness solwly and rolled off the body beneath him. Forcing himself up into a half-sitting position, he looked down at Rimmon lying in the beam of light from his own flashlight several feet away. His eyes stared wide open and glassy at the black sky, his face seemed clenched in a spasm. He's dead, Michael told himself in disbelief, but how? How? I hardly touched him. Getting up on his knees, Michael rolled the inert body toward him; he saw no wound, nothing that would . . . but then his eye caught sight of something glistening in the light, something sticking out of the soft lead. It was a needle, perhaps only an inch long. That's what had been in his "very special" gun, why it hadn't made a noise, only a snap; it fired some sort of poison needle. A chill ran through his body; Rimmon had rolled back onto the needle, killing himself as he had intended to kill Michael. My God, he cried to himself, what kind of a hell is this place?

But he had no time left to think of these things; he had to get off that roof and away before the faint glow he saw in the sky got any brighter. Panic gripped him.

Michael looked down at the body; he couldn't leave it on the roof. Bury it, his confused brain told him, but where? The wind roared down the shaft beside him. He didn't stop to consider the consequences—he only wanted to be rid of the horrible demon that lay next to him. The body lay parallel with the shaft, a trouser leg flapping in the rushing air. Michael sat back and used his feet to push it toward the edge. Its feet slipped in first, righting the body as it went over. Rimmon's open eyes reflected briefly in the torchlight; they stared blankly at him and then vanished, swept down into the bottomless hole along with the howling wind. A wave of nausea rolled through Michael; he took several deep breaths to keep from being sick.

Michael had never killed a man before and was in a state of shock. He forced his head into his hands to compose himself. No time to panic, he repeated to himself over and over again as wild thoughts of Sarah and Hugo and what might happen if the body were discovered before he could escape rushed through his numb brain. In a daze he crawled over to the flashlight, turned it off, and dropped it down the shaft; instinct made him pocket the gun.

Then he backed awkwardly down the ladder to the lower mansard roof and numbly retraced his steps to the place where he'd scaled the interior wall. With movement, his body began to respond more effectively to his commands and, as his brain cleared, the extreme seriousness of his current situation bore in on him. It was now simply a case of living or dying, kill or be killed. The outside laws of society by which he had always guided himself did not apply here behind the high walls of the House of Bardoff.

He was down and across the glass dome of the conservatory within a few minutes. Quietly lowering himself in through the ventilator opening, he slipped the screen back into position and reconnected the ventilator door to the raising-and-lowering mechanism. The conservatory below seemed completely deserted as Michael began his hand-over-hand path down the beam leading to the window through which he'd first entered the room. This time he was very careful to lift his legs high over the palm tree that had set off the chorus of birds on his trip over. Without hesitation, he dropped down onto the window ledge, swung open the window, and slipped inside.

So far so good, he thought—now for my studious friend. He peered around the doorframe and cursed; his guard now stood talking with another, their backs to the door leading to the north wing, looking down the long corridor in his direction. Michael glanced at his watch; 5:12 A.M., and the sky getting lighter with every passing minute. He had to get across that hall, and do it now.

Crossing the room, he switched on a small bedside lamp and examined the needle gun he'd taken from Rimmon. There were seven needles left in the magazine. He wondered if they'd be strong enough and the propelling force of the gun powerful enough to break one of the light bulbs in the wall brackets running down the hall; by shattering one, he might lure the guards beyond his route of escape. No, they looked too fragile and, no matter how great the force, they'd probably deflect harmlessly off the smooth sides of the bulbs. As he pondered his problem, he heard footsteps in the hall outside the door. In a flash he switched off the light and dived under one of the twin beds. The door opened and a stream of light fell across the carpet by his feet; the overhead light was turned on, then off. "Okay here," one of the guards said as he closed the door; his footsteps continued down the corridor to pause before the next door. Just a routine security check, Michael thought—damn lucky for me they think this place is impregnable.

When next he peered around the deep frame of the door, the guards were well down the hall. He waited until both had their heads stuck into rooms, and then darted across the corridor. Moving quickly to the window, he once more scanned the park for movement and then swung it open and lowered himself over the ledge, hanging there until his toes found a suitable hold. Michael felt horribly exposed clinging to the side of the building as the sky in the east showed a rosy glow and would have jumped gladly had he dared risk a twisted ankle. Feeling his way down from stone to stone, he navigated the wall in a few minutes and at last reached his own window, slipping in through the partially closed draperies to sink exhausted to the floor. Sitting, he tried to collect his thoughts, assimilate everything he'd seen and done in the last few hours, but he couldn't. His brain kept returning to one thought—get out, get out of this place as fast as you can.

After fifteen minutes, he rose and stripped off the blackened tennis shoes and his filthy sweater and trousers all of which he carefully folded and buried under some socks and last night's dress shirt in his overnight bag, hoping that should the valet nose about his room, he'd pass over the bag as containing nothing more incriminating than Michael's dirty laundry. Then, washing his hands and face as best he could without running the shower or making any other noise, he quietly unbolted the room door and slipped into bed, the needle pistol securely tucked under his pillow. Three hours to go, he thought, then it's time to run.

6

Michael dozed fitfully until 8:00 A.M., when he picked up the telephone and ordered two breakfasts of orange juice, coffee, and croissants to be sent to Sarah's room in fifteen minutes. The voice on the other end was noncommittal and asked if Monsieur dePasse would like his valet to attend him now. Michael replied negatively and hung up to take a noisy shower, shave, and dress.

He was knocking on Sarah's door when the breakfast trays arrived; they were identical to the six he'd seen in the north wing last night. The kitchen boy followed Michael into the room and drew back the draperies as Michael sat on the edge of Sarah's bed, gently shaking her awake. He nodded to the servant, who let himself out, smiling.

"Come on, you sleepy-headed princess," Michael urged, "your Prince Charming is about to take you on a lovely ride to the mountains. Come on."

Sarah's eyes opened slowly; she tried to focus them on him, while mumbling in a sleepy voice for the time.

"Eight-fifteen on a beautiful Sunday morning. Come on, up you get," he prodded, trying to keep the tremendous urgency he felt out of his voice. When she tried to roll over and pull the covers about her head, he forcibly lifted her into a sitting position. "Breakfast is over there waiting for you by the window. Just look at that sun."

"You look at it," she said miserably. "My God, it's practically the middle of the night."

"Up you get," he said, "and into a nice warm shower."

Michael went into the bathroom and turned the water on full, coming back to pull the covers off her once again. She began to resist, and he feared she might say something that would hurt or delay his escape plan. Before she had the chance, Michael pushed her back onto the pillow and clamped his hand gently but firmly over her mouth, while purposely knocking the bedside phone to the floor with a clatter; he forced another pillow over it with his free hand. Her eyes opened wide in surprise.

"Damn it, shut up, and do what I tell you," he said in a sharp whisper. They stared at each other for a few seconds and then he continued. "Now I'm going to take my hand away and I don't want to hear a word from you until I say so." Sarah lay motionless, looking up at him.

He slowly removed his hand and replaced the phone on the table with suitable apologies for his clumsiness. Taking a firm hold on her arm, Michael pulled her up out of bed and into the bathroom, where the sound of the shower would drown out their brief conversation from all interested ears. They faced each other in the small, white tiled room.

"Yesterday I asked you to trust me. Can you do it now?"

She made no reply.

"We're leaving here as soon as you dress and eat some breakfast. I'll explain everything when we're in the car; I can't tell you now because there are microphones hidden in your room." His words startled and horrified her. Sarah looked over his shoulder back to her dear, familiar room. She didn't know why, but she believed Michael. The room slowly changed before her eyes, changed into an alien, almost dirty thing.

"While we're here I want you to follow my lead, be gay, happy, chatter away as if nothing unusual were happening. We'll be back for lunch. Now I want you to order my car brought around to the front and leave a message for your godmother that we'll be back from our drive by noon."

"You're not telling me the truth, are you?" Sarah asked calmly. "I won't ever be coming back here, will I?"

He stared at her in surprise and then lowered his eyes under the burden of guilt he had to assume for using her, for destroying her fairy-tale life here. "No, probably not," he said quietly, almost regretfully. Her acceptance of his statement led him to add, "Sarah, our lives are in danger if we stay."

A thin smile crossed her lips, one which he could not read. Without another word, Sarah brushed past him and went to the phone, picking up the receiver.

"Who's on the switchboard this morning?" she asked. "Oh, good. Look, this is me, Sarah. Monsieur de-Passe and I are about ready to leave for a drive; will you please have his car brought around now. I don't want to disturb Madame this early, so will you inform her we'll be back in a few hours, about noontime? Oh, and we won't need those picnic lunches I ordered last night. Okay? Thanks."

Michael looked at her with a combination of relief and admiration. Her ready acceptance of his statements and orders frankly astonished him; he would not have been surprised to see her bolt at any moment. She came back into the noisy bathroom.

"What do you want me to wear?"

"Slacks and no heels?"

"Slacks and no heels it is." Sarah dropped her nightgown to the floor with no embarrassment and stepped into the shower. "Darling," she called out much louder than necessary, "hand me my orange juice."

Shaking his head in wonder, Michael walked to the breakfast table and returned with her glass. While she finished showering and dressing, he sipped his coffee and ate several croissants. They couldn't afford to leave too soon or their rush might arouse suspicion. He forced himself to have another cup of coffee.

"Here," he said for the benefit of the hidden microphones, "lovely, hot, fattening pastry for the beautiful lady."

"I hope you like me on the plump side," Sarah said with a forced laugh. "I'm almost ready to go."

Michael slipped quickly back into his room to retrieve the pistol from its new hiding place in the lining of the draperies and wrapped it along with one of his tennis rackets in a white wool tennis sweater.

"Ready?" he asked as he opened her door again.

Sarah looked up. "Ready," she said.

They walked down the long corridor to the reception hall and the car that Michael hoped would be waiting for them.

Meanwhile, quite a different scene was going on in Ava Bardoff's suite in the north wing. "Why was it not reported to me the minute it happened?" Madame demanded of Moloch and Beel, who stood across the large glass desk from her. She clutched a long silk robe with a fur collar around her body with one jeweled hand while banging the other repeatedly on the desk. Ash and Peor, content to be out of the way of Ava's wrath, sat quietly on the edge of the bathing pool behind the metal screen looking down at the fragrant foam they slowly moved back and forth with their bare legs.

"Well, Beel?" she asked, glowering at him.

"I was with the Americans all night, Madame. I didn't hear about it until an hour ago."

Moloch stood his ground. "There was nothing to be gained by disturbing you until we had all the facts—we now have them."

"How long does it take to gather the facts?" she shrieked. "How long, Moloch? Tell me."

"There was very little of the body left to identify; the blades did a good job of cutting him to pieces. As you know many of them look alike and so we had to do it with fingerprints."

"The armpit tattoo? Why not that?" Ava persisted angrily.

"We couldn't find it," Moloch said evenly.

Madam cooled a bit and changed the tack of her questions. "What was he doing up on the roof? We do not keep guards up there."

"I don't know," Moloch answered. "Rimmon was a

loner—he smelled things—that's why I let him roam about the entire complex. He was my best man."

"But on the roof? Does he often roam about on the roof?"

"He is a very strange man," Beel said.

"He *was* a very strange man, Beel, *was*," she corrected. "Why do you say that?"

"He was the most vicious of the guards, a sadist, and a . . . well, he had strange tastes," Moloch answered.

"What is this idiot trying to tell me?" Ava snapped at Beel.

"He's referring to Rimmon's being a necrophiliac. After killing the old lady in Cannes, he raped the body —if you can call it rape."

That stopped Ava Bardoff short. "He raped that old woman? He actually raped her after cutting her to pieces?" As she played the incredulity of the action over in her mind, Ava's face slowly changed. She began to laugh. It was a low laugh that started deep down and bubbled up into one of delight. "Peor, darling," she called across the room to the dark young man sitting at the pool, "think what we could have done with him." She continued to laugh as she sank back into her desk chair. Then slowly sobering, Ava Bardoff returned to the problem at hand.

"Very well, gentlemen, we have a guard who for some reason fell down the shaft from the tower roof."

"I believe he was in a fight up there," Moloch said flatly, "and was stunned by one of the needles."

"What makes you say that?" Ava demanded, leaning forward.

"I found a needle sticking in the lead up there. One or more of our guns must, therefore, have been in use. It probably passed through some part of his body, or perhaps a needle will be found in his remains. He was up there with a flashlight investigating something; we found it in the shaft with his body."

"And his pistol?" Ava asked.

"Not there. We've combed the roof, gutters, and the ground around the northwest corner. Nothing."

"Could it have been one of the other guards?" Beel asked.

"Few liked him," Moloch admitted. "He killed with more emotion than the others, and it made them uneasy. Perhaps one may have been jealous—as I said, he was my best man—but I don't really believe one of the guards would do it."

"That means either you are wrong and Rimmon's death was accidental or," Ava said, "one of our guests murdered him. And that suggests our young friend, dePasse. Report on his activities." Ava Bardoff leaned back in her chair, playing with a strip of leather which she coiled and uncoiled around her fingers.

"From all I've been able to determine, he was in his room the entire night," Moloch replied. "The guards kept watch on his door and nothing came over the microphones that would indicate anything strange. To get to the staircase leading to the roof, he would have had to pass at least five of my men, both coming and going." Moloch paused. "I still suspect him."

"Yes, I begin to share your feeling," Ava said thoughtfully. "Under his playboy exterior I sense a very shrewd mind. Yet Ash reported nothing unusual about his behavior yesterday other than his curiosity about the factory tower, and all the conversations he and our listening devices picked up were innocent enough."

"He and your goddaughter have ordered his car for a drive into the hills behind the château this morning," Moloch said. "Do you think it wise to let them go?"

"Let me hear this morning's tapes."

Moloch dialed the switchboard and placed the receiver in the cradle of the desk amplifier. They listened to Michael's suggestion last evening in Sarah's rooms that the two have an early breakfast and drive into the mountains for a picnic. His apparent change of mind this morning and their decision to return to the château for luncheon was a mark in Michael's favor. Ava asked that the section of tape where Sarah's phone fell off the table and went silent for a minute or two be played over several times.

"With the exception of that accident," Ava commented, "nothing seems unusual. Their little expedition was planned before this Rimmon thing. Let them go —it would seem suspicious not to. But, Moloch, before they leave, make sure one of your radios is in that car."

"I have already taken that precaution," he replied, "as well as attaching a control bomb to it."

Madame Bardoff looked up at him and a smile spread across her face. "Thank you, Moloch. I like your thoroughness, but that bomb will be used only as a last resort. We want information, not revenge. Always remember that."

He bowed to her without showing any sign of emotion.

"Any reports on the *Krait?*" Ava asked.

"Nothing unusual. Montclair and his guests dined ashore last evening and gambled late at the casino. They all returned about one A.M. One of our men stationed at the harbor overheard some of their conversation. Several of the guests will be flying out today. That's àll."

"Let us put one of our neuts aboard," she said. "Start photographing and gathering information on the entire crew so we can determine the best one to replace."

The phone on Ava's desk buzzed. She lifted the receiver, listened, and handed it to Moloch. "Someone from your office."

Moloch took the phone. "Yah, what is it?" He listened intently for a minute. "Good." Replacing the receiver, he smiled triumphantly. "We may have found the answer to our puzzle of Rimmon. My men have found something in the shaft; a ring of lead and some burnt cloth with a monogram of sorts on it. They are bringing it here now."

With a sweep of her hand toward the couches, Ava said, "Gentlemen, please be seated."

Michael and Sarah stood together in the gravel drive at the foot of the steps to the main entrance of the château. He looked at her nervously and tried to cover his tension with a few bad jokes. Why was she so calm, so relaxed, he wondered.

At last the silver Porsche rounded the corner of the

building and pulled up before them. Sarah slipped in smiling as Michael went to the far side. His heart leaped into his throat, and he took a step back, ready to grab the pistol wrapped in his tennis sweater. Getting out of the car was the man he'd killed last night—the same crew-cut blond hair, strong, handsome features, and —Michael glanced at his hand with the keys—even a blue dot on his right thumb.

But the driver gave no indication that he recognized his combatant. "I've filled the tank for you, sir," he said pleasantly, handing Michael the keys and holding the door for him.

Can I be so mistaken, Michael thought, as he moved warily toward the car, ready for a sudden attack from this man. Of course, it was dark last night and with only the flashlight, he thought—yes, the flashlight must have distorted his features. It obviously can't be the same man, yet the resemblance is astonishing.

"Are you all right?" Sarah asked. "You look white as a sheet."

"Fine," he replied with a covering laugh. "Seeing ghosts, I guess."

Michael thanked the driver, put the Porsche into gear, and headed toward the iron gates of the estate. He wanted to jam the accelerator all the way to the floor, but kept the car moving at a controlled slow speed through the park. His heart was racing as they pulled up before the gates. We're almost out, he thought.

The security guard walked from the small gatehouse toward them. "Miss Dilworth and Mr. dePasse, is it?"

"That's right," Michael said in a cheery voice. "Off for a little drive on this beautiful morning."

"I envy you," the guard replied. "Sorry to delay you, but I'll have to check with the château. Just a formality—we're on strict security this morning ever since the accident."

Sarah gave Michael a sharp and accusing look as the guard returned to the gatehouse and lifted the phone. Michael's hand moved slowly into the rolled tennis sweater beside him and gripped the pistol hidden there. Every muscle in his body was taut, ready to spring into action. He wanted to scream from the tension building inside him.

Madame Bardoff replaced the receiver. "It was the gatehouse," she said as the door to her office opened and one of Moloch's men entered.

"Put it on the desk," she ordered.

Stanislau Beel and Moloch hovered over the crude lead ring and stared down at the small triangle of wrinkled cotton fabric that was charred along one edge. It didn't take a handwriting expert to make out the monogrammed M entwined with part of a P. Ava's hand was on the phone almost before the cloth was flattened before her.

The guard walked back out of the gatehouse to chat as the heavy gates slowly began to swing open. Michael's left foot rode the clutch while the other sat poised over the accelerator, ready to roar through the ever widening space between the iron bars. The telephone in the gatehouse rang frantically. Michael and Sarah looked at each other as the guard ran back inside and lifted the phone. He turned quickly to look at them in confusion and then reached for the button. The gates shuddered as their motor reversed itself.

Michael released the clutch and jammed his foot hard onto the accelerator. The gap was too small. Sarah covered her face with her hands as the Porsche leaped forward toward it, tearing the right fender and shearing off the side mirror; but they were through. As the car hurtled ahead, Michael saw the guard run from his house, waving his arms, then dart back inside. The car raced over the meadow road and plunged into the forest cutting the château and its park from their sight.

"Hold on," he called to Sarah, who was bracing herself with both her hands and feet. "We've got to get the hell out of here, and *fast*."

"I want them back here, both of them," Ava Bardoff shouted, beating her desk in frustration.

"I've alerted our men along both roads down to the

coast and in the village," Moloch said, then barked further orders into the phone.

"I want them alive—tell your men that. I want to know just what dePasse knows and with whom he is working." She looked out her window at the two black Mercedes racing toward the shortcut to the village below. "Remember, your bomb is a last resort—only I will give the order for another of those regrettable accidents on these twisting roads."

"But Sarah's with him," Beel protested.

Ava looked at him sharply. "I would not care if *you* were with him, Stanislau. Sarah is of little use to me now—she has fulfilled her role as bait. What are two more lives? Or do you still fancy the little whore?" Ava hurled at him.

"Of course not, but . . ."

Ava waved her hand impatiently. "Beel, you annoy me. Get out." Turning to Moloch, she said, "Switch the microphone in dePasse's car to the speakers in here. I want to hear everything they have to say in case we have to use that bomb."

The silver Porsche careened from side to side on the narrow branch road leading from the Bardoff clinic to the main St. Tropez route ten or fifteen miles distant. Sarah hung on to the window with her right hand and pushed her body back into the bucket seat with her left hand braced against the dashboard. For some reason that she really couldn't explain to herself, she was not surprised at the events of the last few minutes. She knew she was escaping from the clinic; she didn't know why she should have to escape it, and yet subconsciously it seemed the right thing to do. Perhaps all those vague doubts and questions about Ava, her friends, and the clinic that she'd managed to submerge over the last years hadn't really disappeared at all, but were lying just beneath the surface waiting for some catalyst to bring them out into the open, to say, "run, flee, this is bad, get away." She knew it had to come sooner or later; Michael had just made it happen now. Sarah watched the trees and boulders dash by as the wind roared across her face.

The road over which they now sped zigzagged down the side of a steep hill bypassing a small village below them. A single, narrow street through the center of the village intersected their road as it wound down the hill on the outskirts of the town. As he skidded around a hairpin curve, Michael could look down into the village. A cloud of dust made by two black Mercedes was moving at great speed toward the cluster of quiet farm houses and shops from the west.

"Christ, they're fast off the mark," he swore. "They're trying to cut us off."

"Oh, Michael, can they?" Sarah called over the screeching tires as they swung around another bend.

"I sure as hell hope not," he shouted back, pushing harder on the accelerator as they skidded into yet another curve. Then it was a straight two hundred yards to the intersection. Would they give way? Michael wondered. Certainly he wouldn't. Sarah stared in fascination across the small field on their right as the cars roared toward each other at right angles; she could actually see the men inside.

The first limousine shot out inches in front of them, but failed to make the sharp right turn, spun a complete circle, and flipped over on its side as the Porsche streaked by. The second Mercedes navigated the turn with a shriek of its tires and headed after them as the first limousine exploded in flames.

"We're getting more popular by the minute," Michael said sarcastically, relieved at having got through the first of their trials. "They've got the power, but I've got the maneuverability in this baby."

The road wound around three more hairpin turns and shot into a cut between two high hills, and then opened out along a cliff face with a sheer drop of over two hundred feet on their right. He pulled ahead of his pursuers in the larger car and thought if he could keep increasing the lead in the next ten winding miles, he would have a good chance of losing them once on the main St. Tropez route where traffic would be heavy.

His dreams were short-lived. A figure emerged onto the road from the trees ahead, waving his arms at them and brandishing a shotgun. Seeing they had no intention of slowing, he dropped to one knee and fired as the Porsche flashed by. Sarah screamed as the windshield exploded, tearing away Moloch's tiny radio microphone hidden behind the mirror and showering them with sharp little squares of glass that bit into their skin. Michael thanked God his eyes hadn't been hit and kept the accelerator down as they swung into another sharp turn.

"We won't make it in the car," he called to Sarah, the wind rushing through the shattered windshield carrying away his words. "They've probably got lots more of those goons stationed along the road ahead and one is sure to get us. We've got to abandon ship. Get ready."

Sarah didn't know what he had in mind, but unbuckled her seat belt.

"Here we go," Michael called, slamming on the brakes as the Porsche came out of another curve at the edge of the cliff. "Quick."

The two jumped from the car. Looking back over his shoulder to see if the black Mercedes was still out of sight, he threw all his weight behind the car. "Give me a hand."

"You're not going to push it over?" she asked, knowing the answer. Sarah added her weight behind the silver car.

It rolled easily to the edge and with one last desperate shove went over, performing a graceful circle in mid-air before hitting an outcropping of rock, bouncing up and out to fall the remaining hundred feet to the rocky gorge below. Michael pulled Sarah up the bank on the other side of the road behind a dense curtain of shrubbery. They heard an explosion which he assumed was the gas tank going up, but it was followed by a more fierce one which puzzled him. There was no time to think about it; the Mercedes skidded to a halt just below them. Four men jumped from the car and ran to the cliff edge to look down into the valley at the flaming wreck and the column of smoke rising from it.

"We'd better go down and check," the leader said.

"They can't have lived through that," another countered.

"I don't care—we're going to check anyway. She'll want proof. We'll drive to the foot of the gorge and walk back up to the wreck." They got into the car and started down the road.

"Michael, did you see them?" Sarah asked, her eyes wide with surprise. "Did you see them? They all looked exactly alike—just like the man who drove up our car this morning. They were all the same."

"I saw," Michael replied calmly. "I might as well tell you now—I had to kill one of them last night."

"Kill! You—you killed a man last night?" She opened her mouth to say something else but Michael interrupted.

"It was him or me. Come on, we've got a lot of fast walking to do."

Before she could say another word he dragged her to her feet and up the steep hillside, keeping them well concealed from the road below. "We'll stay off the roads for a while—it's longer, but safer."

"Why did he want to kill you?" Sarah asked. "I'm so confused right now I don't know if I'm coming or going."

He stopped for a minute and looked down at her with a sympathetic smile, and then he pulled her against his chest. "You're doing just fine." He kissed the top of her head. "I know you've got lots of questions and I'll try to explain everything as we go. Okay?"

She nodded. "Okay."

Holding her hand, Michael helped her up through the rough undergrowth on the hill. They crossed over to the other side and began stumbling their way back down into the valley eastward toward Cannes.

"It'll probably take those clowns an hour or so before they discover we weren't cremated in the car, then all hell will break loose. Your charming godmother will have these hills swarming for us," Michael said. "I know it's hard going, but we've got to cover as much distance as we can before the alert goes out."

During their laborious flight through the hills Michael told Sarah a plausible story to explain their present predicament but one that had little relation to the truth. He tied Ava Bardoff into the Sicilian Mafia and explained his presence as a sort of undercover agent for Interpol. Neither Hugo Montclair's name nor that of the *Krait* had any part in his tale. As much as he disliked lying further to Sarah, he had to take into consideration that they might both be captured by Ava Bardoff's men; she must not be in a position to give away Hugo's operation. As for himself, he had the poison needle gun he'd taken from Rimmon, and his tennis racket. That was the one incongruous and amusing thing in their mad flight, his carrying his battered Spalding racket. He explained it to Sarah, saying he'd sacrificed his car for the sake of law and order—not his lucky racket, too.

About two hours after Michael and Sarah abandoned the car they heard the occasional barking of dogs in the distance. He estimated that the Bardoff forces would probably have started the dogs off at the point where they'd pushed the Porsche over the cliff and were now following them up and over the hills. He and Sarah had tried to keep to streams wherever possible and so had left a difficult but nonetheless a sniffable trail for the hounds. Michael marvelled at Ava Bardoff's nerve—tracking them with dogs as if she owned the entire south of France. He now understood what Hugo had meant when he said she took her power and the right to have it for granted. If questioned, her men could excuse the dogs as innocent rabbit hounds—who would ever imagine that two people were being tracked down systematically by what appeared to be a small, highly trained army.

Michael didn't dare stop at any farmhouses along the way as they continued their trek toward Cannes. At dusk Sarah finally collapsed at the edge of a large lake rather the worse for wear. Although the south coast is overpopulated with villas and camping sites, the particular area in which they found themselves was completely deserted. Michael recalled that it was a wildlife sanctuary some hundreds of square miles over which developers, the government, and conservationists constantly wrangled. Thus they were completely on their own in a mini-wilderness with Madame Bardoff's men hot on their heels and no local police station to run to for protection.

After Sarah had rested, Michael stood up, saying, "You've got one last job to do today, and then you can sleep to your heart's content. We're going to wade half way around this lake to get rid of our scent."

"But that's the wrong direction—it'll take us away from Cannes," she complained.

"I know, but it may throw them off. It's certainly worth the effort. Come on."

She took off her shoes and slacks and got up with a weary sigh. "If they could only see me now, Miss Chic of 1974."

They sloshed through the water up to their knees, carrying their clothes tied around their necks. After some minutes, Sarah stopped and leaned down to pick up a small yellow canary floating at the water's edge.

"Oh, the poor thing," she said, stroking its matted feathers. "It's just like the ones in the conservatory at the château. I didn't know they flew around wild here." Putting the small body tenderly on the bank of the lake, she took Michael's hand and continued toward the opposite side.

He, too, had noticed several of the small birds floating in the water as they waded by but had refrained from calling them to Sarah's attention. The number of dead birds was puzzling—they just don't fly into lakes and drown. The lake itself also puzzled him; he detected a faint smell of chlorine hanging over it although the water itself tasted pure. He wondered why the government would have to treat a lake in a game preserve, one that should have been in happy balance with nature.

"Here we are," he said finally. They had come to the side of the lake by a high fall of rocks that had come down centuries ago from the face of a cliff directly above them.

"Where is here?" Sarah said rather sarcastically.

"There are lots of little caves in among these rocks," Michael replied, "and I bet lots of nice comfortable leaves to curl up on."

"You've just made a friend for life. Lead me to your cave," she said, trying not to show her real exhaustion.

Sarah stood in the water while Michael explored along the fall, careful not to touch the rocks or reeds. Finally he waved and she waded to him. He had found a largish opening between two rocks leaning one against the other. Over them rested a jumble of boulders and weeds. Stooping down, Sarah could see inside. The water extended inward about eight feet and then large, flat slabs of rock went on back for ten feet or so. As promised, the cave was filled with dried moss, leaves, and a general confusion of flora brought in by some animal to furnish his den.

"I hope the last tenant doesn't come back for the rent while we're in here," Sarah only half-joked as she pulled her tired body up on the rock shelf and lay back on the leafy bed.

"Don't worry, if he does, I'll be here with a little surprise for him," Michael reassured her, patting his pistol. "I've seen this thing in action and it works fast and quiet." He rolled up his tennis sweater to make a pillow for her head.

"Is that—is that how you killed Ava's guard?" she asked in a timid voice, still not wanting to believe Michael capable of taking another man's life. In war, killing was one thing, but when it happened in familiar surroundings, it seemed more like cold-blooded murder. No, she wouldn't even consider the word.

He didn't answer but waded back out of the cave and pulled up several handfuls of rushes growing along the lake bank. He made sure his hands touched them only under the water so as not to taint them with his scent. Dragging them back behind him, he entered the cave once again and arranged the rushes from within to obscure the opening. Then he, too, climbed up on the rock shelf and stretched out next to Sarah.

"I could really lay into a nice juicy steak, right now," he said, lying back.

"You'll just have to settle for me," she replied.

He put his arm under her and she wiggled down to fit the curves of his body, cushioning her head in the crook of his arm. Although the cave was warm from the heat of the day, the warmth of his body running the length of hers felt good, reassuring, and natural. Both were asleep within minutes.

"What do you mean your men have not been able to find them," Ava Bardoff shrieked in anger at Moloch. "You told me they picked up their trail where the car went off the road. Do you mean to say the dogs have not been able to track them? They cannot just disappear."

"They've been using the streams in the area to cover their scent—it has taken longer than I originally thought. I have cars patrolling all the roads out of the area and men in every village between the point where we last picked up their scent and Cannes and St. Tropez—they're obviously headed to one of those two towns. We're also doing a thorough check of all the farms and outbuildings in the area, inquiring at villas, inns, and searching trailer camps. Between the dogs and my men, we'll have them by morning."

"You had better, Moloch." Ava Bardoff plunged a fruit knife into an apple sitting on the silver plate before her at the long dining room table. Ash and Peor sat silently on either side, realizing that at times like these, a mute tongue was the better part of valor. Ava was dressed in a simple black silk kaftan with no decoration, the two men wore tight black trousers and white shirts open to their waists to expose as much of their tanned bodies as possible.

"Have you found how dePasse got up on the roof without your highly trained men seeing him?" she asked sarcastically.

"The valet found torn evening trousers and blackened tennis shoes in his overnight case. Their condition led us to examine more athletic routes to the roof than the staircase. He scaled the outer wall and got into the room above his—we found the hole he cut in the window glass. He obviously crossed the hall to the inner room and from there went up the ironwork in the conservatory to a ventilator opening. The gardener couldn't get it to work properly this morning. Once out on the dome, it would have been relatively easy to reach the roof."

Ava mulled over all that Moloch had told her. Smiling at the two young men beside her, she said, "Well, dePasse is more of a man than I had given him credit for. He must be very strong—a body Madame would like to get her hands on, eh, my young friends?"

They smiled back at her, Peor making an obscene gesture.

"It is too bad we shall never get the chance," Ava said, slowly peeling the skin from a section of apple. Then, looking up—"Yes, Moloch, you have more to tell me?"

The piglike man shifted his weight uneasily. "We found smudges on the window ledge of one of the observation rooms in the north wing. He may have . . ."

Madame's abrupt movements cut him off in mid-sentence. She was on her feet, knocking over wine glasses and brought the back of her hand across Moloch's face with a slicing blow. Her garnet ring opened a long tear in the pink flesh of his cheek; a rim of blood began to ooze slowly out. He stood at attention, making no move to touch his wounded face.

"He may have? He may have?" she hissed in rage. "What are you here for, to give away everything we are doing? Your men let this—this child wander about the clinic as if it were his own private playpen. He may have? Of course he has, you fool." She glared at Moloch, her mouth working. "If he is not in my hands tomorrow, Moloch, you are a dead man. Now get out. Get out," she rasped.

The head of security for the House of Bardoff turned, clicking his heels, and marched smartly out of the room. He showed no trace of emotion. Ash and Peor remained seated safely at the table staring down at their plates. Ava stormed across the elegant dining room to the French doors overlooking the park, her mind whirling with assorted plans and alternatives. She couldn't speed up the work now in hand, three weeks was the absolute minimum. Ava refused to postpone the treatments—it had taken her almost a year to bring together these men so vital to her plans. The conference would be held in Corsica in two and a half weeks —that was the crucial date. The neuts must be ready by then. Her "guests" could be moved to Pandemonium, but that would cause panic and the neuts could not learn to emulate them properly in unnatural conditions.

Then Ava relaxed and smiled. As long as she had those men in this house she, not her enemies, held the upper hand. They had no proof, nothing but the wild accusations of a known playboy; the guests themselves didn't suspect a thing. Let them try to destroy her work—let them just try. Ava Bardoff was not afraid. She'd move ahead as planned while destroying those attacking her. DePasse was now the key. She thought of the *Krait,* where he'd contacted Sarah. If Michael dePasse is on that ship, goodbye Hugo Montclair. Like cars, ships can blow themselves up.

Sometime during the night Sarah was awakened by the noise of dogs and the muffled voices of their trainers moving along the banks of the lake methodically searching for their prey. As she started to rise, Michael's hand firmly restrained her. "It's all right," he whispered, "just relax. The dogs won't find us here." She lay back staring up into the blackness of the cave, feeling rather like a little girl playing hide and seek. With Michael beside her, she somehow felt insulated from real danger.

Michael lay on his side, leaning up on one elbow. He could see the beams of several flashlights bobbing about across the water, illuminating the dogs running in confused circles to and fro over the bank. Not a breath of air moved over the lake, the surface of which was like a black mirror. He was keenly aware of the heavy chlorine odor trapped in the cave, much stronger than during the day when breezes had swept the lake. Although breathing was not pleasant under these conditions, he was thankful for the discomfort; whatever scent he and Sarah might have left must surely be masked by this chemical umbrella. The longer the dogs inhaled it, the less sensitive their noses.

As he lay listening to the curses and whining of the hunting party approaching their hiding place, he absently caressed Sarah's body with his free hand. The dogs scrambled over the rocks near the entrance to the cave and several men waded by within inches, sending little waves back in through the narrow opening to splash over the edge of the shelf on which they lay. Several of the reeds from Michael's screen became dislodged and floated out, caught in the wake of the current made by the searchers. Michael's hand froze on Sarah's breast as he listened for any sign of their discovery. None came. The hunters moved further along the lake shore.

With a sigh he relaxed, becoming aware of the warmth under his hand and the gentle breathing movement of Sarah's body in the dark. Desire began to rise within him, desire spurred by his relief at their safety, the pleasant fatigue of his muscles, and the warm, responsive body of the beautiful girl lying in his arms. He lowered his face to hers, his lips feeling what his eyes could not see—her cheek, the lashes of her closed eyes, down beside her nose, and then the soft, moist lips opening to his tongue. His free hand ran over and around her breast, cupping and massaging it. He pulled her body to his and moved his hand down over her hip and thigh. Sarah's body arched to him and her hands clasped his hair and neck, forcing their mouths together in a devouring embrace. She ground her pelvis against the hard knot in his groin. Michael groaned with pleasure, rotating his hips against hers. Sarah pulled her mouth from his lips. "Please," she whispered urgently. "Now."

The next morning, while Ava Bardoff vented her rage on her staff and paced back and forth in her exotic boudoir at the château, Hugo Montclair sat pensively at the head of the breakfast table atop the *Krait*. He paid little attention to the letters piled high on a silver tray beside him.

"I'm extremely worried about Michael," he told Petras who, as usual, stood nearby. "Exactly what time was he to have met you?"

"He said he'd be at the Palms Beach Club late yesterday afternoon for, as he put it, a swim and water-ski practice after a sybaritic weekend at the Bardoff estate. He seemed to have told everybody there that he was going."

"A good idea—the more people who knew about it, the less suspicious it would seem to Ava Bardoff. No fool, our Michael."

"I hung around the club having a few drinks and pretty much keeping out of the way until six. When he didn't show, I left. I'll go back there this morning."

"No, I think that would be a wasted exercise and might even be dangerous. We'll have to wait for him to find a way to contact us." Hugo got up from the table and walked to the rail, where he could study Cannes' harbor and the city beyond. "The maddening thing is that there's nothing we can do without tipping our hand. We can't make inquiries after him at the club or even call his hotel. To do so might put him in danger if he's being watched and might boomerang back on us. Petras, I hope I've done the right thing in sending a young amateur into the lion's den. Alert the others to be ready for anything. If Madame B. has seen through him, by now she'll know all about us and we can expect swift and unpleasant retaliation."

Petras nodded and moved off. "Shall I schedule some skeet shooting this morning for the guests *and* crew. We ought to brush up on our marksmanship."

"I'd like to, but that would mean taking the *Krait* out from shore, and I want to remain near Cannes and accessible to Michael. We've only got Susan Van Schuyler, Dr. Chandler, and the Winstons on our guest list now. Think of some diversion to take them off the ship this afternoon following lunch. We'll have our hands full without having to maintain a front for them."

Petras left Hugo staring across the water sparkling under the early morning sun. His mind, like Ava's the previous evening, went methodically through each of the alternatives open to him based upon the assumption that Michael had been forced to expose his operation. Susan Van Schuyler's cheery good morn-

ing greeting was one of the most unwelcome inter-
ruptions he'd ever experienced.

"Good morning, my dear. Did you sleep well?" he
replied, giving himself over to his role of perfect host.

By 8:30 that morning Sarah and Michael were sitting uncomfortably eating peaches in a ditch alongside
a minor road leading into Grasse, a small town just
northwest of Cannes. They had left their cave before
dawn and covered a good five miles and, after raiding
a nearby orchard, waited for a sympathetic farmer from
whom to beg a ride into the Cannes market.

Michael had refused to show himself to any of the
automobiles passing along the road for fear Madame
Bardoff's men might be patrolling in them. Instead,
he preferred the safety of produce trucks heading for
the city market on a Monday morning. Sarah had
braided her hair and put it on top of her head in a
makeshift disguise, and he had torn both their slacks
off above the knees and grayed them as much as
possible to make the casual "in" tourist costume of
that season. Spotting a truck rounding the bend down
the road, Michael pulled Sarah to her feet and they
began walking toward Grasse while signaling with their
thumbs. Unlike the previous six trucks, this one
slowed and came to a halt fifty yards ahead of them
up the road.

As they ran toward it, Michael told Sarah, "Get in
last and keep your hand on the door handle, ready to
jump if I give you the word. I don't trust anyone at
this point—anyone, that is, but you. Together we make
a great team." He flashed her a confidence-bolstering
smile.

In answer to Michael's question, the young farmer
allowed he was going to Cannes and beckoned them in
beside him. Michael climbed up into the high seat,
pulling Sarah up behind him, and the truck moved
jerkily off down the road. They entered the outskirts
of Grasse chatting pleasantly about the weather, the
peach harvest, and the local rugby team. Michael
clutched his favorite tennis racket on his lap while
watching every movement of their host out of the corner

of his eyes. Those eyes narrowed when the driver put his right hand on the floor shift lever to gear down as he swung onto a side road leading north out of the village—they narrowed on a tiny blue dot by his right thumbnail. Shifting back into a higher gear, the driver brought his right hand back to the wheel and casually lowered his left into his jacket pocket.

"Have you seen our local boys play rugby this year?" he asked.

"No, not this year," Michael replied, shifting his racket so the handle faced the driver. "By the way, this isn't the road to Cannes, is it?"

The driver looked quickly at Michael and started to lift his hand from his pocket, but never finished the movement. Whatever peace of mind Sarah might have been able to find in the last few minutes was instantly shattered by the explosion from the tennis racket handle and the driver's short, gurgled scream. Michael had both hands on the wheel of the truck as the driver slumped against the door with an expression of surprise frozen on his lifeless face; a trickle of blood ran from the corner of his mouth. She sat for a second or two just staring at the two men beside her and as the truck came to a stop, so, too, did her composure. She began to tremble and a scream was forming in her throat when a sharp slap across the face stunned her into silence.

Michael faced her, his eyes burning deep into hers as he spoke in rough, sharp tones. "I don't want to hear one sound out of you, do you understand?" He reached across the dead man and produced a pistol from his left pocket similar to the one he'd taken from Rimmon. "Before you start getting hysterical about the death of a stranger, look at this." He shoved the pistol in front of her face. "That nice stranger was one of your beautiful godmother's men, and he was about ready to put both you and me out of her way forever. From now on, sweet, it's you and me—or them." He continued to stare at her until she began to breathe more quietly. Then in a softer voice he asked, "Do you understand what I'm saying?"

"Yes," she said quietly.

"Good girl."

"But that doesn't mean I'm not scared out of my wits," she added.

"Between you and me, I'm scared out of mine, too, but everything will be okay very soon—I promise." He squeezed her arm.

Next Michael looked over the truck. He opened the glove compartment and, as he half expected, found a small radiotelephone. "Jesus," he mumbled, "that bastard had time to let them know exactly where we are."

Opening the driver's door, he pushed the body out into the deep, weed-filled ditch. It vanished from view. "At least they still think he's got us. We have a little time before they realize something's gone wrong." He slid into the driver's seat, put the truck into gear, and turned it around to start back for the intersection.

"I think we'd better head for Antibes and try to get into Cannes from the east," he told Sarah. "The road south to Cannes must be choked with Madame's men right now."

As the truck moved off due east, Sarah leaned down and picked up the tennis racket from the floor and examined it curiously. "Your 'lucky' Spalding, eh? I'd hate to be on the court with you when you lose your temper." She looked at Michael and a mischievous smile slowly spread across her face.

He reached over and put his hand on her knee; she covered it with hers and held it for a minute or two before letting it go.

They entered Antibes by a small winding road cutting through a residential section. Michael parked the truck in the driveway of a deserted villa, and they walked the remaining half-mile to the town's market section through a maze of little back streets, avoiding all of the tourist areas. In deference to Sarah, they took time to stop at a small patisserie for some pastry and steaming coffee. The rest and food put iron back into their spirits and, with a degree of optimism strange for their particular situation, they now entered the back door of a small shop specializing in water sports equipment.

The graying proprietor came forward eagerly to greet

them. "Oh, Monsieur le Comte, it is so good to see you after so long a time. And I see you have yet another beautiful young lady with you."

"Sarah," Michael said, "let me present Monsieur Grimond, the world's greatest underwater treasure hunter. And pay absolutely no attention to him or he will charm you away from me, which I think would be a most unthinkable thing for him to do."

"My friend, you do me a double honor. Come, a little Cognac to warm the blood."

"Another time, Antoine. Right now I need your help instead. Can you outfit us with two aqualungs, tanks, the whole works? We've got some serious swimming to do this morning."

"Everything in my shop is yours. Come, my dear." He motioned to Sarah to follow him to a rack containing a variety of harness. While he worked with her, Michael selected his own equipment and tested the pressure in the oxygen containers. He begged the loan of Antoine's little Fiat and explained exactly where he planned to leave it with the keys hidden under the mat. Completing their selection, Michael embraced his old friend.

"Thank you, thank you for your help," he said in an emotion-charged voice. "And Antoine, for your own sake, forget you saw us today."

"But you are so serious—it isn't like you to . . ." The older man held Michael at arm's length and looked at him. "It is not just another of your mad escapades—you are in real trouble."

"Yes."

"Can I help?"

"You already have. We have to go now—I can't tell you more."

"Goodbye, my friend. You can count on me." Antoine Grimond watched the two young people leave his shop and suddenly called after them, grabbing two pairs of dark glasses from a display by the door. "Here, maybe you should wear these—at least for a while?"

Michael smiled, handing a pair to Sarah and slipping on his. "À bientôt, Monsieur."

"À bientôt," Antoine said. "Come back soon."

Michael pulled the Fiat off the main coast road and parked it in the lot of a public beach about a mile east of the center of Cannes.

"Let's hope this is the last place they'll be looking for us," he said to Sarah as they searched the various faces of the sun worshipers and sportsmen moving about the lot. "I hope you're ready for a nice long swim."

"Just how long is long?" she asked. "I haven't done any scuba-diving for years."

"You'll be okay. We've only got about a mile and after that you can have the nicest nap you've ever had."

"I had that last night." Their eyes met and Michael slapped her on the backside playfully.

"C'mon, you tart, we're not out of the woods yet. Give me whatever you're not going to swim in so I can put them in this bag. I don't want to leave anything in the car to incriminate Antoine."

He helped Sarah into her harness and, carrying their face masks and a rubber bag filled with a tennis racket, needle pistols, and other strange paraphernalia for two divers, they walked to the edge of the water.

"Here we go," he said. "Stay close."

"Don't worry—like glue."

Rinsing their masks with saltwater and spitting on the glass, they put them on and adjusted the air tanks. Sarah followed him into the calm blue water, their heads gradually disappearing beneath its surface. The warm water caressed her body and the sensation of gliding through another world of peace and tranquility soothed Sarah's raw nerves. Schools of small silver fish glimmered across their path and darted quickly away to be replaced by others fanning out before them. Rays of sun undulated across the sand below until they swam out into deeper water and the bottom faded away. Sarah seemed to be floating in space and felt as if she were being cleansed of the fears and death of the last two days.

Michael touched her arm to bring her out of her reveries and pointed up at the dark hull of the *Krait* looming over them. He gave her the old V for Victory sign with his fingers. Victory over what? Sarah wondered. She knew she was a long way from the end of whatever she'd got herself mixed up in. Michael swam up and pushed something in the hull; she saw a slit of light slowly widening as a pair of doors opened above her. Sarah followed Michael up into the rectangular hole in the bottom of the yacht, reluctantly leaving the safe womb of the sea for the harsh reality of life.

7

Michael helped Sarah up out of the whirlpool bath and removed her air tank and harness as she pulled off her mask.

"Where are we?" she asked, looking about her at the small tiled room. "In somebody's bathroom?"

"No," he laughed, handing her a towel, "nothing quite so prosaic. You'll find out in a minute or two. The important thing is you're someplace safe."

Michael opened the door to Hugo's study and found himself staring into the barrel of Petras's gun. The steward's grim face lightened with a combination of surprise and relief, and seeing Sarah behind Michael, he slipped the weapon quickly beneath his white uniform jacket.

"Petras, will you please tell the captain that Miss Dilworth and I have dropped in for lunch," Michael said in a master-servant tone; he flashed Petras a wink that Sarah couldn't see.

A faint smile crossed the chief steward's lips as he made a small bow. "At once, Monsieur dePasse. The captain will be delighted."

After glancing quickly around the room to make sure nothing incriminating was visible, Michael ushered Sarah into the luxurious study. "Make yourself right at home," he said as she wandered about the room looking over the shelves of books and running her fingers over the frames of valuable oil paintings to make sure they were really there.

"Isn't he one of the crew on Hugo Montclair's yacht?" Sarah asked after the door closed. "This isn't his yacht, is it?" Michael beamed. "Michael, it *is* his ship—it's the *Krait*."

"You've hit it right on the button," he laughed. "We're on Hugo's yacht."

"So you *do* know him well—you lied to Ava," she said almost accusingly. "This is the place you've been trying to get to all along, isn't it? Is he mixed up in what you were doing at the clinic? Are . . ."

"Whoa," he said, holding up his hands to stop her flood of questions. "Sarah, come sit down here for a minute and listen." All trace of amusement left his voice. She sat down beside him on the leather couch; he took her hands in his.

"You're going to have to be terribly patient. I'm involved in something that's very important and very dangerous as well. So is Hugo and so now, I'm afraid, are you. I shouldn't really have brought you here or, for that matter, come myself, because in doing it, I've risked Hugo's life and what he's trying to do. I know all this sounds confusing to you, but please believe what we're trying to do is good. It's—it's very good."

"It's against Ava, isn't it? And it hasn't anything to do with the Mafia, has it?" she asked. "I didn't believe your story yesterday and I believe it even less today."

"Darling—" he was torn with indecision—"the more I tell you, the greater the danger I put you in."

"How much more dangerous can things get?" Sarah snapped, angry in her frustration. "People have been trying to kill me for the last twenty-four hours. They can't kill me twice, can they?"

"I think Miss Dilworth has a very good point there, Michael." Hugo Montclair's voice made them both jump. "Excuse my quiet entrance, Miss Dilworth, but you are as yet an unknown entity. I commend you on your intelligence and spirit."

The two young people stared up at Hugo as he walked casually to the bar. "Well, aren't you even going to say 'nice to see you back'?" Michael asked with obvious annoyance. "After all the crap we've been through?"

"Forgive me, Michael. 'Nice to see you back.' But you must realize I never doubted you would be back —I wouldn't have sent you in the first place if I had."

This backhanded compliment brought Michael up short while returning to him some measure of the resolve and confidence Hugo feared he might have lost over the last few harrowing days.

Hugo continued. "My steward will bring you and —may I call you Sarah?—Sarah something to eat in a few minutes. Until then, both of you look as if a bit of Cognac would be welcome." He poured two bubble glasses and handed them to his guests. Standing in front of them as he was, Hugo's face broke into a brief, warm grin. "Honestly, it *is* good to have you back—*both* of you," he emphasized, looking at Sarah.

The smile faded and Hugo moved behind his desk. "Now to business. I'm sure you have much to tell me and my curiosity can't wait another minute, but—" he interrupted himself by putting a finger to his own lips —"but first, we seem to have the problem of just how much Sarah is or is not to know for her own safety. I hope you won't mind me paraphrasing your words, Michael."

Michael nodded. "I leave it to you."

Hugo looked at Sarah. "I don't blame you for discarding Michael's Mafia story, whatever it may have been. Ava Bardoff has far too much style for the Mafia and you must have sensed that. But what story do we tell you to replace the Mafia? First, be assured I will not lie to you. It is better to know nothing than to suspect what you *do* know is not true." Hugo sat back in his chair, pulling his ear as he looked across the desk. "I think we shall handle it this way, my dear. You have a right to know the sort of thing in which you find yourself involved—but for you to know more than that, to know all the details—" Hugo shook his head—"that puts others, not you, in greater danger. What you do not know, you cannot repeat. Do you understand what I'm saying?"

"Yes," Sarah answered simply, feeling the strength

of this man she once thought ridiculous, feeling the security that came with that strength. No wonder Michael headed directly here when the going got rough, she thought.

"As I said, I shall tell you the truth, but only as much as I deem safe. Will that satisfy you?"

Sarah nodded her head.

"And you promise not to torture this love-struck young man with questions he would like only too much to answer?"

"I promise." She smiled. Sarah liked his reference to Michael as love-struck.

"Good, then let's get down to business before I explode. What happened?" he asked, his eyes shining with anticipation.

Michael gave a very brief summary of all he'd seen and done while at the clinic and during their escape to the yacht, intending to fill in the details once the outline had been established. Hugo stopped him before he could do this to ask Sarah, "Why did you, shall we say, *flee* the clinic with Michael? Flee so willingly without any real explanation at all?"

Sarah thought for a minute. "I've wondered about that, too," she said. "I think it's because I didn't need his explanation—I had my own." Although answering Hugo, she was really talking to Michael.

"I guess ever since my parents' deaths I've been living in some sort of fool's paradise. I didn't want to lose the life we had together—I tried to hang on to the happy times. I wanted to believe in Ava's beautiful life—the parties, the penthouses, glamour, jet planes —it was all very exciting. So I pushed all the bad vibrations out of the way. I know a psychiatrist would say I was doing a real sublimation job on myself, but, after all, Ava Bardoff was the only friend I had, the only person who took a real interest in me," she said defensively. "But it got harder and harder not to see things, to try to keep living with someone with whom you began to feel uncomfortable. No, it was even more than that—I began to feel very strange and unsure of myself when I was with her."

"How long have you had these feelings?" Hugo asked.

"I'm not really sure. As I said, I tried to pretend they weren't there for a long time. I guess I first really became aware of them a few years ago. The closer I tried to get to Ava, the less I seemed to know her." Sarah got up from the couch and walked aimlessly about the study, trying with difficulty to verbalize intuitive feelings. "She has a beautiful, soft, and charming exterior shell, but inside—I can't quite explain it —her inside doesn't fit. It's completely strange to me —hard, cold, and—well, sort of menacing and sick. Everyone around her seems afraid of her. She's always surrounded by an aura of respect, but when you look at it, it's more fear than respect. Stanislau Beel, her manager—he's scared stiff of her. He laughs and looks real casual when they're together, but you can sense he's frightened just like all the others who work for her, and lots of her friends as well. Sometimes *I* was even afraid of her and I don't know why—it's contagious.

"And another thing that made me uneasy," Sarah continued. "All those perfect specimens she surrounds herself with. They're not real—sometimes I even think she's not real. Look at Ash and Peor— their beautiful white smiles, their perfect bodies, their perfect everything. Perfect people don't exist." As Sarah spoke of her feelings, she realized she was making the final transition out of her fantasy world. "It's as if Ava made Ash and Peor, as if they're her own personal Barbie dolls."

"Dolls—a very strange and interesting analogy," Hugo observed, thinking of the unchanging youth of the second Count dePasse. "You said you left with Michael because you had your own reason. Is that it?" he asked. "Your uneasiness with Ava Bardoff?"

"Just part of it—it's all very confused in my mind. Last week that nice Mr. Martin dies at her party —" Hugo's eyes narrowed with interest—"and Ava ships me off fast to the clinic. I'm sure she wanted to get me out of the way. And then Peter Kent. I know I saw him at the clinic no matter what they say—and that awful, disgusting murder in his flat . . ." Sarah closed her eyes at the thought of the dismembered body of the old woman lying across the bloodstained bed, her blouse torn open to reveal hollow breasts and her skirt thrown up. She gulped the remaining Cognac in her glass. Hugo rose quietly and refilled it, giving her arm an understanding pat. The room was silent for a minute or two, the men waiting for her to continue.

"As much as I tried, I couldn't shake the feeling I had deep down that Ava somehow knew about that poor old woman. She was so calm, so—they were *all* so calm about it. I just don't know. I tried to pretend none of it happened, that life was just as beautiful as it used to be. I wanted it to be the same but it wouldn't work anymore. Things I didn't understand seemed to be closing in on me. I was sure something strange and —and awful was going on around me, that everything was about to collapse. But what could I do? Who could I talk to? And what could I say anyhow? All I had were feelings, vague feelings that even I couldn't explain. And then you came along," she looked down at Michael. "It was almost a relief. I needed someone to tell me what to do, to get me out of there—you did. So here I am. Now what do I do?"

Sarah looked and felt very small and helpless at the moment. She moved back to the couch, sitting on the arm next to Michael, and stared down into the bubble glass cradled in both her hands. He put his arm around her waist.

"You've done all there is to do," Hugo said, smiling at her. "You'll stay with us and you'll be perfectly safe. We, Michael and I, are the ones who have to do things to stop this evil business."

Sarah relaxed back against Michael's shoulder, finding relief in Hugo's words. Maybe the nightmare was over for her.

"But," he continued, "we need all the help, all the information you can give us about Madame Bardoff—the people around her, what she's done in the past, and her plans for the future." Without Sarah realizing it, Hugo had turned on one of his tape ma-

chines to catch everything she'd said. He had decided
she must know nothing of his band of men and the
Krait's secrets. She would think only he and Michael
were interested in finding out the truth behind the
operations of the House of Bardoff.

Petras knocked discreetly and entered with two luncheon trays for Hugo's famished guests. "I beg your
pardon, sir—Mrs. Van Schuyler is asking after you and
wishes to know when you will be joining them."

"Please tell her that I've had a bit of a sinking spell
and am resting. I'll join them for cocktails. Also,
will you have the yellow cabin next to mine prepared for Miss Dilworth. I do not want the others to
know of her presence aboard the ship at this time. That
will be all." He dismissed his steward in an imperious
manner.

While Sarah and Michael ate, she told in great detail
all she knew about Ava Bardoff and her operation.
With the exception of what had happened in the last
few months, Sarah supplied Hugo with the little information of importance that he had not already gathered
himself. He did note every name she mentioned as being more than a distant acquaintance of Madame's. He
was interested in the fact that Ava seemed to hold yearly
reunions in her office in New York and in the clinic in
France—never at a hotel or ballroom or some resort.
At these reunions her closer associates, regardless of
their station or rank—from the most important to the
most insignificant—gathered together to stay sometimes
for several days. He wondered why she would combine such a grab bag of guests and never vary the
location.

"It was at the last reunion that poor Mr. Martin
died—he was so upset about not being invited," Sarah
said.

"How do you know that?" Hugo asked. "I understood he entered the room and went almost at once onto
the terrace with Ava Bardoff. Supposedly no one heard
a word they said."

"I did," she retorted. "I was out there with a friend."
Embarrassed, Sarah glanced quickly at Michael for his
reaction; he looked down at his bare feet. "Paul, my

friend, was pretty aggressive and—well, I'd had a lot to drink so . . ." She paused. "Anyway, we were sitting behind the privet hedge when Ava and Mr. Martin came out onto the terrace. It was awful. Paul works for Ava—he didn't want her to see us together like that, so he made me keep quiet."

"Go on, Sarah, exactly what did you see and hear?"

"I can't remember very much. Mr. Martin was really upset—he was actually crying at one point. He kept saying he'd done his best and that she shouldn't let him die. That's strange, isn't it?" Sarah asked. "As if Ava could stop someone from dying if he were going to die." She thought about it briefly and then continued. "Ava's voice was so funny—harsh and ugly, not like her usual voice—but she kept smiling and looking beautiful and sympathetic."

"Can you remember exactly what he said?" Hugo persisted.

"Something about her letting him go down to the lab before it was too late. She said she'd given him some extra time and not to worry, but he didn't seem to believe her and refused to leave. Mr. Martin started to get mean then and sort of threatened her. Oh, yes, he said something about her not having got them on the plane yet. It didn't make any sense to me. And then he died."

"You mean he jumped or fell off the roof," Hugo corrected.

"No, I think he really died before—a stroke or something."

"Why do you say that?"

"Well, at first I thought he was going to hit her. He raised his hand as if to do it, but instead he gave a gasp—sort of a little scream—and held his head almost like he'd been shot there. He started to crumple up, and as he did he just fell over the rail. He fell—he certainly didn't jump. It was Ava who gave that horrible long scream everyone thought was Mr. Martin's. It makes me sick just to think of it."

"Didn't her screaming that way seem strange to you?" he asked.

"It does now, but at the time everything happened so fast. I really don't know what I thought."

Hugo looked at her intently, fascinated by this new piece of information: "And you say he acted almost as if he'd been shot. Yet you, your friend, and Ava were the only ones on that terrace?"

"Yes."

"And the glass doors into the building were all closed?"

"Oh, yes. I remember it took Ash and Peor a while to get out to Ava. I ran over to her—that's when she saw me for the first time. She was really concerned and had Peor take me right to my room. He gave me a tranquilizer or something and I slept for the rest of the night."

"And Paul?"

"I don't know—I never saw him again," Sarah answered.

Hugo pondered her story. "So here we have a man who seems to know he's going to die, clutches his head as if having a stroke or being shot, and dies. You heard no shot?"

"No."

"The doors were closed and at that height it would be almost impossible for someone to shoot him from below or from across the park. Besides, the police would have found a bullet." Hugo looked down at the two needle pistols lying on his desk. "A needle might have been overlooked. But who would have fired it? From what you say Ava was the only one who was either in the position or had the chance to do so."

"You're not saying she murdered him, are you?" Sarah asked in surprise. "I promise you she didn't. I saw everything—Ava didn't do anything to him."

"Perhaps you're right," Hugo said. The three sat silently musing over the puzzle. "A stroke," he said aloud. "Could he really have had a stroke?"

Michael jumped in enthusiastically. "Perhaps the excitement, the strain he was under was too much and *bango*."

"A possibility, but it doesn't quite fit with the fact that Martin seemed to know in advance that he was about to die and was pleading that she not let him die. 'Let'—that was a strange word for him to use."

Hugo thought for a few minutes. "Martin knows he is going to die—almost exactly to the day or maybe to the hour—and wants to go to her lab, presumably to be saved. Ava Bardoff says no, and he dies of what looks like a stroke."

"What do you make of it?" Michael asked.

"I'm not sure. It sounds almost as if Ava held the power of life and death over him—maybe she holds it over them all. That would certainly account for that aura of fear Sarah senses surrounding Madame and her associates. What could it be? The power of life and death. Do we add that to Ava Bardoff's seeming ability to stop the aging process, to promise eternal youth?"

"Christ," Michael said, "the more we learn, the more she really seems like Satan himself. It's like the Faust legend."

"I'm sure there's some logical explanation for it—we've just got to find out what it is."

In order not to let the conversation degenerate into a morass of speculation, Hugo turned back to Sarah. "Tell us about Peter Kent."

Sarah related the story from Peter's first words to her at Orly Airport in Paris until the discovery of the concierge's body in his apartment in Cannes.

"Did he seem any different after he went to that toilet on the plane?" Hugo asked.

"He sure wasn't as friendly, and he sprang that Rome bit on me after having set up a date in Cannes for the next evening. Now that you mention it, from a hot-blooded lover, he turned rather formal and cool. He didn't talk very much, but maybe that's because I didn't give him a chance—I was furious."

"Could the man who returned have been a different man from the one you met in Paris?"

"Two different men?" Sarah said in disbelief, finding the idea ridiculous. "Oh, no, he was a very distinctive-looking guy."

"Sarah," Michael interrupted, "you saw those men in the Mercedes that chased us yesterday. They were pretty distinctive-looking and they were identical—all four of them."

She was silent for a minute and then began shaking her head from side to side as if trying not to believe what her mind was suggesting to her. "You don't think a double took Peter's place on the plane, do you?"

"It would explain his personality change and the fact that one man went on to Rome while you saw another later that night in the grounds of the clinic," Hugo said calmly.

"But why would they want to do that?" she asked with a look of bewilderment. "What was Peter Kent to them?" It was all coming too fast for her; Sarah buried her head in her hands. "I'm so confused, I don't understand any of this." She almost wept.

"You've had a terrible time, my dear." Hugo felt a great pang of sympathy for this vulnerable and unhappy girl. "You could stand a good sleep—things will seem brighter when you wake. But before you go, would you answer just a few more questions?"

Sarah nodded.

"Have you ever heard your godmother mention the names Moloch or Dr. Mulciber? Think very hard."

"No, I haven't," she replied. "They're unusual enough so I'm sure I'd remember them if I had."

"Fine. And has Ava mentioned anything to you about the secretary of state of the United States or any of the others before Michael told us about them just now?"

"No—it came as a complete surprise. To think that those important people were at the clinic and I didn't know the first thing about it. I thought the north wing had been closed, and none of the staff said a word. I wonder why she didn't mention anything about them. I usually know who's staying there for beauty treatments, cosmetic surgery, or other therapy—I often used their names in my promotional work."

"Unless," Michael interjected, "those people are there for something other than the standard health and beauty treatment and don't know it."

Hugo shot Michael a swift look to silence him. He

obviously didn't want Sarah to learn much about this aspect of their investigation. Before Sarah could react to Michael's statement, Hugo gave her something else to think about. "Finally, has Ava given you any indication of what her plans are for the next few weeks, the coming months, or just the future in general?"

Sarah concentrated deeply. "She hasn't really said anything about her plans. You know, now that I think about it, she very seldom ever tells me about them. Although she talks a lot, she's really a very secretive person."

"That is a great trait, one practiced by the best statesmen and the worst politicians," Hugo commented.

"Now wait a minute," she said, almost thinking aloud. "I did hear her saying something to Stanislau last week about being ready for Corsica in three weeks. I assume she'll be going there for a holiday, but I didn't ask."

"Corsica," Hugo repeated. "Now here *is* a new piece to the puzzle. Thank you, Sarah, you've been most helpful. Now it's time for you to get that sleep. I don't think you'll need any of your godmother's pills this time." Hugo rang the service bell.

"But aren't you going to tell me what this is all about? You said that . . ."

"That I'd tell you all I could without endangering the lives of others. Yes, you're quite right, I did promise." Hugo thought for a moment before going on. "Sarah, to be perfectly honest we're not at all sure what it is about. We do suspect that Ava Bardoff is running some sort of a master espionage organization —one that has infiltrated the internal police and other espionage groups in the West. That would explain the presence of those very important guests at her clinic —there supposedly for a rest, but more probably to drop pieces of valuable information. It also explains why the clinic is so well guarded, her close association with Undersecretary Martin—he was in U.S. intelligence—and many of her other contacts. For the time being, all we have are our suspicions. Her agents may sell to the East or, for that matter, to the various supposed allies of the Western block—we just don't know."

"And I've been sitting right in the middle of it for all these years," Sarah said in awe. "I'm really rather glad I didn't have any idea about it."

Petras opened the door of the study and Hugo turned to him, glad of the excuse to say no more to Sarah. "Will you please take Miss Dilworth to her cabin. I hope you have been able to find some things for her to wear aboard other than that rather preposterous hippie outfit Monsieur dePasse created for her." The steward stood by the door waiting for Sarah. She looked back at Michael hesitantly.

"I hope you won't mind, Sarah, if I detain our friend for a few minutes. I assure you that you're perfectly safe here with me. Oh, and Sarah, please don't leave your cabin until you ring for me. I don't want anyone to know you're aboard."

She smiled and followed Petras Furman to her cabin. The bed, turned down and waiting, was one of the most delicious sights Sarah had ever seen.

As soon as Sarah left his study, Hugo turned to Michael. "Now you, I, and the rest of the men have a lot to talk over and a lot to do."

"You don't really believe that spy story you told Sarah, do you?" Michael asked. "I thought you were going to tell her the truth or nothing."

"I'm afraid deception is often the only course open to one," Hugo answered. "My story was plausible and logical from the standpoint of all Sarah knows to date and it will put her mind at rest. If she is ever taken by the Bardoff people, she will confirm we know exactly what Ava Bardoff already knows we know—no more, no less. I hope it will lead Ava to believe we suspect her only of spying—that should please her."

He picked up one of the pistols and removed the needle magazine, indicating that the subject was closed. "I think we'd better find out exactly what this stuff is before we go much further. Wicked-looking, isn't it?"

Five minutes later, Michael was being introduced to other members of Hugo's crew, all eager to hear of his trip to the Bardoff clinic. In addition to Petras

Furman, Michael knew Tim Carpenter, the ship's radio officer who also happened to be an electronics expert. The others were strangers—George Watson, the ship's gruff and burly engineer, also a weaponry expert, and Chris Halvorsen, nicknamed Big Swede, who had degrees in archaeology and geology, not to mention those in history and geography. He stood in as the ship's navigator. Although he was sure he could match their athletic prowess, Michael felt educationally deprived in their presence.

The men hung upon his words as he slowly repeated in great detail everything he had seen at the Bardoff factory and the château. His story was interrupted halfway through by the arrival of Jim Andrews, the assistant engineer and graduate from M.I.T. with a master's degree in research chemistry. He placed the pistols on Hugo's desk and held up a test tube in which two of the needles rested.

"I've got the first readings from the analysis of these little fellows," he said almost triumphantly. "They contain a hyped-up version of curare that produces almost instant motor paralysis when introduced into the blood. They've doctored it a bit so that the paralysis lasts only about an hour—after that there seems to be no harmful reaction. Of course, this is only a preliminary—I've got a lot more work to do."

"A perfect weapon for knocking someone out of action for a while," Watson commented. "These pistols are silent and should be capable of sending one of those needles quite a distance." He pulled the trigger and a needle flashed across the study, imbedding itself in the center of a small knothole in the panelling. "*And* with great accuracy," he added with a self-congratulatory smile.

Hugo took the test tube from Andrews and studied its contents. "It also offers an excellent means of capturing an enemy alive so that he can be questioned. A convenient accidental death could be arranged after you'd learned everything you wanted to know—typical of Madame." He turned to Michael. "That truck driver outside Grasse wasn't trying to kill you and Sarah—he wanted to take you back for questioning. We were very lucky, gentlemen."

"It also means that poor guard wasn't dead when I pushed him down the shaft," Michael said, feeling sick to his stomach. "Would he have been alive—I mean, would he have been conscious and aware what I was doing?" he asked Andrews.

"Probably, but I'm not sure yet."

"Oh, my God," Michael gasped, trying to keep from retching.

"You have neither cause nor time to concern yourself with that, Michael," Hugo cut in abruptly. "What was in store for you and Sarah was much worse—dying would have been the least of your worries. Now let's stop feeling sorry for ourselves and get on with things."

As usual, this man knew best how to handle the moods of others. His verbal slap brought the younger man back to the cruel reality of the situation. Hugo's right, Michael thought, why should I feel guilty or sorry that I didn't let someone kill me?

They discussed at great length the observation rooms in the north wing, the tapes, intimate dossiers on all the guests' friends, and the nurse's comment about the need for the "neuts," whatever they were, to observe the men and women under normal conditions. Adding this to the apparent ability of the Bardoff team to duplicate human beings in some way, as evidenced by the look-alike guards who had pursued Michael and Sarah and the two Peter Kents, Hugo's men concluded that Ava's objective was not just to obtain information from those staying at the clinic, but to switch her own people for the real ones, and to do it so perfectly that they would go undetected.

"Except for close members of the family," Michael amended wryly, thinking of his own mother.

"But how?" Andrews asked. "That takes science far beyond where we are now."

"Let's take first things first," Hugo interrupted. "We'll make the assumption she can do it physically with some advanced technique of hers and that her doubles are able to mimic the actions, voices, and habits of their victims and so pass themselves off as the real thing. What we must concern ourselves with is not how, but why. What is her reason for all this? Whatever her objective, we can be sure it's an ambitious one, and from the trail of death and misery she's already left in her wake, we know it's an evil one. Let's hope we aren't too late. She may already have launched some terrible abomination on the world—and we are the only ones who suspect. Ava Bardoff must be stopped." He paused and looked from one man to the other. "Do we agree?"

The others nodded their agreement.

"Thank you, gentlemen. Let's get on with it, then. Now that we know for sure the names of several of the people at the clinic, I'll contact the President in Washington—socially, of course—to find out the names of any others, why they're there, and what, if anything, Corsica has to do with it. His answers may shed some light on what Ava Bardoff is planning. I must admit I'm intrigued by what our secretary of state, the shah, and, we must assume, the Russian head are doing at her château in the first place. And I wonder why there was no numbered file on the shah—it may confirm our suspicions about his membership in her organization. I don't like the idea of his being mixed up with the other two—it can only mean trouble. But until I meet with the President, there's no point in wasting time guessing." He spread out the aerial photographs of the clinic. "Let's go over the physical layout of the Bardoff operation again."

"One thing before we hit that," Michael interrupted. "What about those blue dots by the thumbnail on her guards' right hands? If I hadn't noticed it on the driver's hand, Sarah and I would be goners."

"It must be an identification mark and probably all her people have it," Petras said. "The mark is small enough to go unnoticed and, being on the thumb of the right hand, it's quickly seen while shaking hands if you're looking for it. Her doubles would be able to recognize each other wherever they met. It's a nasty little throwback to the concentration camp days."

"It also suggests," Hugo added, "that if they need a

mark like that to recognize each other, there must be a great many of her doubles and agents in circulation, carrying out her orders without necessarily knowing her overall plan or each other."

Each man instinctively looked at the others' right hands and then, realizing what they were doing, burst out laughing. While the others laughed, Hugo said quietly to Michael, "I'd like to know if the Count dePasse wears one of those little blue dots."

Michael nodded. "And Sarah's father and mother."

"Very well, gentlemen," Hugo said, "I'm sure we all agree that from now on we look at a person's right hand before we do or say anything." As he spoke, his mind whirled through all the various guests he'd entertained on the *Krait* and tried vainly to picture all their hands—hands holding cocktail glasses, lifting caviar to lips, resting beside the silver and crystal of his dinner table.

"If, as you say, doubles are floating around all over the world, just think of the organization she'd have to control them, to coordinate their activities," Watson mused. "The logistics are staggering."

"Perhaps it's done at those 'reunions' Sarah told us about," Michael suggested.

"Perhaps some of it is, but from Martin's reaction at being excluded, I think something much more important may go on there," Hugo countered. "Remember, Madame is quite a social lady, traveling on business all over the world. Just as I do, she could conduct her unofficial business over a glass of champagne almost as easily as over a desk. Let's just assume she's got a dangerous worldwide organization and is able to keep them loyal and toeing the line. From what Sarah says, they're all afraid of her for some reason—fear is a pretty effective way to keep people in line.

"But let's leave the hypothetical and get to the practical," he said, pointing to the aerial photos and maps on his desk. "We don't have much time. It's a question of who strikes first, Madame or us. Michael, explain the layout of the factory and the château again, and, Watson, pay particular attention to the shafts. I want to know their implications."

After much discussion, the men seemed agreed upon the fact that the shafts had to have been built to ventilate a large underground installation or complex of some sort; it was the only explanation for their presence. As Watson explained it, "The factory, even if it weren't the dummy we think it is, wouldn't need much of a ventilation system, and certainly the château wouldn't need any at all. Those fucking shafts—if they've got fans to match their proportions, they could ventilate the old *Queen Mary, Queen Elizabeth, Andrea Doria,* and the *Île de France* laid end to end."

Based on the great depth that Michael claimed for the shaft in the northwest tower of the château, they also agreed it was right to assume any complex would have to be much further beneath the ground than could be accounted for by only two levels of subbasements, and it seemed logical that each end must be connected to one of the shafts, the château end pumping down fresh air into it and the factory shaft, almost a mile away, expelling used air from it.

"What a layout that must be," Watson said, whistling in appreciation of the engineering feat. "Can you imagine excavating something that size without people living around knowing a thing about it?"

"It would be virtually impossible," Halvorsen said flatly. He had been sitting in quiet thought during most of the discussion. "That's why I don't think much excavating was necessary other than sinking those two shafts."

"You're out of your mind, Swede," Watson countered.

Unperturbed, Halvorsen continued. "This whole section of the Continent is honeycombed with caves, caverns, galleries—take your pick. The runoff of water from the Alps for millions of years has carved out passages that run for hundreds of miles beneath the ground. This area has been a spelunker's paradise for years."

"Spelunker?" Carpenter asked. "What the hell is a spelunker?"

Halvorsen laughed; he loved teasing Carpenter. "He is a practitioner of the age-old science of speleology."

"Thanks for nothing, Swede," the other retorted.

"Speleology is simply the science of exploring caves. That's what spelunkers do—they explore caves."

"I've got some friends from the Polytechnique who spend every free minute climbing around down in caves," Michael said. "All their finds are mapped and recorded by some institute or other in Paris."

"Exactly," Halvorsen said. "But getting back to this particular area—in the mid-fifties a system of passages and large caverns was found around the city of Grenoble only a little more than a hundred miles north of here. It stretched for miles and some of the galleries were huge. I'll bet the Bardoff complex is built in a cave hundreds of feet underground."

The others fell silent thinking of the implications of Halvorsen's idea.

"If that were the case, do you think we could find it?" Hugo asked. "How would we get to it?"

"As Michael said, all cave finds of any significance are charted. Any underground cave large enough to house a construction of the dimensions we seem to be talking about would most probably have been discovered, charted, and recorded years ago. We can but look."

"I'll do it," Michael volunteered. "I've got those friends who can help me. Using our aerial photos of the surface of the land, we should be able to find a match with some chart of what lies underneath."

"If anything lies underneath," Watson commented doubtfully.

"I'll lay you odds they've got it mapped," Halvorsen countered. "I'm telling you, this area has been gone over by spelunkers for years. When I was studying the fault lines of the Alps and the stratification of the coast, I looked at thousands of photographs taken in caves. You know, there are literally hundreds of miles of underground rivers fed by the Alps, some pretty damn big."

"Hugo," Michael said, his memory suddenly jogged by Halvorsen's talk of underground rivers, "I forgot until this minute, but there were canaries."

"Canaries?" Carpenter interrupted incredulously.

"You guys are all going potty. What do canaries have to do with anything?"

"There were dozens of dead canaries floating in the lake in the wildlife preserve, and there were canaries flying around the conservatory at the château. I think they were being bred there."

"So what?" Carpenter asked. "There are canaries all over the south of France."

"Not true," Halvorsen countered. "You're confusing them with other species. Canaries don't fly wild in these parts, and I think I know what Michael's driving at. If Madame Bardoff has people running around down in caves, she's got a potential problem with gas. She might be breeding those birds for use in detecting gas in her caves just the way miners used them. If the river that feeds Michael's lake also runs through Madame's caves, it's logical to assume any birds killed by gas there might be carried down into the lake."

"Remember I said I smelled chlorine outside the factory?" Michael said with a rush of excitement. "Well, I also smelled it on the lake. The cave where Sarah and I spent the night reeked with it—it could have come along with the water from Ava Bardoff's cavern."

Andrews, the research chemist, took the floor. "Forget Swede's natural gas problem. If, as Michael suggests, she's using chlorine gas down there for experiments or manufacturing—hydrochloric acid is in common industrial use—Madame Bardoff certainly has a warning problem. A leak would kill your birds in a flash, not to mention humans."

"You're all going out of your minds," Watson cried. "Caves, canaries, gas, underground rivers—it sounds as if we're talking science fiction."

"Maybe we are," Hugo said. "I don't think we should rule out this line of thought. As wild as it seems to your practical mind, George, it makes a very great deal of sense to mine. Strangely, it's the sort of thing I'd connect with Ava Bardoff. I can just visualize that beautiful, satanic temptress seated on a throne in her kingdom in the bowels of the earth, her insidious tentacles reaching up and twining around her victims throughout the world."

"Hugo," Halvorsen interrupted, "I've never before seen you so emotional about any of our jobs. May I caution you how dangerous it can be to become too personally involved—you'll lose all objectivity."

"I take your point, and you're right," Hugo said. "This woman has touched my life very much over the years and perhaps I have turned her pursuit and destruction into too personal a vendetta. I think Michael can understand my motivation more than the rest of you." Michael looked down at the carpet, avoiding the curious eyes turned toward him. "But as you say, Chris, objectivity is essential, so let's be objective in looking at the cave theory.

"First, we agreed that an underground complex exists or else there would be no need for ventilating shafts. Second, it must be very large—large enough to house a great many people and probably the laboratories of the mysterious Dr. Mulciber. The château itself could not contain all the security guards and staff Michael saw there, and you'll recall that the interrogation teams with their drugs arrived via the elevator. Also Michael saw great quantities of food supplements —vitamins, or nutritional substances of some sort— destined, we presume, to feed this subterranean complex. Third, as Andrews points out, the presence of the chlorine odor probably indicates work of some type is actually being carried out down there. This ties in with our theory that the surface factory and laboratories are for show only. Aside from disguising the ventilator shaft and freight elevator, they offer a perfectly logical cover for the delivery of all sorts of materials needed below—food, equipment, construction materials, chemicals—everything.

"Now, as to whether or not this complex has been built in an existing, natural chamber? I think it has to be. Chris confirms the possible, if not probable, existence of caverns in this area large enough to hold a complex of the size we're talking about. The chlorine odor brought up by the shaft at the factory and the same smell at the lake many miles away coupled with Michael's canary theory, as farfetched as it may seem, convince me such a cavern has to exist—one with a river flowing through it. Well, gentlemen, what do you think?"

Reluctantly Watson nodded agreement with the others.

"Excellent," Hugo said. "This may make it easier to get at Madame—at least it gives us a back door to her kingdom. Michael, leave for Paris tomorrow and look for those cave charts. Take Sarah with you. I want that young lady far away and out of Ava Bardoff's grasp. Tomorrow night I'll fly to Washington for the reception they're having Wednesday evening at the Kennedy Center; I've got to have a little chat with the President about his secretary of state's visit to the clinic and Corsica. Our course of action seems perfectly clear—we must rescue those statesmen and their wives and destroy Ava Bardoff's organization before she destroys ours—and we must do it on our own."

"But if you know the President and Russians so well," Michael said, "why not tell them what you suspect and have them call their people back home on some pretext?"

"I'm sure those men and women have no idea what's happening to them while they sleep at the clinic and might resist leaving, assuming Madame Bardoff would let them leave or doesn't already have doubles ready to take their places. Also, there could be another of those very convenient and regrettable accidents we've come to associate with Ava Bardoff—we'd be endangering their lives and tipping our hand. As we have only suppositions and no actual proof, we can't count on the help of this or any country's police force and, for that matter, we dare not even ask for it. We might inadvertently be turning ourselves over to one of her agents like Undersecretary Martin, or at least give her enough warning to cover her tracks.

"No, it is up to us. Based on the information we now have and that which hopefully Michael and I will turn up in the next few days, we must develop a feasible plan to eliminate Ava Bardoff, get the names of her doubles and agents around the world, and destroy her base of operations—all the while remembering we've also got some very important people up there in the clinic whose lives are in our hands."

Before the men could reflect on the virtual impossibility of the task set for them, Hugo continued. "At the least, gentlemen, we must rescue those men and their wives and try to destroy whatever Madame has in her caves below to slow her up until we figure out what she's doing and how best to stop it." He looked at them, smiling as if he didn't have a care in the world. "Now shall we take a break and meet after dinner to make our provisional plans for attack? I am sure my guests must be quite concerned over my indisposition after lunch, and Miss Dilworth should be up by now. Oh, Michael, before you two leave, please give me an accurate sketch of those white uniforms the clinic staff wears and put Sarah's considerable artistic talents to use drawing the best possible likeness of the look-alike guards. A very interesting plan is beginning to form in my mind, and, Chris, you can rest assured it is an objective one."

8

Tuesday morning found Hugo busy making plans for yet another lavish dinner party. "Not too large," he had told Petras the previous evening. "Two dozen carefully selected guests. I want it to be the most snobbish, exclusive dinner this season so that news of it will travel like wildfire." He started making his phone calls to the chosen few at 9:00 A.M. that morning, apologizing for the inconvenience by explaining it was a spur-of-the-moment gathering of the most interesting people he could think of. Naturally, none refused.

He waited until early afternoon before inviting Ava Bardoff and her goddaughter, saying he hoped Miss Dilworth wouldn't find it too boring to be with an older group. Hugo wanted to be sure Ava had heard about the party before inviting her so as not to arouse the suspicions of his enemy. Rather to his surprise, Ava graciously refused; he had thought she might like another look around the yacht, particularly since his crew had informed him Cannes' harbor was swarming with her blue-dotted men, keeping a close watch on the ship. Ava had also extended regrets on Sarah's behalf, informing Hugo that the young woman had not been feeling well for the last few days. So much for that, he thought, dropping the receiver back into its cradle. She may not be here, but a thousand to one she'll know everything that went on by noon tomorrow. News travels fast on the Riviera.

The party was being arranged for several reasons: to let Ava know that he had no inkling of what had occurred over the weekend at the clinic, that Sarah wasn't aboard the *Krait,* to announce his trip later that night to Washington for the premiere of a new ballet on Wednesday, and to tell everyone that upon his return the *Krait* would up anchor and slowly cruise along the coast to end at the island of Minorca off the Spanish mainland some ten days later. He wanted no questions over the future destination of the ship and also wanted to give his entire crew the chance to move freely about Cannes and the surrounding area to prepare for his planned armed assault on the clinic under the guise of preparing for the elaborate dinner that evening and the upcoming cruise.

Michael and Sarah had left the yacht before sunup in the most powerful launch the *Krait* carried. Sarah's hair was cut short and bleached to an ash-blonde color. Michael had taken the other route, applying a very realistic moustache and short beard in the current style. The two young people had looked at Hugo with amusement when he requested these changes in their appearance. "Changing hair color and using false beards may seem silly and old-fashioned these days," Hugo had explained patiently, "but they are effective, else why do you think they've been used so much over the years?" They continued to smile condescendingly at him. "All right, so you think it's corny, but please, do an old man this one favor."

They now waited for Petras Furman in the boat beached in a small cove fifteen miles west of St. Tropez. It was too early for bathers and they were completely cut off from view from both sea or land. Hugo's steward, his slacks rolled up to his knees, soon waded around an outcropping of rock separating the cove from a long stretch of pebbly beach and waved to them. He had gone ashore earlier that morning with several other members of the crew and taken a devious route to the outskirts of Cannes, where Hugo kept a car concealed right out in the open in the parking lot of an apartment complex.

"It's the blue Peugeot convertible parked in the

pine grove just to the right of these rocks," Petras said, handing Michael the keys. And then for Sarah's benefit he added, "I've known Mr. Montclair's guests to do some pretty wild things, but you two sneaking off to Paris disguised like that is about the wildest. Well, I wish you all the luck in the world." Michael and Sarah waded back around the rocks. "Happy wedding," he called after them.

"Wedding?" Sarah gasped in surprise. "Did you tell him we were sneaking off to a wedding—our wedding?"

"Yep. Hugo thought it would be the best way to explain all this cloak-and-dagger stuff to the crew. He doesn't want them to know anything about what he and I are doing." Michael began laughing. "Besides, it's not *that* insulting an idea, is it?"

She didn't answer, not knowing quite how to respond to the question and the mood in which it was asked. Instead she ran ahead to the Peugeot hidden from the road by the pines. Within minutes they were well on their way to Marseilles where Michael planned to lose himself in the heavy port traffic and then take the highway north through Lyons to Paris. They should reach the capital and his friends by late afternoon.

He and Hugo's men had discussed in detail how he should plan his escape from the Riviera. They had considered the morning plane from Nice to Paris, but Ava certainly would have her men at the airport to intercept them. The train to Paris had been ruled out as much too dangerous. Hugo was sure that, like the airport, all trains out of the area would be watched, and he didn't fancy the idea of Michael and Sarah being trapped within a moving cage while one of Madame's experienced killers took his time tracking them from one car to the next. Driving was the safest way, particularly as there were many roads into Paris and they would arrive at a peak traffic time.

They also decided that Sarah and Michael should beg room and board with his friends. Sarah had no passport with her and so, as an obvious foreigner, couldn't check into a hotel without drawing a great deal of attention to herself. Hugo was sure that Ava Bardoff's connections reached well into the Paris police force, and as they checked all hotel registrations, Sarah would be tracked to any hotel in the city within twenty-four hours. And thus it was to his friends, Nicholas and Colette Palot, living at 68 Quai des Orfèvres, that Michael and Sarah were running—he to carry out the next step of the operation, she for safety.

During the long drive and aided by a superb, wine-soaked lunch at a small auberge outside of Lyons, Sarah began to unwind from the tensions of the last few days. As the distance between the blue Peugeot and the Bardoff clinic increased, so, too, did her feelings of security and confidence. She dozed comfortably while the car sped along the highway, the wind gently blowing her newly blonde hair. From time to time she'd open her eyes just a little, still pretending to sleep, and look at Michael as he stared intently at the road ahead. His face seemed outlined in the gold reflection of the sun on his tanned skin, his features bold and strong. She felt very possessive toward that face and the now familiar body next to her. She awoke once to find her hand resting gently on his thigh. Michael and she felt right together, and Sarah wanted to keep him close, physically close, as long as—well, for a long time.

They entered the suburbs of Paris from the south, passing the large statue of the Lion of Belfort reclining imperiously on his high podium in Montparnasse. Michael veered to the right and headed down the Boulevard St. Michel past the Luxembourg Gardens and the Sorbonne. The streets were teeming with cars battling for position, impatient horns, and the shouts of irate drivers. The pavements swarmed with students and, at this time of year, with tourists walking aimlessly about to absorb the excitement of the student quarter. Pale stone buildings with tall windows, balconies, delicately carved cornices, and dormered roofs crowded side by side along the boulevard, their ground-floor shops shaded by orange and yellow awnings and spilling displays of shoes, clothing, cooking pots, and fruits and vegetables out onto the sidewalks. Tables and chairs crowded the pavement from cafés where patrons sipped aperitifs and discussed the latest scandal, political defeat, class assignment, or just sat back, content to gaze at the incessant stream of people passing along before them. Michael crossed the bridge over the Seine at the foot of Boulevard St. Michel and swung the blue Peugeot left onto Quai des Orfèvres. Sarah bubbled with excitement as they drove down the narrow street running along the south bank of Île de la Cité, one of the two small islands representing the heart of ancient Paris that sat in the center of the river.

"This is my favorite part of the whole city," Sarah said gaily. "I love it, I love it. Where is the house?"

"Just up ahead," Michael replied. "That you really *will* love."

They passed by the imposing walls of the Palais de Justice on the right after which the street became residential. Very narrow old stone houses, six and seven stories high, leaned together on one side; their shuttered windows with striped awnings looked across the street over a low stone wall to the cobblestone bank of the Seine twenty feet below, where the old and very young sat dangling fishing lines into the river shaded from the late July sun by towering elms. Michael pulled up in front of Number 68, the ground floor of which was a dusty old bookshop.

"Well, here we are. What do you think?"

Before Sarah could answer, they heard a voice call down from the balcony running across the second floor of the house. "Darling, you're here—how absolutely fantastic. Come up at once."

Looking up, Sarah saw a plain but animated woman about her own age leaning over a long row of boxes filled with bright red geraniums; a watering can waved dangerously in her hand.

"Ah, fair Juliet," Michael called, "this reminds me of our great Shakespearean triumph."

"Remind me of that debacle one more time and you shall get this entire can of water over your silly head. Now get up here." She gave him a little sprinkle of water and disappeared through one of the three French doors leading onto the balcony.

"Who is that?" Sarah asked.

"Colette Palot, our hostess—you'll adore her." He took Sarah's hand and pulled her into the tiny entry hall leading off the sidewalk where the impatient buzzing of the door latch indicated Colette was leaning on the button upstairs. Michael took the narrow, circular staircase two steps at a time.

"My little sparrow," he cried, grabbing the small woman who stood with open arms on the landing. He twirled her around and lifted her into the air.

"I almost feel like crying," she laughed as he set her down and gave her a great hug. "Oh, how good it is to see you after all this time. But that beard—when did you go all fuzzy?" Then, seeing Sarah standing somewhat awkwardly behind, she pushed Michael away. "Now introduce me to the 'most wonderful girl in the world' you said you were bringing to us."

He turned and, holding the hand of each woman, introduced Sarah to Colette. Disengaging her hand from his, Colette kissed Sarah on both cheeks.

"Anyone who can capture this big lug is more than welcome in this house. He's our favorite elusive bachelor." Colette pulled her into the living room. "Now make yourself at home while I get some ice—I assume tea is the last thing on your minds after the long drive up here."

"The perfect hostess, as ever," Michael complimented, bowing outrageously low to the floor.

"You clown, if you break your back it will serve you right." She stood on tiptoes and kissed him on his "fuzzy" chin. "Now see to Sarah. I'll be right back." Leaving the door open to the tiny landing in the circular hallway, she darted up the stairs.

Sarah looked appraisingly around the room. "Oh, Michael, it's out of a dream."

The high-ceilinged living room ran the width of the narrow building and was panelled in mellow walnut dating back to the time of Louis XIV. One wall contained French doors with interior shutters that opened

out onto the balcony overlooking the Seine; the back
wall facing it was hung with large floral paintings of
poppies and sunflowers mixed with old family portraits.
One of the end walls was lined with bookcases
crammed with every size and color of book, while
the other contained a large, high mirror built into an
elaborate frame in the woodwork over a beautifully
carved marble fireplace. The furnishings were mostly
comfortable Louis XIV style, covered in faded ma-
roons, tans, and yellows. Two delicate chairs in petit
point stood formally on either side of the fireplace, but
other than these, the room was furnished for soft comfort. Large vases filled with gladioli added fresh, brilliant splashes of color to the room.

"I feel as if I'm in a combination museum, library,
and cosy den," Sarah said. "And that view—why I can
see all the way down the Seine to the Place de la Concorde and across the river—just look—the entire left
bank spread out before us." She was like a small, enthusiastic child, pointing out one domed landmark after the other. "I could stand here all day." Impulsively
she reached out and hugged Michael to her. "I'm so
very happy."

He brought his arms around her, his right hand playing with the nape of her neck and the blonde curls
floating around it.

"Hey, you two, do you want the police from the
préfecteur down the street to raid the place?" Colette
said as she entered the room with a tray of glasses and
an ice bucket. "I have nothing against it, but can you
imagine what Madame deFarge would say—she'd be
knitting your names into her scarf before you could
blink an eye." Opening a panel to the right of the
fireplace, Colette asked, "Now what is it to be—
Scotch, gin, vodka?"

"Scotch, please," Sarah answered. "Can't I help?"

"Not at all. One Scotch coming up, and I'm sure the
fellow you're with will have one, too."

"She knows every vice I have," Michael told Sarah.

"*Mon dieu,* I hope not!" Colette laughed, pouring
the drinks.

Sarah couldn't help but warm to Colette at once. This

diminutive woman with mouse-brown hair and a plain, open face was like a favorite sister or cousin whose cosy personality invaded the room and swept away any reserve. Sarah felt completely at home with her. She had thought of Michael as being surrounded only by sex kittens and sirens; this woman gave her yet another glimpse of the real man behind the glossy play-boy and athlete façade he always wore. It was a nice glimpse.

The three stood on the balcony looking across the Seine in the pink light of the late afternoon Paris sky for a long time talking casually about nothing in par-ticular—a happy, relaxed kind of talk. Then Colette hit her head with her hand.

"But what a fool I am. I haven't even shown you your room. Don't you want to wash after your trip? Come—and bring your drinks."

She led them up the circular stairs in the hallway to the floor above, letting them peek on the way into a beautiful dining room and kitchen, both overlooking the river. "These are my most favorite rooms in the whole house. Nicholas and our friends love to sit over coffee here after dinner solving the problems of the world." She led them up to the next floor. "We have only two small bedrooms up here and I hope you don't mind sharing the bath. I've moved the baby in with Nicholas and me—you will have the honor of sharing the nursery. I trust that won't meet any objec-tions." Colette gave them both a naughty look and started for the door. "I've got some things to do in the kitchen. I hope you like pigeon. Make yourselves at home. If you want another drink, you know where the liquor is. The baby will be home from its wheel through the Tuileries soon, and I'll expect you to make quite a fuss over him." Before either could say another word, Colette bounded down the stairs calling over her shoulder, "Nicholas should be home any minute."

Sarah lay back on the bed and looked up at Michael. "Hi," she said quietly.

"Hi!" He smiled, sitting beside her and leaning for-ward to gently kiss her. "Welcome to the other side of Michael dePasse."

"It's his best side," she said, pulling him down so his head rested on her shoulder.

They had been lying in each other's arms for only a few minutes when they heard thundering footsteps on the stairs and Nicholas Palot's voice call out, "Where are they hiding?"

"Upstairs," Colette shouted from the kitchen. "Better knock first."

He roared with laughter. "The hell I will—I'll join them." The door to the nursery was flung open and Nicholas Palot jumped in, smiling from ear to ear. He was slightly slimmer in build than Michael and had a more serious, aquiline face, obviously lacking the American blood of his friend. "Don't get up," he said as Sarah and Michael started to rise. "Beautiful women are at their best lying down."

"Sarah, this chauvinist pig is our host," Michael joked. "You haven't changed at all, have you? Just as lecherous as ever."

"But of course, my clients expect it of me—women like to tingle with anticipation when they enter my examining room."

Nicholas Palot was one of the best young surgeons in Paris and a lecturer at the École de Médicine. His smile faded slightly when he grasped his friend's hand. "Michael, how are you?" he asked with warmth but also with concern. His eyes searched the other's face.

"Physically, I couldn't be better, but . . ."

"But," Nicholas finished, "you are in some trouble you won't tell me about—yes, I know. Anyway, I've done as you asked and . . ."

This time Michael interrupted. "Nick, Sarah knows about my problem, but we've agreed that while we're here it won't be discussed in front of her." Nicholas glanced at Sarah with a puzzled frown and then back at Michael. "It's for her own safety, and yours."

"Mine?" he asked, somewhat surprised.

"Yes, yours and Colette's. As long as you don't know anything, you'll be perfectly okay. And no one must know Sarah and I are here except . . ." Michael raised his eyebrows in a question.

"As you asked this morning, I've called him. No one

else but us knows you're in Paris. Colette has even
given the cook a week's holiday, for which the old
lady would thank you if she weren't supposed to know
you're here." He was smiling again. "Very well, we'll
keep away from your mysterious problem. I had to
give Colette some explanation, so I told her you two
are trying to avoid the police in Cannes over some
silly brawl at the Casino. I thought it would not only
appeal to her sense of humor, but fit in with her sense
of outrage at the police. She hasn't changed either since
the student protest days."

Michael turned to Sarah. "Colette used to organize us
for every cause imaginable under the sun. Do you
think we ever accomplished anything, Nick?"

"Absolutely nothing, but the battered bodies of our
comrades gave us medical students a great deal of
practice. I recall patching up a broken arm for you—
or was it a foot?"

"Only a toe, but broken in the cause of reinstating
the drunken dean of physics. And speaking of drunken
deans, shall we?" He raised his empty glass.

"That, my friend, is an excellent idea. Sarah—" he
extended his arm—"may I have the honor of escorting
you to the most chic bar in Paris?"

The three descended the two floors to the living room,
refilled their glasses, and sat looking out through the
French doors at the sunset reflecting off the glass
domes of the Grande and Petite Palais far down the
Seine. The room was filled with warm shadows, comfortable shadows, when Colette joined them and curled
up on a cushioned stool beside Nicholas's deep armchair. Madame Ava Bardoff and her château on the
Riviera did not exist at that moment.

After a long, lazy, and delicious dinner, Michael and
Nicholas left the two women in the kitchen, telling
them they were going to take a stroll across the Pont
Neuf to the Left Bank where they would "probably
get stinking drunk talking about their student days together." Colette gave them each a kiss and a bright
wave goodbye. Sarah looked apprehensive. "Be careful,
both of you," she said.

"Yes," Colette added with a laugh. "Don't go falling into the river."

Michael nodded to Sarah in understanding of her warning. "We won't fall in, don't worry."

The two men descended the winding stairs to the street and crossed over the bridge not more than fifty yards away. Making a little zigzag on reaching the other side, they walked two blocks south and then turned right onto Rue de l'Université, a long narrow street paralleling the Seine. Most of the private houses lining both sides of the street had long since been converted into apartments—many over small antique shops, art galleries, and smart boutiques.

"Jean-Pascale is just as mad as ever," Nicholas said. "He's in and out of holes in the ground every chance he gets and, can you imagine, he's even found some pretty great-looking girls who'll go along with him. I think we may have to remove his name from the bachelor ranks in the very near future. What about you? I have to agree with Colette, Sarah's a great . . ."

"We're just good friends," Michael interrupted to the amusement of Nicholas. "What did you tell Jean-Pascale about me and my wanting his help?"

"Only that you were in town and wanted to talk to him about some caves friends of yours wished to visit, that's all. When I mentioned caves, he practically screamed with delight."

"What's he doing now? He keeps hopping from one job to the next like a rabbit. Last year he was running an art gallery, wasn't he?" Michael asked.

"That's right. But he gave it up and now owns a camping equipment store—doing very well with it, too. Be careful, or he'll have you outfitted for a trip across the North Pole. I understand he overstocked snow-shoes last winter. Ah, here we are, Number 37." Nicholas pushed at the small door built into the larger wooden doors opening into the courtyard of the old building, but it was locked. "Have to ring for the concierge." He pushed the bell in the stone wall and was answered after a time by a buzzing as the latch of the smaller door pulled back. They waved at the lighted window on the left where the concierge stood inspecting them with the eyes of a hawk. "Paris's secret police system." Nicholas laughed. "Those old crows know the intimate details of the love life of everyone in the whole neighborhood."

Michael remembered the unfortunate "crow" in Peter Kent's flat in Cannes. "All the same," he said, "I don't envy their lot."

"Look who's getting a social conscience," Nicholas joked. "I see our friend is home and waiting," he said, pointing at three lighted windows on the third floor overlooking the courtyard. They walked up to the third-floor landing, where an old panelled door stood ajar. "I swear, someday a burglar is going to steal everything that man owns—which isn't that much when you come to think of it. What burglar would want three pairs of filthy coveralls, climbing shoes, and a spelunker's tin helmet?"

"Monsieur Melia," Nicholas called out, beating on the half-open door, "are you home, or is this open house for every rummy wandering by?"

"Come on in," a voice shouted from somewhere in the back recesses of the apartment. As they entered the front door, Jean-Pascale Melia, dressed only in a pair of undershorts and holding a towel, walked in from a small hallway that led to the bedroom and bath.

"You old son of a gun," Jean-Pascale cried, striding across the room to capture Michael in a bear hug and smearing his cheek with the remnants of shaving cream. "How the hell have you been? I understand you're about to join the ranks of the great international spelunker society—that's really great, man. And dig that beard. When did you go hippie?"

"Hold on." Michael laughed. "One thing at a time."

"Absolutely right," Jean-Pascale said, holding up his hand, "and the first thing on the agenda is a drink. Scotch?" He didn't wait for the answer. "Good, that's all I've got. It's in the cabinet over there, Nicholas, and the ice is in the kitchen. You get it while I tidy up. I just got back from the shop. I've been keeping it open late this summer to take advantage of the insatiable demand of us French to go camping in style—in other words, we're too cheap to pay for a hotel. My customers spend hundreds on gimmicks they'll never use, but who am I to complain? I'm crying all the way to the bank. You know, this is the first time in my life that I'm actually making a living."

Michael looked over the small apartment. It was sparsely furnished and mirrored well the personality of its owner. Clothes lay about on chairs, this morning's cup of coffee sat cold and half full on a table covered with newspapers and girly magazines.

"I see you're just as much of a slob as ever," Michael called down the small hallway.

"That's right, but a loveable one—you have to admit that," came the retort. "Stop bitching and get yourself a drink."

"He's just the same as always," Nicholas whispered to Michael. "He gives every last cent he earns to the person with the hardest hard-luck story, chases the girls and usually catches them, and exists from day to day with one of the most optimistic outlooks on life I've ever known. Actually, he's one of the few really happy men I've ever had the privilege to meet." Nicholas popped some ice cubes in three soap-streaked tumblers and covered them liberally with whiskey. He held up his glass. "*À vôtre santé,* Monsieur."

"Cheers," Michael replied.

"Do you want me to stay while you talk with Jean-Pascale or . . ." he paused.

"I think you'd better make some excuse and leave the two of us together. I hate being so damn mysterious about all this, but it really is best to know nothing. Okay?"

"Sure. But please, Michael, ask me for help if and when you need it. What are friends for?"

Michael squeezed Nicholas's arm. "They're for being like you. I appreciate the offer and I'll call if you really can help, I promise."

"Hey, what are you two so serious about?" Jean-Pascale asked as he entered and picked up his drink from the table.

The three of them reminisced over their many adventures together for the next hour, recalling with great laughter their near expulsion from the Polytechnique for "off-campus behavior not fitting for a student of that great institute." Michael lost himself in the humor of the past and was only brought back to the problems of the present when Nicholas finally put down his empty glass and made a point of looking at his watch. *"Merde,* I must get back to Colette—I didn't realize how late it had got. Eleven o'clock—she'll skin me alive."

"But the night is just beginning," Jean-Pascale countered. "Surely the lovely Colette isn't sitting in the window with a lamp burning—you know she doesn't care how late you're out."

"All the same, I really must go. You stay, Michael. Let the two gay blades live it up." Nicholas departed despite Jean-Pascale's further protestations. "Remember, you're coming to dinner tomorrow," he called back as he left the room and made a point of closing the door.

Alone, Jean-Pascale filled Michael's glass once again and sat down at the littered table. "I think he was just making an excuse to avoid having to listen to us talk about caves. What exactly are you planning to do?"

Michael got up and approached the table, unfolding a copy of a topographical map of the area surrounding the Bardoff clinic that Halvorsen had made. "Some friends have just bought property here and were wondering whether or not there were any caves underneath it—they don't want to do a lot of heavy construction if they're going to fall down a hole."

Jean-Pascale looked at him condescendingly. "That's about the most stupid thing I've ever heard. Surely if there were any danger of that, your friends' surveyors and the registry office would know about it."

"Well, actually it's more for curiosity than anything else. You see this lake?" Michael pointed to the body of water where he and Sarah had sheltered. "Well, they think it might be fed by an underground river that flows through this area right about here. If so, they thought they might explore the caves and see if they could tap the river for a water supply."

"Well, now you're talking my language," Jean-Pascale said, sweeping the magazines on the table off onto the floor and reaching for a book that contained detailed maps of the European Continent. Thumbing through its pages, he came to the section devoted to the area of southern France. "From what this shows, the whole place you're talking about probably does have lots of caverns. These maps are only topographical ones, but from the notes on them you can get a pretty good idea of subterranean conditions. Tomorrow morning on the way to the shop I'll stop off at the Institute and get a photostat of any charts they've got of the cave systems in the area—it's a simple thing to do. Then we can look for your mysterious river."

"That would be great," Michael said. "I hate to bother you, but you know exactly what to look for and how to find it. I'd spend months wandering around in the archives, and in the end I'd probably find myself exploring the sewer system of Paris."

"When do you plan to explore the caves—that is, if there's anything down there? Can I join you? I haven't done any spelunkering in that area at all."

"I don't know when we'd get to it—as you say, we'd have to see what's down there first. We're all amateurs at this sort of thing so you'd be more than welcome to join us if and when we go," Michael lied.

"It's a deal. Let's meet at the Deux Magots, St. Germain, for lunch tomorrow and I'll bring the stats. We can go over them there. Okay?"

The two men talked aimlessly for another thirty minutes before Michael left. "Till tomorrow, then," he said standing on the landing, "and for Christ's sake, keep your door locked."

"Why? I always forget my key and I haven't anything worth stealing," Jean-Pascale replied, laughing. "Besides," he called after Michael as he disappeared down the stairs, "who would want to hurt me? I don't have a guilty conscience."

Wednesday morning passed slowly as Michael sat in the living room of 68 Quai des Orfèvres trying to concentrate on the newspaper. It was impossible. He kept thinking of what Jean-Pascale's charts might show.

Nicholas had gone to the hospital and Sarah and Colette were off somewhere shopping for clothes. He was
sure that little expedition would take most of the day
since Sarah had arrived in Paris with only the clothes
on her back, and those had been borrowed from the
Krait's intelligent but not very fashionable stewardess.

After pacing the room for nearly an hour, Michael
left the Palot apartment and wandered around the Île
de la Cité to kill time. He meandered slowly through
the long rows of flower stalls overflowing with colorful
blossoms of every size and description in the great
market situated in the center of the island and then
headed for Nôtre Dame Cathedral. He smiled to himself, remembering how he'd stared at the right hand
thumb of every flower peddler in the market looking
for the telltale blue dot. He'd even found his eyes wandering to the hands of the priest lighting candles by the
main altar. I'm really getting paranoid, he thought,
while looking at the distinctly treacherous eyes of a
passing nun. Smiling to himself, Michael went back
out into the sunlight. He felt more relaxed and unre-
stricted away from the oppressive atmosphere of the
heavy, dim cathedral. He looked at his watch in frustration for perhaps the hundredth time that morning
and finally went across the bridge to St. Germain, relieved that at least this action would bring him closer
to Deux Magots and the information he sought.

Michael ordered an aperitif and sat at a small table
inside the restaurant by a window that gave an unob-
structed view up and down the boulevard over the
heads of those lunching at the sidewalk tables. Waiting
for what seemed hours, he at last saw the happy, am-
bling figure of Jean-Pascale bobbing along the sidewalk toward the café. The husky, disheveled young man
nodded appreciatively at the girls passing in the opposite direction, occasionally making a slight, respect-
ful bow to the prettier ones. He stopped to embrace a
young brunette, kissing her on both cheeks as well as
firmly on the lips. They talked and laughed for several
minutes, increasing Michael's impatience. Jean-Pascale
motioned toward the café where Michael sat and
shrugged, obviously explaining he would be unable to

lunch with her because of a business meeting with a "boring old associate." The bastard, Michael thought, smiling to himself. At last Jean-Pascale tore himself away from the girl and covered the last hundred yards in a run to flop down in a chair across from Michael.

"Sorry to be late," he apologized, "but I had trouble getting away from the shop. Ran here as fast as I could."

"That's all right—I haven't been waiting long." Michael wanted to laugh at this preposterous, lying humbug of a friend. "What luck with the charts?"

Jean-Pascale waved his hand at a waiter for service and then turned to Michael, his brow creased in a curious frown. "Most unusual," he said. "I got to the Institute when it opened this morning and went straight to the archives to look up your caves. There's been a lot of exploring done around that area in the last ten or twenty years but nothing at all in your precise sector. Finally, with the help of a clerk, I found an old volume that covered all exploration up to the late 1930s in the southeast corner of France, and you know what? The eight pages covering your lake and that tight little area were missing."

"You mean stolen, or . . ."

"Well, let's not get dramatic." Jean-Pascale laughed. "Some enthusiast probably didn't bother to wait to photostat the charts and ran off with the pages. I don't see why anyone would actually go out of his way to literally steal them. The clerk took my name and address and said he'd continue to look around and send over stats of whatever he found. Nosy bastard, that one—asked a lot of questions about why I wanted the charts. Told him I was planning to open a whorehouse down there." Jean-Pascale chuckled to himself, remembering how he'd shocked the superior smile off the clerk's handsome face. He took a long, slow sip of the beer the waiter put before him.

"Anyway, you can be sure there are caves aplenty down there," he continued casually.

"How do you know?" Michael asked.

"Elementary, *mon cher* Watson—eight pages were missing. If eight pages were devoted to just that small sector, that means a lot of exploration and charting of it was done at some time. I must say, you've got me curious now. After lunch I'll head over to the students' spelunker club and see if by any chance they've got something in their files. They usually keep up-to-date charts on all cave systems their members are likely to investigate. Failing that, maybe old Professor Musquère can help. Do you remember him, the geology professor at the Polytechnique when we were there?"

"No, I can't say the name rings a bell," Michael answered. "Remember, we didn't take all the same courses."

"Well, he used to do a lot of cave exploration, and, as I recall, he came from Marseilles, which isn't all that far from the area you're interested in. I don't think he's at the Polytechnique anymore—he must be about a hundred and ninety by now—but I'll track him down."

"I'd really appreciate that, but will it take a long time?"

"I don't think so." Jean-Pascale looked at the menu; it reminded him of the coming evening. "Look, Nicholas and Colette have invited me for dinner tonight— I'll bring whatever I find with me. Now how about that lunch you promised? I gave up eating with a real beauty today, so the least you can do to make up for it is to buy me a bottle of good wine."

During lunch Jean-Pascale rattled on happily about the humorous problems of their student days, not really aware that Michael was lost in thought over other subjects. They parted after a Cognac and Jean-Pascale dashed off down the boulevard to the student spelunker club, leaving his friend more impatient than ever *and* with a long afternoon to kill. Michael decided he might as well make good use of the time by brushing up on the science of speleology.

It was only a brief walk to the Sorbonne library where he immersed himself in books on all aspects of the subject, soon losing all track of time. He had no idea of the dangers involved in cave exploration and the equipment one needed. He read of an unfortunate spelunker who had built a small fire in the mouth of a cave in Texas that was filled with years of accumulated bat guano. It was the last anyone ever saw of him; the fire set off a tremendous explosion in the decomposing, combustible guano and the cave burned for two years. Another man had built a fire inside a small cave and lost consciousness because he burned up all his oxygen; he fell to his death. These were, perhaps, the more spectacular ways of meeting one's end. The ordinary spelunker seemed to meet his by slipping on muddy rocks, falling from rotten cliff faces, getting wedged in narrow crawlways, or drowning in underground torrents. All in all, Michael decided it wasn't a very happy environment in which to spend one's time.

He reviewed the impressive list of equipment needed just to survive in a subterranean system. Thank heaven the crew of the *Krait* was already in the process of assembling it on the assumption that he would be returning with a map of the caverns leading to Madame Bardoff's "back door." Many of the techniques that Michael had used during his few mountain-climbing expeditions would be extremely useful in descending below the earth's surface. He reviewed them mentally —the use of ropes and guide lines, the rappel for vertical descents, and the relative safety of various belaying techniques. The more he read, the less enticing became the idea of crawling down and around in the darkness over wet, muddy rocks lit only by the faint glow of a carbon lamp or a flashlight. The library's closing bell brought him back to the surface with a jolt.

It was late afternoon as he retraced his steps down the Boulevard St. Michel, crossed the Seine, and turned left to the apartment on Quai des Orfèvres. Sarah called down to him from the narrow balcony and by the time he joined the women there, an iced drink was waiting. Sarah looked fresh and cool in a simple but sophisticated long dinner dress.

"I just had to splurge," she said. "I wanted to feel *madly* beautiful and chic this evening." Sarah slowly turned to show herself off while Colette stood behind beaming like a proud parent.

"You look more fantastically sensational than even I

could have dreamed ever possible," Michael responded, rising eloquently to the occasion.

"You don't have to go overboard," Sarah said, laughing, "but don't you dare take it back."

The three sat on the balcony, sipping their drinks in silence while looking over the Paris skyline or down at the river where a slowmoving bâteau mouche now glided past crowded with tourists looking up at the lovely façades of the old buildings rising on the banks above them. The serenity of the scene was spoiled only by the frequent blaring and tooting of tinny automobile horns fighting the slow traffic inching along the far bank of the Seine.

Nicholas returned from the hospital around 7:30 P.M. and, after a quick shower and change into casual clothes, sat hunched over a backgammon board with Michael, both men absorbed in the serious battle going on between them. Sarah watched the two from her chair on the balcony. The single lamp on the table cast a soft glow over them as the rest of the living room slowly faded in the rosy shadows of the setting sun. It was hard for her to imagine that the man who sat smiling across the table from his gentle friend, the man who had begun to mean more and more to her every day, was the same person who had killed two people in Cannes without seeming to bat an eye. She wished that backgammon game were the only battle Michael would ever have to fight again, but although he'd said nothing, she knew he would be returning to kill or be killed.

Colette came back from the kitchen and sat next to her. "I can't understand what's keeping Jean-Pascale," she said. "He's usually late, but never this late—it's after eight-thirty."

"Why don't you telephone," Sarah suggested.

"Can't—he hasn't been able to get a phone put in yet. Can you imagine, he's lived there for almost two years and still no new phones are available in that quarter."

Michael had been eavesdropping on their conversation. "If he's not here in the next ten minutes or so, I'll go across the river to his flat; it's only a fifteen-minute walk. Can you hold dinner that long?"

"Barely—why not go now? If he's involved with an-other of his girl friends, bring them both. I know he's not at his shop because there wasn't any answer when I phoned earlier."

"I'm off," Michael said, rising from the table.

"Let me come with you," Sarah begged.

"Not dressed like that—every man on the street would be after you. Besides, I can make it faster on my own."

In the back of his mind, Michael attributed Jean-Pascale's lateness to the fact that he had had trouble getting the cave charts. By going to his flat, he might be able to discuss them quietly with him there and so not let Sarah and the others know what he and his old friend were up to.

It was dark by the time he arrived at 37 Rue de l'Université and only a few couples strolled slowly down the street, pausing occasionally to peer into a gal-lery or antique shop window. The small street door was not locked as it had been the previous evening, and Michael looked up at the lights in Jean-Pascale's win-dows as he crossed the courtyard. He had just started up the stairs to the third-floor flat when a figure running down bumped into him. Their eyes met briefly, Mi-chael catching just a glimpse of his face in the shadows as the handsome stranger fled quickly across the court-yard to the street door. Michael turned to watch him, finding something vaguely familiar about him, when his nose picked up the faint smell of gas. Almost before he could react, he was hurled back across the landing and smashed to the floor by the force of the horrendous explosion that blew out the entire south wall of the building into the courtyard, bringing down with it large sections of floor, flying glass, shattered wood, plaster, and the screams of those dying beneath.

Michael staggered to his feet, choking in the gray dust swirling about him, and leaned stunned against the wall, his head ringing from the tremendous concussion. Blood ran from his torn right cheek. He looked through the thick dust clouds up the stairwell; it was blocked by a jumble of wood and plaster that had collapsed into it. There was no way up to Jean-Pascale. He climbed over a pile of rubble back through the lower hall door into the courtyard and looked about in a daze at the disemboweled building. Flames began to dance up through torn walls and empty windows as sirens shrieked in the distance. His friend's third-floor flat no longer existed—no floor, no ceiling, nothing— just a few pipes sticking out from a wall, one of them gushing flame. Michael looked numbly about this nightmare. He saw an arm extending out from under a pile of stone and timber and began scratching frantically at it. Hands dragged him up from his knees and pulled him away; the police and firemen were now swarming over the death-strewn courtyard, hoses trained on the fires and stretchers moving in and out. The limp form of a small child not more than four or five was carried by and to his left; two bodies, unrecognizable except for the shreds of their clothing, lay on stretchers. He gulped back his sob as he saw the blood-soaked remains of a yellow-and-blue striped shirt on one of them, the same shirt Jean-Pascale had worn at lunch.

Lost in the frantic activity of the courtyard, Michael stood overwhelmed by grief, seeing everything but hearing nothing. Tears ran from his open eyes, leaving streaks down his dust-covered face. It was perhaps the first "unmanly" emotional reaction he'd allowed himself since leaving home—and he found no shame in it.

He stumbled slowly out into the street now clogged with the curious trying to peer in through the courtyard doors at the hoses, fire, and rescuers. "The gas, it is the gas in these old buildings," he heard someone saying. "Just last week another went up—boom!—on Quai Voltaire. Did you see it?"

Michael kept seeing the yellow-and-blue shirt on the stretcher and the face of the man who'd run past him on the stairs. Everything replayed through his mind in slow motion, giving him a chance to observe each detail as if he were a spectator watching himself and the disaster scene through powerful binoculars. That face! He suddenly remembered—it was the beautiful face common to most of Madame's elite corps of killers. "Oh,

God, Jean-Pascale," he sobbed quietly, "I'm so sorry, so very sorry."

He leaned against the wall of the building across the street for almost a quarter of an hour, pressed back by the people crowding in front of him to watch the fire. His brain slowly came back to take hold of reality and began piecing together the tragedy he'd brought to his friend. The missing charts and the nosy clerk in the archives who'd asked for Jean-Pascale's name and address—he was obviously another of Ava Bardoff's watchdogs guarding the secrets of her organization, guarding her subterranean kingdom. He found himself seeing her as Hugo must, as a queen of hell spoiling everyone beautiful who came within her reach. How naïve he'd been, how stupid, to open the doors of her kingdom and ask Jean-Pascale to enter, to risk his life without warning him of the danger or giving him the chance to defend himself. The Palots, he thought —I'm doing the same thing to them. No, Madame's organization would have no reason to even know of their existence unless—unless he were to lead Madame to them.

Michael put his hand to his cheek, feeling for the first time the pain of his wound. As he gently touched the skin, sticky from his blood, he suddenly realized his beard was gone, blown off by the force of the explosion and whatever had flown into his face. Instinctively he put both hands up to shield the face of Michael dePasse, fugitive, as if it were the most sought-after face in Paris. He looked around him at the people in the crowd. Who were they? Had someone recognized him? Had the killer of Jean-Pascale recognized him on the stairs and was he watching him now as he stood in the street? He had to get back to Quai des Orfèvres as quickly as possible; he had to get not only the spare beard Hugo had put in the small overnight case he'd brought with him from the Krait, but also the small gun with the silencer that rested beside it.

The thought that he might have been recognized, might be being watched at this very moment and might be the target for a needle gun, filled Michael with panic not only for his own safety, but for the safety of the three people he loved now sitting back in the warm light of the living room overlooking the Seine and the small baby asleep above them. He couldn't risk leading one of Madame's weasels back to his nest. Holding a handkerchief to cover as much of his face as possible, he moved to the edge of the crowd and then, turning his back on it, walked steadily, but not too fast, back up Rue de l'Université. Instead of turning left toward home, he swung right for two blocks to the Boulevard St. Germain that he knew would be teaming with people out for an evening stroll on a warm summer night.

The Café de Flore was always crowded to capacity. Michael made for it. Weaving through its sidewalk tables, he entered and climbed quickly upstairs to the men's room to clean the wounded face he saw staring back at him in the mirror. He washed off the dried blood and brushed his clothes as best he could to make himself less conspicuous. The cleaning operation had started his wound bleeding again and so he was forced to hold his dampened handkerchief to it as he walked back down the stairs. From the corner near the bar he looked over the crowded café; none of the faces looked familiar. Perhaps Jean-Pascale's killer had been so eager to escape the impending blast and the risk of being seen that he'd fled the scene, not waiting to witness the results of his work. Then another thought hit Michael. What if the killer had questioned Jean-Pascale under drugs and had already found out all he wanted to know about who had asked him to get the charts and where that person was hiding. If that were the case, no one at 68 Quai des Orfèvres would be safe. He envisioned the front of that building exploding outward across the Seine and heard a voice in the crowd watching the fruitless rescue work saying, "The gas, it must have been the gas. Just yesterday another one went up—boom!—on Rue de l'Université. Did you see it?"

Panic again gripped Michael. He left the Café de Flore by the side entrance leading onto a narrow, almost empty street heading toward the river. He had to know if he were being followed; the uncertainty was too unnerving for him. After walking two blocks, he veered off into a small, deserted alley lined only with the tightly shuttered doors of warehouses. Michael hurried past them to the far end of the alley, turned the corner and waited, his ears alert to the slightest sound coming in his direction. He heard nothing. He waited for several more minutes and then peered slowly around the corner, almost hoping he'd see a crouching figure moving silently toward him. The alley was completely empty and there was not an open doorway or recess in which a pursuer could hide. He was safe for the minute, but what about those at Quai des Orfèvres? Were Ava Bardoff's men right now making plans to take him prisoner and eliminate the others?

Michael made a wide circle, crossing onto the island several bridges east of the Pont Neuf, swinging through the now shuttered flower market, and approached Quai des Orfèvres from the right bank. He pressed the bell to the Palots' apartment and pushed quickly through the street door when it buzzed open. As he climbed up the stairs to their first floor, he met Nicholas standing in the hall silhouetted by the light from the living room.

"Did you see the excitement across the river?" he asked. "We heard the explosion from here and the flames were . . ." He broke off in mid-sentence, seeing Michael's face and disheveled appearance. Turning, Nicholas called over his shoulder to the women inside, "We'll be with you in just a minute—our star boarder wants to go to the bathroom." He closed the door on their merry laughter and came forward to grab Michael's arm.

"What in hell happened to you? Come upstairs where I can do something about that face."

Michael's legs were wobbly and he was grateful for Nicholas's support as they climbed the stairs. "Jean-Pascale is dead," he said in a flat voice.

The hesitation in Nicholas's stride was barely noticeable. "Was it the explosion?" he asked quietly, guiding Michael to a sitting position on the edge of the bathtub where he could examine the deep tear in his cheek.

What could Michael answer? Did he say yes, or did he say Jean-Pascale had been murdered? Did he admit his friend had been killed because of him? The truth will have to wait, he thought, taking a page from Hugo's book.

"Yes, there must have been a gas leak—the whole back half of the building blew up just as I was going in."

"You were lucky." Nicholas tilted his head back to apply antiseptic to the wounded cheek. "Anything else I should know now?" he asked almost casually. The two men looked into each other's eyes, each trying to fathom the other. "Shall I send Colette and the baby—and Sarah—away?"

During his long roundabout walk home, Michael had had time to think calmly and rationally about the death of Jean-Pascale. He might have been murdered without being questioned simply to discourage further investigation by an innocent spelunker into Madame's caves, or he might have been questioned and so tied to Michael and, through him, to the Palots. If this were the case, the Palots would be in danger no matter where they went so long as Michael remained free. Rather than risk their lives further, Michael had decided on a plan to remove the danger to his friends. He would appear to offer Madame easy access to himself and, by so doing, eliminate her need to go after others to find him. He would turn himself over in a most innocent and believable way, simply by arranging to meet one of her agents—his supposed father, the Count dePasse. He'd keep his father dangling for several days to give Hugo Montclair the time he desperately needed to organize his attack on Ava Bardoff's empire; her destruction would end the threat hanging over them all. Until meeting the Count, he'd lead a clear but winding trail, one in the opposite direction from Colette, Nicholas, and Sarah.

"No," Michael replied to Nicholas's question, "no, that won't be necessary. You will all be safe."

Nicholas finished administering to the wound and stood by with a concerned expression while Michael carefully applied the second false beard to his face and changed into another pair of his host's slacks and a sport shirt. They went down to face the women with the tragic news of Jean-Pascale's death.

Colette, her face twisted in grief, quietly removed the fifth chair and place setting from the table and the already spoiled dinner was eaten in silence, each lost in his own thoughts. Colette's were of simple sorrow for the loss of a dear friend, Nicholas's filled with worry for his family, and Sarah, not realizing the "accidental" death of a man she'd never met represented another threat to her and Michael, was filled only with relief that he had escaped injury in the blast. Michael felt strangely calm and strong as the self-appointed defender of this family around him. His thoughts were not of the past few hours, but of tonight, tomorrow, and the days following; he was building his strategy, his defenses.

That night Sarah clung to him until sleep loosened her grip. He gently disengaged himself and slipped quietly out of bed, taking the pistol from his case and walking slowly downstairs to the dark living room. He sat hidden in a deep armchair so placed that he could see and hear any movement on the quay before the house and also see through the partly open door into the hallway. No one would be able to invade the sleeping household that night. Tomorrow there would be no reason to do so.

Thursday morning, at Michael's urging, Nicholas managed to get Colette, the baby, and Sarah safely out of the house for an all-day excursion and picnic in the Bois de Boulogne before he left for the hospital. When the house was empty, Michael lifted the telephone and dialed his father's home in Neuilly, the expensive and fashionable residential section not far from the center of Paris. He knew the count would be at his office, but wanted only to buy time with the call. The phone was answered by the butler and Michael asked to speak with the count.

"Monsieur le Comte is not at home now. May I take a message?"

"Do you know where I can reach him?" Michael asked, trying to sound as desperate as possible.

"Who is calling?"

"This is his son, Michael. I got to Paris yesterday and must see my father."

There was a brief pause on the other end of the line. "I shall give your father the message. Where can he reach you?"

"Damn," Michael said, "he can't telephone me back —I'm at a pay station and must go. I'll have to call again later in the day. I've been staying on the left bank but I'm leaving this morning to visit friends in Montmartre for the next day or two."

"Do you wish to phone his office? The count's number is . . ."

Before the butler could give the number, Michael cut him off; he didn't want to speak to his father so soon. "Tell him I'll phone this evening. Goodbye."

He replaced the receiver, well pleased with the call. If he had been seen in Paris last night, it should create some confusion, establish that he was ignorant of his "father's" connection with the seamier side of the House of Bardoff, and that he was on the move, staying far from Quai des Orfèvres. And, knowing the Paris telephone system, Michael was sure the unexpected call couldn't be traced back to Nicholas and Colette. Checking his beard, he left the house and headed for the chaotic flower market several blocks away. He lost himself in the crowd and, when he was sure no one was following him, he leaped into a taxi for the Polytechnique. It took him over an hour of cajoling, flirting, and begging various secretaries in the university's records office to track down the current address of the retired Professor Musquère who now lived in rooms in the Palais Royal near the Louvre.

Michael took a taxi to the Champs Elysée, walked several blocks, and then jumped into another cab just as it crossed an intersection on a warning light, leaving the cars following it trapped on the other side of the wide boulevard. The taxi dropped him off at the rear entrance to the Palais Royal beside one of Paris's most famous Old World restaurants, le Grand Vefour, the favorite meeting place for those well known in the arts over the years.

The Palais was a vast, elegant, rectangular structure four stories high surrounding a large and beautiful garden with a large central fountain and neat rows of carefully pruned trees. The southern end of the building contained government offices and the Theâtre Français. An interior colonnade circled the garden within the remaining three sides of the Palais. Small, exclusive shops opened onto it, and above was a mixture of the grand apartments and smaller rooms of a wide variety of occupants from the very wealthy to pensioners.

Michael climbed the stairs to Professor Musquère's small flat on the top floor under the mansard roof. His knock went unanswered for many minutes but finally the door opened a crack. An old gentleman with long, unkempt, white hair and a weather-beaten, lined face looked out. "Yes, young man? What do you want?"

"Professor Musquère?"

"Of course," he snapped. "Who else would I be?"

"My name is Jean-Pascale Melia." Michael thought it best to continue all investigation of the caves in the name of his dead friend; he couldn't be tracked down and killed twice. "I was a student of yours eleven years ago—do you remember me?"

"You flatter yourself, young man." The eyes twinkled with the sarcastic humor common to most of the egoistic educators of the Polytechnique. "I assume I did not fail you or else you would not be standing at my door today."

The old man undid the chain and held open the door to his small, dusty sitting room, the walls lined with bookcases, their contents overflowing onto tables, chairs, and the faded Oriental carpet. Two small dormer windows looked out over the treetops to the far side of the Palais.

Michael entered and stood respectfully while Professor Musquère, his once powerful frame now bent low with arthritis, walked painfully across the room and eased himself into his well-worn desk chair. He waved his cane at Michael.

"Sit down, young man. It is not often I am visited by my pupils. What is it you want? I doubt you have come merely to pass the time of day?"

"No, Professor," Michael answered, "you're right. I've come in hopes that you may have information about some caves in the southeast. You see, I'm a spelunker of sorts and . . ."

"A spelunker, are you?" His eyes danced with enthusiasm. "No matter what marks I gave you at the Polytechnique, I officially upgrade you this very minute. Tell me, what systems have you explored recently? Have you tried the vats of Sassenage? I remember when my team and I descended two hundred meters into . . ."

"I've been exploring only a very short time," Michael interrupted gently, but the professor carried on as if not hearing.

". . . into Landeau's Shaft. At the bottom we found the Great Gallery, a magnificent living gallery—what a sight. The stalactites, columns, and flowstone displays were unbelievable, and the room of icicles—breathtaking. I used to visit it every few years. One of the small halls bears my name. Yes, when I was younger . . ."

The professor talked in glowing terms of the wonders beneath the ground and his explorations while rattling off names, places, and dates with precision. Michael was relieved that although his body had worn, the professor's mind remained bright and sharp. Coming to the end of a small lecture on calcite pearls, he looked quizzically at Michael.

"What systems did you say you've explored? But then you said you've not been at it long," he said, partially answering his own question.

Sidestepping a direct reply, Michael said, "Actually I'm particularly interested in going down into the caves near Comps."

"Comps," the old man said in surprise. "I, myself, spent many happy times exploring them before the war. But which caves? Several systems lie under that area. There are some interesting chambers, but on the whole, most of the passages are disappointing. I would recommend you go closer to Colmoars."

"Perhaps another time, Professor. Right now it's this area that interests me most." He pulled out Halvorsen's contour map and spread it out before the professor.

"Whoever drew this map is certainly no amateur. Did you do it?" the old man asked.

"No, I'm afraid not—a friend in our party did it. I tried to find the charts of the systems in the archives at the Institute, but they were missing."

"That is not very surprising. To my knowledge, little exploration of this area has been done since the war, and the Nazis often destroyed the records of cave systems that they might have used for military purposes or as storage bunkers. You're not after looted treasure, are you?"

Michael smiled and shook his head. "No, a different kind of treasure, perhaps."

"Let me see." The professor studied Halvorsen's map carefully, nodding his disheveled head from time to time. "Yes," he said finally. "Get me that large volume with the brown and red binding over there. Be careful—it is in a most fragile condition."

Michael gave the heavy book to Professor Musquère, who thumbed through it quickly, shaking his head. "No, not in here. Let me think." His eyes stared long and hard at the ceiling. "The Comps, the Comps," he repeated over and over under his breath.

"I believe there's an underground river there that may feed the big lake in the wildlife preserve," Michael prompted.

"Underground river? But of course," the old man said, hitting his head. "You must be referring to the Styx system. We called it that when I was exploring it because of that river—it can be very nasty. We always joked about Charon coming across it to ferry any of us who were careless down to Hades. Oh, yes, I certainly remember that one. I've never seen official charts of it, but I've got my drawings and notes here somewhere."

He lifted himself painfully from his chair and moved slowly to a section of the bookcases filled with notebooks—the professor's private archives of the subterranean. As he pushed, pulled, and thumbed through the pages, he continued to talk about the Styx system.

"If you're going down there, be very careful. I've heard that it has become extremely dangerous. I know of two parties that have tried it in the last few decades and they both met with trouble. Several fell to their deaths and others died of gas—they ran into a great deal of gas." He cocked his head to one side in thought. "Strange, that. As I recall, that particular system was not really difficult to navigate and we encountered no trouble with gas pockets." Then, continuing to riffle through a notebook, he added, "But you never know what the earth is up to, maybe a fissure has opened somewhere in the system."

After some twenty minutes of search, the old man smiled triumphantly. "Here it is—I knew I had it somewhere. Nineteen thirty-seven—that's the last time I went down into that system. I was on holiday back in Marseilles and we explored them for a week—covered a lot of territory that time."

He moved back to his desk and settled once again in his chair, spreading his drawings out before him. "Now, let us see where we are." His gnarled left forefinger traced the contours of Halvorsen's map while his right hand turned the pages of his personal notes on the caves. "Well, here we have your lake. Yes, the feeding river flows through a very old system, much of it dead now, consisting of large but boring galleries. We've charted it as far back as twenty-eight miles to the northeast. Look here."

Michael leaned over the professor's shoulder, his eyes moving from the drawings to Halvorsen's map. "What part of the cave system lies under this point?" he asked, pointing to an X exactly halfway between Ava Bardoff's château and factory.

After a few minutes of study, the professor said, "I should think the Great Hall is there. You see there are two halls running almost parallel to each other. The upper one, the one we call the Great Hall, is the largest

and the one through which the river flowed millions
of years ago. The smaller hall below it is a living
gallery and now carries the river although some of the
spring overflow still is forced through the other."

"How big is the Great Hall?"

"Oh, it runs almost a mile, and most of it has a high
ceiling, forty meters in places. The Great Hall is a
huge room all right, but as I said, relatively boring. If
you do go down, young man, do it in the summer
when there is little chance of bad weather. Although
there are large halls and galleries in the Styx system,
there are more small passages that completely fill
with water even under conditions of moderate rain. In
the spring it is impossible."

"What's the best way in?" Michael persisted, greedy
to get all the information possible from the expert. "I
mean, the entrance closest to the Great Hall."

"Let me see." Again the gnarled finger began to trace
back over the passages in the notebook. "There are
several entrances. This sinkhole is a good way in, but as
I recall that is where the last party got in trouble.
Three died just climbing down the ladder—the others
were disheartened and gave up. Further back about a
mile we have a smaller entrance with a more difficult
descent of some seventy-five meters into water—make
sure you take some good, strong rubber boats. Now
here we have an interesting series . . ."

Michael and Professor Musquère spent the rest of
the afternoon discussing the Styx system, even while
lunching on an impromptu meal of cheese, fruit, and
wine. The old man delighted in the rapt attention of
his young companion and by the time he left at 4:00
P.M., Michael had complete copies of the professor's
charts of the cave system and his notes. He promised
to return to the top-floor room in the late fall to tell
his new friend of his explorations; it was a promise
Michael hoped he'd be able to keep.

He walked quickly along the west colonnade of the
Palais Royal and out through the side gate beside
the Théâtre Français to the public telephones in the
small square before the theatre. After completing a
brief call to Chris Halvorsen, who was waiting for him

at the decaying Hôtel des Étrangers just off Boulevard St. Michel, he took a taxi to deliver the charts of the caverns of the Styx.

"It's all here," he called to Halvorsen as he entered the cramped, uncomfortable hotel room. Michael went over in great detail all the old professor had told him, describing the past misadventures of other spelunkers and the relative difficulty of the different entrances into the cave system.

"Sounds as if Madame's men make sure no one gets close to the Great Hall," Halvorsen commented. "We're obviously going to need masks against her homemade natural gas, and to be well armed."

Michael told him of Jean-Pascale's murder and his plans for leaving a false trail with the Count dePasse.

"Be careful and stall until Monday if you can—that's when we'll be ready to go after her. The yacht will be on the far side of St. Tropez then. Use our special number—after we've had a chance to digest these charts, we'll give you instructions for the rendezvous. By the way, Hguo got the information he wanted from the President. It seems the heads of the major Western states are meeting in Corsica in ten days' time, ostensibly for a mini-summit, but really to draw up plans for a possible invasion of the Arab oil fields."

Michael looked aghast. "You're not serious."

"They're in the planning stage, nothing more," Halvorsen assured him. "Apparently they've got wind of another oil embargo coming their way very soon."

"Tell Hugo that while we were driving up here, Sarah remembered that our friend, Madame Bardoff, had meetings with several tycoon types from the Ruhr Valley. That's the big coal and steel region, isn't it?"

"That's right."

"She also met with some of the shah's sheik friends in New York before she left for France."

"Coal and oil," Halvorsen mused. "It looks like Madame may be sticking her fingers into the energy pool. Add to it the fact that the secretary of state, who will be attending the Corsica meeting, is now with the shah and our Russian comrade and you have a very intriguing situation. I wonder who's double-crossing whom and what part she's playing in it. Whatever it is, I'll bet it stinks."

"Everything about this stinks," Michael said acidly. "I've got to go now. You're leaving directly for the *Krait?*" The Swede shook his head affirmatively. "Well, give my regards to the others. Unless you need me sooner, I'll leave Paris Sunday after I hide Sarah away somewhere safe." He grasped the other's hand. "Good luck."

"You, too." Halvorsen closed the door after Michael and went to the window overlooking the boulevard below. He watched as the newest member of Hugo's group walked a block or two before hailing a taxi. He saw no one following him. Carefully placing the charts and notes and a few clothes in his bag, Halvorsen left the room to return to the yacht, which, if all were going according to plan, should now be moving toward its anchorage off St. Tropez.

Michael directed his driver to drop him at the Place Dauphine, the tiny triangular square behind Quai des Orfèvres. Many of the ground-floor shops opened onto this square as well as the quay. He entered the little art gallery next to the bookstore in number 68 from the rear and walked nonchalantly from one painting to the next, pretending to study them. He lingered longest in front of those by the window looking onto the quay to study not the art, but the people on the street. Smiling at the proprietor, who shrugged at another lost sale, Michael left and walked the ten yards to the recessed entrance of Number 68. Using his key, he entered and climbed quietly up to the living room, pausing with his ear to the door. After a minute he unlocked the door and, getting down on his knees, pushed it open an inch or two. Reaching carefully around it with his fingers he could feel that the broom straw he'd leaned against it before leaving was still in place; the same was true of the Palots' other doors leading onto the hallway of the building. He made a quick search of the entire six floors of hallway but found no suspicious bundles that might be bombs.

Highly relieved that Madame Bardoff's forces still did not seem to know of the existence of Nicholas and Colette, Michael sank into a chair by the French doors with a drink in his hand to await the return of Sarah and Colette. About thirty minutes later he saw them strolling down the quay in deep conversation, Sarah pushing the baby carriage. How natural she looks doing that, he thought. He pretended that it was his son in the carriage being wheeled home to a proud father. Father, that word brought him back to reality. He briefly reviewed his mission. The first part had been accomplished; he'd established the existence of a huge cavern beneath the château and found the way into it. Now he had to play cat and mouse with Ava Bardoff, using his false father as a pawn. He hoped he could carry it off.

Once more cocktails were served on the balcony overlooking the Seine, the soft, pink light of the late afternoon sun filtering through the trees lining the river. Michael arranged to sit just inside the door, where he could enjoy the conversation with the others, but could not be seen from the street below. As if by mutual agreement, no mention was made of Jean-Pascale. The women maintained a running commentary on everything they'd seen and done on their outing in the Bois with the baby. Nicholas entertained them with amusing anecdotes of some of the more spoiled and eccentric patients he'd had to deal with that day, including the scene made by the Baroness "Quelque Chose" when she had not been allowed to keep her seven poodles beside her bed, and their eventual stampede through the hospital corridors, upsetting nurses, orderlies, not to mention the decorum of that august institution.

After a simple dinner, Michael excused himself and went to Nicholas's bedroom to use the phone secretly. In answer to his name, he was passed almost immediately to the Count dePasse.

"Michael," the Count said with unaccustomed warmth, "what brings you to Paris in the summer? When did you arrive?"

Was this genuine ignorance or planned innocence? Michael wondered. No sense being caught in a lie at this point. "Tuesday night, Father," he answered.

"I was told you wanted to see me. Why don't you come to the house now."

"I can't, not now. I'm in a bit of trouble and have to keep out of sight."

"Where are you staying? I'll come to you."

"Right now I'm in Montmartre at a small hotel, but I have to keep moving, changing addresses. You'd better not come to me—I don't want to put you in any danger."

"Touching concern on your part after all these years," the Count countered in the imperious tone to which Michael was more accustomed.

Unknown to Michael, Sarah had come into the adjoining bedroom.

"That's more like it, Father," Michael said, "just as cold as ever. I was beginning to think you really cared."

"Get on with it, Michael. If you're in trouble of some sort, let's get it cleared up. You know in my position I can't stand to have scandal attached to my name. Come to the house tomorrow morning—I'll wait for you here."

"I can't, Father. I must meet some people in Versailles tomorrow—it's very important. Can we meet Saturday afternoon, either at the house, or, better still, at the villa in the country?"

"I would prefer to meet you tonight."

"I cannot."

"Very well then, Saturday at the house at five o'clock. Don't be late—I, too, have important meetings to attend."

"And your meetings are more important than your son?"

"Michael, do not try to start a quarrel." There was a marked pause on the other end of the phone. The Count's voice softened again. "Michael, let me send the car for you now. Where are you staying?"

"I've got to go now. Saturday at five o'clock—sharp." Michael hung up and sat on the bed, smiling. Things had gone well. Believing he would deliver himself into their hands on Saturday, the hunt for him in Paris, if indeed there had been one, would be called off. And Madame might think that Michael's ally or allies in this operation were now in Versailles, hopefully taking the pressure off Hugo' and his men back on the Riviera. Saturday he'd call and postpone the meeting with the Count until the next day; by then it would be too late to either find him or stop Hugo's move against Ava Bardoff.

He left the room, not seeing Sarah standing back in the shadows of the nursery. So, she thought, Michael was seeking help from his very powerful and influential father. How wonderful; this could solve all their problems. He could certainly bring in the police or the army or something to arrest Ava and put her away where she couldn't hurt them. What a shame, though, that Michael and his father didn't get along well. Sarah was sure they could solve their problems if they'd only give each other a chance. That man is probably terribly proud of his son and all those awards and Olympic medals, but he just doesn't know how to go about telling Michael he loves him. Men are such stubborn fools, she thought. Perhaps I can help bring them back together.

Sarah walked over to the phone table. The top page of the small note pad beside the instrument was covered with doodles, one of which was a series of boxes surrounding a telephone number with a Neuilly exchange. Sarah reached down and tore off the page, folding it carefully. She put it in her pocket.

Sure that the danger to 68 Quai des Orfèvres had been removed, Michael felt more relaxed about leaving Colette alone in her own home the next morning. He insisted on taking Sarah out for a little personal tour of some of his favorite spots on the Île—those places that had meant a great deal to him as a boy, those places that had given him comfort during troubled times.

They started with Ste. Chapelle, the magnificent little royal chapel seemingly made of nothing but stained glass and tall, thin, incredibly graceful columns that rose to the heavens, where they formed a lacy network of arches over their heads. Then on to the flower market in the center of the island where Michael, filled with laughter and gaiety, loaded Sarah's arms with one bunch of brilliantly colored summer flowers after another. When she couldn't hold another stem more, they went on to Nôtre Dame cathedral and proceeded to give all but one away to passing strangers, delighting in the surprised and happy expressions that flooded their faces.

They strolled hand in hand back down the quay to the tip of the island and walked down a long flight of stone steps to the small triangular park on the water, twenty feet below street level and the statue of the Vert Gallant, who sat up there on his bronze horse scowling at the bleating traffic that invaded his island. The neatly kept little park was empty and seemed cut off and centuries away from the automobiles and taxis above. Sarah and Michael sat on the cobblestones of the embankment under a great willow tree and watched the Seine flow silently by, carrying the leaves they tossed into it away past the stately buildings and graceful trees lining its banks. The morning sun cast mottled patches of light around them as it filtered through the willow.

Michael's earlier exuberance and gaiety faded, and he lapsed into silence.

"Would it be corny to say, 'A penny for your thoughts?' " Sarah asked.

He looked over at her with a faint smile and took her hand in his. "No—they were all of you, anyway." He sat quietly staring at the water for another minute or two before continuing. When he spoke he didn't look at her. "I was thinking how you looked last evening pushing Nicholas's son in the carriage along the quay. I wanted him to be my son and . . ." He didn't complete the sentence—he didn't know how.

"You want a family again, don't you?" she asked quietly.

"Yes." His answer came out naturally, without any embarrassment. It surprised him a little; he'd never talked before of his needs, of his private thoughts. Now Michael wanted to share them. As he sat with Sarah warm against him, the Seine faded and his eyes saw only ripe, golden fields and gentle hills. "I've got some land in the southwest near Langon—no one knows about it. There are a few empty outbuildings on it now. I've let the land out to local farmers for grazing, but someday I'm going to build it up into one of the best stud farms in the country." He looked back at Sarah. "You like to ride, don't you? I remember you said you and your father rode a lot."

"I love horses," she said simply, wanting him to continue with his dreams.

"I wish you could see it—I want you to see it. We'll go there after this—" he tensed—"this mess, this rotten, terrible . . ."

She shook her head. "Don't, don't talk about it, please," Sarah pleaded. "This is our day—don't spoil it."

Michael sighed and relaxed against the trunk of the willow, pulling Sarah back against him, his arms securely around her. He needed the feel of her hair on his cheek, the faint smell of her skin.

"And what are your plans?" he asked. "Are you always going to be a loner?"

Sarah looked away, wondering why the two of them couldn't just come right out and say they wanted to be with each other, wondering why they had to keep going around in circles. "I don't want to be a loner anymore." She watched a shabby red barge drifting down the river.

"I've got a secret place, too. I've kept the tiny cottage my parents had in Cornwall—it's in a little fishing village. You can see the harbor and the boats coming back at night from the front windows. When it stormed I used to curl up in a little ball and feel cosy and warm covered with quilts in my great four-poster bed. I haven't changed a thing since the accident, since my parents died—staying there was like being with them again, remembering all the times we had together. When I think of the cottage now it seems part of the past, so far away—empty. I don't know if I want to go back there again—not alone. I guess I'm tired of having only memories. I want a future."

She felt suddenly cold in the hot sun as she realized they might not be allowed a future together. She saw Hugo's image and Ava's beautiful and smiling face blended together before her, threatening her life with Michael. She forced them away, pretending she and Michael were like Colette and Nicholas. Michael, too, was lost in thoughts. The scent of her hair filled him, and he kissed it. She took both his hands and snuggled more securely back into his arms.

"It would be nice," Sarah said half aloud, picturing their life in 68 Quai des Orfèvres. Michael nodded, seeming to know what she was thinking.

Later they walked slowly to a small restaurant surviving in the old Les Halles area. It was as if they were on the honeymoon each subconsciously feared they might not have; they drank too much *vin cassis* and devoured assorted sausages, meats, and bowls of thick bean soup, laughing and giggling with each other. "Not another thing," Sarah called, "I'll explode."

"You shall, my love. The *gâteau au chocolat* is to cry over. *Deux gâteaux,*" Michael demanded of the waiter smiling at them from across the room, *"et encore de vin."*

"No, no," Sarah protested. "You'll have to carry me home."

"To Cornwall or Langon?" Michael asked.

She didn't answer; she didn't have to—the question said it all for them. They smiled at each other and said very little as they finished the cake and coffee. Sarah suddenly looked at her watch.

"I've got to leave—oh, damn. I've got a fitting at a boutique on the Faubourg St. Honoré and another little errand to do."

"I'll go with you," he offered happily. "You shan't escape me, not today."

"I can't have a man standing around while I'm having a fitting or shopping," she exclaimed. "You are the most impatient beasts God ever turned out. I'll be back home in time for cocktails and I expect you to collapse at my feet with admiration—I've got a lovely surprise for you."

"Ah ha—what is it?"

"It's a secret," she said, teasing.

"Tell me or I won't let you go."

"Oh, yes you will, and you'll wait for me to tell you all about it tonight."

"Just like a woman, devious."

"Just like a man, demanding."

Sarah gulped the last of her coffee and, blowing Michael a kiss, darted away laughing as he frantically called the waiter for the check. By the time he'd thrown his money on the table and dashed out of the restaurant, Sarah had vanished. He wandered aimlessly about the area, looking blankly into shop windows, trying to kill time. "This is ridiculous," he finally said aloud and hailed a taxi to return to the Sorbonne library and plunged himself back into the subterranean world beneath him. At least, he reasoned, it was a more productive use of his time than pacing the streets waiting for her.

At 6:30 that afternoon, Michael *was* pacing—not the streets, but the living room of 68 Quai des Orfèvres. He'd been waiting for Sarah to return for over an hour and a feeling of apprehension had been building within him during the entire time. He should never have let her out of his sight—he should have insisted on going with her.

"For heaven's sake, Michael, I don't know what you're so worried about," Colette said from the chair by the desk where she sat doing her needlework. "Sarah's a big girl, she'll be back soon."

"She said she'd be back in time for cocktails with a surprise. It's after cocktail time and she's not here," he complained petulantly. "Where was she going for her fitting? I'll call the shop."

"Michael, that's ridiculous, now stop worrying. Besides, it's too late—the boutique will be closed."

"I don't care, give me the number."

With some annoyance, Colette put aside her work and crossed the room to the telephone, where Michael stood impatiently. She riffled through the pages of the directory and gave him the number of the boutique on the Faubourg St. Honoré. He dialed it and stood anxiously waiting for an answer. Michael really didn't expect one, but he still held on to the receiver hoping —there was nothing else he could think to do.

"I really don't understand why you're so upset," Colette said. "Honestly, I've never seen you like this before."

He looked down at her, fumbling for some sort of an explanation. "Well, you see, Sarah was mixed up in that little hoopla I had down on the Riviera and I'm naturally concerned she might have been recognized by the police and be in some trouble over it."

"Well, if that's all you're worried about, you can relax. She's perfectly safe." Colette smiled smugly.

"You sound as if you know where she is."

"Michael, it's Sarah's surprise—I don't want to spoil it. Can't you wait until she gets back? You know how bad the traffic can be at rush hour. She's probably hung up somewhere in a taxi. Be patient—have a drink."

"I'll give it thirty more minutes and then I'll wring the story out of you," Michael threatened, only partially in jest.

After leaving him in the restaurant, Sarah had gone to the boutique on the Fauberge, where she changed into her new dress and left her other clothes to be retrieved the next day. Then, hailing a taxi, she settled back to enjoy the long ride out to Neuilly. The cab crossed into the Place de la Concorde, circled the obelisk and fountains at her request, and swung up the Champs Elysée, weaving through the traffic toward the Arc de Triomphe dominating the skyline ahead. Passing around the monument, the driver continued down the Avenue de la Grande Armée to the Port Maillot and veered left along the boulevard passing the Bois on the left and magnificent houses on the right in some of which she and her parents had been entertained in the past.

Sarah wondered what Michael's father would be like.

He had seemed extremely warm and friendly over the phone when she'd called this morning, and he'd even cancelled a meeting that afternoon to invite her for tea to talk about Michael's problem. Sarah was sure she'd be able to effect some sort of a reconciliation between father and son if she could just get them to admit how much they respected, loved, and even needed each other. I know he'll help Michael and me, she thought, I can feel it in my bones.

Sarah was trying to form a picture of him in her mind as the taxi pulled to a halt in front of a large brick house set back from the street behind an ornate iron fence. Paying the driver, she walked to the high gate, lifted the latch, and pushed hard. It opened slowly and then swung back shut with finality behind her. The house and grounds were very stark—no flowers, only ivy and other assorted ground cover shaded by large fir trees. The draperies in most of the windows were drawn. She had to admit that Michael had been right in his description—it was not the most friendly and inviting place she'd ever seen.

A few doubts had begun to creep into her mind by the time she'd reached the front steps leading up to a formidable front door. Both this heavy glass door and the narrow windows on either side were covered with an Art Deco pattern of iron bars. What if Michael were furious at her intrusion and meddling in his personal family life? What if she managed to make things worse between the two men? Well, she was there, invited by the count himself; if he cared enough to do that, things couldn't go too far wrong.

A powerfully built butler answered the bell and showed Sarah across a large square entrance hall and up the wide alabaster staircase leading to a balcony running around three sides of the hall. Light filtered down from a glass dome three stories overhead, reminding her briefly of Ava's conservatory. The uniformed servant ushered Sarah into what she thought must be the count's library—a large, beautifully furnished room in the Empire style looking out over the grounds to the street and Bois beyond the iron fence. A fastidiously dressed man with distinguished streaks of silver at his temples and a welcoming smile on his face stood up behind an immense Napoleonic desk. He walked around it, approaching Sarah with his hand extended.

"Miss Dilworth, is it not? How delighted I am that you phoned." He took Sarah's hand and led her to a large sofa in front of which an elaborate silver tea service sat on a low table. "I hope you will pour—it is not often that this house is graced by so beautiful a woman."

Sarah was completely taken aback by the warmth of his greeting and quite surprised by the youthfulness of his appearance. He could have been Michael's older brother, certainly not his aging father.

"You're very kind to receive me on such notice," she said.

"Not at all, my dear. Any friend of my son is always welcome. You are aware that he called last evening and acted very strangely. I was most concerned."

"Yes, he's terribly worried and in great danger." She began to play with the tea things absently.

"No sugar or milk—only lemon, please," the count said to help her as he leaned forward to take his cup from her hand. "Exactly what is the trouble in which my son seems to have become involved, Miss Dilworth?"

"I'm sure it would be much better for him to explain it all to you when you see him on Saturday—I'd make a complete muddle of it. I wanted to see you for another reason." Sarah paused, covering her nervousness by taking a sip of her tea. "You see, Michael and I are very close friends and—well, I just felt I had to make you understand how much he needs your support and help, particularly now. No matter what he says or how he acts, I know beneath it all he loves you and is very proud of you, even though he's too stubborn to admit it. He's told me a lot about his childhood and his life after that. He's missed you and his mother very much since—since she became ill."

The count smiled affectionately at her and patted Sarah's hand. "It is very kind of you to concern yourself with our problems, and you are quite right, our differences could easily be overcome with a little understanding on both sides. As you probably know, we have not been very communicative over the last years," he said sadly, and then added more positively, "but I think it's time we changed all that. Where is my son now, Miss Dilworth?"

Sarah hesitated, not really knowing why.

"I would like to see him as soon as possible," the count continued. "If he is in serious trouble, I want to help." He looked directly into Sarah's eyes.

Whether it was instinct or her desire not to go completely against Michael's wishes, she didn't know, but Sarah lied, using what she'd overheard last night. "I don't really know. He's staying somewhere in Montmartre."

"You don't know where he is? Two such close friends?" He seemed to be mocking her. "Come, Miss Dilworth, you can do better than that. When did you see him last?" The charming smile had become set on his face; there was no warmth in it now. Sarah felt suddenly on the defensive.

"We dined last night at a small restaurant in Les Halles, and he's in Versailles somewhere today."

"Miss Dilworth, would you tell me where Michael was—even if you knew?" The smile was gone. The count put his teacup back on the tray.

"Of course. He's in Versailles now and he's staying at some hotel in Montmartre," she repeated desperately.

"No, he is not staying at some hotel in Montmartre." The count's positive rebuttal of her statement startled her. "I've had every hotel and pension in that quarter checked."

"He may be staying with friends, then."

"You're a friend of his, aren't you, Miss Dilworth? A very close and, shall we say, intimate friend?"

Sarah looked down at her hands, not knowing what to do or say. She wanted to run.

"Tell me, Miss Dilworth, how did you leave your charming godmother, Madame Bardoff?"

The complete change of subject shattered Sarah's composure. "I . . . I . . . I'm sure she's fine, thank you."

He laughed. "Don't you think it's about time we stopped playing games, my dear? We don't have all the time in the world, do we?" Count dePasse raised his hand and snapped his fingers over his right shoulder.

Sarah turned to see two men walk out from a screen behind her. They were replicas of the men in the black Mercedes. Her teacup shattered to the floor as she stood up, looking helplessly to her left and right. She started for the door leading to the wide alabaster staircase.

"All right, Colette, the thirty minutes are up and she's not back. Now where is she?" Michael demanded.

It was not his angry tone of voice that made Colette decide to speak up; she'd weathered many of his scenes before. But she, too, was becoming concerned about the long-overdue arrival of her new friend.

"She heard you quarreling on the phone with your father last night," Colette confessed, "and decided to visit him to see if she couldn't bring you two closer together."

"What?" Michael yelled, staring at her in disbelief.

"I told her there was no love lost between the two of you and she'd be lucky to even get inside the house, but she wanted to try."

"When did she go?" He was grasping at straws. A wild thought flashed through his mind that he might be able to intercept her; he couldn't lose her, not now.

"He invited her to tea, around five o'clock, I think. I was quite surprised that he was so eager to meet her."

"Oh, my God," Michael wailed, bringing both fists down on the table, toppling a figurine. "Sarah, why . . . why?"

"What's the matter?" Colette asked, very frightened now at his extreme reaction. "Michael, tell me, what's the matter?" she pleaded as he looked past her out the French doors, his mind no longer in this room.

Like some horrible nightmare, he saw Sarah falling away from him down a deep, black hole, reaching out to him as she turned slowly over and over in the air. Suddenly Michael looked down at the small, frightened woman before him as if he'd seen her for the first time. His brain clicked back into action.

"Colette, don't ask me any questions now—it's too late. Please, just pack what you need, and you and the baby get out of this house—get out right now."

"But . . . but . . ."

Almost in tears from frustration and anger, Michael grabbed her by both arms and shook her. "Don't you understand? You've got to get out."

The door of the living room flew open and Nicholas burst in. "What's going on?" he demanded in alarm.

"Michael's gone mad," Colette cried. "He wants . . ."

"They've got Sarah," Michael told him in agony. "The same people who murdered Jean-Pascale." Colette's face froze in a mask of horror. "And they'll be coming here next. You've got to go now, right now."

Nicholas turned to Colette and said sharply, "Get the baby—we're leaving. Don't bother to pack, just get the baby." Colette ran from the room; he turned back to Michael. "I was afraid of something like this after Jean-Pascale. Why didn't you tell . . ."

"I'm sorry Nicky, really sorry. I should have told you. I should have told Jean-Pascale, but I thought . . . Oh God, I never thought this would happen. Lose yourselves for a week or two, don't even go to the hospital."

"What are you going to do?"

"I don't know—it depends on this phone call. Don't listen." Nicholas left the room to help his wife while Michael called the Neuilly number, paused, and asked to speak to the Count dePasse. "Tell him his son is calling."

After a minute or two he heard the familiar voice. "Hello, Michael, how nice of you to call," the count said sarcastically.

"What have you done with her, Father?" The word father almost stuck in his throat, but he had no other name for the pretender.

"If you are referring to Miss Dilworth, we're about to head south. You'll know where to find us."

"I've got to see you."

"That might be enjoyable, Michael, but I don't really think there's much point in our meeting now, do you? I'm sure Miss Dilworth will be able to tell us what we want to know. However, I do have a message for you—that is, if you're as intelligent as you appear to be. It's from an admirer of yours."

"Father, please—"

"Ava has a very generous offer to make to you." The count continued. "It would be well worth your while to listen to what she has to say. If I were in your position, I'd accept it without hesitation. Why not phone her at the clinic. I must leave with your little friend now. Perhaps we will all meet again very soon."

"Father."

"What?"

"I'm leaving Quai des Orfèvres for good—they know nothing here."

The phone went dead in Michael's hand. He stood staring dumbly at it.

"Well?" Nicholas asked as he entered a minute later.

"I'm going back to Cannes. Don't you or Colette come back here until you hear from me. They may still want to kill you. If I tell you more, then they most certainly will. Can you ever forgive me?"

It was difficult, but Nicholas managed a smile. "Sure we can. Colette will be all right when she has a chance to simmer down. You pulled that old rush act out of nowhere and she's scared out of her wits." His smile faded. "I'm not feeling very brave either."

"I'll go so you can have a few minutes here alone, but please don't drag your heels. Where can I get hold of you? No, don't tell me." Michael scribbled on a piece of paper. "Instead, call this number in one week. And pray someone answers." He gave Nicholas Hugo's secret number; he owed him that much. He embraced his old friend.

"Be careful," Nicholas said with emotion.

"You, too." Michael tore himself away and walked quickly from the room down to the quay where his blue Peugeot waited. The motor purred into action as he turned the key in the ignition and the car moved forward. He glanced up. Nicholas and Colette, her baby tight in her arms, stood on the balcony looking after him. For a second he thought he saw Sarah beside them. He wondered if they were thinking the same thing as he was—would they ever see each other again?

He only drove a few blocks, parking by a line of public telephones before the *prefecteur*. Michael dialed the number Halvorsen had given him. Within a few seconds he heard Carpenter, Hugo's electronics expert, answer.

"Paris here," Michael said. "I've got to talk to the captain. We've got a crisis."

9

Hugo said little as Michael related the details of Sarah's capture. He asked Michael to repeat several times the exact words used by the Count dePasse and requested his assurance that Sarah was no wiser about their plans now than when she had left the *Krait* earlier in the week. That given, Hugo asked, "Would you be willing to sacrifice Sarah for the good of the overall project?"

Michael almost went through the roof of the phone box. "Of course not," he flashed back angrily. "What kind of a person do you think I am? I got her into this thing, and I've got to get her out."

Hugo was silent for some little time after this outburst and then asked, "Is it only your sense of honor as a gentleman or something else that makes you feel this way?" He had an uncomfortable way of making Michael face up to himself.

"If I interpret your question correctly, I guess I have to admit that there's something else."

"You love her," Hugo said flatly.

"Yes, God damn it, I love her. Satisfied?"

Again there was silence on the other end of the phone. Finally Hugo said, "Then we shall have to modify our plans a bit to try to do something about Miss Dilworth, but, my young friend, I fear the success of anything we do along that line will depend almost entirely upon you."

Hugo outlined the details of a plan that would have made Michael weak in the knees had he not been so wrapped up in the urgency of the situation and ended the conversation with a simple wish of good luck and a surprising understatement designed to pick up Michael's spirits. "See you both for dinner tomorrow evening. Don't bother to dress." Hugo's humor rankled rather than encouraged him.

Now that he had been forced to admit his real feelings for Sarah, Michael spent the next fifteen minutes reviewing everything Hugo had said in light of saving her. He didn't like the odds—they were impossible. Michael realized he had no choice and, shaking his head sadly, reluctantly lifted the receiver once again. He slowly dialed the number of the Bardoff clinic. It took only a few seconds to get through.

"Madame Bardoff, my father informs me that you have a very generous offer to make to me."

He was answered by a gay laugh. "Michael, dear Michael, how nice of you to call. I was hoping you would. You made me very angry—you were rude to leave us without saying goodbye."

He felt like a mouse being toyed with by a cat. "I'm sure my manners have little to do with what you wish to say to me," he said curtly.

"I admire an athletic body, a clever mind, and courage." Her voice hardened. "But I wonder how clever and courageous you would be if you were not so very far away." Point well taken, he thought to himself. Ava continued. "We have Sarah." She paused to let the implied threat sink in.

"Sarah knows nothing."

"You are probably quite correct, but *you* know a great deal. I like men who know a great deal—they are very useful. And despite all the trouble you have caused me, I hold no grudges—I admire you for it. I want you to join my—" she paused—"business operation."

"Join you? You must be . . ."

"Do not be naïve," Ava laughed, cutting him off. "You either cooperate with me, join me, or I will have you killed—it is just a matter of time, you know that.

And of course poor Sarah will suffer so, and your nice innocent friends, the Palots. How old is their little baby?"

"The Palots! You touch them and . . . and . . ." he sputtered into impotent silence.

"That is better," she purred. "You see, we really have far more to offer you than you have to give us."

"What exactly is your offer?"

"Life—yours, Sarah's, the Palots'—and a chance to share in the future of the world. I will give you all that for just a little cooperation, just a little information." She paused, waiting for his reply.

"Michael, believe me, I am very fond of you." Ava's voice was filled with genuine warmth. "You would fit in very well with my plans. I think we should talk about it."

After further discussion, Michael agreed to drive directly to the clinic, to arrive there no later than 6:00 A.M. the next morning if he wished to see Sarah again. As Ava had so succinctly put it, "Your way you lose everything—my way you gain everything. There really is not much choice, is there?" He knew she was right.

Replacing the phone, Ava swung around in her desk chair to face Moloch. She put back her head and laughed. "I have won." She laughed. "I have won."

Michael stood back on the bustling street in Paris, staring at the receiver he still held in his hand. How he envied those people walking quickly by him—walking to their homes for dinner, for laughter over coffee, for the chance of being bored by a bad television show. He felt he had the weight of the world resting on his shoulders.

By agreeing to meet Ava Bardoff he'd bought time, he'd removed the immediate danger to Nicholas and Colette to give them a chance to escape, and he'd see Sarah again—at least she'd be alive until he got there. After that it would be up to him. And he'd also delayed any move of Ava's against Hugo and the *Krait;* he was sure Ava would want more information than Sarah could offer before striking out at such a prominent man.

But would it be a futile gesture to resist her when they met? She'd get all the information she wanted from him one way or another. Sarah's capture meant Hugo's attack scheduled for Monday would have to be pushed forward almost forty-eight hours, a change that put an already tenuous operation in extreme jeopardy. With Michael's phone call, Hugo had begun moving his remaining guests to hotels ashore on various pretexts, and his men had been forced to leave the *Krait* to scatter where they could not be found until it was time to strike. And they had to be the first to strike or else Hugo, left alone in luxury on the ship with Petras and a skeleton crew, would be a sitting duck before Madame's hunters, and the only opposition to Ava and the House of Bardoff would vanish.

Racked with indecision, Michael walked to the car parked at the curb and slid in behind the wheel; he sat with his head buried in his hands for several minutes. His happiness, his life with Sarah, his entire future depended on the course of action he chose to take during the next twelve hours. Finally he looked up and, taking a deep breath, jammed the Peugeot into gear to send it screaming in a sharp U turn across the street and over the bridge up the Boulevard St. Michel.

His trip south was agonizing. Sometime in the middle of the night a fine, misty rain began to fall, and the windshield wipers clicked slowly back and forth to form a monotonous background to his thoughts. He reviewed again and again Hugo's improbable scheme and the high odds against its success. If it failed, not only he but Sarah and the Palots would die—they'd die because of him. The sight of Jean-Pascale's bloody body lying on the stretcher in the courtyard at Rue de l'Université focused in his mind. He hated Ava for it, but hadn't it really been his fault for involving his friend in the first place?

It was time to be realistic. Hugo offered him honor and the fulfillment of some vague kind of obligation or responsibility—but to what? Even Hugo didn't seem to know. Ava offered life. He had an obligation, all right—an obligation to his friends and his love for Sarah. There was nothing vague about that. And what about his obligation to himself? Weren't these greater than the one to Hugo, who had only recently recruited him, recruited him almost against his will? What was he doing in this damn thing anyhow?

The glare of car lights passing in the rain stabbed into his tired eyes just as these and other arguments stabbed into his tortured brain, pulling it first one way and then the other. Should he sacrifice his life and the lives of those closest to him in the cause of a man obsessed with good and evil, obsessed almost to the point of insanity? Or should he live, swallow the remnants of his pride, and seize whatever opportunities fate presented? Be realistic, he told himself over and over again.

Reluctantly, he made his decision.

10

Like moths to a flame, the combatants in the forthcoming conflict were drawn inexorably toward Ava Bardoff. There was no turning back now for any of them.

As Michael drove south from Paris, the Count dePasse's private plane swept down along the rain-slick runway of Nice's airport. It executed a sharp turn and taxied to the Bardoff hangar, where an ambulance waited. The count looked at his watch—10:00 P.M. All had gone precisely according to plan. Two attendants climbed into the plane and emerged carrying a stretcher on which Sarah Dilworth lay strapped in a drugged stupor. DePasse got into the ambulance with Sarah and the glistening white vehicle rolled smoothly over the service roads of the airport and out onto the highway leading west to the clinic.

Meanwhile, ten of Hugo's men, led by Watson, the engineer, crept east through the darkness toward the sinkhole entrance to the Styx cave system and the innocent-looking farmhouse nearby that protected it from unwanted intruders.

By the time the ambulance reached the northern entrance of the château, Sarah's head had cleared. Where once the sound of the gravel drive under her car wheels had evoked the warm and secure feeling of home, now it brought terror. She had visions of Ava waiting for her, no longer the beautiful Ava but looking like some ugly, evil witch from a children's fairy tale. She thought of the dismembered body in the flat on Rue St. Denis and felt the pain in her arm that had been so brutally twisted by the Count dePasse's men in their attempt to find Michael's whereabouts. Her left eye was swollen and her lower lip cracked.

"Here we are, my dear," the count said as the doors of the ambulance were opened. "Isn't it nice to be home where you belong?"

The two attendants unstrapped the terrified girl and dragged her roughly from the vehicle into the château and along a lower corridor to a pair of metal doors. She heard a clock somewhere in the great building chiming the hour; it was midnight. The idea of the witches' hour increased her dread. The doors opened and Sarah was pushed forward into an elevator. This confused her; she knew the clinic had no elevator—where was she? The pressure built up in her ears as they descended and she tried to swallow to relieve it, but her throat was too dry. She almost screamed. Where was she? She was going down and down, but to where?

Finally they came to a stop, the doors opened, and Sarah found herself in a well-lighted corridor of modern construction not at all like the château. A low humming sound filled the air; it seemed to be coming from all around her as if the very walls were alive. Men— some dressed in the white uniforms of the clinic attendants and others in the black T-shirts and trousers of the security guards—walked past her in both directions. She was half-pushed, half-dragged down the corridor to a door that slid open at the push of a button to a sterile, efficient-looking office. The walls were made of prefabricated steel sections, two of which contained large, oval portholes that looked down into an alien, subterranean landscape of shadow and rock. A third wall was lined with shelves filled with plastic-bound record books and tape cartridges; an impressive computer stood against the fourth. The furniture was simple, expensive, and contemporary in design. It was the sort of office a high-powered business tycoon might assemble for himself.

Sarah was forced roughly into a chair facing the

steel-and-glass desk and the two attendants stood behind ready to restrain her; the Count dePasse sat comfortably in another chair, waiting. Waiting for what? Sarah's brain screamed. It wasn't long before she found out. The door opened abruptly and Ava Bardoff walked in to face the helpless girl.

"Welcome home, dear," Ava said warmly. "We were very worried about you."

Contrary to Sarah's fantasies in the ambulance, Ava looked just as she always did—beautiful, calm, and collected, wearing a black velvet robe with white silk lining showing at the cuffs and open neck. She looked at Sarah's face and turned angrily to dePasse.

"Who did that to her face?" she demanded.

"My men in Paris tried to force young dePasse's whereabouts out of her."

"Without success, I assume," Ava said. "Sarah is neither a fool nor a weakling. It was stupid, a ridiculous primitive throwback, particularly when you know we can get everything we need out of her with drugs."

"Yes, Madame," the count said submissively. "I did use them to get the Palots' address."

Sarah's blood went cold at hearing for the first time that she had given away the place where Michael was hiding.

Ava turned and chided her. "Darling, you have betrayed me shamefully. After all I have done for you I expected some loyalty. Now it is too late, unless you decide to work with us as has your friend, Michael dePasse."

"Mich . . ." Sarah started to say and then stopped. "I don't believe you. You tried to kill him, and besides, he wouldn't work for a spy."

"A spy?" Ava laughed. "Is that what they told you I was, a spy?" She looked carefully at Sarah. "You really *do not* know much at all, do you? Your lover said you did not, but I expect you know more than either he or you think. Why don't you tell us everything that happened since you met him on the *Krait*."

Sarah sat tight-lipped.

"Do not be infuriating, Sarah," Ava said in annoyance. "You might as well tell us or we will merely put you under sedation and get the information that way. You will not be betraying anyone," Ava tried to persuade her. "Your lover will be here soon and will tell us everything we want to know."

"You're lying," Sarah snapped out.

"You underestimate my charms and persuasive abilities, my dear. Young dePasse has agreed to give us the information in a gallant swap for your life. I may even let him join us if he behaves."

Sarah was stunned. She wanted to believe what Ava had said, that Michael loved her enough to make this sacrifice to save her, but at the same time she didn't want to believe he'd agreed to destroy his life for her —she loved *him* too much for that. She didn't know what to believe and so, rather than make the decision, she turned on the Count dePasse to relieve her frustration.

"How could you do this to your own son? How could . . ."

Her words were cut off by Ava's laugh. "He is not Michael's father, you little fool. Michael's father was eliminated years ago. He could not be recruited the way yours was and so we had to substitute counts."

Sarah heard only the reference to her own father. "What do you mean you recruited my father? What do you mean?" she demanded, forgetting everything else.

"Your father was a charming lightweight in the diplomatic corps—a talented, selfish man who advanced more through wealth than his ability. Britain was the ideal post for an egotistical socialite like Harrison Dilworth. When I offered to give him back his youth, he jumped at it—'an eternal life of the pleasures of Adonis,' he called it. The greedy fool," Ava sneered. "He even tricked your mother into having my little operation to guarantee her cooperation. No wonder he could not face you. I could never decide if he sent you away because you were growing up too fast for such a young-looking father or because he had some spark of conscience left."

Sarah tried to fling herself at the older woman, all her fear having vanished at these horrendous accusations, but the men behind held her.

"A commendable display of loyalty, although misplaced," Ava said with some amusement as she continued undermining the girl. "I might as well tell it all to you as long as we have gone this far."

She sat on the corner of her desk and faced Sarah. "I needed a man in Britain, and your father was the best placed not only to supply us with information on American intentions in Europe, but the reactions of the British government to American moves. He joined my organization willingly for the power it promised to give him and because he could not stand the idea of growing old." Ava saw the look of disbelief in Sarah's eyes. "Yes, Sarah, I can give people back their youth and prolong their lives. That is what your father wanted, and in return he underwent our little loyalty operation —as did your mother, although she knew nothing about it. When she began to suspect the brain implant, she became hysterical and so I was forced to act rather than risk disclosure by her at that critical time. I arranged the skiing trip to my chalet in the Alps, but the avalanche my men prepared was less selective than I had anticipated—it took your father along with your mother. It was a lamentable error and a great waste of my time and talent."

"I don't believe you," Sarah said, staring at her, "I don't believe a single word." She hated Ava, hated the cool way in which she had just explained the corruption and destruction of her parents, hated her all the more because she knew in her heart that Ava was telling the truth. Her father's ego had drained Sarah of affection and then discarded her when she no longer suited its purpose.

"And me? Why were you so nice to me? What could I possibly give you?" Sarah asked. "Was it because you killed my parents? Did you want to soothe your conscience?" she challenged Ava bitterly.

"Soothe my conscience?" Ava laughed. "Darling, I do not have a conscience. I do not need one. I am above one. I have kept you around me because you were useful—you were good for my image of the kind, loving *god*mother." Ava howled with laughter.

Sarah stared at her in wonder. For years she had ad-

mired and loved this, this horrible creature; she'd
looked up to the murderer of her own parents. These
revelations on top of all that had happened to her in
the last few hours were too much for her. She felt exhausted and sick; Sarah buried her head in her hands,
wanting to cry.

Ava Bardoff had been waiting for this reaction of
submission and said, "Now, Sarah, I think it is time
you told us what we want to know. Who is Michael
working for?"

The mention of Michael's name, the only thing she
had left in the world, put iron back into her. She'd defend him until her death. "Never," Sarah shouted at
Ava. "I'll never tell you anything, never, never—you
vile, disgusting . . ." Ava's slap across her face rocked
her head back.

"I have had enough of this," Ava Bardoff shouted
at the stunned girl. "You silly little whore, do you dare
call me ugly names? Do you dare say no to me? To
me? Disgusting, am I?" Ava's face twisted as she
worked herself into a rage.

"Get her out of my sight," she ordered the attendants. "Take her to Moloch and find out everything
she knows."

Sarah was roughly hoisted to her feet. Ava stood,
shaking with anger. "Disgusting? Take her through
Mulciber's laboratory cells. I want her to know exactly
what that word means. I want her to see what I plan to
do with her." She glared at Sarah. "You will beg, my
arrogant little friend, oh, how you will beg—that is if
you have any mind left to beg with. Now get her out,"
she shrieked.

They pushed Sarah through the door, bumping into
Beel, who was just entering. Her eyes met his briefly;
it was she who broke the contact first.

Ava snapped at him, "Order Ash and Peor to my
room at once." She was panting heavily and had an
urgent need to release her pent up emotions. "Call me
as soon as you have got everything out of her." She
nodded at the now empty doorway. "And Beel, if you
lose her from an overdose, do not worry—I have fin-

ished with Miss Dilworth." He left and she turned to the Count dePasse, who had sat impassively through the entire interview. "Take one of the guest rooms in the barracks down here. I may want you on hand should your 'son' prove difficult, too. Now leave me."

Alone in her office, Ava took a swagger stick from her desk and whipped her right leg in a frustrated staccato as she paced back and forth across the room in thought. Finally she brought the stick down on the desk top with a vicious smack and, still grasping it in her fist, strode out of the office toward the elevator that would carry her up to her subservient and beautiful young men.

Sarah was manhandled down a wide, circular staircase that spiraled through three floors of the administration tower and on down through the three stories of the long, rectangular, technical center below it. Her feet slipped on the soft, soundproof carpet of the staircase as she fought to grab its highly polished steel railing. On each landing she saw elaborate directories efficiently indexing the activities being performed in the many rooms and laboratories off the corridors radiating out from the center. Uniformed men, many of them exact duplicates of each other, passed her silently on the stairs, hardly bothering to look at the young woman struggling against the attendants as if this were an accustomed occurrence down here.

On the ground floor they stopped before a thick door and one of her attendants rang the buzzer to its right. After a few seconds a face appeared at its small inset window and nodded; the door slid open with a swooshing noise to let them in. Although Sarah had been in the complex only a short time, she had become used to its hushed, efficient atmosphere with hardly a sound except for the gentle background hum. But now other sounds came to her ears—the sounds of moans, groaning, quiet, hopeless sobbing. The door swooshed shut behind her as she was forced down the white tiled corridor by her captors, supported by their firm grips under her arms. Sarah needed that support

as her knees buckled under at her first real understanding of the meaning of Pandemonium.

Cells, or more accurately, human cages stretched
along both sides of that long corridor. Some of their
occupants were restrained only by bars, others behind
thick, antiseptic glass all too visible to her. These were
the living experiments of Dr. Mulciber, distorted men
and women, their violated bodies often barely recognizable as human. Some lay in stupor, softly moaning,
some paced mindlessly back and forth, others huddled
in corners. Sarah saw bodies strapped into frightening
apparatus with complicated, bubbling tubes and wire
coils leading in and out from them to supply nutrients
while draining off the by-products of their organs. Creatures without eyes, missing limbs or supporting extra
limbs, cage after cage of bodies stripped of flesh or
wearing the grotesque marks of grafts—she saw them
all—victims of multiple organ transplants, horrible
growths extending from their sides and bellies.

Sarah began to retch uncontrollably, fouling herself
as she was dragged along. To her right she saw one
naked creature behind glass, strapped spread-eagle to
a vertical harness, its tongue dangling limply from its
open mouth. Through red-rimmed holes in its flesh,
thick plastic tubes penetrated into its throat, the chest
cavity, and up into its groin. Its head moved slowly
to follow her as she passed, and the glassy eyes seemed
to clear momentarily in vague recognition; it was Peter
Kent. Sarah screamed through her vomit and collapsed.

Her limp form was carried to the floor above into
one of the operating theatres and dumped on the table.
Moloch's piglike face smiled down at her as he slowly
inserted the long needle into her arm.

Watson looked at the luminous dial on his watch.
"It's 1:40 A.M.," he whispered to Carpenter, "let's get
this show on the road."

Carpenter lifted a small radio and whispered orders
to the other nine men lying hidden by the rainy blackness around the farmhouse. The old stone building had
been under surveillance for twenty-four hours—ever

since Halvorsen had returned from Paris with Michael's maps. Using directional eavesdropping equipment, they had been able to ascertain the routine exacted of Madame Bardoff's watchdogs, who ran four six-hour watches, reporting by radio to the cavern below at the end of each watch. The house guard consisted of a couple posing as a farmer and his wife and four field hands, two of whom were on constant patrol. Watson had waited until the patrol changed at midnight and then killed the two new men. He had wondered at the time if either of them had been responsible for the murder of the concierge in Rue St. Denis. They now had about four hours to take control of the farmhouse and get through the warren of passages and galleries below to Madame's complex before their intrusion was discovered.

A flash of lightning caught one of the crew running toward the front of the building. Watson held his breath but no reaction came from within. He and Carpenter rose and, crouching low, ran a zigzag course toward the kitchen windows. The other men stationed themselves at the other windows around the house. When all were in position, Watson peered cautiously in through a narrow gap between the curtains, seeing only one man reading at the heavy wooden kitchen table, his back to the radio transmitter in the cupboard just behind. They couldn't afford to give him even a second to hit the warning button that must be somewhere in that complicated piece of equipment.

Smith, the smallest and scrappiest of the crew, was hoisted gingerly up onto the roof of a small shed built against the main house. He moved like a cat across the slippery, wet tiles to the window and, after a quick look in, held up two fingers showing the number of guards who slept there. It left just one, probably the woman, in the front bedroom. The men positioned themselves for the attack.

Upon the signal, Watson kicked open the back door with one swift movement, the silencer on his gun muffling the bullet that blasted through the forehead of the startled guard as Halvorsen and two others ran past him up the stairs. Simultaneously, Smith crashed through the upper window, dispatching the men there before they could reach for their weapons. After the seven-second commotion, the house fell silent. None of the crew moved, everyone listening for the sound of the fourth guard. Halvorsen and the two deckhands flattened themselves against the hall wall on either side of the door to the front bedroom and waited. They all waited as tension mounted and nerves stretched. The minutes ticked slowly by, the quiet of the farmhouse broken only by the distant rumble of thunder. Without warning the bedroom door suddenly flew open and, with the shrieks of a fanatic, the woman, stark naked and hair streaming behind, ran out spraying the hall before her with a submachine gun in a desperate attempt to reach the radio below. Halvorsen put a bullet into the back of her head before she could turn.

The first step of their mission completed, the men gathered in the kitchen to unpack the duffle bags they'd brought with them. They changed into rubber wet suits over which they donned canvas coveralls and metal helmets to protect them from the jagged rocks they'd soon encounter. While several of the men organized the ropes, torches, and other equipment they'd brought for their long descent into the Styx system, Andrews pulled two needles out of Smith's arm; he'd been caught in the woman's wild firing. "At least we know our antidote injections are effective," he said. "How do you feel?"

"A little groggy at first, but I'm okay now," Smith answered. "I've got another of those fuckers sticking in my back. Talk about putting a cure to the test."

"Okay, you guys," Watson interrupted, "let's cut the chat and get going."

The crew strapped streamlined back packs on over their coveralls and fastened gun belts around their waists. The guns, wrapped tightly in waterproof plastic, were equipped with silencers so they wouldn't alert the entire cave system to their presence with their first shot and, from an equally practical standpoint, Halvorsen had warned, "There's no use in shooting one man and having the sound vibrations bring the whole cavern roof down on us all."

Halvorsen was worried about another aspect of this operation—the rain. Aside from the drizzle that had been falling for the last five hours, the heavy storms over the Alps were moving steadily in their direction. He remembered Professor Musquère's warning to Michael that even in moderately bad weather, many of the smaller passages in the system filled completely with water.

"Make sure your underwater gear is working," he cautioned the others.

At precisely 2:00 A.M. that morning, the crew left the farmhouse carrying the bodies of the guards with them. Carpenter had planted incendiary devices in the house set to go off a few minutes after 6:00 A.M., when the cavern would be trying to contact the outpost to find out why it had not reported in. He hoped that the fire would destroy all evidence of the radio, and without bodies, the French police would be spared having to solve a confusing and embarrassing puzzle.

The ten men walked to a nearby field and down into the depression that had been made centuries ago by the collapse of the roof of the rock cavity beneath. They stopped at the jagged opening in the center that led into the Styx cave system far below.

"I wonder how many poor innocents have taken this trip before them," Smith mumbled as he and the others rolled the bodies of Ava's six guards into the black hole. "It's a fitting final resting place for these bastards."

"Okay," Watson said, belaying a delicate-looking nylon rope ladder with aluminum rungs to an outcropping of stone, "we've got a timetable to meet, and standing around looking at each other isn't going to help us meet it. Halvorsen, you're the expert, you go in first."

The big Swede shrugged his shoulders, lowered himself into the hole, and climbed carefully down the fragile, swaying ladder fifty-five feet to the cavity's uneven floor. He steadied the ladder for the others as they clambered down, bringing with them the packs filled with inflatable rubber rafts and explosives. The men stood grouped together, averting their eyes from the broken bodies of Ava's guards at their feet while looking around at the shadowy rock walls in the eerie glow of their dim helmet lamps. The only sound was that of water dripping down from somewhere high above in the blackness; a few bats swooped low over their heads.

Watson shook himself out of the claustrophobic, panicky feeling that began to grip him in this alien underworld, and flashed the beam of his powerful electric torch over the rough walls until he found the lower opening to the narrow and cramped crawlway through which they must squeeze.

"C'mon, you guys, down on your knees. We've got two miles to go and not much time to do it in."

The phone beside Ava Bardoff's bed buzzed gently for almost a minute before a hand lifted the receiver.

"Who is it, Peor?" Ava's voice asked in the darkness.

"Beel, he and Moloch have finished with Sarah," the young man replied.

"Give it to me. What time is it?"

"Three-thirty." He handed the phone to her.

"Do not go away," she commanded, grabbing his hair and forcing his naked body back over hers. In the darkness of the room, the three entwined figures could not be seen, only their passion heard.

"Well, Beel, what did you learn?" As she listened, Ava absently brought down her swagger stick, slapping into the flesh of the young men who gasped with mixed pain and pleasure.

At the other end of the line Beel said, "More than we'd hoped for. Hugo Montclair is our man—he put Michael dePasse up to coming to the clinic."

"Excellent," Ava said. "We will take care of that meddling little fool today. What else?"

Beel went on to tell of the underwater entrance to the *Krait* and that Hugo knew of their guests at the clinic. "He also suspects we're using doubles but doesn't know their real purpose. He thinks we're spies."

Ava laughed, whipping down the swagger stick, enjoying Peor's delighted cry of pain. "For what organization is Montclair working?"

"Sarah knows nothing about that—they were careful not to tell her much. She only implicated dePasse and Montclair—we already knew the Palots were innocent bystanders in the entire affair."

"Even so," Ava replied, "we'd better get rid of them. I don't want any loose ends. With young dePasse in our hands, that leaves only Hugo Montclair. We will make sure he collects no more information about us. Send out a team of our best men at once. I want everyone on that yacht killed and then blow it up to look like another regrettable maritime accident." Ava began to chuckle at the rude analogy that came into her mind. "Perhaps our men should make their entrance through the *Krait*'s underwater orifice—it is anatomically descriptive of what we plan to do to its owner." She brought down the stick again.

"I'll see to it right away," Beel replied. "The ship is sitting off St. Tropez now. We should be able to dispose of it before sunrise."

"No, wait, Beel," Ava said quickly in an afterthought. "We had better wait a few hours until Michael dePasse gets here—it could be dangerous to act prematurely. If he cannot satisfy our curiosity, we may want to bring dear Hugo here for interrogation before disposing of him. I want to make sure we rid ourselves once and for all of everybody who even suspects us."

"And Sarah?" he asked.

"That little bitch," Ava snarled. "Turn her over to Mulciber and tell him I don't care how he uses her."

Beel hesitated on the other end of the phone. "May I suggest she might be useful in assuring dePasse's cooperation, at least until he undergoes the operation."

"You have always wanted her, have you not, Beel?" Ava was amused. "You have always wanted her but she has sent you packing. Very well, I give her to you —but only until dePasse is ours. After that she goes to Mulciber."

"Yes, Madame," he said flatly.

"And Beel," she said, smiling cruelly in the darkness, "go hard on the little slut." Ava dropped the receiver back into its cradle and laughed. She rolled over as Peor, aroused by her whip, flung himself onto her.

The crew of the *Krait* emerged covered with mud from their cramped and uncomfortable journey through the long, torturous crawlway leading out of the first chamber. Their hands were raw and bleeding, and despite their heavy coveralls, several of the wet suits suffered tears from the jagged fingers of rock that had tried to bar their advance. They found themselves in a passage ten or twelve feet high, heading downward at a steep pitch. The walls had been worn smooth by flowing water sometime in the dim past, but the floor was littered with heaps of rock from collapsed parts of the ceiling.

The roof of the passage lowered as they struggled warily along it, eventually forcing them to walk in crouched positions. Finally the passage ended and they were faced with their next problem, a narrow chimney in the rock thirty feet or so straight down. Bracing his back against one side of the narrow shaft and his feet against the other, Watson started inching his way down. After some minutes of blistering profanity, he reached the bottom and flashed his electric torch in a signal for the rest to follow.

The chimney ended in another passage that soon opened out onto a ledge running high along one side of a huge gallery. As they carefully picked their way along the ledge, Watson's torch picked out walls shining with calcite crystals, stalactites, and columns. Halvorsen looked down at a series of rimstone dams on the floor below that had been turned into a series of small waterfalls by the stormy weather above. Several thin cascades of water poured out from the sides of the gallery, increasing his concern about the flooding of the cave system before they could get through to the Bardoff complex. Somewhere he could hear the roar of the underground river that Professor Musquère had called the Styx.

"It's like a cathedral," Andrews said in appreciation of nature's architecture.

"This isn't a fucking art class, you know," Watson commented dryly. "Let's move it."

It was 3:30 A.M., exactly at the time Ava Bardoff was issuing her commands by phone for the destruction of the *Krait* and Sarah, that Hugo's men completed their treacherous descent by rope from the ledge to the floor of the hall.

They crossed the slimy floor of the large gallery, threading their way gingerly between the giant rock formations, wading knee deep in water in several places, to reach the far end, where the chamber narrowed and led down to join a maze of passages through which the lost river of the Styx flowed. The water level was almost to the roof of the smaller passages, but the larger one they were to take still had some eight feet of air space left above the water surface. How long this would last was now a matter of general concern. They had not brought oxygen tanks with them—only snorkel equipment—and the men didn't relish the idea of swimming underwater through this unfamiliar maze with only a very limited air supply. Although unspoken, the fear of losing their way in the underwater labyrinth weighed heavily on all their minds.

They stripped to their wet suits and inflated the four small rubber boats. Watson and Smith took the first boat and went ahead to scout the passage, reasoning that they must soon run into patrols of some sort from the Bardoff complex.

The passage down which the swift current carried them was about ten feet across, and its walls had been worn smooth by thousands of years of flowing water. It was therefore difficult to find the needed handholds to slow or stop the boat should they come upon a patrol. Watson and Smith backpaddled as hard as they could to keep from being swept forward too fast. After fighting the water for ten minutes, they noticed the current slowing as the passage began to widen and its roof rose higher above them.

"This may be it," Watson said. "The map showed

a good sized gallery just before the Great Hall beneath the château. Let's try to stop this damn thing."

Both men backpaddled frantically, moving in against the right-hand wall. Watson pointed to white water twenty yards ahead, where the smooth flow of the current was interrupted by a recent breakdown of the passage roof restricting the width of the channel. They moved in behind the jumble of rocks and beached their boat on them.

"God is smiling on us," Smith whispered. "Look."

Up ahead, the passage made a gentle turn to the right—the two men could tell because they saw a dim glow from some light source reflected on the far left wall. Over the rushing sound of the river as it swept past, they could now hear a faint mechanical hum.

"We're here, buddy boy," Watson said.

"It's a good thing we found this heap of rock," Smith replied, "or else we'd have sailed right into their laps."

Watson started tying a rope around his waist. Handing Smith the other end, he said, "Wait here for the others while I go up ahead to see what it's all about. One tug means stop playing out rope, two means pull me back. Wish me luck," he said as he put on his scuba mask and slipped into the water.

He surfaced again at the bend in the passage, gradually moving along the wall to a position where he could see into the watery gallery indicated on Michael's chart; he tugged the rope once. As he pushed up his mask for a better view, Watson's nose picked up the faint odor of chlorine. Chalk another one up to dePasse, he thought.

The gallery into which he now looked was perhaps a hundred yards long and thirty-five wide with a ceiling rising thirty feet above the current level of the water. At the far end he saw a series of mammoth sliding doors made of heavy steel that could presumably slide shut to protect the Great Hall from the river during its periods of flooding. Through the opening between these forty-foot doors, Watson could see part of the high roof of the hall beyond.

A large passage branched off to the right about half-way down the wall of the gallery. The water of the lost river pulled at his body as it rushed toward the passsage that ended in a violent waterfall crashing down to the smaller, lower hall through which the Styx now flowed. Watson couldn't see into the right-hand cavern, but its rock walls were lined with large heavy-duty electric cables that ran out into the gallery and on into the Great Hall. Those bastards, the engineer thought with grudging admiration—they've harnessed the falls and built a fucking power plant down there. Then a smile crossed his face as he remembered the explosives his men carried. Cut off their power, he said to himself, and we immobilize their entire underworld complex.

But first they had to get to the power plant and clear their way into the main hall. It would not be as easy as they had hoped when sitting securely back on the *Krait* several days ago. The entire gallery in which he now treaded water was illuminated by a row of powerful spotlights running the length of its ceiling. A glass guardhouse sat at the intersection of the gallery with the passage leading to the power plant; at least two men were moving about inside it. About six feet above the water level, three catwalks radiated out from this security center along the walls. One ran down the branch passage to the plant, another back to the giant doors at the far end of the gallery, and the third extended in Watson's direction. On it two guards stood together in conversation, looking down into the water, their fractured reflections stretching across its surging surface toward him.

Jerking the rope twice, Watson was pulled back against the strong current to the breakdown, where the other nine men now waited for him. A plan had formed in his mind—a dangerous plan, but the only one that offered a chance of getting through.

In the light of their torches, he set Carpenter the task of reassembling the explosives into larger-sized bundles and attaching timing devices to them while he explained his new attack strategy. "Make sure those damn timers work," Watson warned, "or you'll bring the fucking world down on our own heads before we can get out of here."

"What time is it now?" Carpenter asked.

"Five-o-two A.M. We've only got one hour before the alert goes up and we've got a hell of a lot to do before then."

Fifteen minutes later all ten men moved through the black water with two of the rubber boats loaded with their back packs, the bundles of explosives, and their guns. Ropes tied to the breakdown held the boats back against the current just out of sight of Madame's men patrolling the catwalks. These two floating supply depots now represented Hugo's advanced base of operations.

The invaders counted at least six guards, two in the glass house, one by the steel doors to the halls, two on the catwalk extending toward them, and at least one down the passage leading to the powerhouse.

"Remember," Watson cautioned, "don't attack until I get into the guardhouse—if the men in there see anything strange going on out here first, they'll raise the warning and the shit will really hit the fan."

He pulled on his face mask, checked his pistol in its waterproof side holster, and nodded to the five others who were also adjusting their masks. "I hope you're as accurate shooting light bulbs as you are skeet off the back of the ship," he said to Carpenter. "Keep 'em looking up, Sport." Then giving the signal, he and the other five sank down below the surface of the water and, hugging the uneven floor of the gallery, swam around the bend into the illuminated chamber.

As soon as they disappeared, Carpenter moved along the wall until he could just see the string of spotlights running down the center of the rock ceiling. Halvorsen braced the marksman against the wall as best he could while Carpenter checked the silencer on his gun, took careful aim, and fired. The center spot suddenly popped and went dark, the sound of its shattered glass covered by the noise of the water. The three guards on the catwalks all looked up, pointing to the light and calling to each other. One of the men in the guardhouse came out to investigate the apparent electrical failure. Their attention diverted above, they failed to notice the six black shapes deep below slowly swimming toward them, fighting the current to reach the three catwalks under which they hoped to find some degree of protection from observation.

"Keep looking up, you bastards, up," Carpenter whispered through clenched teeth.

11

Two hundred and fifty feet above, Michael dePasse's blue Peugeot passed through the gates of the château's park, rolled up the tree-lined drive, and stopped before the wide steps leading to the main entrance of the imposing building. Two security guards, arms folded, stood waiting for him in the rain.

"Will you please inform Madame Bardoff that Monsieur dePasse has arrived," Michael said with all the aristocratic snobbery he could muster as he walked past the guards and up the steps before either could take hold of him. His arrogance confused the men who fell into step behind him as he crossed the entrance hall toward Stanislau Beel, who greeted him cordially.

"It's just past five A.M.—you're early. Madame Bardoff will meet you in her office below. Before we go down, would you like to freshen up? Your trip from Paris in this weather must have been exhausting."

"Thank you," Michael replied, following Beel to a washroom off the hall. Not knowing just how to act in these desperate circumstances, he felt it best to prolong the civilities as long as possible. He kept repeating over and over to himself not to panic and to stay cool no matter what happened. His experience under the stress of international athletic competitions helped him maintain a remarkable degree of control over his emotions and nerves. Splashing water on his face and brushing back his hair, Michael squared his shoulders, ready to meet the unknown challenges that lay ahead.

He followed Beel to the mysterious north wing—this time the door was open to him—and entered the elevator. As they began their descent he said, "I've been looking forward to seeing what you've got down here."

"You know about it, then?" Beel asked with mild curiosity.

"No, just suspected. After all, you don't have great ventilator shafts going into the ground for nothing."

"Quite right," Beel replied. He looked steadily at Michael, studying him. After a brief silence he asked, "Do you really intend to join the organization, dePasse, or . . . ?"

"It depends upon what Madame Bardoff has to say," Michael interrupted. "How is Sarah?"

"She is safe for the time being." The elevator doors slid open and the two men walked down the corridor. "Her life depends entirely upon you and your persuasive powers with Ava. I hope they are good."

"You're very fond of Sarah, aren't you? I noticed the way you looked at her when I was here last weekend."

Beel didn't answer, opening the door into Ava Bardoff's office. The clock on her desk showed 5:10 A.M. as Michael crossed the room and looked out through one of the large oval portholes. He whistled.

"My God, you've got a whole city down here. What's all that?" He pointed to a long, one-story, glass-domed building on the other side of the huge cavern.

"That's the gymnasium. Aside from calisthenics and athletics, we use it to drill the guards."

Michael shook his head in awe at the scope and strange beauty of all he saw. From the tower where he stood, the entire complex was visible. The Great Hall must have been almost a mile in length, half of which—the half in which the complex was built—was about three hundred yards wide with a roof one hundred feet above. Although supposedly a dead cave, the hall contained sufficient moisture so the calcite formations glistened in the artificial daylight Ava Bardoff's engineers had created through the use of a network of huge sun-

lamps suspended far above in a vast steel grid hung
from the cavern roof. Two parallel rows of polished
metal buildings, each running almost half a mile in
length, were built against opposite sides of the hall.
They were connected by three enclosed glass bridges
nearly a hundred yards long, that arched gracefully
across the cavern thirty feet above a vast series of hydroponic gardens. These water gardens were terraced
from the huge doors at the top of the cave down
the entire mile length of the Great Hall between the
two rows of buildings and the walls of the narrower,
lower end of the cavern. Water pumped from the Styx
into the top of the gardens flowed gently down from
terrace to terrace until reaching the far end of the hall
where it followed its old route through the cave system until rejoining the current lower channel of the
lost river. From there it flowed on several miles before
bubbling up into the lake in the wildlife preserve or
continuing on through another maze of passages into
the Mediterranean Sea. The fertile green foliage of the
gardens spoke eloquently for Madame's ability to feed
a large number of underworld inhabitants with only a
little help from outside.

The buildings themselves were constructed among
the stalagmites and columns of the Great Hall, making
brilliant use of the natural formations for support and
added strength, a perfect blending of man's and nature's architecture. The major buildings were constructed of prefabricated sections of some sort of
polished stainless steel and glass that mirrored the
crystalline formations of the hall and the greenery of
the gardens. The smaller structures toward the narrow
end of the cavern were made of stone with a thin inner
lining of metal. The entire complex was joined together
to form one large airtight compartment within the cavern to protect its inhabitants from poisonous gases, both
natural and manmade, and to expedite efficient ventilation. In times of emergency, the complex could be
sealed off into a series of smaller airtight compartments.
The portholes, some as large as thirty feet in height,
contained thick glass strong enough to withstand ex-

tremes of water pressure should the great sliding doors at the head of the hall fail to protect the complex from the flooding of the Styx system in the spring.

It was all like a fairyland to Michael as he looked at the geometric shapes of shining steel and glass built into the crystal formations of the vast hall and illuminated by underground sunlight. A canary fluttered down to perch on the outside ledge of the porthole.

Beel noticed Michael's smile upon seeing the little yellow bird. "We use them to detect the first signs of a gas leak," he said. "We use a great deal of chlorine gas down here to make the calcium chloride powder we need to absorb the moisture within the complex. Without it, the wet atmosphere would play havoc with our computers and the other equipment. The gas tanks are over there." He pointed to two eighteen-foot, egg-shaped glass tanks sitting next to each other outside the largest building in the complex. "One contains hydrogen, the other chlorine gas. That building's our manufacturing center, four stories high. Beautiful, isn't it?"

Michael nodded his appreciation of the half-steel, half-glass building inside which he could see a labyrinth of immaculate machines, pipes, aisles, and catwalks.

"Aside from the manufacture of calcium chloride," Beel continued with pride, "we process food there and have developed a waste-disposal process to supplement our energy supply. It can run most of the complex at reduced levels for a day. We also manufacture the active ingredients for the Bardoff cosmetic preparations and, of course, the double formula Mulciber and Ava developed for ourselves. I expect you'll be using it soon."

Although his curiosity almost exploded at the mention of this formula, Michael contented himself with familiarizing himself with the layout of the complex. "What are those buildings across the way?"

"The three-story block by the doors at the opening of the cavern is the armory and main security headquarters. The first bridge connects it with this tower. The rest of the building blocks between it and the gymnasium way down there are barracks, social rooms, cloning nurseries, and so forth. Counting the slaves, we've got just over four hundred people living in the complex."

"Slaves?" Michael asked, trying to keep his voice even.

"The men and women Mulciber has finished with and who are still capable of work," Beel replied. "We can't let them go, so we might as well make some use of them. They tend the gardens and also do some quarrying for the stone we need to expand the warehouses."

"Whose idea was that?"

"Ava's, of course. She has a completely practical outlook on life."

Michael thought he detected a trace of sarcasm in Beel's voice. He looked down at a group of misshapen figures limping about in the hydroponic gardens below; several guards prodded them occasionally with long poles with electrified tips. "This is all really quite fascinating," Michael said, concealing his abhorrence for what Beel was telling him.

Beel, for his part, saw no harm in explaining the complex to Michael. After all, he reasoned, Michael would either join their organization or end out there in the hydroponic gardens with the slaves. Besides, it was not often he had the opportunity to boast about the underground city he had helped to create.

"This building is the core of the whole operation," he continued. "Right now we're on the top floor of the administration tower. Under the tower is the technical center. The third floor is devoted entirely to the neuts and below that are the operating rooms and Dr. Mulciber's laboratories. The first floor contains more laboratories and the cells for the experimental . . ." Beel hesitated—"animals. And below that the sublevel with the slaves. The technical center joins the factory, which connects to that series of warehouses extending the rest of the way down the hall."

"So the shaft in the factory connects with the warehouses and the shaft in the château with this tower and your technical center?" Michael asked.

For the first time Beel looked at him with suspicion. His rapid grasp of the complex and acceptance of many of its more unusual aspects was unnerving. He couldn't put his finger on the reason, but suddenly he felt ill at ease. Although this young man was in their power now, Beel felt he represented an extreme danger to them.

"I've said far too much as it is," he replied to Michael's question and lapsed into silence.

Michael continued to stare mesmerized through the porthole at the complex spreading along the walls of the vast cavern. What had at first seemed strangely beautiful to him, now became cruel and loathsome in his eyes. As he looked down at the twisted bodies of the slaves below and thought of the "animal" cages in the research laboratories, the Styx Complex seemed to him more like a crystal Auschwitz—and somewhere in its bowels, Sarah's life hung by a thread. He had to save her no matter what the consequences.

The office door opened and Michael turned to face Ava's triumphant smile as she walked toward him, confident and relaxed. Despite his dislike and revulsion for her, he had to be impressed with her cool, sensual beauty.

The guards on the catwalk broke off their conversation about the faulty spotlight and returned to their stations, one going back into the glass house to telephone a report of the electrical problem. Two of Hugo's men swam underwater beneath the catwalk, keeping pace with the lone guard until he reached the farthest point by the steel doors. Two others stayed beneath the two guards on the catwalk extending out toward the passage down which the crew had come; Watson and Smith fought the current along the passage leading to the great underground waterfall and the powerhouse below it. Surfacing, Watson saw only one of Madame's men pacing back and forth above them.

The walls of the passage curved gradually away from each other as the passage widened toward the waterfall. Thus, while standing at the far end of the catwalk by the falls, the guard was effectively blocked from the view of the glass guardhouse by the bend in the rock wall; it was here that Watson and Smith would have to take him.

They had great difficulty in keeping from being swept away by the powerful current to the falls. While the guard's back was turned, Smith tossed a rope up over and around the floor of the catwalk, tying the two ends together just below the water's surface to form a loop that supported the two men under their arms. His hands thus freed, Watson carefully removed the waterproof wrapping from his pistol and held it ready for the guard. He looked at his watch in the dim illumination of the passage. "Five-thirty A.M.," Watson cursed. "We're way behind schedule."

The roar of the waterfall drowned out the footsteps of the guard and he was back overhead almost before Watson realized it. Waiting until he passed on by, Smith braced his back against the rock wall and used his feet to push Watson several feet out from under the catwalk, where he would have a clean shot at the back of the man's head. He pulled the trigger; the guard spun around, bounced against the railing, and fell forward with one leg dangling in the air over them.

"Jesus," Watson said with relief, "I thought the bastard was going to fall off, that would have screwed up everything."

The two men pulled themselves up the rope to the catwalk six feet above. Without pausing, they began to strip off his uniform, the black T-shirt, trousers, and boots. They were so engrossed in this work that they failed to see the door of a cement control house by the sluice gates at the top of the falls open and a second guard emerge, stretching himself after waking from an illegal early-morning nap. He froze in the middle of a yawn, then slowly and smoothly drew his gun and fired.

Smith felt the sharp pain of the needle slicing into his back and turned in surprise. Straightening up, he tripped back over Watson as the second needle hit his chest. The guard vaulted the two men sprawled on the catwalk to run to the glass house with his warning, but Smith reached up and caught him by the foot to bring him down. As the guard scrambled to his feet, Smith's lunge carried them both off the catwalk into the water. They surfaced some yards away still grappling with each other, too occupied in their struggle to realize they were being swept along toward the falls. Watson stood gripping the railing helplessly. Breaking away at last, Smith had time only for a few desperate strokes toward the catwalk before he was carried over, his arms flailing for a hold in the air. Whatever cry he may have uttered was lost to Watson's ears.

Shaking his head in combined grief and anger, the engineer returned to the guard, finished stripping him, and donned his uniform. One down, he thought as he worked—I wonder how many more of us will go before this thing is over.

Dressed in the black uniform, Watson walked casually toward the guardhouse at the intersection of the three catwalks, pretending to study the water in an attempt to shield his face from recognition. He was only a few feet from one of the doors of the house when he turned his back to it and stood for a minute giving his comrades in the water a good chance to see him there. He backed nonchalantly to the door, put his hand on the knob, and in almost one continuous movement, was inside, his pistol spurting lead into the faces of the two guards, who barely had the chance to realize they were dead. Simultaneously, the three remaining guards on the catwalks fell to the guns of the *Krait*'s crew.

Carpenter looked at Halvorsen and smiled in relief. "Well," he said, "now it's up to us."

They, and the remaining two members of the crew accompanying them, unfastened the rubber boats from their mooring ropes and guided them across the gallery. Carpenter and one man took the explosives boat with them toward the powerhouse while Halvorsen and the other crewmen swam directly for the steel doors leading into the Great Hall. Watson retraced his steps along the catwalk to the sluice gates to help lay the charges and determine at what hour to set the timing devices. They were already past their deadline. A little more than fifteen minutes after Smith's death, the nine remaining members of the crew stood on the gallery side of the great doors against which Carpenter had laid two more explosive charges, hoping to jam them open when the branch passage to the powerhouse had been brought down. Now Watson and the others all changed into the white uniforms of the clinic staff, which they'd brought with them in their back packs. All, that is, but Carpenter, who wore the black uniform of one of the slain guards. He had one last major charge to lay—the all-important one that would close up the smaller, far-end exit of the Great Hall like putting a cork in a bottle. If all went according to plan, the swollen lost river would once again flow through its original channel into the Great Hall, but this time it would not flow out, not until the hall was filled with water and the complex and all its inhabitants within were destroyed.

Watson's main concern now lay in getting up the elevator shaft into the clinic unnoticed to rescue Ava's distinguished guests and take her prisoner along with her files for the evidence they would need to put her agents around the world out of commission.

"You'd better take off, Carpenter," Watson said. "That last charge of yours has got to blow exactly ten minutes after the others so you can get out with de-Passe. If he doesn't make it, you'll have to go without him."

Carpenter shook his head. "His odds are a hundred to one."

"I know, but that's the way we had to play it—de-Passe insisted on trying for the girl." Watson nodded toward the complex. "He should be somewhere in there now. He doesn't have much time left to get her and meet you. Have you got enough climbing gear for three and the flashlights? I don't know which way I'd rather be taking out of this hole, yours through the cave system, or mine."

"See you later," Carpenter said. He started off in a crouching run down through the lush foliage of the hydroponic gardens.

The rest of the men took the last item out of their back packs—flexible plastic masks—exact replicas of Ava Bardoff's look-alike men made from the sketches Sarah had drawn for Michael before leaving the *Krait*.

They knew that those of the clinic staff highly visible to the guests maintained separate appearances but hoped that the invisible staff would be identical to the majority of the security guards. Pulling their new identities over their faces, the eight doubles scattered to infiltrate the complex and make their way singly or in pairs toward the shaft that extended up from the nearby six-story tower through the ceiling of the Great Hall. It was the only construction they could see in the complex that could hold an elevator going up to the clinics. Small blue dots now appeared not only on their right thumbs, but on their left to facilitate easy identification of each other; they carried their guns concealed under their white uniform jackets. It was 5:58 A.M.; they were almost twenty minutes behind schedule.

Michael had been engaged in a sparring conversation with Ava Bardoff since her arrival. The first thing he'd asked was to be taken to Sarah. Ava had looked hurt.

"I fear you will make me quite jealous of that young woman—you obviously know little of the pleasures that the sexual sophistication of a more mature woman can bring."

Michael remained cool. "I'm sure I've got a lot to learn, but for the present . . . Sarah?"

"Your concern over the welfare of my goddaughter is very touching," Ava said with a charming smile. "You make me feel quite neglectful of my responsibilities." She walked to the wall by the computer in which several TV monitors were set. "Where is she, Beel?"

"Number 14," he replied.

Ava flicked a switch, a TV screen came into focus, and Michael could see into an elaborate operating theatre. Sarah lay strapped on one of the two tables in the center of the white-tiled room, her head turned to look at a distinguished gentleman in a pinstripe suit and a white lab coat, who was arranging instruments on a tray beside her. Sarah's hair had been tightly pulled back over her head and wrapped in a white towel; she wore a white surgical gown.

"What are they doing to her?" Michael demanded. "You promised not to harm her if I . . ."

"Calm yourself, my young friend. I have no plans to harm Sarah as long as you continue to cooperate with us." Ava spoke into the microphone beside the TV monitor. "Tell me, doctor, how is your patient?"

He looked up at the camera and spoke in a voice of cold appraisal. "She is in perfect condition. Tense, of course, but a perfect specimen."

His words ran a chill through Michael's body. "Let's talk," he said to Ava.

"But of course, Michael, that is why we are all here." She sat down in the chair behind her desk and indicated that he, too, should sit. "But first a little information from you. With whom are you working? Who put you up to your visit and snooping around the clinic?"

"You guarantee no harm will come to Sarah or the Palots—that you'll let us go?"

"As I said earlier, I will have no need to harm any of you once you become a member of my organization. Now my question."

Michael appeared to be struggling with himself. Reluctantly he said, "Hugo Montclair, he's been investigating you ever since my mother told him something was wrong with my father."

"Then you know the Count dePasse is not your real father?"

"Yes."

"I see." Ava Bardoff looked at him with interest, trying to read his face for any reaction to the murder of his father. "And for whom is Hugo working?"

"No one, he's doing it all on his own."

Ava leaned back in her chair and laughed. "Come now, Michael, you cannot expect me to believe that. The truth."

"It *is* true. He and his crew have formed a superintelligence operation—they're not regular sailors if that's what you think. They're all experts in some field or other—chemistry, electronics—his whole ship is a laboratory and an arsenal. He usually concentrates on drugs and things like that, things he calls 'evil' —he has an obsession about you."

Ava looked straight through Michael. "An obsession, am I? Evil? How very interesting." She smiled, pondering his words in relation to her observations of the *Krait* and the quality of the crew. Suddenly she flashed out with, "And how did you and Sarah manage to sneak aboard his ship without my men seeing you?"

"There's an underwater entrance. It leads to his study."

Ava was pleased with his answer. "What does he know about me?" she asked in a calmer voice.

Michael looked at the clock on her desk, cold perspiration beginning to form under his arms and on his back. It was only 5:25 A.M.; thirty-five minutes to go. He slowly began to relate to Ava everything he could remember about what Hugo had told him about her as well as what he suspected.

As he spoke, Ava Bardoff became more and more pleased with herself; she seemed almost to enjoy the fact that someone had actually taken so much time and effort to investigate her and was close to guessing her strategem, objectives, and methods. Like the person who commits the perfect crime, Ava had often felt the overwhelming desire to confess her plans so the entire world would know of her supreme brilliance and power.

"Hugo is more clever than I had given him credit for. I made a great error in underestimating him—I will not make that mistake again. And you, Michael," she stood up and approached the chair where he sat, "you surprise me, too. You are telling the truth—I was afraid we were going to end up playing games. I congratulate you on your realistic assessment of your situation."

She stood behind him as he sat looking straight ahead at her empty desk. Ava put her hand lightly on his shoulder. "I think you may be more useful to me than I had really thought and that would be nice—very nice." Her hand slid over his neck and across the skin of his shoulders under the loose sports shirt, down over his chest. Ava felt the muscles of his chest tighten and shrink from her touch. She withdrew her hand and walked back to her desk, leaning against it to face him.

"You do not like me, do you?"

"No," he replied.

"Ha, ha," she laughed. "Excellent, excellent, another bit of honesty. Do not worry, my men do not have to like me—I am sure most of them detest me." She looked at Beel. "You hate me, do you not, Stanislau?"

He started to protest but she cut him off sharply. "Take a lesson from our young friend here, Beel. Do not grovel." She turned her attention back to Michael. "You say you are willing to join us, to betray Hugo Montclair. Have you any other reasons aside from saving Sarah and your other friends?"

He paused, realizing what he was about to say was more truth than he liked to admit to himself. "I'm intrigued with all this." His hand swept in an arc, embracing the office and the city complex seen through the portholes. "It repels me and at the same time fascinates me. I don't really know what you're doing, but from what I now know, it's bigger, much bigger than anything I would ever have expected. It excites me."

"Exactly, Michael," Ava Bardoff said, her eyes shining with fervor. "And do you know why it excites you? It is because you are a champion. Athletes like you have a driving force to compete—an all-consuming desire to win, to be first. You sense power here, you sense success and supremacy, your adrenaline flows, does it not? Your blood boils, surges with the need to meet whatever challenge all this represents."

Ava Bardoff wanted to impress and tempt the handsome young man sitting before her. She wanted to corrupt his clean, open face, corrupt him mentally, morally, and sexually. She wanted him to make love to her and enjoy it, lust for it. As she spoke, her body seemed to sway like that of a cobra hypnotizing its victim.

"I understand you, Michael—we have the same drives. You do not yet know what you see, but you feel it, do you not?" Ava walked to the porthole and looked out over her underworld kingdom, her arms extended and her red fingernails spread like claws against the glass. "Like me you feel things. So, Michael, try to think how it would feel to be first—first over the entire world. Can you feel it? Well, Michael, soon I *will* control the world, I will rule it, I will be the supreme ruler—God." The laugh welled up through her body in a triumphant emotional release.

"That's impossible," he gasped. "A mad dream."

"Impossible? Mad?" Ava shrieked, whirling angrily around to face him. "You fool, I am doing it!"

Then she relaxed and smiled sympathetically at his inability to believe her. "Of course it is impossible," she said. "That is what everyone thinks, do they not? And that is why it has been so easy. Their minds are too small to grasp the concept, to even contemplate the possibility of one person controlling the earth unless that person has mighty armies, tanks, guns, planes, and bombs behind him, armies that are visible and thus menacing to them. But visible, brute force is not the way. The Führer tried and failed. Intrigue is the way —to attack from within. Look at the Communist successes in the Far East, what they achieved in Portugal right under NATO's nose, in Italy, even England. Like theirs, my army is invisible—it infiltrates, divides, and wields power from within. But mine is far more efficient and my strategy far more effective. You think it a mad dream to rule the world? Ask Beel." Before her underling could answer, Ava continued, "Impossible? How wrong you are—it is almost mine now."

Michael sat stunned, staring at her. Ava's words had momentarily obliterated all thoughts of Sarah and Hugo.

Abandoning herself to self-aggrandizement, Ava asked, "Do you want to know how I did it? Do you want to know where it all started?" She pointed through the porthole. "Here, right here in these caves, caves filled with the riches of Europe. Gold, jewels, paintings, priceless art works carefully collected by German officers who no longer have any need of them—Moloch and I have seen to that." She smiled, thinking of some private joke. "I needed laboratories to carry on the experiments that are the foundation of my power. I slowly sold those untraceable art works, those hidden away for generations in family collections, to private collectors." Ava laughed. "Some to your friend, Hugo

Montclair. Yes, Hugo's insatiable passion for art has helped build my laboratories—ironic, is it not? Other pieces found their way into the private vaults of Japan—the Japanese pay well for the privilege of ownership. The better-known paintings were returned to museums to build the respectability and credentials of my agents. The French government has been most appreciative and generous to your supposed father for his efforts in uncovering and returning 'looted' art, has it not?

"With this wealth, I started the construction of the complex you see here and established the House of Bardoff in Paris. How simple it was to build the world's greatest cosmetics empire on the secrets of the skin and body my research had already uncovered at that time."

"Research done on prisoners in concentration camps," Michael interrupted. He felt a desperate need to continually remind himself of the revulsion he felt for the beautiful and obviously brilliant woman before him—a woman who, as she spoke, became more and more fascinating to him.

Ava brushed his comment aside with a contemptuous smile. "Your indignation is naïve—they were going to die anyway, so why not make good use of them? While other researchers were forced to play with animals, I could indulge my theories with human guinea pigs. The only purpose of the weak is to serve the strong—their bodies gave me the one tool I needed to recruit my people. Do you know what that tool is?"

Michael shook his head. He knew what she was about to say but he wanted to hear it from Ava Bardoff's own lips—he wanted to know that such a thing really was possible.

She smiled slowly. "Youth and beauty. How would you like to be young, strong, and handsome for the rest of your life? I can give you all these, Michael, just as I have given them to the others. Oh, not my clients —they get just enough in their lotions and creams to preserve their skin a bit to make them look a little better—but look at Beel and dePasse. Time has stood still for them for twenty years. I can preserve or restore the whole shell and musculature of your body to keep you strong and young with injections of the serum that I develop within the bodies of those kept in the laboratories. It will circulate in *your* body and penetrate the fibers underlying your skin to nourish and rejuvenate them, keep them elastic and flexible so your skin will stay supple, soft, and smooth. It will never age, never. With massive overdoses I can even free and rearrange the pattern of these fibers, mold them like clay into any shape I want before another injection sets them permanently in their new arrangement."

Michael now realized how she had created her army of look-alikes, how she had duplicated his father.

"I have developed other formulations," Ava continued, "formulations that rejuvenate the muscles, cartilage, all the connective tissue that keeps your body flexible, lithe, and strong. Would you not always like to be as strong as you are today?" She laughed at his hesitation. "Of course you would.

"Mulciber and I have worked on thousands of those men and women you pity, experimented on them for over thirty-five years to learn the secrets of all the glands—now we control them. I can control the manufacture and release of hormones and so I can control the timetable of your body—speed it up, slow it down. I can transplant or rejuvenate organs, turn men into women and women into men. I can actually prolong life and soon I will control life itself. Do you understand what I am saying?" She looked at him with wild, excited eyes. "Soon I will have the process for complete cell regeneration, the process for eternal life."

Michael stared back at this incredible woman, stared into her eyes that seemed able to cut through all his defenses. Was this really happening? Was she telling the truth or had she seduced her entire organization only with the promises they wanted to hear? Was she mad?

"That is my tool, Michael, the basis of all my power —the promise of life, youth, and beauty—and to it I can add unlimited power and wealth. Few have been able to resist me—that is why my organization has grown so quickly, grown with those already in power who know what it is to live with power and want more, grown with those who want to live twice their lifetimes. The hypocritical fools who do resist me I replace with my doubles. Soon I will have control over all those I need for the completion of my plan—the world."

He was overwhelmed and looked for flaws in her grand strategy; there had to be flaws somewhere. "But the world is too big," he protested, "there are just too many people to . . ."

"Michael, your mind hasn't yet comprehended what I am saying, all the implications. Don't you understand I already have hundreds of men and women strategically placed throughout the world? They are in the East, the West, they report to me, men and women in the highest places who have either joined me voluntarily or neuts who have assumed the identities of those who have refused my offer. I have kings, senators, businessmen . . ."

"The shah?" Michael asked, remembering the unexpected visit of the ruler to Cannes and his meetings with Ava Bardoff.

"Mine," Ava gloated, "they're all mine. And my people control the internal security organizations of the major powers and their armed forces. I control generals, admirals—I need just a few more and then they're completely mine. Soon I will control the very powerful American secretary of state and, through him, all of NATO. And the Communist bloc will soon jump at my command. These fools sleep above us now, brought to me by my shah. They sleep now, but not for long. When we have finished with them, they will be given to Mulciber, and my neuts, identical in every detail, will replace them. They will deliver the information and power I need for my final step." She laughed triumphantly at the young man sitting before her.

"You look at me strangely, Michael. Do you think I am mad?" Ava suddenly grabbed his arm, pulling him up from his chair with surprising strength. "Come, I will show you—I will show you the future rulers of the world."

She laughed again as she led him quickly down three flights of stairs to the top floor of the technical center and threw open the door to a corridor running the length of the building. Ava Bardoff half-pushed, half-pulled him along past the living quarters and study rooms of her neuts.

"I call them 'neuts,'" she said, "because what they were is of no importance, only what they become. They are reborn in the body, personality, and image of the man or woman they are to impersonate. I recruit people of the same nationality and with a physical similarity to those they will replace and then Mulciber and his team perform the surgery necessary to make the match complete—bones, skin, defects—perfect duplication. Even the vocal chords are changed and the hair pattern over the body. I personally mold the skin to duplicate each tiny line and wrinkle. And then they study." She took him past libraries, rooms with tape machines, motion-picture projectors. "They learn every detail of the past, every personal secret, voice inflections, how to move, walk, smile, frown, they become the other person—it becomes their only identity. Look at your own father—one of my perfect neuts."

"And if someone should detect a difference?" Michael asked, thinking of his mother.

"Minor physical differences can be explained away by the fact that they have spent several weeks at my clinic undergoing rejuvenation treatment. My neuts always look more beautiful or handsome, a little younger than the people they replaced, and they age only at my direction. That is the key to my fame, the reason I have been able to lure so many of those in power."

"And if the difference is in personality or . . . ?" Michael persisted.

"Then we take steps to eliminate the problem which, in our case, means the person who detects the change. There are many ways. Simple ones—you may remember the shah divorced his first wife—or more complicated ones. Accidents can always be arranged or . . ."

"Or people can be committed to mental institutions," Michael finished.

Ava Bardoff looked at him sharply for a second or two, understanding the reason for his statement. "Yes," she said, "we can arrange that, too."

"What happens if you can't lure someone here, someone you have to control?"

"Then we make the switch elsewhere, as we did with Peter Kent on the plane, or we eliminate the troublesome person completely and work on the person who fills the gap. Assassinations are very common these days, are they not?" Ava's smile was one of cunning. "They are still fighting over the direction of the bullet in Dallas; did it come from behind, in front, or beside him? As I said, we have our neuts everywhere, in the secret service as well as in the marriage bed. And the poor late-lamented king of the oil wells—his nephew was such a nice boy when he last visited us. I now control OPEC."

As they walked through the neuts' quarters, Michael saw many familiar faces, faces pictured frequently in newspapers and on TV, faces of important people as yet unaware their lives would soon end. He was aghast. He now firmly believed everything Ava Bardoff had told him; he believed in the doubles that worked for her all over the world, and he believed it was just a matter of time before they moved. Who were they? Which leaders? Which generals? Who could be trusted? How could they be tracked down and stopped? It would be impossible. Would they all have the telltale blue dots or not? Her operation was too vast, too advanced to be stopped now by Hugo or by anyone else.

Ava was pleased with the effect of her little tour on Michael; as they reentered her office, her seduction was nearing its climax.

"Ever since World War II, the world has said that the road to lasting peace is through interdependence, one people upon another, one country upon the next. But that has been the road to world weakness, not strength. When the grain crops fail in North America, India and Africa starve. When the Arabs raise the prices of their oil, other economies falter. The country that is self-sufficient is powerful, not the country dependent on the resources and political blackmail of another. It is through this new interdependence of the world on each other's energy resources that I shall attack."

Ava Bardoff strode to a large detailed map of the world set into the wall; her fist began to beat with more and more enthusiasm at one area after another. "The Ruhr; I control its coal. The Middle East, Lybia, Venezuela, all OPEC—oil, I control it. Texas, California, Alaska—oil, I control it. The North Sea fields, Russia—oil, I control it." Her hand swept across the map in a wide arc. "I control it all. The rulers of the countries or the owners of these energy complexes— whether they're the real ones or my neuts—they do as I tell them.

"I will be able to activate my plans once the Corsica meeting is over. Do you know what the fools will do at that very secret meeting in Corsica? The presidents, prime ministers, chancellors of the Western countries are going to draw up their invasion plans for the Middle East oil fields in the event of another boycott. In the name of détente, the secretary of state is telling our Russian friend about it and will get his approval. In the name of détente, those two will carve up the oil fields for themselves. But they are too late. Once I know the invasion plans I will make *sure* that boycott occurs, I will force them to invade. Their brief war will give me the excuse I need to *destroy* the oil fields, and, through a series of regrettable and unforeseen circumstances, the other energy sources of the world will dry up as well. Production of coal will falter, oil refineries and wells will break down or be mishandled, prices will explode and so will the world economy. You saw how oil prices almost bankrupted Italy. Well, I will destroy the economies of the others and in the chaos and anarchy that follow, only my organization will be prepared, coordinated, and strong enough to take over. My collaborators—my neuts—will lead, and there will be no one to oppose us and the subtle changes we make in the internal structures of the major countries. The security forces won't expose us—they are mine. The armies won't rise against us—they are mine. By the time the world wakes up it will be too late—I will have absolute control."

Ava leaned forward, her radiant, excited face close to his. "Then I will begin the creation of my society, to replace the existing social order. My elite race will rule, the rest will merely exist to serve us. Yes, Michael, my handsome men and beautiful women will be the kings and queens, the dictators of the world, all loyal to me as the supreme being. We will use selective breeding to limit population and clone vast armies of identical soldiers who will strike terror into all who even contemplate rising against us. It will be paradise on earth.

"Would you like to be a king, Michael, would you like to control a state in my new order? If only I could be sure of you." Ava Bardoff stared deep into his eyes, trying to penetrate his thoughts. "If only I could be sure."

Michael glanced at the clock on Ava's desk; it read precisely 6:00 A.M. His life and Sarah's—their future—everything depended upon what he would say next.

"Madame Bardoff, this cave of yours will be destroyed any minute—you'd better sound an alert and get out now." Ava froze, a shocked expression across her face. "Hugo's men should be here at any minute, if they're not inside already. They're brought bombs with them."

"Impossible," she snapped, regaining her composure. The idea was ridiculous. "They would never—" Ava paused, remembering she'd underestimated Hugo before. She reached for the phone on her desk and barked into it, "Get me Moloch."

Holding the receiver in her hand, Ava stared at Michael as he continued his betrayal. "I went to Paris to get the charts of this cave system. You must know—your men killed a friend who was helping me at the archives, Jean-Pascale Melia. They blew up his building on Rue de l'Université."

Ava turned to Beel, who stood with his mouth hang-

ing open. "Bring me dePasse—at once." Turning back
to Michael, she demanded, "How many men?"

"Ten, I think. Their orders are to destroy the cavern and all in it."

"Moloch," she said flatly into the phone, "ten men
from Montclair's ship are attacking the complex from
the river entrance. Full alert and report back at once."

A siren began wailing throughout the corridors and
reverberated in the Great Hall outside. Ava Bardoff
paced back and forth across the office like a caged
tigress impatiently waiting for news of the raiders. Her
frustration and anger at the audacity of the attack increased as the minutes ticked past; Michael braced
himself for the explosions that should already have
rocked the complex.

"Montclair is stupid, a fool. He sends peashooters
after a cannon. They are all as good as dead. I hope he
is enjoying his last few hours on earth."

Michael felt a wave of guilt, hearing her signature
on Hugo's death warrant.

The door opened abruptly and Moloch strode in,
perspiration glistening on his fat, bald head. He looked
suspiciously at Michael while making his report.

"There is no reply from the farm guarding the northern sink, and the guards at the water entrance have
just been reported missing by their replacement. Montclair's men are obvious already with us. I've doubled
the guards on the catwalks should they try to escape
that way and have begun a thorough search of the
entire complex and the cavern for the men and any
explosive packages they may have planted. We should
find them very soon." Pointing at Michael, he asked,
"He gave you the warning and numbers of the enemy
force?"

"Yes, I believe our friend has most firmly decided to
join us. Unlike his late master, Hugo Montclair, Michael wants to live."

Her words did not convince Moloch. He continued
to eye Michael suspiciously as he went on. "I have
ordered the clinic staff to their positions up above—I
want them out of the way. Two were reported off lim-

its wandering in the hydroponic gardens. When we find them, they'll be disciplined."

"If you move the attendants up to the clinic, we can afford to bring down the security guards there to help in the search. I want Montclair's men found at once—the longer they are free, the more damage they may do. Make sure every inch of this complex is scoured for explosives, is that clear?"

Moloch was issuing orders over the phone when Beel entered with dePasse. Ava turned angrily on the count and shouted, "Your men blew up a building on Rue de l'Université to eliminate a Monsieur Melia, who was prying into these caves. Why was I not informed?"

DePasse was taken aback at her anger and rightly assumed her question was connected somehow with the alert now going on. "Yes, I put it in my report which . . ."

"Which," she snapped, "you have as yet failed to give me."

"I did not wish to bother you with the matter when you had so many other things on your mind last night. The death of Melia is only one of many we've had to . . ."

"And you also did not wish to bother Moloch with it last night?" The count's mouth worked, trying to find the correct words. "Idiot!" The slap of her swagger stick across his face raised a red welt on his cheek. "You may be the grand and talented Count Jean Claude Henri dePasse to all those in Paris, but to me you are still just a number on the recharger. I do not even remember the name you had when you came to us. Do not think yourself too important or you shall be in for a very rude shock. I will decide what should and should not be reported, is that clear?"

Before he could answer, she continued, *"You* are not head of France, *I* am. Remember that. I will not tolerate . . ."

"Madame," Moloch interrupted, "they have taken one of the enemy and are bringing him in now."

"Alive?" she asked, momentarily diverted from her attack on dePasse.

"Unfortunately not—the guard didn't get a chance to use his gun. In the struggle, he was forced to strangle him." As Moloch was describing the circumstances surrounding the incident, the office door opened and two guards carried in the lifeless body, his head hanging grotesquely to one side from a broken neck. They dumped him unceremoniously on the carpet before Ava Bardoff's desk.

"Where did you say this happened?" she asked, prodding the body with her foot.

"In the hydroponic gardens below the complex, just this side of the rear entrance to the cavern. He was carrying explosives and underwater gear."

"Do you recognize him, Michael?" Ava asked.

Michael forced himself to look down at the body. "He's Carpenter, the radio man from the *Krait*."

Ava kicked the body viciously. "Get it out of here—use it to feed the slaves." Michael's stomach turned. "Moloch, get back to headquarters. I want the rest of Montclair's men and I want them now. Beel, inform Dr. Mulciber that I will be bringing our young friend down shortly for the loyalty treatment." She smiled at Michael.

He looked at the clock on her desk. It was 6:15 A.M., twelve minutes past the time the explosives were to have gone off. Moloch's men must have found the charges wherever they had been placed and neutralized them. Carpenter had failed in his attempt to close the far end of the Great Hall and establish an escape route. As he'd feared, Hugo's gamble had lost.

Although Ava Bardoff was anxious about the safety of her underworld complex, there was nothing more she, herself, could do. Having seen one of Hugo's men dead, she was confident her elite, well-trained security force would be capable of quickly rounding up the rest of the small invasion group and find any explosives in the complex. That done, she would take her revenge on the *Krait,* its owner, and the remains of its crew to wipe out all opposition. The excitement of the last minutes, the sight of the dead man, and the anticipation of her revenge on Hugo combined to arouse her.

"DePasse," she commanded, "wait outside, I want to talk to our handsome young friend alone."

As the count left, Ava slowly walked around Michael's chair, studying him.

"What is this loyalty treatment you keep talking about?" he asked warily, feeling awkward under her appraising eyes.

She didn't seem to hear him. Instead of an answer, Ava said, "We have one other little thing to discover about you first. Stand up and take off your shirt."

He stood uneasily, looking at her questioningly. "Why do . . ."

"Take it off," she repeated coldly. In answer to his hesitation, Ava reached out and tore open the front with a jerk of her hand.

Opposition was fruitless under these circumstances. He slipped out of the torn garment.

Ava looked him over with admiration and desire. "Yes," she said, her voice lowering to a whisper. Her fingers traced the outline of his muscles under the tanned skin. "I promise you, Michael, that you shall always be as strong and desirable as you are today. Age will not steal *your* beauty." She circled him, grasping his chest suddenly from behind and pressing her cheek to his shoulder. "You will live young and beautiful for me, forever."

He stood rigid, looking straight ahead at the map of her world in the wall; his throat was dry and his heart beat wildly.

"I . . . I can hardly believe it's possible," he stammered, stalling for time.

She pressed his body back against hers, giving a low laugh, her breath hot against his neck. "The bodies of the weak will keep you strong, I will use their glands, their hormones, their organs to keep you young. I will use them to rob nature of your life." He couldn't see her, just hear her purring voice and feel the excitement building in her body, excitement being transmitted to his. "Oh, my young beauty, I will keep your skin smooth and warm," her tongue moved across his shoulders, "and your body firm and strong." One hand massaged the muscles of his chest. "You will always be the virile young bull you are now." Ava's other hand slid below his waist.

Michael gasped aloud as he felt her fingers close around him. Her arms and body seemed to be encircling him like a serpent. His head was spinning as her urgent voice filled his brain with a torrent of seduction. Oh, God, help me, he cried in a silent plea.

"In nature the strong and beautiful survive—they devour the inferior. Why shouldn't we do the same? Morals and religion were created to protect the weak. I will create a new religion, one for the strong. I will give the world its gods, gods to worship and serve, gods to rule them. My gods will be of flesh and blood, gods of physical beauty and intelligence." Michael's body betrayed the excitement building in him. "My gods will live forever. We, Michael, you and I, we will be those gods," Ava hissed, writhing against him.

His knees trembled, his initial revulsion of her was overwhelmed and now served only to excite him more. Michael's breath came in short gasps and his brain and body responded to the lust in her words and touch. He relaxed back into Ava's arms, hearing her voice droning on hypnotically like a psalm in his ear. Somewhere inside he heard his own voice answering, yes, yes; his lips formed the word.

The sudden, sharp jab of a needle shattered him. Michael broke away, turning to look with surprise at Ava's smiling face. Poison, not the elixir of life, surged through his veins as his legs buckled and he fell forward at her feet.

Ava Bardoff looked down at the proud athlete who had succumbed to her mind and body. She put a booted foot on his chest; her laugh was cruel and victorious. "Welcome, Michael, welcome to the House of Bardoff." Stepping over his body, she jerked open the door and said to the count, waiting outside, "Get some guards —we will take your new son down to Mulciber."

As they descended to the second floor of the technical center, the spiral staircase and corridors swarmed with guards like black ants, moving against the current of the white uniformed attendants on their way up to the clinic above. One of the attendants, his face blank of emotion, paused to stare at Michael and moved almost as if to help him. His companion pushed him ahead callously.

Ava Bardoff strode down the corridor to the operating theatre with her protective force surrounding her and looked from side to side with satisfaction at her research laboratories with their bubbling crucibles, glass tubes carrying liquids of all colors, and elaborate, fragile constructions glistening under the bands of fluorescent lights overhead. Men in spotless white coats moved silently among the benches in the antiseptic environment so wrapped up in their work that their scientific minds paid little attention to the sirens and activities in the outside world.

She swung through the doors leading into Theatre 14 followed by dePasse and the guards carrying Michael; Beel and Dr. Mulciber stood waiting for her. Sarah's eyes widened as she saw Michael's limp form.

"I believe you two have met," Ava Bardoff said sarcastically as he was being strapped to the table beside hers.

"Please, oh, please don't hurt him," Sarah pleaded.

"I have absolutely no intention at all of hurting him. Unlike you, I have many uses for young dePasse here."

"What are you going to do to him?" Sarah would gladly have plunged a knife into her own heart at that moment for having brought him to this. "Oh, Michael," she said in a useless apology, "forgive me, I only meant to help, I . . ."

"My poor little sparrow," Ava gloated over the girl strapped to the table, "it makes no difference whether he forgives you or not—you have lost him, he is one of us now. We are just going to put a little time bomb in his head to make sure he does not stray."

Ava leaned down over Sarah, dangling a test tube containing a tiny device, less than half the size of a pea, before her eyes. "This little bead will sit quietly inside his head. At the end of each year, if I do not recharge it with the right combination of radio waves, *poof!* It will disintegrate and dissolve with enough power, just enough power, to make a small hole in his brain —in the past they have always diagnosed it as a 'fatal cerebral hemorrhage.' Would you like one in your skull, my dear?"

Sarah moved her head as far away from the tube Ava dangled and the leering face behind it as the restraining straps would allow. Her tormenter stood up laughing and turned to Beel and dePasse. "And only I know the right combination for each of these little beads, do I not, gentlemen? Moloch can recharge all the guards and the little people's beads, but I recharge his. All your lives depend upon my memory and your loyalty." They looked at her with blank expressions, not wanting to arouse her anger.

"My poor friends," she said with sarcastic sympathy, "you think you hate me, but you do not. You hate the weakness in yourselves. Would you like to return the youth and power I have given you in exchange for the removal of this little bead?" She looked from one to the other. "Well, would you? No, I do not think you would. Power sits too well with you and your vanities need the reassurance they get every time you look in your mirrors, every time you seduce a young virgin, does it not, Beel?" He looked away from Sarah. Ava laughed. "Yes, gentlemen, I think you have made a very good bargain."

Michael had been strapped securely to the second table and lay as if in a deep coma. Ava ran her hand through his hair. "What a pity to shave this away. Would you like it, Sarah? Would you like to keep his hair? It is all his body will ever give you now. But you are going to give him a great deal—your body is going to keep him young and handsome for *me*."

She turned to Dr. Mulciber. "Make the first batch of his serum from her," she ordered, and then looked back down at the helpless girl. "I want him to know that part of you is in his cells, his blood, his muscles. The thought will disgust him, and his disgust and guilt will turn to hatred. He will hate you, Sarah, despise you and your memory for giving him youth and life. His hatred for you will drive him to me."

Ava held up the test tube containing the tiny bead and smiled at it while running her hand over Michael's chest. She looked at him. "You will learn to depend upon me, and I can be a very exciting person to be dependent upon." Stepping back, she nodded to Dr. Mulciber. "You may proceed, Doctor. I want to watch *this* operation." Sarah struggled uselessly against her bonds as Mulciber moved forward to begin his preparations.

12

Halvorsen and five other members of the *Krait*'s crew tried to blend inconspicuously into the general movement in the corridor before the elevator, stalling for time. Three times the doors had opened to deliver the black T-shirted security guards from above and three times the crew, through their apparent lack of interest, had allowed other white-uniformed attendants to take their places on the slow-moving elevator. Halvorsen glanced constantly at his watch, finally sighing with relief upon sighting two attendants walking toward him, their hands held so that blue dots were visible on both thumbs.

"Well, it's about time," he said quietly through the frozen mouth of his mask, "we've only got a few minutes left."

"Sorry," Watson mumbled, "we ran into a little trouble with an overzealous guard and had to find a good hiding place for the body in the gardens."

"We saw Michael dePasse," Andrews said. "It looks as if he's had it."

"This sentimental fool was about to blow the whole scene and grab him," Watson added.

"I sympathize," Halvorsen replied. "Was there nothing you could do?"

"Nothing," the engineer said flatly. "We would have had the entire place down on our necks."

"But we could have taken Bardoff, too. She'd have been a hostage and . . ."

"Taken her? With that cordon of guards around her?" Watson interrupted. "You're dreaming, mate." He checked his watch and jabbed the elevator button impatiently. "Where the hell is this thing?"

It arrived empty. The eight men entered and waited for the doors to close. The elevator rose only one floor and stopped. Their eyes met nervously and their hands moved instinctively for the pistols hidden under their jackets as the doors slid open.

Two clinic attendants entered the crowded car, nodding a slight greeting to the others. The eyes of one suddenly narrowed and he made a move to jump back through the slowly closing doors. Halvorsen's arm snapped around his neck, cutting off his windpipe; the other found himself pinned and muffled by Watson before he could call out. The doors slid quietly shut and the elevator started its long journey upward, the silence broken only by the dull thud of two bullets going through the bodies of Madame Bardoff's men. Watson ordered each man to attach a three-inch, red fabric disk to his uniform over his heart and in the center of his back. "No sense shooting each other," he explained. "By the time Madame's goons realize why we've got these badges, they'll be dead."

When the elevator doors opened on the second floor of the north wing of the château, the crew ran softly forward down the hall. One of Ava Bardoff's attendants walking away from them turned in surprise; he fell before he could utter a sound. Watson used the bodies of the two they'd killed in the elevator to wedge open its doors, effectively putting it out of order and so assuring none of the guards returned behind them. The others moved silently ahead, bursting first into the observation rooms to shoot what neuts they found and then into the rooms of their intended victims to take care of the interrogators and nurses hovering over them. Within two minutes the entire second floor in the north wing had been taken without a single shot being fired against them and without disturbing any of the drugged guests.

Watson stationed one member of the crew at the doors at either end of the north corridor. Leaving them behind, he and Halvorsen, each followed by two men, ran down the east and west wings of the château toward the central staircase that led down to the main reception hall and the switchboard and communications center connecting the château to the subterranean complex. They threw open every door along their route, quietly and efficiently shooting every living person they saw in uniform. Michael had warned them that four innocent women were also staying at the clinic; these four sleepy and confused guests were quickly carried back to the north wing and locked together in a room to keep them out of harm's way.

The entire second floor had been secured without a cry or the alarm being given. Now the six stood at the head of the grand staircase circling down into the main entrance hall.

"Okay, men," Watson whispered, "the honeymoon is over."

He and two others removed their red badges temporarily and walked casually down the staircase and across the wide marble hall toward the main reception desk, where four of Ava Bardoff's attendants had gathered to discuss the search being carried out below for the invaders. They looked up as the three newcomers approached. Some instinct warned them of danger; the man seated behind the desk pulled his needle gun from the drawer and fired point blank at Watson, the others following suit with their weapons. Watson and his two men fired back, their bullets designed to kill, not paralyze. The fourth attendant cried out as he broke from the group. Watson brought him down.

As the other three members of the *Krait*'s crew dashed downstairs, the door to the communications center opened in answer to the warning cry and then slammed shut. Halvorsen blasted away at the closed door as they burst through over the body of the man lying on the floor. His companion, eyes wide with surprise, recovered quickly from the shock and, swinging around in his chair, reached out for the alarm to warn the clinic staff and those in the cavern below. Halvorsen's bullet shattered his hand before it touched the red button and Andrews's charge carried the screaming man out of his chair from in front of the radio switchboard and across the room.

While Halvorsen and Andrews efficiently immobilized both the equipment and its operator, a wild battle was building up in the main hall. The first shouts had alerted Madame's men to the presence of the enemy in their midst, and they had come swarming to the attack. It took them only a brief time to discover that those of their comrades with the unusual red badges were, in fact, the enemy, but that delay cost many lives. Now identified, the clinic staff was able to move against them. White-coated men and women poured down from their quarters on the top floors and along the corridors of the ground floor, shouting to each other and converging on the six crewmen. After recovering from the shocked realization that their needle guns were useless against the immunized crew, they were forced to rely upon their superior numbers and sheer brute strength in their fight to destroy the invaders. With knives and assorted clubs, they massed into suicide charges, using furniture as shields, until they were close enough for hand-to-hand combat.

The situation soon became desperate. Watson had never expected such fanaticism; he could not know that these men considered themselves as good as dead if their leader were taken. He shot two of them as the third brought him down with a flying tackle, tearing off his mask. Rolling over on his back, Watson fired up point blank between Peor's eyes. Getting to his feet, he looked across the hall to see one of his own men stagger back, his throat torn open. "Holy mother of God," he muttered, dodging a missile thrown at his head, "they're madmen—they're fucking madmen."

The entire building suddenly trembled beneath their feet, the crystal chandelier overhead tinkling from the shock waves. Watson and his men had only a brief second of satisfaction, knowing that at least one of their charges had gone off below, before they threw themselves back into the shrieking life-or-death struggle raging about them.

Far below, the shock wave was much greater, knocking Dr. Mulciber, knife still in hand, Ava Bardoff, and the others in Theatre 14 to the floor as the power house cracked wide open in the first blast and continued to disintegrate in a series of subsidiary explosions. The second major blast collapsed the entire roof of the branch passage, blocking it solid, while a third one buckled the huge steel doors. The lights of the complex and those in the Great Hall dimmed and flickered out. Small chunks of the vast rock ceiling rained down on the buildings and the slaves cringing in confusion in the hydroponic gardens, while bats screeched through the air, adding to the initial panic of the inhabitants who bumped and scrambled over each other in the darkness.

After the first few minutes of terrifying subterranean night when the fate of the main ceiling was in doubt, lights slowly brightened in one section after another inside the complex as the emergency electricity supply Beel had described automatically switched into operation; only the gardens were left in darkness. Although the personnel of the complex were badly shaken and frightened, the structures themselves remained intact. Ava Bardoff picked herself up from the floor and steadied herself against the table on which Michael lay strapped. Her mind was clear and precise.

"Mulciber, quick, to the laboratories," she ordered. "See what damage there is—we can't lose those experiments." Ava saw several men running in the corridor and moved quickly toward the door. "Beel, dePasse, come with me. I may need you to stop any panic and help bring things here back under control. I want a damage report from all areas. Use the public address system to . . ."

They left Theatre 14 deserted, Michael and Sarah temporarily forgotten, as Madame Bardoff continued issuing her orders in a rapid staccato. Silence fell over the room; only footsteps running past in the corridor outside could be heard.

Sarah lay staring up at the ceiling, imagining it crashing down on her and thinking how much better it would have been to have died that way than in the manner Ava was planning for her. Once again she saw those poor, horrible creatures in the glass cells; she would soon be one of them.

Her heart almost stopped from fright when a quiet voice beside her asked, "You all right?"

She looked across the gap between the two tables, not really believing what she'd heard. Michael lay looking over at her with a faint, mischievous smile playing on his lips. "I'd just about given up hope of ever finding you again," he said. "Trying to walk out on me?"

Sarah didn't know what to say as tears of relief welled up in her eyes. "I . . . I thought you'd been drugged and . . . and . . . oh, darling."

"So did they, but you can't keep a good man down," he said cheerfully for her benefit and then sobered, a look of concern on his face. "Actually, I injected myself with an antidote Chris Halvorsen gave me in Paris before coming down here, but are *you* all right? They haven't hurt you?"

"No, no, I'm fine," she replied, trying to put on a brave face. Then she began to laugh and cry at the same time. "It sounds as if we're chatting at an English tea party, and look at us." She moved her hands the few inches allowed by the table straps. Her laughter deserted her and only tears were left. "Oh, Michael, I'm so afraid."

"Of course you are, and right now I don't particularly feel like Superman, but we're going to get out."

Michael craned his neck in all directions, looking about the antiseptic operating theatre for some means of escape as Sarah told him all she'd seen in the complex. Lying strapped on the table, he felt like a man stranded on a tiny desert island in the middle of an empty sea. Sarah's table was the closest thing to him, about four feet away. Then his attention was caught by the wheeled instrument trolley sitting beside her table near her left hand. Several of Dr. Mulciber's scalpels glistened in a neat row on it.

He interrupted her ugly description of the cages below them. "Darling, there's a trolley beside you on the left. Can you touch it? Be careful not to push it away."

Sarah bent her left wrist away from her body, her fingers spread feeling the air. "No, I can't touch it."

"Try again, I know you can do it," he urged.

She pushed her arm down through the restraining strap as far as she could until it bit into her skin. Gritting her teeth, she twisted her hand out, groping. "Yes, yes, I feel it now—there's a cloth on it. But I can't move my head far enough to look down."

"Pull it against your table. Does it seem to roll easily?"

"Yes, yes, I think so. Do you want me to try to get something from it?"

"No, I want you to give it a good shove over to me. Do you think you can put your hand between it and the table and give it a strong enough push to get it over here? You'll only have one chance."

"Oh, Michael, I don't know. I'm afraid—I don't . . ."

"You can do it, darling, just give it a try. Don't worry, if this one doesn't work out, I've got some other ideas."

Sarah relaxed a bit. Although she didn't really believe he had other ideas for escape, his words gave her confidence. She inserted her fingers in the space between the trolley and table, feeling the stiff cloth on the back of her hand. Pressing her fingers against the table, she concentrated, willing all the power in her body into her left hand. Then, eyes clamped shut, she flipped her hand out with all her might; a pain shot up her arm from the quick release of tension in her muscles.

Michael lay watching the trolley, the four feet seeming like four miles to him. After its initial fast movement away from Sarah's table, it slowed and began to rotate as its wheels turned to the right from the uneven force of her push. Continuing its slow rotation, one corner swung agonizingly closer and closer to him, stopping at least seven inches from his hand.

"You've done it," he said to Sarah to keep up her spirits. "We'll be out of here in a flash." It was one of the longest flashes in their lives.

Pushing his arm down through the leather loop holding his wrist to the table, Michael could only manage to caress the cloth on the trolley with his last two fingers. He strained down further, rolling his arm back and forth against the leather bond that now acted like a tourniquet, cutting off circulation to his numb fingers. He could barely feel the solid metal underneath the fabric when at last he was able to press down on it and slowly and painfully roll the trolley to him. He relaxed for a minute or two to let the feeling flow back into his fingers, then, bit by bit, he pulled the cloth toward him, bringing with it the scalpels he so desperately needed. At last his fingers felt the razor-sharp edge of the cutting tool. His hand was about to close over it when he heard footsteps approaching; he froze as they stopped and the doors of the theatre were thrown open. Michael's and Sarah's hearts stopped as a guard looked in, his eyes sweeping the theatre for a lurking enemy. Seeing nothing but two of Dr. Mulciber's experiments on the tables, he abruptly turned and left, the doors swinging back and forth before coming to rest.

Heaving a sigh of relief, Michael grasped the surgical instrument, pointed its tip up toward his wrist, and began sawing awkwardly at the strap. Sarah stared at him as he worked, biting her lip at the sight of his bloody wrist as the scalpel took chunks out of it. She listened intently to the movements in the corridor outside, keenly aware that at any minute they might be discovered or that Mulciber might come back and proceed with their operations as planned.

Michael's fingers ached and he was forced to take more frequent periods of rest to relax the muscle cramps in them. During these respites, he strained every muscle in his arm trying to snap physically the constantly weakening strap. During one of these attempts he felt the leather begin to give and doubled his efforts. Exerting every ounce of strength, it finally broke with a popping sound. He lay back and took a deep breath.

"We've done it," he said simply.

It didn't take him long to unbuckle the other restraining straps and slip stiffly off the table. He unbuckled Sarah's bonds, diverting his attention only to give her a brief kiss. "Welcome back to the land of the living, my sleeping beauty."

The sirens still wailed outside the complex and in its corridors. Michael wondered how many of the *Krait*'s crew had been captured or killed. From where he stood, Hugo's attack on the Styx Complex was failing miserably. He had played the role assigned to him perfectly up to this time; he had convinced Ava Bardoff of his defection from Hugo and given away the invasion plans precisely at 6:00 A.M. so that she, believing the sole purpose of the invasion was to destroy the cavern, would send down her guards from above, thus leaving the clinic unprotected to give the crew the opportunity to rescue the guests and take her prisoner. But Madame was not up in the château and the delay in the detonation of the explosives had given her men too much time to track down and eliminate the crew. Michael had no way of knowing of the pitched battle raging far above his head at this very minute; he remembered only the lifeless form of Carpenter, the man who was to have sealed off the Great Hall after their escape, lying at his feet. As far as he was concerned, he was on his own—for all practical purposes, he was.

Michael had to start improvising. His new plan was to capture Ava Bardoff and use her as a hostage to escape the caverns via the elevator. Also, he now knew she alone had the recharging codes for the brain beads locked in her head and so was the key to the destruction of the entire Bardoff organization around the world. As in Hugo's plan, he would try to create chaos to keep her men occupied and then make a grab for her when she was undefended.

He handed Sarah a long white surgeon's gown and tucked her hair under a white surgical cap. The final touch was a sterilizing mask.

"You look like a sexy Dr. Kildaire," he whispered. "Okay, out you go and do your tricks."

While Michael flattened himself against the wall of the operating theatre beside one of the doors, Sarah went into the corridor. She waited only a few seconds before a guard rounded the corner and walked quickly toward her. Sarah waved at him and beckoned urgently that he follow her into Theatre 14. Madame's guards had long since learned that the research and medical personnel in the complex were top dogs in the pecking order and that their wishes were to be obeyed. This security guard was no exception. He nodded acceptance of the surgeon's command and followed the white-gowned figure into the theatre. Before he could call out, Michael's arm clamped around his throat from behind and one of Mulciber's scalpels sank into his heart.

Michael changed clothes with the guard, Sarah washing out what little blood the thin wound had let escape onto the black T-shirt. The guard was then strapped in Michael's place on the table. In exactly the same way, a uniform was procured for Sarah and a second body was substituted in the white patient's gown she had once worn. She looked down at herself in the black uniform; the trousers bagged and the T-shirt, made for a barrel chest, sagged. Seeing her concern, Michael cracked, "Mae West you're not, but no one will notice."

He wrapped a hastily made bandage around her head to cover her hair and part of her face. "Let's hope they think you got beaned by a stalactite. If anyone gets nosy enough to ask, we'll let him have it with one of his own needle guns." He handed one of the pistols to Sarah. "Don't use it unless you really have to—we don't want to leave a line of bodies flagging our trail."

They started down the corridor in the opposite direction to Ava Bardoff's tower while he looked about him for any means of creating trouble and confusion in the complex. Sarah and Michael pretended to be in deep conversation and walked quickly by any guards or other personnel they met in the corridors. They passed through the door at the end of the corridor in the technical center to find themselves standing on a balcony fifteen feet above the factory floor. At one end of the balcony they saw a major glass control booth; several technicians were working in it.

"Stay behind me," Michael told Sarah over the noise of the machines. "I can take their needles if they're armed—you can't. I don't want to have to carry you all over this labyrinth."

They walked into the control room with cool authority, Michael waving at the only technician who bothered to look up. He pulled the trigger of his pistol four times and four of Ava Bardoff's men slipped to the floor. "Give me a hand," he called to Sarah. "Put everything on full power while I chop off the controls and do a little short circuiting."

"What will happen?" she asked as she twirled knobs.

"I haven't the slightest idea, but with them on emergency power and us turning everything on full, something has to happen," he answered, bringing down the ax on a master circuit.

It took only a minute, but when Michael and Sarah left the room it was filled with acrid smoke, sparks, and threatening hissing and popping sounds. They looked down to the factory floor at the confusion that was beginning to break out there. The few machine operators on duty that early in the morning were running back and forth pushing buttons and banging control panels, obviously concerned about what appeared to be a massive malfunction of their equipment. Several alarm bells, different in tone to the alert siren, began to jangle throughout the huge four-story structure.

"Come on," Michael urged, "I think we'd better clear out of here before something pops." He took her hand and drew her up a flight of iron stairs leading to another balcony just outside the neuts' floor. He felt it would be easier to lose themselves here for a while in the maze of libraries, tape and film rooms, and dormitories rather than in the more open areas of the laboratories below. As they strode with outward confidence through the door to the neuts' quarters, a small explosion accompanied by a shower of sparks and a spurt of flame rose up from one of the more intricate machines in the factory complex.

"Bull's-eye!" Michael smiled.

Things were going wrong all over the technical center. The electric controls on much of the equipment failed to operate correctly, either giving no response at all or building up unacceptable power levels to blow overloaded fuses, explode, or burn. The doors to the cages of Dr. Mulciber's living experiments slid open and shut in a jerky frenzy and finally ceased to function, half open. A series of short circuits caused the same problem in the slaves' cells in the sublevel of the technical center, and the bewildered creatures wandered out in the corridors not knowing what to do or which way to turn without a leader. Their dilemma was solved when a spark from fused wires set fire to one end of the cell block and, like primitive animals, the slaves shuffled in the opposite direction away from the flames, some moving out into the hydroponic gardens while others lumbered up the stairs to the laboratory floors above. No alarm sounded to alert the complex to the fire or the movement of their human refuse.

Down the hall from Theatre 14, Mulciber and his assistants worked desperately to save what experiments they could after the explosion had shattered or otherwise disrupted many of their delicate tube systems. Already two of the victims who were laid strapped to tables where they were fed drugs and hormones intravenously had died from an imbalance of the fluid mixture. Michael's attack on the electric circuits had caused further difficulty, completely eliminating all power to half of the laboratories as well as immobilizing all the alarm systems in the technical center. It was not until the smell of smoke being carried by the ventilating system caught Mulciber's attention that he realized a far more serious problem than saving the experiments might exist. Ordering his assistants to remain at their posts, he opened the lab doors and stepped into the corridor. It was slightly hazy with smoke. A few guards ran past but were unable to enlighten him about any fire, assuming that the appropriate department in Madame Bardoff's highly organized and efficient organization was dealing with the problem; their job lay in other directions. Mulciber pulled a hand-operated alarm outside the doors of the major laboratory. It ran for a few seconds and then ceased. Cursing, he picked up the phone nearby to contact Ava Bardoff.

Completely absorbed with the growing chaos in the complex and the search for Hugo's men, who had so far evaded her guards, Ava received his call with annoyance. "What do you mean, systems destruction?" She listened for a minute and then turned to Beel. "More trouble. Mulciber is having problems in the laboratory—his electric systems have been damaged. Check it at once. And Beel, Mulciber says there is a fire somewhere in the center, although none of the alarms have gone off. He smells smoke—probably from the fires we have already got under control in the factory—but alert the fire force to search the entire center. We cannot afford a serious internal fire now, particularly with that water building up out there."

Beel hurried from the room, leaving Ava Bardoff holding the phone and staring out of a porthole at the water of the Styx that was just beginning to flow over the threshold of the giant doors her men were so desperately trying to close. It would have been bad enough to have the river diverted through the Great Hall under normal conditions, but the foul weather above had swollen it dangerously and she was sure the worst was yet to come. Once before Ava had been below when a wall of water had swept through the cave system, flooding it completely. Although the powerhouse had been badly damaged, the doors had protected her complex.

"Where are those men?" she screamed in frustration at the Count dePasse, who stood across the office waiting for further orders. "Why have we not found them yet?"

Her question was answered almost immediately. Moloch entered the room breathlessly. "We've lost all communication with the clinic." He anticipated her question. "Yes, we have tried the radio as well as the phone—the tremor from the explosion could not have put both out of action. Also, the elevator does not respond, it is being held up above. We are cut off from the clinic and there is only one explanation."

Ava Bardoff stared at him in disbelief for several seconds. "But how could they . . .?"

Before she finished, Moloch stated flatly, "Montclair's men must have got up through the elevator, surprising them, or else a second group of his men got into the grounds and château after we pulled the guards down here for the search. I'm sending a force up through the elevator in the factory. They are to surround the clinic from the outside and move in to kill. I am taking no chances with our needle pistols—I am issuing them real guns and ammunition."

"We have had no news at all from our men up there?"

"None."

"Hurry, Moloch, we must not let them take the American and Russian. Hurry, damn it," she shouted.

"Our men are on their way now," he answered with infuriating calmness.

In sheer frustration Ava Bardoff turned the TV monitor on to Theatre 14 and looked at the two covered figures strapped to the tables. "Those two are responsible for this," she raged. "I was willing to indulge my whims with that young man, but not now. DePasse," she barked at the count, "kill them. I want them both killed. Do you remember what I told you Rimmon did to that concierge in Cannes?" He nodded uneasily, dreading what was to come. "Then bring me their heads. Do you understand? I want their heads brought to me here. Now go."

DePasse left and she turned back to Moloch, her angry frustration somewhat alleviated by her act of revenge against Michael and Sarah. "We will lose most, if not all, of the gardens to the water," Madame Bardoff said, itemizing the debits and credits of the situation like an accountant. "Aside from the factory damage and the loss of the powerhouse, we have lost some of Mulciber's experiments. He will be set back about a year. But, Moloch, they are not that vital to our grand scheme. We can still move ahead on schedule if we do not lose those two men in the clinic. We must not lose them."

The phone buzzed. Ava picked it up, listened, and slammed it down. "Your men report a serious fire in the slave blocks."

Dr. Mulciber hurried down an internal staircase to the floor below to check the cages and the living experiments there. Smoke was heavy when he emerged from the enclosed stairwell and it took him a few seconds to register on the events before him. In the smoky haze he saw figures milling about. He was almost among them when he recognized them as slaves. He shoved several of the unfortunate creatures out of his way imperiously before realizing just how many were crowded into the corridor.

In the back of what little was left of their minds, the slaves vaguely remembered this place and the pain it represented. They remembered cruelty and the evil face with the Vandyke that had peered down at them, cut into them, hurt them, and they remembered what it was like to hate. One reached out tentatively to touch that face. Dr. Mulciber knocked the hand roughly away. Another tried to speak at it, grunting pathetically. A third moved toward it, wanting to react to it but not knowing how.

Mulciber hesitated and then decided to withdraw before the explosive tension he felt in the air become focused upon him. His hesitation and the weakness it showed was communicated to the animals around him; they moved forward. He backed toward the door through which he'd come, not calling out for help for fear it might trigger off this mindless mob. It was not his call, but the cry from Peter Kent incarcerated in his cell—the cry caused by some mutilated nerve screaming in his body—that triggered the slaves. They surged toward Mulciber as he moved backward through the door and up the stairs, staring in the detached fascination of a scientist at the hideous creatures shuffling after him. They picked up speed to match his pace and burst after him through the glass doors into the major laboratory. His assistants turned at the noise and stood wide-eyed in horror as the slaves shambled down the parallel aisles between the laboratory benches, their arms reaching out and swaying back and forth, smashing into test tubes and glass constructions and crashing them to the floor.

The lab assistants scattered, running before the creatures to alert the guards. Their panic only served to stimulate the slaves, who continued to move determinedly after Mulciber as he backed away, still hypnotized by them. It was not until the jagged fingernail of one tore painfully across his cheek that the doctor snapped out of his detached, analytical state into one of personal terror.

Turning his back on them, he ran down the corridor to the balcony and made for the stairs leading down to the factory floor. He stopped with his foot on the top step. In the chaos now going on within the vast subterranean factory building, no one had noticed the dozen or so slaves who had entered the building and now stood in a tight knot near the foot of the balcony stairs. One after the other, they looked up at the only face they knew and slowly began to mount the steps toward it. Mulciber turned to run back along the balcony but his route was cut off by the slaves who now lurched along it toward him.

The doctor called out for help, but the noise of the machines and the firefighting crews drowned out his voice. The creatures shuffled toward him from both directions; his only escape was now over a series of catwalks that crossed the factory. He climbed over the balcony railing and moved cautiously along one of the narrow catwalks high above the factory floor; the slaves followed awkwardly, pushing and shoving each other to get close to that face, to hurt it. Mulciber's route was planned for him, the catwalk he had chosen ran halfway across the factory and then out through a door to the huge, egg-shaped glass tanks of chlorine and hydrogen gas.

As the slaves struggled to get onto the catwalk, a guard happened upon them. Pulling out his gun, he fired several needles to drop the two creatures closest to him, but before he could fire again, he was inundated by the others, each reaching for a piece of him. Whether he suffocated first or was pulled apart screaming, no one would ever know. When the slaves moved forward again, all that was left behind of him was a bloody pile of bones and flesh that bore no resemblance to a human being.

Mulciber fled out on the delicate metal frame supporting the tanks into the night of the rock cavern. Shafts of light from within the factory cast strange shadows across the dark water of the gardens. He crawled carefully on all fours to one of the ladders built into the corner supports when he heard the same subhuman gurgling noises beneath him that he had just left behind inside. In the shadows below, Mulciber saw more of his mutilated mistakes clustered about the foot of the tank frame. Like their companions, as they looked up at the white-gowned doctor, his face caught in a shaft of light, a vague recognition sparked off the emotion of hate. They, too, moved irresistibly toward him. Several started clumsily up the ladder. Mulciber pulled himself back up on the frame and inched his way gingerly across the fragile steel construction to another of the ladders. His movement only served as a lure to bring other slaves to the second ladder. Within minutes, the creatures slowly pulling themselves up the four corners of the supporting frame were joined by those from inside the factory who had broken through the outer door.

This horrible parade of contorted humanity coming closer and closer to him evoked images in his mind of the columns moving to the death pits and gas chambers. He saw the crematoriums, smelled burning flesh and bone. He saw his laboratories and his research director; would these creatures of the past take vengeance on him, too? Would they bring down the promised kingdom again?

Mulciber stood with his arms outstretched in the underground night, once again mesmerized by the shadows of the subhuman forms that he had created, accepting retribution, his death, and the destruction of the complex and all its inhabitants. The first to touch him did so almost gently as if to embrace him. He sank slowly under the combined weight as one hand after another took hold of him, his brain so numbed by visions of the past that he hardly felt his cheek being torn away.

And still they came, each one moving toward the center like bees swarming over each other—up the ladders, over the catwalk, over the delicate steel network. By the time the guards discovered what was happening and moved in to take control, it was too late. Cross wires and braces had separated and thin beams sagged under the heavy burden of the bodies writhing above. Hoping to stun those slaves who still clambered dumbly upward, the guards made a fatal mistake—they ordered the giant sunlamps in that section of the garden turned on to full brightness. They had no knowledge of the horrendous effects of sunlight on the combination of chlorine and hydrogen gas—the man who could have warned them was dead. The delicate frame began to twist and break apart; one of the huge, glistening glass tanks slipped slowly toward the other. A guard was the first to give the warning. His shout and struggling flight through the knee-deep water in the gardens was useless.

The steel network collapsed, toppling the chlorine tank sharply against the other. With a series of loud snapping sounds, cracks fanned out from the point of impact across both glass surfaces like lightning bolts and, as the men below stood frozen in terror, the tanks shattered under the pressure of the gases inside, uniting the chlorine and hydrogen in a cataclysmic explosion, blinding in its brightness and deafening as it reverberated over and over through the Styx system, its force carrying with it the torn fragments of the slaves and their masters. The narrow, thirty-foot glass portholes of the factory walls disintegrated, slicing millions of deadly splinters into the firefighters and workers within; huge pieces of machinery and furnaces were tossed through the air across the floor, spilling and scalding those still living with their white hot contents. The metal seams of the buildings in the complex split open and portholes popped. Across the Great Hall, the graceful glass dome of the gymnasium erupted in glistening fragments that rained down throughout the complex. And simultaneously another sound came to the terrified ears of the subterranean inhabitants, the sound of massive stalactite formations tearing free from the cavern ceiling and crashing down along with a hailstorm of jagged rock, smashing through the roofs of the complex to crush and impale those beneath.

The first horrific explosive flash was followed by darkness, but soon the remains of the Great Hall were reilluminated—not by Madame Bardoff's electric sunlamps but by flames, one huge burst of which rushed through the warehouse system and up the ventilation shaft to Ava's phony factory above ground, incinerating Moloch's reinforcements in the elevator as it plunged screaming back through the inferno into the cavern.

Those surviving the explosion and its immediate after effects faced, perhaps, a more terrible death—the heavy, colorless gas that burns the skin and lungs making the last minutes of life an agony. It was now free to invade the complex through gaping portholes and open seams. Like those in the death camps of Dr. Mulciber's last fantasies, the Styx Complex was slowly turning into a vast gas chamber.

The top floor of the technical center escaped major damage although many of its portholes were shattered and the roof had been brought down in several sections by large falls of rock. There was little need now for Michael and Sarah to worry about discovery; everyone in the complex was interested in only one thing—self-preservation and escape. They ran with the others, climbing over ruptured beams, toward the administration tower and the elevator leading up to safety. As they ran, Michael noticed many of those about him carried gas masks and he snatched two from an open emergency cabinet fastened to the wall.

"Put this on," he called to Sarah over the din. "It'll cover your face and we may end up needing them."

Already the heavy gas was fanning out over the hydroponic gardens, bringing down anyone caught there unprotected. They tore at their throats coughing blood before slipping beneath the water to be carried down into the dark subterranean cave system by the flooding river that now poured unchecked through the Great Hall.

Michael dragged Sarah up the circular staircase of the tower, but instead of battling his way with the others to the elevator, he ran along the corridor to Ava Bardoff's office. When Sarah pulled against him protesting, he shouted to her, "She's the only person who can get us out."

As they burst through the door into her office, Madame Bardoff looked up from her wall safe, where she stood cramming a briefcase with the documents critical to the survival and continuance of her organization elsewhere. Michael slammed the office door behind him and leaned against it. He pulled off his gas mask to confront her defiantly from across the room. Sarah also removed her mask, but did it slowly, still feeling frightened and naked before this woman.

Ava seemed surprisingly calm as she spoke. "So you have weathered the storm, my young friend. What a poor time you chose to switch allegiances—that is, if you really did switch them." She paused, looking at him with cold eyes. "But it makes no difference now— I no longer have any use for you." She continued her work as if dismissing the two of them from her presence.

Michael marveled at her confidence and her contempt for the danger he represented at that moment. "But I have a use for you," he replied.

"Oh, really?" she taunted. "And what might that be?" Her smile was familiar, one of amusement, like a cat playing with a mouse. She smiled, yet in the background she certainly heard the minor explosions and smelled the panic in the complex that spelled its doom.

"You're going to get us out of here, you and that briefcase."

She gave a derisive laugh. "But I have no intention of getting you out. I want you and Sarah to die. Do you not understand? I want both of you dead."

Michael rushed at her in a furious outburst of anger. He wanted to wipe the taunting smile off her beautiful face, wanted to smash this woman who had forced him to see himself, his fallibility, his weaknesses. Smiling, she stepped back a few paces, and before he realized what had happened, a glass wall fell from the ceiling cutting him off from her. She stood behind the protective barrier, laughing at his hatred and frustration.

"You see, Michael, Ava Bardoff always plans ahead —plans far enough ahead to destroy all who oppose her." Her smile faded and in its place he saw a look of pure malevolence. "You and your friends have dared to oppose me, to attack me," she hissed. "I swear to you that the House of Bardoff will live long after you and they have gone shrieking to your deaths. You and your slut are already dead, the rest will follow shortly. My vengeance will be very swift, you can be sure of that."

"At least we've stopped your mad dreams of a world dictatorship," he lashed back with almost childish spite.

"Have you? Have you indeed?" Ava sneered. "What have you really accomplished? Very little. The work of this complex was nearly completed, it was expendable. What little is left to do can be done in New York." She held up the briefcase. "Dr. Mulciber's notes are all here and the laboratory across the ocean waits. All you have done is to destroy the evidence that would have had to go sooner or later. Perhaps I should even thank you. Would that help make your death any easier?" Ava Bardoff laughed cruelly.

"Those men at the clinic," Michael rebutted desperately. "They know."

"Ah, those poor men. How their countries will mourn them. Unfortunately they will all perish in the tragic fire that will sweep my château exactly sixty seconds after I leave here. Yes, I must admit you have put a dent in my plans for Corsica, but there are other ways. My agents around the world will be loyal to me —you know the reason for that—and so tomorrow I will still control all I control today."

The Count dePasse, his clothing torn and his left arm hanging limply at his side, had entered the room during her farewell speech. He rushed forward. "Madame, take me with you."

She looked at him blankly.

"Don't leave me here." He beat against the glass wall with his good hand. "Beel is dead and Moloch can't control the panic. It's all over." Another small explosion shook the room.

"For you, perhaps, but nothing is over for me," she snapped. Ava picked up her briefcase and moved back toward a panel in the rear wall that had just opened. "I regret I cannot take you, dePasse—there is only room for me."

"Please, Ava, please," the count begged, slipping to the floor at the foot of the glass wall. "I've always served you, I've always . . ."

His pleas annoyed her. "Stay with your son, Monsieur le Comte. How fitting that you two should be reunited in these circumstances." She gave one last bitter laugh and stepped through the panel into a vacuum tube that would shoot her to the surface. The panel closed behind her.

Michael stared at it for a few seconds and then turned quickly to Sarah, grabbing her hand. "Come on, we've still got a chance." They started for the door.

"Please," dePasse called to them, "don't leave me. My arm—I can't . . . For God's sake, please take me with you."

"You call on God?" Michael asked as he looked back at the man who resembled his father, the man whose respect he had mistakenly tried to win ever since he had been rejected as a child. He wondered if his father had begged like this fifteen years ago, before they killed him. Never, he told himself. Michael took Sarah's needle pistol from her and tossed it across the office to the count. "Here, if you take the whole magazine it may ease things for you."

He pulled Sarah after him to the head of the spiral staircase; they looked down at the pandemonium on all the floors below.

Watson, Halvorsen, Andrews, and a deckhand had been forced to retreat halfway up the grand staircase of the château, leaving a second of their comrades dead below among the bodies lying in the hall, when the force of the explosion hit the château like an earth-quake, hurling attackers and defenders alike off their feet. As he sprawled on the stairs, Watson saw the huge chandelier swing violently and crash down onto those below; all through the building he could hear glass shattering—sections of the elaborate stone cornice fell from the roof through the conservatory dome, or-nate sculptured ceilings ruptured and collapsed in clouds of plaster and dust.

"Let's clear out," Watson shouted to his friends as the staircase under them trembled violently and began to crack. "It's all over."

While his shouted words served to mobilize his men, they also acted to throw the defenders into a state of confusion. The château seemed to be coming down around their very ears, and they knew that a subter-ranean explosion of that magnitude following on the heels of the earlier tremors must mean an end to all those in the complex below. As far as they knew, Madame Bardoff, Moloch, and their other leaders were down there lying buried under thousands of tons of rock. It *was* all over for them—in more ways than one.

The clinic attendants thought now only of saving what little time remained to them to enjoy. They aban-doned the fight and ran from the château into the early morning drizzle toward the limousines parked before the entrance. There were only a few more than a dozen men and women left, and all they wanted was to es-cape as far away as possible from the old building that reminded them of their inevitable fate.

The crew of the *Krait* clambered over the rubble-clogged upper hall toward the door to the north wing. As Watson called out, he thought, My God, what if the roof fell in on those VIPs or those bastards got in and killed them. His momentary panic vanished when his guard opened the door to them. "What in hell's been happening? You guys were shouting like . . ." His voice trailed off as he counted only four of the six men who had left him.

Overlooking his question, Watson asked gruffly, "The men and women okay?"

"Yes."

"Then let's get 'em out quick before anything else happens. I think what's left of the clinic guards have deserted a sinking ship."

Just to make sure, Andrews and the deckhand scouted the ground floor of the north wing and the gardens nearby while Watson and Halvorsen unlocked each bedroom door in turn to explain very briefly to the confused and frightened people inside that there had been a bad earthquake and Madame Bardoff had asked them to evacuate at once before another tremor brought the entire building down. They were all to meet her near St. Tropez, where alternate accommodations had been arranged; their luggage would follow. As the crew were dressed in clinic uniforms and the guests were in a state of near panic from the bad shake-up they'd just received, no further explanations were necessary at that point, not even to Madame's legitimate guests, who had been routed out and locked away earlier. The secretary of state, his wife, and their Russian counterparts, along with their small personal staffs of interpreters and secret service men, offered little or no resistance. Their mission accomplished, the shah and his queen had returned to Iran the previous day. The diplomats were still groggy from sedatives and had to be helped down, but the evacuation was done quickly.

Meanwhile Andrews and his fellow crewman had gone on ahead to the nearby garages and, by crossing ignition wires, started two of the largest limousines. They were just pulling away when the garage complex exploded in flames, and seconds later the gasoline storage tanks went up. "Jesus Christ, that was close," Andrews mumbled under his breath.

Watson was mumbling the same thing as he and the others lay on the wet grass after flinging themselves face down to escape the splinters of stone, wood, and glass that erupted from the château behind them. Flames now roared out of every shattered window in the once-magnificent building.

13

"They've gone mad," Sarah gasped as she and Michael stood looking down at the frantic chaos going on in all the corridors leading off the spiral stairwell. By this time many of the inhabitants of the complex had realized the elevator would never come and had forced entrance into the shaft itself, attempting the impossible climb up two hundred fifty feet of vertical rock and cable; they were knocked back and crushed by an avalanche of stone and flaming debris when the château above erupted from Ava Bardoff's demolition devices. Others were now trying to fight their way through the burning warehouses in hopes of finding escape up the second shaft. This exit, too, was blocked. The majority of the survivors, accustomed to functioning under strict regimentation, were lost without it and ran aimlessly through the ruptured, smoke-filled corridors looking for someone of authority to issue the orders that would save them.

Only a few, like Michael, realized the cave system itself offered the sole means of escape, but unlike Michael, they had not seen the charts of the system nor did they know how to survive in it. To fight against the swollen waters of the Styx now pouring into the Great Hall to reach the entrance through which Hugo's men had come was impossible. The lower exit of the Hall into the cave system was the only escape, but not as long as the water continued to flow through it. Had

Carpenter succeeded in his mission, he would now be waiting for Sarah and Michael at the lower exit of the Great Hall, ready to set off a final charge to block the entrance once they were through and temporarily seal off the lower cave system from the water. It would have given them the time they needed to reach a chimney up which they could have climbed to a passage opening out into the cliffs overlooking the lake in the wildlife preserve. Without Carpenter, Michael would have to risk it on his own, but where was he going to get the explosives upon which the plan depended?

He was puzzling over this when a minor explosion in the complex spurred him to action. "Come on," he said, pulling Sarah after him down the staircase, pushing through the desperate men and women running past. He had to get to that armory Beel had mentioned earlier; it was somewhere in the security headquarters by the main entrance to the Great Hall. They fought their way down two floors, leaving the staircase for a corridor leading to the enclosed bridge that connected the tower with the security building. Sarah grasped his arm more tightly, wanting to pull back at the sight of several bodies that lay sprawled in contorted positions along the bridge. A guard staggered toward them clutching his throat, a trickle of blood running from the corner of his mouth.

"Quick, put your mask back on," Michael ordered, "things must be pretty bad on that side."

They ran the rest of the way, vaulting bodies and not pausing until they reached the heavy door clearly labeled in the efficient manner typical of the complex as the security headquarters. The door was partly open, showing them a large, deserted control room filled with telephone and radio equipment, TV monitor screens, and electronic equipment. Two walls of the room had been made of glass to afford a complete view of the Great Hall, but the glass now lay in splinters on the floor or imbedded like knives in the equipment and furniture scattered about the room. Moloch lay face up in a pool of blood, his eyes staring blankly at the ceiling. No flying dagger of glass had ended his life;

a very real knife had been plunged into his heart. Realizing the end was at hand, one of his men had indulged himself in the last pleasure left to him—that of vengeance.

The adjoining rooms were records offices of some type and of no use to Michael now. Down an interior staircase they found what appeared to be a changing and equipment storage room for the guards. Underwater gear hung along one wall and small tanks of compressed air were stacked in bins along another. Michael recognized them as the latest type available, each tank, only four inches by eighteen inches, containing a mixture of gas to last for thirty minutes. There were also closets containing inflatable rafts, ropes, and the equipment Moloch's men must have needed for their occasional patrols deep into the cave system.

"Find a wet suit that fits and get into it fast," he told Sarah. "I want every inch of your skin covered. And don't take off your mask until you're sure your breathing apparatus is working properly—if that gas isn't in here yet, it soon will be."

Sarah shook her head and started looking through the rubber suits hanging on the wall. Michael squeezed her shoulder in an encouraging gesture; she would need every ounce of her courage in the next few hours.

While she dressed, he continued his search in the armory on the floor below, wearing only his gas mask. The thick walls had stood up well to the explosions in the complex. Behind barred and locked doors Michael saw rows of needle pistols and regular bullet-firing guns. Cartridges for both types of weapon were stored beside them but, search as he did, he could find nothing other than these cartridges that could pass for explosives; they would have to do—plus a lot of praying.

As he pondered his problem, his skin began to itch. Quickly grabbing a box of shells, he ran upstairs to where Sarah was adjusting her face mask and the two air tanks in her back harness. "Good girl," he said as he started pulling on a wet suit.

"Michael," she asked, "do we have a real chance of getting out of here alive? Please be honest with me."

He looked at her standing in the flickering light of the fires burning fiercely around the Great Hall. Sarah had put up a game fight so far—he couldn't let her down now. Crossing to her, he took both her arms. "I swear, darling, I'll get you out of here if it's the last thing I do."

Covered with the rubber and the mask as she was, he could only read her reaction in her eyes. They moved over his face and then wrinkled at the edges in a smile. "I believe you," she said simply.

He finished getting into his equipment and then started prying a dozen cartridges apart, putting the powder into a plastic envelope. Unzipping the front of his rubber suit, Michael placed the envelope, along with some oily cleaning rags, paper, and matches, next to his skin. As he zipped back up, he thought, I'm a walking bomb.

"Okay, let's go," he said to Sarah. "You carry the rope, I'll get the raft."

A few minutes later they emerged into the flooded hydroponic garden, most of which had been swept away by the river that now raged through it. Sarah looked about her at the water swirling past her knees; the bodies of several slaves floated in circles, caught in the back eddies of the current close to the buildings. She swallowed, staring at them and wondering if her body would soon join them.

Michael inflated the raft and helped her in. He followed, handing her one of the paddles. "Don't let us get carried out into the main current or we'll be swept through the lower entrance of the hall without having a chance to stop. Keep paddling for the sides."

As the raft moved down through the Great Hall, they could see the extent of the damage to Madame Bardoff's once-proud glass and steel subterranean empire. Now it looked more like it was, her kingdom of hell. Jagged metal and stone walls were silhouetted against the raging flames that licked up to the glistening ceiling of calcite and reflected across the hidden river Styx. Bodies of her henchmen, her fallen angels, floated on the surface of the red water.

The current grew swifter as the hall narrowed and

Michael and Sarah were forced to use all their strength
to beach the raft before being swept through the lower
exit into the passages leading to the sea. Michael
climbed out, looping a securing rope around a rock
and handing the end back to her.

"Be ready to shove off the second I get back. We
won't have much time."

"But where are you going?" she asked, her voice
betraying her fear of being left alone in this hell of
fire and water.

"Up there." He pointed to a large opening about
fifteen feet in diameter some twenty feet above the roof
of the exit passage from the hall. "It's called the 'Bat
Gallery' in Professor Musquère's notes. It runs back
about a hundred yards and, if we're lucky, should be
filled with guano."

"I don't understand what you're . . ."

"I haven't time to explain. Just get ready to scram
and don't worry."

Michael climbed with as much speed as caution
would allow over the pile of loose rock and rubble at the
left of the exit passage up to the Bat Gallery, looking
back anxiously over his shoulder at the flaming complex as a series of explosions shook the rocks under
his feet. Pulling himself up over the lip of the cave, he
shone his torch over its floor as far back as the
beam would reach. Michael sighed with relief; as he'd
prayed, it was inches thick with the accumulation of
hundreds or thousands of years of the nitrate-rich
guano.

Quickly removing the materials from his wet suit,
he crumpled the paper to make a pile several feet in
diameter and covered it with some of the oily rags. The
longest rags were torn into strips and rolled into a six-
foot fuse filled with a sprinkle of gunpowder. He scattered the rest of the powder over the heap of paper
and rags and around its edges onto the guano. His construction seemed woefully inadequate, almost ridiculous. "If this works, Professor," he said aloud, "I'm
personally going to dedicate a whole new university to
you—that's a promise."

Not knowing just how fast his fuse would burn, Michael slipped over the edge of the gallery, ready to make a quick getaway. He struck the first match and ignited the oily rag; it flared up and then went out. Cursing, he lit it again and watched anxiously. The flame grew larger and began to sputter erratically as it moved slowly up the fuse. This is it, he thought, sliding roughly down over the rubble and jumping into the raft beside Sarah. Without a word, he pushed off toward the center of the river. At first they hardly seemed to be moving, but then the current picked up the raft and carried it quickly into the exit passage.

"What's going to happen?" Sarah called to him over the roar of the water.

"Just hope it happens in the next few seconds or we're going over a waterfall in this damn thing," he called back, desperately back paddling to slow the raft.

Up in the Bat Gallery, Michael's fuse was about to sputter out when a concentration of gunpowder gave it new life and sent it hissing onto the heap of paper and rags. It flared up in a burst of flame which then swept out over the decomposing and highly combustible guano. Almost instantaneously the entire gallery erupted in a fiery explosion, the confining walls compressing and magnifying its force. The face of the cavern wall from which the gallery opened splintered and crashed down into the opening of the exit passage below. More rock plummeted from the already weakened roof of the Great Hall to add to the landslide of rubble falling from the surrounding walls. The water of the Styx swirled and beat angrily at the rock barrier, its efforts to reach the sea once again frustrated. The Great Hall slowly began to fill.

Even though they still wore the head gear of their wet suits, Sarah's and Michael's ears rang painfully from the concussion and reverberations of the explosion in the narrow passage. She screamed in terror but he almost welcomed the pain and shouted with relief when he felt the current slow as the water ran out from under them. The raft finally settled on the floor of the passage. Michael grabbed his frightened and confused companion in a great bear hug.

"We've done it," he shouted happily, "we've done it."

"What have we done?" she cried in frustration, almost in anger at not knowing what was happening to her.

"We've plugged up the Great Hall, that's what we've done. We're going to be all right. Do you understand?" he squeezed her in his arms. "We're getting out of here."

His excitement and obvious relief were comforting, but Sarah still found it very hard to be filled with joy when she flashed the beam of her torch over the dripping rock walls around her and knew she was hundreds of feet underground in some tight little passage leading to God knows where.

Leaving the raft behind, Michael took her hand and carefully led the way over the slippery floor. Several hundred feet ahead they came to the deep, vertical shaft over which they would have been carried if the water still roared through the passage. Using ropes, he lowered her down and climbed quickly after.

"I never thought I'd be marrying a mountain goat," she joked in a halfhearted attempt to keep up her courage.

"I didn't know I'd asked you," he replied lightly.

"I'm going to make sure you do," Sarah said, a bit embarrassed at having put into words what they both knew but had not yet dared talk about.

After a brief silence, he took her hand. "Come on then, Countess."

Michael led the way through a series of passages, falling often on the wet rocks that soon tore into their rubber suits. After thirty minutes of this, Sarah begged for a rest. He agreed and, still not trusting the purity of the air in the passages, used the break to replace their nearly exhausted tanks with four fresh spares he'd brought along in a canvas pack.

"When do we start going up?" Sarah asked. "How can we get out of this place without going up? We've been going down most of the time."

"My poor darling," he laughed. "No wonder you've been so worried. Actually, while we've been walking more or less on a horizontal line, the surface of the land above has been dropping to meet us. The Great Hall was under a lot of hills and from there most of the terrain slopes down to the coast. Do you remember the high cliff over the lake where we spent the night?"

Sarah shook her head.

"Well, up ahead we come to a chimney that goes up about thirty feet into a passage that we follow until it comes out on the face of that cliff. In the spring, when there's a lot of water running through these caves, sometimes the water is forced up that chimney and comes out the passage, making a waterfall into the lake. All we have to do is climb down from there —it's really not very hard, honestly."

"How do you know where that chimney is?" she asked. The blackness of the caves frightened her and she had a foreboding that things were not going to be as easy as Michael tried to make them, that something horrible still awaited them up ahead.

"I spent an afternoon with a man who knows every inch of this cave system and besides, if we go past it, we'll know. About fifty yards beyond there's another shaft that drops way down below the level of the lake. Musquère called it the 'Devil's Shaft.' From there the system breaks up into several passages, some come up to feed the lake, the rest go on in a giant maze to the sea." He turned his light on her face. "Satisfied?"

"Yep, you've done your homework," she said cheerfully, not feeling a bit cheerful.

"Ready to go on?"

"Couldn't we rest just a little bit longer?" she asked, reluctant to face the uncertainties that lay ahead.

"I guess another minute or two can't hurt us now," he conceded.

As they rested "another minute or two," many miles back in the Styx system a wall of water like a sub-

terranean tidal wave rushed forward, a wall formed of
two days of rain and the violent storms in Switzerland that had followed the Styx south—a wall of water under tons of pressure filling the passages and
caverns as it thundered closer and closer, smashing
against rock formations and the walls restricting it on
its express train journey to the sea.

Sarah and Michael were carefully picking their way
toward the chimney and safety when it roared across
the water gallery and smashed into the Great Hall,
tearing the huge steel doors from their frames and
hurling them like gigantic battering rams at the flaming technical center and the tower above it. They
disintegrated with a shriek of tearing metal, sweeping forward to complete the destruction of the buildings below. The bridges snapped like matchsticks,
the burning barracks, headquarters, gymnasium,
warehouses—all erupted from their foundations and,
along with the last screaming survivors of the Bardoff complex, were carried on the crest thrown up to
the roof of the Great Hall like toys to fall back into a
turmoil of power that ground them into an unrecognizable jumble of wreckage.

The water rushed ahead to attack Michael's plug,
tossing the newly fallen rocks aside in its desperate
quest for the sea. Water shot through the crevices
between the larger rocks with the pressure of fire
hoses, eroding and undermining the tenuous structure.

Up ahead, Michael put his hand on Sarah's arm to
stop her and held a finger up to the glass plate of his
face mask before his lips for silence. They both heard
it, water running somewhere back in the passages
through which they'd come. He tried not to show his
fear as he pulled Sarah after him. They scrambled
ahead, slipping, running, falling. They were almost
there. He flashed his torch frantically along the black
walls and the ceiling overhead looking for the chimney. Where was it? Where?

They stumbled along, splashing through pools of
water left in the passage, picking themselves up and

splashing on, guided by the beams of their torches. He suddenly realized with horror that they were no longer struggling through isolated puddles or pools, but through one continuous flow of water—the Styx was getting through, it was engulfing them. Soon the water was up to their knees, pushing them forward toward the Devil's Shaft.

Water now completely filled the Great Hall and the pressure on the plug was terrific. The larger rocks slowly began to grind against each other, turn, twist, and finally the keystone gave way. As if enraged at the delay, the water crashed through, carrying with it the obstructing rocks—rolling them, breaking them, hurling them ahead and over the first shaft with a deafening roar.

Floundering in the water only a few miles ahead, Michael and Sarah heard the thunder behind them and knew exactly what it meant. She froze in terror but he manhandled her forward, his promise running through his brain over and over, "I swear, darling, I'll get you out if it's the last thing I do." They fell and were swept roughly along in the waist-deep water. When he managed to regain his footing and surfaced again, Michael looked up—the chimney.

Sarah had lost her torch. Holding her with one hand, he shone his light into the chimney with the other and then gave it to her while he unfastened her air tanks. Michael lifted her up toward the hole over their heads about four and a half feet in diameter. Sarah grasped desperately at the rock wall, trying to pull herself upward with Michael's help from below. The water was up to his armpits as he forced her feet into the chimney, wedging her there with her feet and back pressing against opposite walls. The noise of the death wave as it rounded the bend in the passage and rushed toward them was unbearable. She looked down at Michael's hand on her ankle as he locked her foot into place. She tried to make room for him while reaching down to take hold of it. His grasp tightened, pulled briefly at her in an instinctive attempt to live, and then opened. His hand was lost in the roaring torment of black water that swept him away into the bowels of the earth.

Sarah screamed his name in a long, drawn-out cry, unaware that the water was pushing her up, up the chimney. Its great pressure lifted her body like a doll's up the thirty feet and spilled it over into the passage, pushing her along toward the pinpoint of light far ahead. Sobbing, she pulled herself over the rocks in the passage as the water flowed more gently around her to create its midsummer waterfall.

Sarah crawled exhausted and dazed onto the ledge beside the falls as the morning sun broke through the overcast sky, creating rainbows in the mist around her. She sat back numbly against the face of the cliff, staring straight ahead oblivious to everything but Michael. In her mind he was beside her, holding her, comforting her. She felt his lips on her cheek, saw his funny smile, the one he used just for her, she heard his voice. Sarah reached down and touched her ankle; she felt his hand in hers.

"Michael, why?" she asked. "Why when I loved you so very much?" Tears flowed from her open eyes.

14

Hugo Montclair, his face drawn from lack of sleep and worry, stood on the deck of the *Krait* watching anxiously through his binoculars as the launch pulled away from an empty beach several miles west of St. Tropez. Earlier that morning the same launch had made two trips to bring on board the foreign diplomats and four other guests of the clinic—sadly, of the ten crew men who had left the ship, only six returned to it.

Hugo had explained the entire bizarre situation to his guests, most of whom he knew socially, by telling them an actual attack had been carried out on the clinic by a terrorist group in an attempt to kidnap them for political ransom and that Madame Bardoff had felt his ship the safest place for them under the circumstances. They had accepted his story, which was made all the more plausible by their continued belief that their rescuers were in Ava Bardoff's employ. Only the Soviet chairman had been told the truth; he knew of Hugo's organization and had helped him in the past. Hugo felt it best not to expose the Bardoff plot until he had the chance to speak personally with the other heads of state who might be involved, detail the situation to them, and determine the best course of action for each to take. But right now he didn't really know the details of the situation. In fact, he now knew very little more about

Ava Bardoff's grand stratagem than he did before the attack. His men could only confirm the existence of a highly sophisticated industrial complex beneath the earth, which they assumed had been badly damaged or destroyed. As to its purpose or the fate of Ava Bardoff and the names and locations of her agents, Hugo was ignorant. He must now rely upon Michael for this information, but as he looked at the lone girl huddled in the launch, he feared he had played all his cards only to come in a poor second.

Sarah sat dumbly in the approaching boat, supported by one of Hugo's sailors. She hadn't said a word or uttered a sound since emerging beside the waterfall, not even when she'd been taken in hand by one of Hugo's men, who had been waiting with ropes and other climbing equipment to help her, Michael, and Carpenter down the cliff when and if they succeeded in escaping. She had answered all his questions with only a numb stare. Now, as the launch pulled alongside the larger ship, she looked up at the smiling, white-haired man holding out his hand to her and, remembering Michael's words before the water had come, "If anything happens to me, go to Hugo—he'll be waiting for you," she shook herself free of the sailor and stumbled out of the launch up the steps to throw herself into Hugo's arms. Only then, in the security and warmth of his embrace, did her emotions and grief surge out into the open. She wept uncontrollably.

Hugo stood holding the sobbing girl, saying nothing, but giving her comfort and strength just from his presence. He said quietly to the sailor who had mounted the steps behind Sarah, "You'd better get the launch out of the water—I don't think we'll be needing it again today."

After some minutes her sobs subsided, and he led her gently below to the cabin next to his, where he sat with her until the sedative he'd given her slowly took effect. As she lay on the bed holding his hand, Sarah began to tell him what had happened below the ground in the cave system—of the explosions and fire, of Ava, the horrible deaths, of Michael and the water. Sharing the horrors through which she'd gone helped calm her and soon she drifted off into an exhausted and fitful sleep. Hugo tucked the blankets around her and bent down to give her a sad, tender kiss. You are a very brave little girl, he thought. Sitting there while she slept, he shared her grief over the loss of Michael, who had been like his own son for all these years. He had been a difficult and, perhaps, a spoiled son, but Hugo had encouraged and enjoyed his free spirit and initiative. As he recalled some of Michael's youthful madcap escapades, a melancholy smile crept across his face. He had given Michael the love and guidance his father had refused, but in the end, it was Hugo, not his father, who had demanded the impossible of Michael and in so doing had taken his life. Why had he asked for so much?

Looking down at Sarah, Hugo remembered Eleanor. Once again he saw their black sedan moving through the wet streets of Boston after the symphony thirteen years before. He remembered her velvet evening dress and the simple strand of diamonds around her slender neck as she sat in the back seat trying to be gay with his friend Granger, while he'd charmed Granger's wife sitting up front next to him. How beautiful she'd looked as he saw her in the rearview mirror, lights reflecting about her on the rain-streaked windows. And then the other car—addicts, drug pushers being chased through the streets by the police. It screamed through the red light at the slippery intersection—he might have seen it if he hadn't been glancing back at her. They hadn't even tried to put on the brakes. In that one instant, his wife and friends gone, he without a scratch. He saw Eleanor lying in the rain. He promised her then that no one would ever have to die like that again, that he'd devote his life and fortune to ridding the world of its corrupters, the dealers in misery and death, those who lived with evil.

He thought about Michael and the four men who had died that day. He thought of the others in the past who had also died helping him. Had he asked them to give their lives to help society or had he

asked it merely for his own personal atonement? Even
worse, had he become the fanatic Halvorsen had recently implied, a man so obsessed with what he
thought to be his divine mission that he'd lost all per-
spective? Did he look upon himself as an aveng-
ing angel of God, or perhaps even God himself? Hugo
buried his head in his hands as these questions
flooded his tired brain and filled him with doubts.
Had he played God with Michael and the others, ego-
tistically manipulating them in his power games while
justifying their deaths as their suicidal duty to *his*
perfect society; was he, in his own conceit, just as
bad as Ava Bardoff?

"Don't let it all have been for my own selfish vengeance," he whispered to all those faces before him,
"don't let it have been just for me." Hugo prayed
silently for guidance, for strength.

Touching Sarah's hand gently, he finally rose,
wiped his eyes, and left the cabin to walk slowly back
to his study to face the men who would be waiting
to hear what he had learned from her. They saw the
stricken look on his face when he entered but
could only guess part of the agony he was going
through.

Watson walked over to him and took a firm hold
of both his arms. "Hugo, don't tear yourself apart over
the others. They knew what they were getting into,
we all did." Hugo's face did not brighten. "We'd do it
again," Watson said with emphasis.

"If you'd seen what Bardoff had down there, you'd
know we did the right thing," Halvorsen added. "Hugo, we had to do it." And then to change the mood he
asked, "What did you learn from Miss Dilworth?
What happened to the complex? Does she know anything about Ava Bardoff? Is she dead? And—" he
hesitated but knew it had to be asked sooner or later
"—and what about young dePasse?"

Hugo sat down behind his desk and repeated all
Sarah had told him. Fortunately Michael had revealed
to her everything he'd learned in an attempt to dis-
tract her from their troubles while they fled through
the complex and cave system. As he discussed and

analyzed the information with his men, a large part of Hugo's confidence and purpose returned. The sheer scope of Ava Bardoff's operation and her all too feasible plans for world domination convinced him once more that no sacrifice was too great to stop her. If not world domination, she and her organization could most certainly cause world chaos resulting in a bloodbath as nations fought to assure their energy supplies and governments toppled from within.

"It's a terrible tragedy that Ava has slipped through our fingers," Hugo sighed. "If she had only died in the complex today, her entire organization would have been destroyed by those beads of hers within a year and we would be done with it. Now we are in a very dangerous stalemate. We must get to her before she can pass on those codes for recharging the brain beads to her underlings and so carry on her operation. On the other hand, she and her anonymous agents must eliminate us and the others aboard to destroy all evidence against her. As long as we live, she won't have the freedom of movement she needs and most certainly won't dare go back to her New York laboratory."

"So we're right back to square one," Watson said wryly. "It's her or us. How in hell do we go about tracking her down now?"

"First things first," Hugo corrected. "We've got to get these diplomats and the other women back home safely and warn the various heads of state what Madame Bardoff is up to. Then we can go after her. But I have the feeling Ava Bardoff will come to us —I just hope we can protect ourselves when she does. We know that you didn't get all her private army at the clinic and we also know she has men in Cannes and probably in St. Tropez. I'll bet they're still watching every move we make."

"They could launch an underwater attack or even torpedo us at any minute," Halvorsen said in alarm. "Good God, we're sitting ducks."

"Why not bring in a few patrol boats from the French Navy for protection?" Watson suggested. "After all, they wouldn't want our Russian friend killed in their territorial waters and . . ."

"I'm afraid to do that," Hugo interrupted. "We now know that the armed forces have been infiltrated at the top and a call for help or an escort may tip our hand to Madame. I'm sure that whatever she may be dreaming up for us will look like an accident— sending out torpedo boats in waters crowded with holiday craft is a little too obvious for her. An underwater, frogman-style attack is more along her line. Watson, assign lookouts and keep a man or two down on the electronic equipment to warn us of any swimmers or snoopers."

"Right," he said, leaving the room on the run.

"What about our guests?" Anderson asked.

"I've been giving that a lot of thought ever since they arrived. I think we should steam slowly west along the coast so Madame's men will think we're headed for Marseilles with our cargo. We'll gradually pull away from land until they lose us visually and then we turn tail and run full steam southeast for Corsica. Ajaccio will only be about a hundred and fifty miles from us at two this afternoon; we can make it easily by eleven P.M. and have a plane waiting to fly them to Paris."

"But Corsica must be crawling with Bardoff's men," Halvorsen protested. "We'll be walking right into the tiger's teeth."

"Madame wasn't planning to be there for two weeks," Hugo reminded him, "so they're probably not completely organized yet. Besides, it's the last place in the world they'd expect us to go. We'll arrive at night and lie off shore so no one will identify the *Krait*. If I can get a close friend of mine to fly down in his company jet, we can bring our people ashore by launch and have them aboard and flying back to Paris before anyone at Ajaccio's airport knows what's happening. Corsica is French, so he'd only be making an internal flight and wouldn't have to worry about official red tape."

"And then?" Andrews asked.

"That's it. We'll be free to move against Ava Bardoff officially and unofficially. No matter how many agents and infiltrators she has, when executive orders from the number one men in various countries go out for her arrest, there's little she and her people can do unless they want to try to take control now. Hopefully that would be a premature move. Let's hope that instead she goes to cover until we find her."

"Okay," Halvorsen said, "let's get moving."

The men rose and left the study, only the big Swede hanging back. He turned to Hugo and said quietly, "We're all sorry about dePasse—we know how much he meant to you. We caught sight of him only once in the complex but if we'd tried to save him, we would have blown the entire operation."

"You were right to do what you did," Hugo replied, doing his best to keep his face expressionless. "Just remember that he did escape from Ava Bardoff—it was nature, not you, that let him down. Tell that to the others."

"Thanks," Halvorsen said. "They'll appreciate knowing how you feel."

"And tell them that right now all our efforts should be devoted not to looking back, but to throwing Madame off our scent until we can get rid of our diplomatic cargo."

Halvorsen closed the door, leaving Hugo to stare out of the porthole across the water to the beach that was now filling with sun worshippers and swimmers. A week ago, Michael might have been one of those tanned bodies relaxing on the beach. Soon he felt the gentle vibrations of the *Krait*'s engines under his feet and thought, If you're out there now, Ava, you'd better start swimming—fast. The shoreline began to move past him.

By noon Hugo had been able to contact Paris and had arranged for the Corsica flight that was to arrive on the island at precisely 11:30 that night. The French president had listened intently to all Hugo had told him of the operation and objectives of the famous House of Bardoff. Although he had complete trust in

Hugo, his first reaction to the wild story was one of absolute disbelief, but his doubts began to fade when Hugo filled in the details of the exact movements of his trusted friend, the Count dePasse. He verified Hugo's statements by calling the count's home in Paris to request his immediate presence at the Elysée Palace and was informed regretfully that, as Hugo had said, the count had left Paris by private jet last evening for some destination currently unknown to his secretary. She assured the president she would track him down at once. A second call to the Cannes airport at Hugo's suggestion confirmed the Count dePasse had arrived last evening and his plane was now in the Bardoff hangar. Faced with this proof of Hugo's story that lookalike agents had infiltrated his and other governments, the president had agreed to contact the other heads of state by private wire or hotline to explain the current situation and request the detention of Ava Bardoff. It was vital to obtain the Americans' agreement to have Ava stopped should she fly to that country. Hugo stressed that she must not be allowed to reach her New York facilities or contact any members of her organization there.

After his calls to Paris, Hugo joined his guests on the top deck to quell any fears that still might remain and to explain the arrangements for their flight to Paris that evening. Thus reassured, they were able to relax and, with the aid of the champagne that Hugo directed should flow liberally, the mood of the *Krait* turned into a festive and almost frivolous one—after all, they had survived one of the greatest adventures of their lives. Hugo himself was beginning to relax a little, confident that his plan for Corsica would succeed, when one of the crew whispered to him that the radar had picked up a powerful boat approaching from the direction of St. Tropez.

Excusing himself with a weak joke, Hugo quickly left the sundeck for the radar room, where he watched the bleeping light on the screen closing on them. He ordered his men to their "battle" stations and to stand by the deck guns concealed cleverly in false ventilating shafts. Petras was sent above to get the guests out of the way by bringing them down into the main salon, where a luncheon buffet was being quickly arranged. All precautions taken, Hugo and Watson went to the afterdeck with binoculars to study their uninvited guest.

It was with great relief that Hugo finally recognized the figure of Paul Mytilini standing up at the wheel of a small motorboat, waving madly at the *Krait*. Smiling patiently at this unwelcome, yet amusing interruption, Hugo told Watson to slow the ship and prepare to bring Mytilini aboard.

"Hugo, where have you been," Paul Mytilini shouted as one of the *Krait*'s crew helped tie his boat to the partially lowered steps and put buffers over the side to protect it from bumping against the ship as it picked up speed again. "I've been trying to get hold of you for two days—wait till you see what I've got for you." Paul Mytilini carefully picked up a large box from the floor of his boat and, with the aid of the crewman, climbed the steps to greet the millionaire.

"Paul, this is a most pleasant surprise, but I'm afraid you've caught me at a bad time. We're heading for Minorca, must be there day after tomorrow, and so we can't stop."

"Oh, that's perfectly all right. I'm only staying a few minutes and you can tow my boat along with you. I just had to bring this out to you the instant I got it —you must see it." He tapped the box.

"My friend—" Hugo laughed—"anything I 'must see' means you've got an extremely expensive art object in there that most certainly will tempt me and my pocketbook."

"Exactly," Paul replied. "Now where can I show it to you?"

Hugo thought a minute, and before he could answer, Harriet Granville, one of the jet-set guests who had been at the clinic and reminded Hugo of a junior Susan Van Schuyler, walked down the deck and cried, "Paul, how marvelous—you must come and join us all for lunch. You'll get the surprise of your life when you . . ."

"Harriet," Hugo interrupted, "Paul and I have a little business to discuss and then I'm afraid he must leave us before we carry him too far out to sea."

"Hugo, you dog, what are you holding out on me?" Mytilini asked in a teasing voice. "Who are you entertaining for lunch and why won't you let me meet them? Ashamed of your old friend, eh?"

On the defensive, Hugo was seeking the right words when Harriet Granville blurted out several of the names and begged, "Hugo, do let Paul join us. You will be discreet, won't you, Paul?"

Hugo was trapped; it was too late to do anything but invite Paul Mytilini to lunch. To do otherwise might cause all sorts of speculation and start his tongue wagging around the Riviera as soon as he returned to shore, creating too much unwanted publicity. And so Hugo extended the invitation, adding, "I know you will say nothing of this to anyone, Paul. It's a most urgent request."

"Of course, my friend. If you ask me to be discreet, you must have a very good reason and so I shall be the proverbial clam. But first, let me show you what I have here."

Hugo took Paul to his luxurious cabin and poured him a drink while the other carefully removed volumes of tissue paper from the box and finally lifted out a magnificent, foot-and-a-half-high porcelain horse dating from the Ming Dynasty. Hugo paused with the whiskey decanter in one hand and whistled quietly.

"It's fourteenth century—one of a matched pair. I have the other one back in the vault. Hugo, they're about as beautiful as you'll ever find. I can't tell you how rare they are."

"Where on earth did you get them?" Hugo asked.

"One of my clients, a private one—he needs cash."

Hugo put Paul Mytilini's drink on the table beside him and gently took the fabulous horse from him, slowly turning the heavy object around in the light in admiration.

"How much is your client asking and what will he settle for?"

Mytilini quoted a figure that made even Hugo gasp. "I don't expect you to make up your mind right now," he said. "I'll leave this beauty with you until you return from Spain—by that time you'll have decided one way or the other. You either return it to me, or I give you its twin. What do you think?"

Negotiating over the price of art was a welcome respite for Hugo's tired brain. Absorbed completely in the exquisite figure in his hands, he momentarily forgot about the heavy problems of Ava Bardoff and his guests.

"It's a deal. When I get back to Cannes in a few days you'll have my answer."

Paul Mytilini raised his glass in a silent salute to Hugo and a broad smile spread across his face.

"I see you're counting your commission already," Hugo said pleasantly.

"No, actually I'm just happy to have been able to bring you something that will give you pleasure for as long as you live. Now how about a bit of that lunch. I'm famished."

Hugo replaced the Ming horse gently among its wrappings in the box on his bed. "It's waiting for you in the salon. As Harriet has already told you, I have some very public guests who've been vacationing secretly in the south of France. I would appreciate your keeping their being here under your hat. I'm sure you can understand how important that is not only for their security, but for diplomatic reasons."

"Certainly, I understand. Now, where can I wash my hands, and don't bother to wait for me."

"Use my bathroom—there are fresh towels. See you in a few minutes." Hugo left Paul to himself and went up to the salon.

Paul looked down at the figure lying among the tissue paper. He picked it up fondly and, on impulse, kissed it.

Sarah's sedated sleep, although restoring some of her strength, had not been a happy one. Her subconscious had taken all the terrifying incidents of the past days and twisted them into even more grotesque and horrible dreams. She and Michael were running in slow motion through the passages once again, chased by some frightening force she could not identify. As they ran, the sound of someone humming gradually surrounded them; it was a familiar tune that brought with it Ava's beautiful face. The face came closer and closer to her, growing larger, larger, almost to the size of a house, and then it began to contort into a horrible leer, its mouth opening to envelope them. Michael ran into it, but Sarah leaped back, startling herself awake—or was she? She lay on her bed staring at the white cabin ceiling trying to shut out the awful symbolism of the dream but it was still going on. Her eyes were open and she shook her head to clear it, yet the humming continued, coming faintly through the very walls of her cabin. Sarah recognized it—it was a tune that Ava used to hum when she was happy. Oh, my God, she screamed to herself, she's here, she's come after me. Sarah sat up in terror; the sound was gone.

Ava Bardoff sat unrecognized in the salon of the *Krait* enjoying her lunch and chatting with the others. Underlying her veneer of charm surged a passionate hatred of Hugo who stood across the room with the wife of the American secretary of state, a hatred of his crew who circulated so innocently among them serving drinks, a hatred of even her intended victims who had escaped. Soon she would have her revenge. They would all be dead and the evidence against her gone; she would be free to continue her operations.

Ava's lust for revenge on the *Krait* was the strongest emotion she'd ever experienced. It was so strong that she gladly risked even her own destruction and that of her plans to see them all dead. She had decided to perform the executions personally not only because she dared not trust the success of this vital mission to her remaining underlings in St. Tropez or Cannes, but because she wanted the thrill and satisfaction of killing them herself. As Ava looked across the room at the social clown who had brought her down, a rage grew inside her. She would have torn his flesh away with her bare hands and fingers right then and there if it would not have meant her exposure and the escape of the others from the fate she'd planned for them. The garnets in the rings on her fingers glistened in the sun streaming in through the porthole as she lifted a glass of champagne to her lips—a thin, cruel smile crossed them in anticipation of her final triumph.

Sarah was in a state of extreme agitation when she entered the salon. Petras Furman had tried to calm her, stop her from going in, but she'd insisted she must warn Hugo and threatened to become hysterical if thwarted.

"Who is that poor child?" Paul Mytilini asked when she burst into the room.

"A young friend of mine who's had a very bad time recently," Hugo answered. "I must go to her."

Sarah grabbed his arm and spoke hastily in a low, rasping whisper as her eyes swept over those in the salon. "Mr. Montclair, Ava's aboard the *Krait*."

Her words froze him momentarily, and then he relaxed, realizing she must be suffering the effects of delayed shock. "How do you know?" he asked sympathetically.

"Ava always used to hum a particular tune, sort of a German beer hall song. When I woke up in my cabin a few minutes ago, I heard her humming that very same tune. Please don't look at me that way, I've heard it so many times before and I know how *she* sounds. Believe me," she begged.

"Are you sure you weren't dreaming? You know sometimes . . ."

"I wasn't, I swear I wasn't dreaming. Ava's here."

Hugo gently put his arm around her and nodded for Petras to follow them from the salon. Once in the corridor outside, he said to her patiently, "Sarah, the only people on this ship right now are my crew, those we brought from the clinic, and Paul Mytilini, a friend I've known for years. However," he turned to Petras, "just to be on the safe side, have a complete search of the *Krait* made and station someone at each of the two doors leading into the salon." He issued these orders

more to soothe Sarah than because he believed her—
and yet her certainty unnerved him. "Have any of our
guests left the salon during the last twenty minutes or
so?" he asked Petras.

"Several of the women have gone to their cabins, I
presume to wash for luncheon," he replied. "But they
were all back fairly quickly. We are keeping a close
watch on them."

"I see," Hugo mused. "All right, get the search
started." Turning back to Sarah, he asked, "Do you
feel strong enough to join us for a little lunch? A bit
of feminine chatter might help relax you."

"I guess so," she answered reluctantly, "but . . ."

"But nothing. You leave finding Ava Bardoff to us—
if she's on this ship, we'll get her. Now come in and
meet Paul Mytilini—he's very amusing and he's just
brought me the most beautiful Ming horse I've ever
seen. As I recall, you are quite an art lover yourself."

Sarah didn't answer but let herself be guided across
the salon to the art expert, who, much to Hugo's surprise, spoke only briefly to the girl and then excused
himself. Hugo gave little thought to the pointed snub,
attributing it simply to the fact that Sarah was in no position to be a profitable client to Mytilini, and turned
his attention to a study of the women in the room. Of
the four jet-set guests the crew had rescued from the
clinic, Hugo had only met Harriet Granville before. Was
Ava disguised as one of them? Sarah had told him what
Michael had learned about Ava Bardoff's ability to mold
the skin of her neuts into the identical features of others. Was it possible that she'd already substituted some
of her neuts for the diplomats or those in their parties
and was it one of them who, in an off minute, Sarah
had heard humming the tune picked up from Ava?
Unlikely, he thought. Hugo drifted over to the unknown guests and engaged them in a casual but probing conversation.

Sarah stood alone by the buffet table, sipping champagne and, like Hugo, studying the others in the salon.
Most of the faces were familiar to her. Her eyes fell on
Paul Mytilini; she didn't like that man. Aside from his
rudeness to her, she didn't know why she felt so hostile

toward him. Perhaps it was his mannerisms, his phrasing—but something made her feel uncomfortable in his presence.

She was about to serve herself from the elaborate buffet table when her nose picked up a vaguely familiar scent. Sarah stiffened and looked wildly around her for the source. The room was quite warm now and with the guests crowded together and wearing borrowed jeans and sweaters, it was impossible to tell from which one that faint scent of perfume came. Terror gripped her once again as she looked from one face to the next. Ava was there in that very room; she knew it. Hugo had to believe her. He was standing by the door to the afterdeck, saying goodbye to the little art expert. Sarah walked quickly toward them and was about to interrupt but the words froze in her throat; she walked on by to Petras who stood outside on the deck. Mytilini's eyes narrowed with interest and followed her.

"Quick," she said to the steward, "how long has Mr. Montclair known that man?"

"Mytilini?" Petras asked, looking across the deck at him as the door to the salon opened. "Oh, for years —ten, maybe fifteen. Why?"

Sarah was taken back and confused by his answer. She saw Paul Mytilini make a small bow to Hugo and walk out onto the deck and along the rail toward the steps leading down to his waiting boat. Hugo called after him, apparently remembering something more he wanted to say. The two engaged in further conversation at the head of the steps as the *Krait* slowed. Mytilini looked anxious.

"He brought Mr. Montclair a Ming horse?" Sarah asked. "Can I see it?" The steward hesitated, a puzzled expression on his face. "Now—quick," she pleaded.

Shrugging his shoulders, Petras led Sarah swiftly along the deck on the other side of the ship and down to Hugo's cabin. "It's probably in here somewhere— this is where they were."

"But it's right next to mine!" Sarah exclaimed.

"That's right."

"Then the humming must have been coming from

in here." She rushed through the door, her eyes searching the cabin, and seeing the large box resting on Hugo's bed, ran to it. Sarah put both hands to her mouth as she looked down at the magnificent Chinese horse she'd seen so many times before on the glass and steel desk. As impossible as it seemed, what she feared must be true. Snatching it up, she ran from the room pursued by the steward.

"Easy there," he called after her, "that thing's valuable."

Reaching Hugo's study, she tried the door. "Let me in, Petras. Hurry, hurry, unlock it," she cried in hysterical panic.

He stared at her for only an instant. The urgency in her voice was, in its way, as commanding as any order he'd ever received. He removed the keys from his pocket.

"It's a bomb—I know it!" Sarah screamed.

He fumbled at the lock.

"It's a deal then," Hugo said, shaking Paul Mytilini's hand. "I can't resist your horses. I'll contact you as soon as I return and you can bring out the other one to the pair."

Mytilini nodded, looked at his watch, and started down the steps to his boat.

Sarah pushed by a shaken Petras Furman and ran through Hugo's study to the small room containing the underwater entrance. Still carrying the horse, she leaped into the little pool and disappeared.

"Oh, and Paul," Hugo's voice stopped him once more. "Thank you for your help, I really appreciate it."

"My pleasure," he called back. As Paul Mytilini stepped at last into the boat, he began to chuckle to himself. The engine coughed into life and, catching the mooring line tossed to him by one of the crewmen, he put the motor into gear and swung sharply away from the ship.

Several hundred yards out, he looked back over his

shoulder at the *Krait* and laughed wildly. "He really appreciates my help, does he—well, I've appreciated his," he shouted to the wind in his face. "Hugo," he called back across the water to the yacht, "your money helped build the House of Bardoff, and your money has just bought you oblivion."

Paul Mytilini's face broke into the triumphant, gloating smile of Ava Bardoff. Dr. Albert Bohme, the chief medical researcher of Auschwitz who dropped from sight in January 1945 just before the Russians reached the camp, tore off his tie and opened his shirt to cool the breasts of the undisputed genius of the cosmetic world, to cool the ever youthful body of Ava Bardoff that he and his camp assistant, Dr. Heinrich Mulciber, had created. Bohme looked for the last time at the second hand of his watch as it swept up to the hour of 2:00 P.M. and threw his head back in a shrieking laugh. The supreme ruler of the Styx Complex failed to see the rare fourteenth-century horse vibrating on the deck under the seat of his motorboat as it sped away. The final mad laugh blended into the monstrous fireball that engulfed him, lifting a vast explosion of water hundreds of feet into the air.

Sarah, her clothes dripping with water, stood silently by Hugo at the rail of the *Krait* staring at the spot where the small boat had been long after the seething white patch of foam had settled, leaving only the normal swells of the clear blue sea. Each had his own thoughts, she of her parents and Michael. Like the floating splinters of the little boat, her life once again lay in pieces. She wondered if she had the strength to pick them up and put them back together without help. Instinctively Sarah moved closer to Hugo Montclair; he put his arm around her protectively.

How many strange tricks fate plays on us, he thought. Of the three—Carpenter, Michael, and Sarah—she had been the one chosen to escape from the cave system. Was it because only she had the unique knowledge to save us all and close the book on the omnipotent House of Bardoff? Ava Bardoff's agents now had no more than a year to live, their lives and her dreams terminated because a young girl recognized a beer hall melody and the lingering scent of perfume. He looked down at her. Fate took my son, he thought—has it given me a daughter to take his place?

The *Krait* veered sharply to the southeast and picked up speed as he led her gently away from the others crowding the rail. They would be in Corsica in nine hours. Hugo sighed, wondering if fate had any more tricks up its sleeve for them.

15

The next morning Hugo Montclair sat at his desk in the *Krait*'s study staring blankly at the fat file marked House of Bardoff that lay open in front of him. The previous evening he had seen his guests safely off on the private plane at Corsica. Ava was dead and her empire destroyed, but still he couldn't bring himself to close the file, to relegate the lost lives of those dear to him to the past. He was aimlessly moving papers about on his desk when the call from Cannes came through on the ship-to-shore phone. He expected it to be the harbor master confirming permission to anchor offshore when they arrived at the city that noon and so was completely unprepared for the voice on the other end of the line. When he replaced the receiver several minutes later, he was white, stunned—he slowly buried his head in his hands. For the first time since the death of Eleanor, Hugo wept like a child.

It took him a long time to bring himself back under control after his emotional outburst. Finally he pushed himself to his feet and walked out onto the foredeck of the ship where Sarah had been sitting desolate and alone since sunrise, looking out over the empty water before her. The older man sat quietly beside her, wondering how best to tell her. At his touch, she looked up, guessing the emotion locked within him.

"You have something terrible to tell me," she said flatly.

"Not terrible—perhaps the most wonderful news I'll ever be able to tell anyone. You must be calm, not build up your hopes and . . ."

"What is it?" she interrupted, a flicker of hope already building up inside her for the only words she wanted to hear.

"They've found Michael. He is alive, but," he added quickly, "in very critical condition. He's undergoing surgery at the hospital in Cannes right now. They won't know his chances until it's over."

The only words Sarah heard were "Michael is alive," all the others were lost to her. She looked at Hugo in disbelief, wanting desperately to believe.

"How? How is that possible?" she asked, almost afraid to challenge his statements for fear of losing Michael again.

"Some wardens came across him yesterday morning lying unconscious at the edge of the lake in the preserve. Just as you were forced up to the waterfall exit by the rush of water, he must have been carried down and through one of the passages leading up into the lake bottom. His oxygen equipment apparently saved him, but he took a terrible pummeling. He has a lot of broken ribs, one of his lungs has been punctured, and there are multiple bone fractures. He's a very sick young man."

"But he's alive," Sarah said. "He's alive." She threw her arms around Hugo and squeezed. "Oh, Hugo, he's alive. When can I see him? When will we get to Cannes?" Sarah began to laugh and cry. "Can't we go any faster? Can we . . . ?"

Hugo laughed, too, at her excitement and happiness. "We're going as fast as we can. If all goes well, we might be able to see him this afternoon." Then he sobered, saying, "Calm down, remember he's very, very ill and . . ." But her enthusiasm was too much for him; he squeezed her back and the two fell into each other's arms laughing, their eyes streaming with tears of joy.

The following day Hugo stood at the foot of Michael's bed returning his weak but mischievous smile. Sarah sat beside him, holding his bruised hand gently in a grip that, for all its tenderness, would never be undone.

"If I'm not mistaken, not only have I regained my
favorite son, but I'm about to pick up a daughter-in-
law as well."

"You're not mistaken," Sarah replied gaily and
looked over at Michael. "I'm not letting this hulk slip
through my net again. You know, I actually believe he
loves me. What do *you* think?" she asked, confident
of the answer. Hugo nodded his agreement. "Besides,
I've got him trapped. He's not going to be able to
stand without me next to him for a good many months
to come."

"Months?" Michael asked in a painful but happy
whisper. "You're not very faithful. I thought you were
going to be standing next to me for life."

Sarah beamed. "And Hugo, in your official capacity
as captain of the world's most luxurious honeymoon
yacht, Michael and I want you to be the one to marry
us as soon as we can get him up and out of here."

Before Hugo could accept this, their most beautiful
gift to him, the door to the room flew open and in
swept Susan Van Schuyler, followed by angry, cackling
nurses.

"Marry? Who's getting married? Hugo, Petras told
me you were here and I dashed right over—I was so
worried. What's happened? Michael? Is that you behind all that plaster, Michael dePasse? And Sarah,
what are you doing here? I understand there was the
most terrible fire at your godmother's clinic—she must
be frantic. What a . . ."

Michael closed his eyes feigning sleep while Sarah
looked hopefully at Hugo. The captain of the *Krait*
took Susan Van Schuyler's arm and drew her out of the
room and down the hospital corridor while planning
the revenge he would take on Petras for betraying him
to this terrible woman.

". . . and where did you take the ship? I didn't believe for one instant the excuse you gave for getting us
off the *Krait*. I'm all ears. Is it true that . . . ?"

ABOUT THE AUTHOR

A graduate of Yale and the Harvard Business School, RUSSELL RHODES spent ten years in Europe as the senior vice president and director of European operations for a leading international advertising agency. He has written one previous book entitled *Man at His Best*. *The Styx Complex* is his first novel and second internationally published book. He currently lives and works in New York City.

JAWS 2

CHAPTER ONE

Bantam is pleased to bring you this bonus preview. It's the exciting opening chapter of the completely new novel based on characters created in Jaws. Read on...

JAWS 2

CHAPTER ONE

A flattened, blood-red sun rose dead ahead.

The white Hatteras powerboat, *Miss Carriage* out of Sag Harbor, slithered around Montauk Point. She emerged from Long Island Sound and rose to the swell of open ocean. The two half-suited Scuba divers high on her flying bridge took wider stances.

The taller of the two, an obstetrician from Astoria General on Long Island, flicked off the running lights. The shorter was a Manhattan attorney for Union Carbide. The two had little in common except an interest in diving, diminishing as they aged, and a partnership in the boat. They almost never met except on summer weekends.

Years ago the doctor had decided that his little partner was a Jewish pinko, and simply accepted it. The lawyer sensed bigotry but ignored it. Friends or not, each had some $30,000 in the boat, and there was the security of a known companion. Each was sure that the other was a steadier diver than himself.

Every year, the physician dreaded the first few scallop dives of spring. Equipment always felt strange at first. The water would be cold and cloudy. And here, off Amity Township, lurked a ghost.

The beast was dead. The doctor had all but forgotten the stories in the *Long Island Press*. The Manhattan lawyer seldom thought of the pictures in the *Times*. But a secret half-tone specter swam in the subconscious of each.

The doctor was suddenly cold. He glanced at the recording fathometer tracing the depth. They were searching for a clump of bottom-rocks they knew, but the graph on the instrument was still flat as the trace of a terminal patient in Intensive Care. The doctor pictured mud below, and silt.

He shivered and swung down the flying-bridge ladder. He tugged his neoprene upper-suit from behind a tank-rack in the cockpit, and squirmed into it. He had put on weight.

Even after he smoothed it on, he was still shivering. He stepped into the cabin. He had not got his sealegs yet. Crossing to the stainless galley stove behind the service bar, he lurched into a rattan barstool and knocked it over. He swore softly and set it up. Then he moved behind the counter and took two cups from a rack. He poured a double slug of Old Grandad into his cup and a single into his partner's, then filled the cups with coffee from the stove. He started out, remembered that it was impossible to carry two cups up the ladder to the flying bridge, and sat down at the lower steering-station to sip the stronger one below.

The groundswell, which was making him queasy, told him that they were paralleling the beach too closely offshore. He gazed for a moment, through binoculars, out the starboard window. The gray summer cottages of Napeague, Amagansett, East Hampton and Sagaponack slumbered less than half a mile away. In them, early tenants would be awakening to the gut-growl of the boat's twin Chryslers. A child poked along the tide-flats, teased to run by a huge woolly dog. The doctor found a strange comfort in the cottages and decided after all not to ask his partner to move further out.

The sound of the engines suddenly diminished to a quiet chortle. Obviously, the first trace of the fathometer had sprung to life.

The doctor slipped down from the lower helmsman's seat. He hesitated, then slugged down the drink he had intended for the man topside. He went forward and dangled a stainless Danforth anchor until he felt the bottom some 30 feet below. As his partner backed slowly, he paid off chain and line. Finally he snubbed the line on a bow-cleat, and signaled his partner that the hook was properly set.

Sidling aft along the narrow deck outboard of the cabin, he glanced at the shoreline. All the shoulder-to-shoulder communities lining Long Island dunes had always looked the same to him, but he was pretty sure he had anchored on the doorstep of Amity.

The Great White swam south, 20 feet below the surface, leaving Block Island to her right. She came left, dead on course for Montauk Point.

She was gravid with young in both uteri and her hunger was overwhelming. She had fed last night off Nantucket on a school of cod and all night long she had held course southwest along the coast of Rhode Island. She had swept into Newport Bay and found nothing, banked gracefully like a cargo plane, and resumed her track south. Her six-foot high tail propelled her bulk with stiff, purposeful power.

Before her, an invisible cone of fear swept the sea clean, from bottom to surface. For a full mile ahead the ocean was emptying of life. Seals, porpoises, whales, squid, all fled. All had sensors—electromagnetic, aural, vibratory, or psychic—which were heralding her coming. As she passed, the Atlantic refilled in her wake.

Man would have ignored such sensors, if he still

had them, in favor of intelligence. But man was not her normal prey.

To overcome the clairvoyance of her quarry, she was ordinarily swifter than whatever animal she pursued. Her food included almost any creature of worthwhile size that swam, floated, or crawled in the ocean. But she had become so large, near term, that her speed was down.

She grew more ravenous with every mile that passed.

Halfway down the anchor-line the doctor paused. His panting, amplified in his regulator, was ear-splitting. He was sure his partner, descending in a green flowering of bubbles 10 feet below him, could hear every gasp. Clinging to the half-inch rope, he tried to relax.

Hyperventilation in the first dive was normal. But if he could not slow his breathing he would be out of air and forced to surface in ten or fifteen minutes. There was pride involved. Despite his size and greater metabolic requirements, his tank always out-lasted the smaller man's. He could not understand the apprehension that was making him pant.

When his respiration eased, his ears began to ache. He jammed his mask tightly against his face, wheezed air through his nose, and cleared his Eustachian tubes.

He resumed his descent. Visibility was better than he had expected—15 feet or more—but he had already lost his partner. When he reached the bottom, he followed the anchor line along the sand until it became chain. Fifteen feet further he found the lawyer in a cloud of silt, trying to bury the Dan-forth against the outgoing tide. He assisted in this and finally they had the anchor-flukes buried.

The lawyer glanced at his wrist compass,

jerked his thumb toward the north, and began to swim back along the track they had taken, searching for the clump of rocks. The doctor followed, cruising five feet above the bottom and off his partner's left hip. He began to feel at home again. His heart had stopped hammering. His three-shot breakfast was working through his system, calming him wonderfully.

Swimming along, he glanced at his partner and found himself smiling. The little attorney was burdened with all the equipment that money could buy. His mask was prescription-ground so that he needed no glasses. He wore a pressure-equalizing vest. This was its maiden voyage, and he kept climbing and descending as he tried to regulate it.

On the lawyer's left wrist was the compass, and on his right an underwater watch to give him bottom time. From his neck dangled a Nikonos underwater camera. They had used it last year and found the light below too weak, so now it had a strobe.

Strapped to the lawyer's left calf was a Buck diving knife; on his right leg was an aluminum scallop-iron for their prey.

He looked, thought the doctor, like Dustin Hoffman in *The Graduate*, hiding from the festivities at the bottom of his parents' swimming pool.

Dawn had begun to shimmer faintly down to her as she passed Montauk. Her eyes were black, flat, and unblinking, giving her an air of profound wisdom. Her pupils were mirror-polished inside, so she had excellent vision even in this dim light. But she continued to navigate as before, blindly and mindlessly as a computer would, using the electroreceptor *ampullae* which covered her head to sense the orientation of the earth's magnetic field.

Two years before, not far from here, she had been hit by a male not much smaller than she. Grasping her dorsal in his jaws, he had somehow borne her, despite her superior strength, to the muddy bottom. There, passive and supine, she had received both of his yard-long, salami-shaped claspers into her twin vents.

Her back, though her skin was composed of thousands of tiny teeth itself, was still scarred from his grip.

Even before her pregnancy she had outweighed her passing mate and any creature in the seas except for some cetaceans and her own harmless relatives, the basking and whale-shark.

At 30 feet and almost two tons, she was longer than a killer whale and heavier by half.

Now, near term, her girth was enormous. In her left uterus squirmed three young. In her right lived five, three females and two males. The smallest was a little over three feet long and weighed only 22 pounds. He was, nevertheless, a fully functional being. He had survived *in utero* for almost two years, eating thousands of unfertilized eggs and, with his remaining brother and sisters, some 30 weaker siblings.

He himself was not out of danger yet, especially from his sisters, who were uniformly larger than males. If the mother hunted successfully for the next few weeks, her egg production would satisfy his siblings and he would probably live.

If he successfully fought off his sisters, he would be born at the top of the oceanic feeding triangle.

Already, he feared no kind but his own.

The lawyer slowed and the doctor almost overran him. His partner was pointing to the left. The doctor turned his head. He saw a shape, tinged darker green than the pale water through which they swam. It was not the clump of rocks they had dived last year. It was abrupt, angular, man-made.

Excitedly, his partner swam toward it. The doctor followed. The stern of a wrecked fishing boat, bigger and heavier than their own, loomed from the murk. Green shards of light played on her barnacle-covered transom. She was an immensely rugged old craft. The growth on her twisted planks told them that she had been here for some time.

The doctor spotted a heavy hawser lying along the sand. It led below the half-buried quarter of the hulk. He pulled himself along it, jerked at the line, could not move it. He rounded the stern to see where it led on the other side. The lawyer porpoised along beside him, trying to adjust his buoyancy.

The doctor found the other end of the rope. Secured to it by a giant shackle, a 55-gallon iron drum bumped restlessly against the hull. It was crushed and dented, but the remains of yellow paint showed that it had once been meant as a float.

The current swept it suddenly against the hulk with a mournful clang. The Old Grandad left the doctor's veins in a rush. He was very cold.

The lawyer had swum aft. He was rubbing at the seagrass whiskers growing on the stern. He suddenly yanked his scallop-iron from its scabbard and chiseled loose a half-dozen barnacles, loosening a mist of mud. When the water cleared, the doctor could read, in faint orange letters, the name *Orca*, home port *Narragansatt*. The name chorded some deep memory. He looked at his partner.

Behind the lawyer's face-plate, enlarged by the prescription lenses, he saw his companion's gray eyes crinkle in thought. Suddenly the lawyer jammed a fist into a palm, remembering something. Excitedly, he began to grunt, their signal for something out of the ordinary. He waved toward the orange letters. Then he took both hands, fingers clawed like teeth, and swept them through the motion of huge jaws closing.

He pointed again at the name on the shattered stern. The doctor understood.

The half-forgotten news story of a shark-fisherman, a tank-town police chief, and some oceanographic expert or other, read long ago in the *Long Island Press*, surfaced in his mind.

He discovered that he did not like it here. They were after scallop, not wrecks, and anything of souvenir value must have been salvaged by other divers long ago. He found, in fact, that he was no longer even interested in the scallops. His breath was rasping again and his heart hammering, and he felt the first indications of low tank pressure.

He pointed to the surface, but his companion shook his head, tapped the camera, and drew him to a position by the stern. He planted him under the overhang of the sternboards. Then the lawyer backed off, camera-to-faceplate.

The doctor pointed obediently at the letters on the transom, smiling idiotically around his mouthpiece. His partner, trying to stand erect on the bottom, seemed to take forever.

The doctor had suddenly to urinate. The strange apprehension he had felt all morning gripped his bladder and squeezed it tight. When he could wait no longer he simply voided into his wet-suit pants. The warmth of it was good along his side, but did not help the chill in his gut.

He heard the *clunk* of the steel barrel against the hulk, and felt it through his glove where he held to the plank. He could hear his own hoarse gasping and his companion's breath as well.

The strobe light fired, turning everything momentarily white. All at once he heard a sound like a subway train, fast approaching from his rear. His partner, dancing on sand as he tried to balance in the current, wound his camera, then stopped. He stared at something approaching from above and behind the doctor. His mouthpiece fell from his face.

The doctor, startled, began to turn but instinctively hunkered down instead, clinging to a broken plank. His eyes were riveted on his companion. A great bubble soared from his partner's mouth. The lawyer threw up an arm to protect himself. The camera strap fouled and the strobe fired again, illuminating everything and making the doctor feel naked.

The green surface light faded. An enormous bulk, descending like a gliding jet, swept by, a foot above the doctor's head, blotting out the dancing sunlight. It seemed to pass forever. The last of the shape became a tail, towering taller than himself. It swished once, almost sweeping him loose and blotting his view of his partner in a cloud of bottom-silt and mud.

There was silence. The barrel clanged.

The doctor clung to the splintered plank, peering into the settling murk. He could hear only his own tortured breathing. He was terrified at the loudness of it, and of his bubbles, beckoning whatever it was back to the spot. But he could not quiet the panting, and he could not budge from the stern.

One of his partner's diving fins bounced past, heading to sea on the tidal current. He could have reached out and touched it. He made no move.

It was fear that finally drove him from shelter. He became more frightened of dying where he was with an empty tank than of discovery. Tentatively, he moved a few feet from the stern and waited. Nothing happened. In a burst of courage, he kicked off.

He remembered to rise no faster than his bubbles,

remembered to kick slowly and steadily without panic—for whatever it was would be attuned to panic—remembered, as the depths turned from dark green to shimmering jade, to breathe and breathe again, so that the expanding air in his lungs would not burst them—though the noise of his breathing terrified him. He remembered, when he surfaced into golden sunlight, to shift his mouth from regulator to snorkel. He remembered to drop his weight belt for easier swimming. And he remembered, for a while, to kick with a careful, pedaling motion so as not to splash the surface with his fins.

He eased his head from the water. The Hatteras slapped at anchor hardly a hundred feet away. His fear diminished. A rush of joy that it was he who had survived, a flow of ecstasy almost sexual, warmed his veins.

Carefully, he slithered toward the boat. He hardly broke the water. Once he stopped and glided, gazing straight down. He saw nothing but shafts of emerald light lancing the depths below.

He raised his head. A thousand yards beyond the boat slept the houses by the dunes. Two tiny figures raced along the tide line. It seemed an eternity since he had seen them from the cabin, but it was the same child, same woolly dog. He could hear the dog barking.

He shivered suddenly. Deep in his soul he felt another onrush of terror. He quickened the beat of his fins. One of them plopped loudly, and then the other, but he had less than 30 feet to go. He could no longer stand the dragging pace.

With 20 feet to go, he was sprinting, thrashing recklessly, breathing in enormous chest-searing gulps.

All at once, 10 feet from the boat, he felt a bump and a firm, decisive grasp on his left femur, some three inches above his knee. It was surprising, but not at all violent. His first thought was that his partner had somehow survived, caught up with him from below, and plucked his thigh for attention. He dipped his mask, looking down.

He was amazed to see half a human leg, swathed in neoprene, tumbling into the depths. He observed that, though fully detached from the upper femur at the *superpatellar bursa*, it exhibited little bleeding from its own portion of the femoral artery, though a cloud of blood from somewhere else was forming quickly. Whoever had amputated had performed neatly: the skin along the incision was scalpel-clean.

He was filled with sudden lassitude. He floated, fascinated by the leg spinning into the depths. He had the sense of something vast moving below the limb, out of his zone of visibility, but he was strangely giddy and somehow did not care. The leg rose as if bumped, and disappeared.

His left side was weak. He wondered if he had had a heart attack or even a stroke. He was getting too old to dive. He might even sell his share in the boat. He began feebly to swim again.

He heard the faint subway roar. He did not care. He stopped moving. He was too tired to fight his sleepiness, though the boat was only three strokes away. He would doze awhile like a basking seal, and swim the last few feet later.

Then he was borne aloft. He sensed that his ribs, lungs, spleen, kidneys, bowels, duodenum, were being squeezed firmly together as if in a giant hydraulic press.

He felt no pain at all.

And the great white shark moves on, gliding silently and undetected underwater, still in desperate search for food.

On land, Chief of Police Martin Brody, his wife Ellen and their two sons are unaware of the dangers in store for them once again. In fact, the town is just recovering from the disaster caused by one shark four summers ago.

JAWS 2

an all-new novel, contains many of the pulse-pounding elements of Jaws, as well as new people, new situations and intimate knowledge of diving and the sea life—all of which make this totally new book an edge-of-the-seat reading experience.

Amity, four years later. The terror continues.

JAWS 2

A novel by Hank Searls. Based on the screenplay by Howard Sackler and Dorothy Tristan. From the characters created by Peter Benchley.

JAWS 2 THE BOOK

APRIL 19 Read the complete
Bantam Book.
On sale wherever paperbacks are sold.

JAWS 2 THE MOVIE

JUNE 16 See the Universal
Release.
At theaters across the country.

ROY SCHEIDER   LORRAINE GARY

JAWS 2

A ZANUCK/BROWN PRODUCTION

Also Starring
MURRAY HAMILTON

Screenplay by CARL GOTTLIEB • Screen
Story by HOWARD SACKLER and DOROTHY
TRISTAN • Directed by JEANNOT SZWARC •
Based Upon Characters Created by PETER
BENCHLEY • Music by JOHN WILLIAMS •
Produced by RICHARD D. ZANUCK and
DAVID BROWN • A UNIVERSAL PICTURE •
Color by Technicolor • Filmed in Panavision